About the Author

This is Devin Moon's first traditionally published novel. He
lives in Virginia with his wife and daughter.

The Seeker's Truth

Devin Moon

The Seeker's Truth

Olympia Publishers
London

www.olympiapublishers.com
OLYMPIA PAPERBACK EDITION

A CIP catalogue record for this title is
available from the British Library.

ISBN: 978-1-80074-694-7

This is a work of fiction.
Names, characters, places and incidents originate from the writer's
imagination. Any resemblance to actual persons, living or dead, is
purely coincidental.

First Published in 2023

Olympia Publishers
Tallis House
2 Tallis Street
London
EC4Y 0AB

Printed in Great Britain

Dedication

For Aurelia

Chapter 1

With sweat dripping from his brow and a heavy heart, Vallus the Seeker walked down a long and broken road. The sun was hung high in the sky, its light weakened by the toxic upper atmosphere. With nothing in the burned wastes to keep his mind occupied, Vallus scanned the surrounding area as he walked. There was not much of note for miles, save the distant ruins of the ancient Gods' grand cities on the horizon, and a mountain range far to the west. Occasionally, Vallus would pass the odd crumbled building, a grim reminder that this road was simply the skeleton of a long-dead world.

Vallus had spent nearly the entirety of his twenty-five living years learning of that dead world and its fate. He had vowed to devote his life to learning the secrets of the Gods, and thus became known as a Seeker. Vallus was six-and-a-half feet tall with bronze skin and broad shoulders. He had unremarkable brown eyes and a curtain of medium length black hair draped over his ears. Covering his sharp, chiseled face were several scars, each a reminder of his mistakes. His sloped nose held evidence of a past break. The Seeker's clothing was all elaborately and carefully chosen to help him survive his voyage across the barren wastes, and consisted of a long, dark brown leather coat over a wrinkled, white tunic with pieces of metal armor strapped to his shoulders, wrists, and chest, and a small gas mask that hung from his neck by a strap. Vallus' pants were made of a padded, breathable material to make long walks easier, and he had more armor strapped to the front of his boots. He carried a large backpack with a thin mechanical frame surrounding it that had several bottles and a pouch clipped to it, and an old, dusty bedroll strapped to the bottom. Around his waist were two intersecting belts with several pouches and implements attached to them. Strapped to each of the belts were two scabbards that sheathed two swords. Each sword hilt bore a small, circular insignia with the letters R.S. carved into them as though by unsteady hands.

Vallus was indeed built well for the monumental task laid out before him; for as a Seeker, he had vowed to find the answer to the questions that plagued the minds of his people. Many believed that the Gods had left the world, and for whatever reason, their departure had brought the Fall of Man, sometimes called just simply the Fall, and scorched the world, cursing what remained of mankind. And thus it had become Vallus' honor-bound mission to answer the questions his people asked: Why did the Gods leave? Where did they go? And why did they curse those who remained? In reality, it was a single question: Why did the world Fall?

Vallus recalled a conversation he had had with his father during his training. He walked as he lost himself in the memory, taking each step essentially automatically. His father had sat him down on the small platform that served as the porch of their hovel and they watched the people who lived in their encampment move about, set to their tasks. After a few moments of quiet reflection, his father had spoken.

"The world wasn't always like this, son. If a Seeker is what you aim to become, you need to know the legends."

"Legends?" asked the bemused child.

"Yes. A belief spread, years ago. Legend holds that long ago, people lived alongside the Gods. They were powerful beings, and they crafted grand cities, and forged wondrous weapons. And they gifted men with machines that used artificial intelligence, reflections of the Gods themselves that could think and learn like people."

"Then what?" His father had gained the boy's rapt attention. His father gestured broadly around, as if to say "Then this."

"The Gods left, and in doing so, they burned the world. They wounded it. And they left it to us, to survive with what little is left. And no one knows how or why. That is what many Seekers dedicate their missions to. Because knowledge is power, and one we sorely need. Because just knowing why the world is like this is enough to build hope that it could be better."

Vallus had been but a child, with a child's mind and a child's empathy, but the thought had resonated with him. It made him feel an unusual warmth in the depths of his chest. Hope? But of course he could find that.

"Then I will, too," he said, his face determined.

"Then you must learn of their vaults."

Vallus snapped back to reality with those words echoing in the back of his mind.

There was a sound, far in the distance behind him. It was like a high-pitched whirring, almost like an engine but with an electric quality. Vallus wasn't quite sure what gave him the impression, but the sound seemed as if it was approaching fast.

"Pip," he said calmly with a pleasant voice, and an accent that was in between simple and refined.

At the word, a hand-sized drone with a trapezoidal metal body floated out of a pocket in Vallus' bag and hovered in front of him using two small vents on its sides. The drone spoke with a soft and wispy voice.

"Did you wish for me to identify that sound, Vallus?"

The Seeker nodded and Pip slightly adjusted in air to peer over his shoulder with her single ocular lens. She beeped quietly a few times then shifted to look at Vallus.

"There are two machines approaching us at high rates of speed. They appear to be what you call 'Pursuers'. Odd, though. It looks as if their primary weapons have been dismantled and removed. ETA one point five minutes."

Vallus glanced around.

"No cover. But they don't have weapons. They'll try to ram me. No chance they won't just ignore me. Gonna have to fight," he said, half to Pip and half to himself.

Vallus turned to face the approaching Pursuers as he drew both of his swords and held their single-edged blades flat against his forearms. He crouched, ready to strike at their center of gravity. Pip's estimate had been slightly off. They closed distance in forty-five seconds.

The Pursuers were man-sized machines that strongly resembled motorcycles, although there was no place for a rider. Their bodies consisted of strong segmented plates that sat over their internal components, with two wheels wrapped in thick, puncture-proof tires. The first Pursuer passed Vallus so fast he almost missed his window to sink his blade into the machine's side. Despite the speed, the blade caught between a metal plate and cut clean through the frame. The machine sparked and smoked as it drove off the road and flipped several times before crashing to a halt against a pile of rubble. The other Pursuer blasted past Vallus but turned around at speed as its partner hit the ground.

"Strange. It almost seemed like it didn't want to attack me," said Vallus with a hint of guilt.

Vallus could not truthfully know whether or not the Pursuer intended to attack him, but he knew that the second one had become motivated to do so. It had stopped still on the cracked pavement about sixty feet from Vallus and had begun to rev its engine as it peered at him through its ocular lens and beeped aggressively. Vallus gathered that it was scanning him.

Learning. After a few moments, it revved its engine louder, spun its tires, and charged forward. Fifty feet away. Forty feet away. Thirty feet away. The Pursuer was twenty feet away from Vallus when the grenade he had thrown detonated and a shrapnel-laden explosion tore through the machine's body. The sundered machine broke apart and skidded to a halt just past Vallus. The latter crouched to shield himself from the blast.

Vallus shook his head as he sheathed his swords. He had become accustomed to having to defend himself, but his encounter with the Pursuers left a bitter taste in his mouth. Their behavior had thrown him for a loop. He quickly scanned the area around him as Pip hovered beside him. Once Vallus felt safe, he walked off the road to where the smoking remains of the first Pursuer sat still against the rubble. As he crouched down in front of the dead machine, Pip floated over the wreckage, beeped, and began to scan it. As she did so, Vallus took a small toolkit wrapped in thick leather from his bag and began to move the burned metal plates out of the way. Pip beeped again.

"Vallus, I am detecting a faint signal connecting to this Pursuer. It also seems to be processing a request to receive repairs."

"So the rumors were true. There is a vault nearby," he said as he looked down the road in the direction he had been walking for a moment before he returned to tinkering with the machine's remaining inner parts. Vallus had hoped the stories he had heard

13

on the road were true. They had said there was an ancient vault that housed a Forgotten God. It was his best chance of finding his answers.

"It would seem so," said Pip.

Vallus picked up his tools and returned to the road, then walked over to where the second Pursuer's remains rested scattered around. The bulk of its wreckage sat in the middle of the road in a smoking heap. Vallus looked around at each chunk and took a quick inventory of what remained. He quickly determined scavenging the machine would be a waste of time. After wrapping up his toolkit and returning it to his bag, Vallus turned and continued his long walk down the dry, shattered road.

The Seeker continued to walk for nearly an hour before he stopped to rest and take a drink of what little water he had left in his canteen. The sun was still peering down upon Vallus with its gaze, as though it were watching him eagerly. Vallus' breaths came slowly but the air tasted bitter. He was sweating and his legs ached. Vallus had put away his canteen and taken in all of these things when he looked to his right and was quietly startled to see a relatively young man with sandy brown hair and a thin frame sitting on a chunk of rubble about ten feet off the road, staring at him intently with a pleasant thin smile framed by an equally thin goatee. He was draped in a dark brown poncho that blended almost perfectly with his surroundings.

"Do you not speak?" asked Vallus.

"I apologize, good sir," said the man as he stood and picked up his large satchel from the ground. "You seemed to be in deep thought and I didn't wish to disturb you. My name is Garr, and I'm something of a merchant," he said with a flourish of his hand and a light bow.

Vallus eyed the man. He didn't appear to Vallus to be

carrying any weapons, and nothing about his mannerisms seemed to indicate he was dangerous. He decided to hear Garr out.

"What do you trade?"

"That depends on what you need," Garr replied with a coy grin. "I could use clean water and medical supplies."

Garr rifled through his bag and pulled out a small box and a sealed bag filled with water with 1L printed on the side. He held the box up toward Vallus, who was surprised to have found such a well-prepared trader.

"I looted an ancient medical facility some time ago for these. Two syringes, a roll of fabric bandages, and needles and thread for sutures. Very rare. The water, that's cheap. Ish. How about that drone? Trade that for everything?"

Pip beeped despondently from her perch behind Vallus' shoulder. Vallus scowled. He shook his head once, and with a near-whisper, he said:

"No."

The man grinned.

"Very well. You look like you've been to some fantastic places, though. What kind of things have you scavenged, I wonder?"

"Fantastic? Not so much. I am a Seeker. I've been in the vaults. I have an extra power cell taken from a machine. Will that suffice?"

The merchant appeared to think it over for a moment before he nodded and grinned again.

"Sure! Those are quite rare, after all," replied Garr.

Vallus reached behind him into his bag and pulled out a small metal box. He opened it to reveal the inside held four thin, cylindrical plastic casings with metal parts strapped into the box, along with eight empty slots. Vallus saw Garr's eyes light up, and Vallus looked at him sidelong.

"I can only give up one of these. I wish I could give you more," he said as he handed the merchant the power cell.

Garr took the cell and held up a hand.

"All is well, noble Seeker," he said as he handed Vallus the items. "I understand. Your journey is hard enough without grifters pilfering your hard-earned supplies."

"Perhaps there is one more thing you could provide me?"

"Yes?"

"Information. Is there a settlement near here? Or perhaps a vault?"

Garr nodded and pointed down the road.

"There's a small village about a day's walk that way. Nice little place called Ashenvale. Not sure about any vaults, though. I try to stay far away from those, anyway."

"Very wise. What's that going to cost me?"

Garr grinned wide. "Not a thing, Seeker. Consider it a tithe to the cause."

"Thank you. Safe travels, Garr," said Vallus as he turned to walk.

"And to you," replied the merchant as he followed suit and walked up the road where Vallus had come from.

Vallus continued his journey down the road, and would occasionally glance over his shoulder to see the form of the merchant in the distance, growing smaller each time he looked. Eventually, when Vallus looked once more, the man was but a pinprick on the horizon, indiscernible from a lump of rubble. Vallus walked until he began to tire, just as the sun was ending its own journey to dusk. Where he decided to rest, off to the side of the road, was the remains of a small brick building. He walked through a hole in the wall to find what might have been a store lifetimes ago. One of the walls was completely destroyed, and there was a small countertop in one corner.

With the little daylight he had left, Vallus began to set up his camp. He took his bag off his back as Pip floated around the structure to assure it was safe. He then removed the bedroll from his bag and unfurled it in one corner of the room. Vallus then gathered a few boards from another corner and what little kindling he could and built a pile with them. He took a small silver box from his bag, flicked a switch on it, and shot a thin line of heat at the boards that quickly ignited them.

As Vallus sat and began to rummage through his bag for food, Pip floated into the room and hovered at his eye level. She beeped as Vallus began to cook on a small pan from his bag.

"I have concluded my sweep. We appear to be secure," she said.

"Good. Thank you, Pip."

She beeped happily then hovered silently, watching Vallus mix together various vegetables that he kept vacuum sealed. After a few moments of silence, Vallus looked up at Pip.

"Hey, Pip? Can I ask you something?"

"Of course," she replied.

"I've walked this path for seven years, and all I have to show for it is a mountain of destroyed machines, several scars, and rumors of forgotten Gods. Do you think I will ever actually complete my mission?"

"Redefine your mission," said Pip.

"To find the answer," replied Vallus, puzzled.

"And what is the question?"

"Why is the world like this? We can see the remains of the Gods' world. So something horrible must have happened. But why?"

"The causation of anything can eventually be traced back to its origins. So I would say that it is likely, or at least possible."

"And what if I do find this Forgotten God that I've heard about? What would I even ask it?"

"I would suppose the same thing you asked me."

Vallus nodded as he began to eat his meal. He noted that his cooking was improving. Seven years alone had forced Vallus to practice things he wasn't good at, because he would need them to survive. Cooking had always been hard for him, and growing up he had relied on his father for food. Since the Seeker's mother had died giving birth to him, his father had no help but what little his village could offer, and either out of pride or embarrassment, he had more often than not turned it down. He had been determined, it seemed, to raise his son with what meager resources he had. But as the man who trained Vallus to become a Seeker, he had also taught him how to adapt and learn. Because his life depended upon it.

After finishing his meal and putting away his utensils, Vallus drew one of his swords from its sheath and a block of course material from his bag and began to sharpen the blade. With his hands at work, he watched the fire dance with Pip silently floating beside him.

Suddenly, a thought occurred to Vallus and he sat up on his cot. Alerted to the movement, Pip floated up at attention.

"Pip, you have an internal database, right?"

"Yes," replied Pip, tilting slightly to her left as if inquisitive.

"You have files about the world before the Fall. Could you search for records of wars or leaders?"

"I can check," she said. "There are a number of files, and much of my data is corrupted... It's like I've been... cut off."

Pip beeped quietly for several seconds, then tilted to look at Vallus again.

"I have found three files that match your query. I also found seventy-two corrupted files with similar time stamps."

"Delete the corrupted files, then tell me about the three," he said.

"Deleting. The first file is an incident report. Most of the information is redacted, but it was a terrorist attack on a town that killed twelve and wounded twenty-two. A soldier was sent to restore order. Deleting. The second file is a request for additional troops from that soldier, noting concern of a possible imminent invasion. Deleting. The final file is a note of concern from a technician. According to the letter, this technician was worried about a technical problem in 'the network'. This file seems less informative and more panicked. All corrupted files deleted."

"Not much to go on. Do you have any additional information on this soldier? Why did they only send one?"

"Scanning… It appears that this soldier was a special unit. His name and rank are both redacted, but the file indicates he was of a particularly high rank."

"And the attack? What else is there on it?"

"Nothing of consequence. Most of the details are redacted. But it seems violent attacks of that nature were a problem of the era."

"Where there is fear to exploit, there will always be those willing and able to exploit it," said Vallus pensively.

Vallus sheathed his last sword after he had finished sharpening it and laid his weapons next to his cot. He sighed, feeling no more informed than before, but at least assured of the validity of the tiny spark of hope that rested in the back of his mind. Pip turned back to the fire as Vallus wished her a good night, then slowly hovered to the ground to enter rest mode. Laying back on his cot, Vallus quickly drifted away to sleep under the black, starless void of the night sky above.

**

Vallus looked around. He was back in his village, far to the north. He looked at his hands. They were small, like those of a child. He was in the courtyard, observing the few people who called the place home. They were distraught. Woeful. He heard a voice calling to him from behind. He turned and...

Vallus was in his home, a small hut on the edge of the encampment wall. He had his own small room. He was still young. There was a knock at his door and a voice told him to get ready. He put on a coat and grabbed his gas mask. He knew what he was preparing for. He turned the knob on his door and...

Vallus was in an empty courtyard. He felt more present here. He was a bit older, perhaps twelve. He had made his resolution clear long ago. There was a sword in his right hand. He had hardly noticed he was gripping it so hard his knuckles had turned white. Vallus recalled his father's teachings. Keep your breathing calm. Don't think about anything but you and your target. Strike at their weak points, but strike with confidence and precision. Vallus took a deep breath in before he realized his father was standing in front of him, ten feet away, holding a sword of his own. His father spoke with a calm, commanding voice, befitting his sharp jaw. Vallus realized he looked quite a bit like his father.

"You chose this path. Now you must learn how to survive as you walk it."

He raised his sword and bolted forward. Vallus was ready. He braced himself and... Vallus was once more in his room, but he was now a teenager, probably fifteen, and a machine was spread about the table by the wall. Its parts were scattered around tools and old tattered manuals. He remembered this vividly, a memory close to his heart and thick with sentimentality. It lingered.

"My brother learned much to become a Seeker, and he left that knowledge with me. Now you will learn it. You will learn how to understand the machines of the ancient Gods," his father had told him.

They were almost like living things to him. The parts within their metal bodies reminded him of organs. His task had been to rebuild the machine from a pile of parts, and it had taken months to complete. He learned very early on that the test had nothing to do with if he understood the machines or not; it was a test of his ability to use his tools. And it was a test he took every day. He worked with deft hands, every day making a step forward in progress. But he sat in front of the disassembled machine not to train him to survive, but to teach him to be smart enough to know how to.

"If you can't fix this machine, you probably shouldn't risk your life entering a vault. And if you can't do it quickly, it means you'll probably die trying to open the front door."

His father's words were but an echo, but they still rang through Vallus' mind. It took every day, every hour Vallus had to complete the project. With each failure, he learned something new. As the day of completion drew near, Vallus began to understand what the machine was. And when he finally slipped its optical sensor into the socket, he realized that it was the head of some ancient machine. Vallus couldn't identify what kind of machine, but none of that mattered when he finally tightened the last screw and told his father he was done. He then watched as his father slowly disassembled the machine, checking his son's work.

Vallus figured out why this memory seemed so vivid. It was because this was the day he finally, truly succeeded. With the machine lying on the desk in parts once again, Vallus' father looked at him with a smile.

"Well done," he had said.

He held up his hand, offering the optical sensor to Vallus. He took it, held it in his hand, and felt its weight. He looked into the lens and…

***

Vallus awoke a few hours after dawn and packed his camp as he ate a quick breakfast of baked crackers, his previous night's dream fading into the back of his mind. Before he finished packing his camp, he reached into his bag and withdrew the optic lens. He had kept it as a memento of his accomplishments, and used it to reassure himself on occasion. He clutched it in silence for a moment, Pip regarding him with curiosity, then tucked it away in his bag again. With Pip silently bobbing and swaying along at his side, Vallus continued his long and arduous walk down the road. The mood of the walk would have been improved if there weren't nothing for miles around. The mountains in the distance loomed like a vague dream on the horizon, and the surrounding rubble was too damaged to be interesting and too old to be of use. His only entertainment was his own thoughts and Pip's quiet fans.

This boredom came with its advantages. With nothing else to occupy his mind, Vallus had found he could reflect on what he had gained. He now knew he was heading toward a vault. He had been in three other vaults in the span of his seven year journey. Each one had nearly taken his life. He recalled his father's teachings, his own experiences, and focused upon them. He knew, deep down, that if he could learn from every single misstep of his journey, he could survive again. And perhaps this time, it would be with the answers he so desperately sought.

It was nearing noon when Vallus began to see what appeared to be a large encampment sitting upon the road. Within the hour, Vallus was at its front gate. A crude sign welded to the metal walls read 'ASHENVALE'. Spray painted to another were the words 'HE IS COMING' in faded, red letters. The gate itself was actually more of an archway with a lone guard standing next to it. As Vallus approached, the man looked up with an expression that read half boredom, half despair. He spoke with a disinterested tone.

"Halt and state your business in Ashenvale."

"I am a Seeker, and I have come to enter the nearby vault," Vallus replied. "Whoa. Been a while since another Seeker showed up here. Come on in," said the guard.

"Another?" asked Vallus as he passed under the archway with the guard.

"Oh, ya. They come here all the time. Gotta tell ya, though, none of 'em have come back. They all went down the valley into the vault, same as you wanna."

"And they just vanished?"

"Probably died, actually. Well, welcome to Ashenvale. Stay safe. Oh, and if ya wanna head to the vault, take the left path."

The guard returned to the front of the archway, leaving Vallus alone to walk through the streets of what he found to be an amazingly thriving township. The buildings that lined the cobblestone streets were largely the ruins of ancient buildings that had been built upon. Large sheets of metal and various fixtures had been bolted to the walls. Some of them were homes; others were shops. From the gate, there were two paths that diverged around a large central court. Sat within that court was a house-sized structure with glass walls and an apparently complex machine in the back. Stationed around the machine were several guards, and as Vallus approached it, he soon figured out why. The structure was a greenhouse, containing at least a half dozen rows of various vegetables and fruits. It was the town's food supply. As Vallus took another step closer to look, one guard raised the rifle he was holding and pointed it at him.

"Halt! This area is off limits!"

"Apologies," said Vallus as he held up his hand. "I was only admiring this structure. Does this feed the entire town?"

The guard looked skeptical at first, but then lowered his weapon and stood at ease. "Yes, sir. Ashenvale only has a population of one-hundred-and-six individuals. Divided evenly, this greenhouse provides enough food for each citizen each year."

"Who built it?"

"Everyone. Ashenvale lives by the code of our King. So that no man should want, each man should work."

"Your king?"

"Yes. Although he has gone away, this town is ruled by the Ashen King. Tales say he will return, but until he does, we have a town to protect."

"Then I'll leave you to it," said Vallus as he nodded to the guard and began to walk down the left side path.

Vallus walked the path slowly, taking in all the sights of the lively town. Children played in the street. There were men and women at work, each doing something of importance. Further down the path, the sounds of the town died out. Vallus noted that he was on the outskirts. After all, the town was visibly larger than what its population needed. Vallus walked past an apparently abandoned building, then noticed the two men who had just begun to follow him. He stopped, turned, and stared the men down.

"What do you want and why are you following me?"

"Us? Oh, we just wanted to see if you intended to enter the valley without paying the tax," said a tall, bald man with a mischievous smirk. Vallus noted the sword strapped to his side.

"Let's skip the bit. You're obviously bandits. One warning: do not cross me. I don't like to fight people. But if you impede my mission, I will kill you. No hesitation. No restraint."

"Big words. Wanna back 'em up?"

The man had begun to draw his blade, but Vallus was much faster. Blood sprayed from the bandit's wrist across the shirt and face of the other bandit, an unremarkable man with long, matted hair and a build like a pile of cinder blocks. The bald bandit screamed as Vallus wiped the blood from one of his swords.

"How about a hand for a tax? Draw another weapon and you both die."

Terror and blood plastered across their faces, both men turned and ran, trailing echoed screams behind them. Vallus shook his head in disgust as he sheathed his sword. To think with the world scorched and dead, and so much suffering surrounding the few who survived, that there would still be men trying to profit on pain disgusted him. It upset him even more when it stood in the way of his quest.

Vallus continued along the path and soon found himself walking alongside a cliff to his left with a path that descended into a sheer valley flanked by tall cliff faces. To the left, sitting upon a cliff that jutted out from the path was a massive, gray metal castle. The building was probably sixty feet tall to the vaulted roof, with each of its four spires in each corner reaching about one hundred feet before tapering off to thin, intimidating spikes. The castle disturbed Vallus, as if it was something out of a half remembered nightmare. The thought that something about it was profoundly wrong nagged at the back of his mind, but he bottled the thought and kept moving into the valley.

Vallus continued onward. He passed the castle on his left and took a pathway that branched off to the right toward the valley cut into the steep hills. The mouth of the valley was no more than one hundred feet away when Vallus spotted a man in the road. He was a full foot shorter than Vallus, and wore a simple tunic and pants made of tattered and old fabric. The man was prostrated on the pathway, facing the castle as he muttered to himself.

Before Vallus could walk around the man, the latter looked up at him with a wild look in his eyes and lunged for Vallus. Before Vallus could react, the man clutched the ends of the Seeker's coat and pulled against Vallus' attempts to wrest himself free. For a man who appeared to be quite emaciated, the stranger had a strong grip.

"He is coming! Our glorious King shall return! He brings a new dawn! He is coming!" The man screamed, frothing at the mouth as his eyes grew ever wilder. He wasn't panicked; he was mad with joy.

Tired of the distraction, Vallus grabbed the man by the back of his neck and pried him away. Gently enough to not hurt the man, but with enough force to get the point across, Vallus tossed him to the side of the road, then drew one of his blades and leveled it toward him.

"Stay out of my way," he growled with authority.

The disheveled man laughed a high-pitched, grating laugh

and allowed Vallus to pass.

Vallus sheathed his sword and continued along the path as the man's wild cackling faded behind him. As he approached the entrance to the valley, Vallus looked back to see the man standing absolutely still at the foot of the pathway that led to the castle. Unsettled but undeterred, Vallus continued onwards.

He entered the valley to find himself flanked on either side by cliff faces that must have been at least two hundred feet tall on either side. The vault's entrance was in clear view as soon as he entered the valley, and a short walk brought him to a large, paved courtyard with several metal barricades scattered around the area. In front of the vault's massive door was a set of four stairs to a porch, and sat upon the porch was a car-sized machine mounted on three legs with a long turret gun barrel protruding from its center. As Vallus approached, the machine beeped loudly and began to spin up its gun.

Vallus only had a moment to react. Thinking quickly, he dove behind the closest barricade, the one farthest from the door. Just as he made it to cover, the sentry began to fire. The turret's fire echoed through the valley as the rounds hammered against the barricade with a thunderous clamor. The noise was deafening, but Vallus was not deterred.

"Pip!" Vallus shouted over the roar of the gun.

The drone floated out of Vallus' bag and hovered just in front of him, careful to avoid the sentry's gunfire.

"Got anything on this?"

"No files found," said Pip after a moment. "This machine must be custom built."

"Damn," Vallus muttered to himself. "Take cover in my bag. I need to get closer."

Vallus waited. After a few moments of sustained fire, the

machine stopped. Vallus peeked over the barricade to see the sentry's backside open. Two mechanical arms extended from the back and began to reload the gun. As it did so, Vallus ran to the next closest barricade. A little faster and he could have made the run to another, but his hesitation forced him to take cover when the sentry began to fire toward him once more. On the run, Vallus had counted three more barricades between him and the turret, all unevenly spaced, but too far away to risk the run while the turret fired.

The sentry's rounds continued to thunder against the barricade. When the firing stopped and the machine once more reloaded, Vallus rounded the barricade and made a mad dash for the one closest to the gun. The sentry began to spin up and adjusted to aim at Vallus. He slid toward the barricade as his heart pounded. Just before he made it to cover, the gun opened fire and Vallus heard the whistle of a bullet fly past his ear. He hit the barricade hard but it didn't give. He exhaled hard, took a deep breath, and drew one of his swords from its sheath. Each second of gunfire that passed was agonizing, but Vallus remained as calm as he could. By his estimation, the gun was twenty feet away from the barricade Vallus was behind. He would have to be fast.

The moment the gun ceased to fire and once more began to reload, Vallus vaulted over the barricade, sword firmly in hand, and sprinted toward it. He took all four stairs in one leap and watched the gun's barrel begin to spin up as he slid under it. As he did, he took one hard swing at one of its three support legs. The blade glanced off. After muttering a quiet expletive, Vallus rolled to his feet and began to run in a circle around the machine as it tried to aim at him. He rolled toward the gun and thrust his blade into its side, narrowly avoiding its fire. The blade dug deep into the machine, shooting sparks from the gash. Vallus twisted his sword and ripped the blade out from within it. But the barrel continued to spin and the gun continued its attempt to take aim.

Vallus' attack had interrupted the turret's fire, but the reprieve didn't last for long. With only a moment to spare, Vallus dove behind a small pile of rubble that barely covered him as the turret once more opened fire. Oddly, Vallus heard very few rounds hit the rubble. Most of them hit the ground around him or the cliff walls instead. He surmised he had damaged the machine's targeting system. Another few seconds passed and the gun once more ceased firing and began to reload. Vallus sprinted to the gun and shoved his blade between the end of its barrel and the chassis. Drawing upon as much strength as he could muster, Vallus twisted the sword and tore the barrel out from its mounting. Bits and pieces of the gun's inner machinery came out with the barrel like spilled guts, but the machine continued to beep, whir, and attempt to take aim. But without its barrel, the gun was harmless. After a few moments, the sentry clicked loudly, beeped, and ceased to move.

Vallus sheathed his sword and carefully approached the sentry as a thin wisp of smoke began to float out from where the gun barrel had been. He quickly inspected the machine, then took his bag off his back. Pip floated out to join him. Vallus rummaged through his bag and pulled a long metal tool rod with a hooked tip out. He wedged it under one of the metal plates that formed the machine's body and pried the panel off. With access to the machine's inner parts, Vallus began to salvage anything useful. Anything that seemed usable went in a small pouch in his bag.

"That's odd," said Vallus as he continued to salvage the machine. Pip perked up at attention.

"There's no power source. This machine shouldn't have been able to function," he said.

"I am detecting a weak signal from the machine," said Pip. "It seems it was being controlled remotely by some type of indirect, digital system."

"Very odd, indeed. Let's keep our wits about us," said Vallus as he turned to the towering steel doors of the vault. On those doors, painted in faded black block font, was a short designation number: DA-0708.

"I wonder what the letters mean," said Vallus, almost to himself in a somewhat whimsical manner.

"I have no data concerning these designations," said Pip. "No matter. It doesn't change the mission."

Vallus walked to the right side of the door, where mounted on the wall was a small console. He bent forward to look closely at it, and after a moment of thought, drew a small knife from his belt. He used the tip of the knife to pry open a small panel on the console to find several wires within running over computer parts. Vallus put away the knife and pulled two thin metal tools from another belt pocket and began rooting around in the console. Within a few minutes, a light beep issued from the console and a loud thump echoed through the valley from the vault. With a shrill, groaning churn, the doors began to slide open. Vallus stood just in front of them until they ground to a halt. With one last deep breath, Vallus stepped into vault DA-0708.

Chapter 2

While the doors of the vault slowly closed behind him, Vallus found himself in a long, dim hallway. There were several functioning fluorescent lights, but most of them were dead or laid broken on the floor. A dull thumping sound emanated from the walls, like a large fan spinning somewhere deep in the vault. Vallus walked toward the end of the hall and noticed a faint, dusty scent, like a home that hadn't been lived in for some time. He stepped over bits of scattered junk and debris every so often, then finally came to a door at the end of the hall, flanked by two small cameras that appeared to have broken lenses. Considering the door didn't open as he approached it, Vallus surmised that the sensor he'd become familiar with in other vaults was faulty or broken. To the right of the door was another console mounted in the wall.

"Pip, think you can get this?"

The drone flew out of the bag to the console and extended a thin metal arm from underneath her lens. The arm had three tiny fingers tipped with even smaller tools. She fiddled with small parts of the console for a few moments before she beeped and the door slid open weakly.

"I think so," said Pip cheerily before ducking back into Vallus' bag. "Thanks," he replied with a smirk.

Vallus entered a large, circular room with a domed roof and a skylight that was mostly broken out. Through the skylight,

Vallus saw piles of rubble, as if the vault was sunken inward upon itself. Vallus guessed it probably had done exactly that. The lights were mostly dim in the room, but Vallus could still see the sign hanging from high on the roof that read 'LOBBY'. At the back of the room was a pair of large metal elevator doors. And to the left was the one thing out of the ordinary. There sat a large structure, made mostly from found sheets draped over long metal poles on tripods. Vallus walked along the wall of the structure until he found a small opening between the sheets. Within was a small cot with three large bags sat next to it, and a pile of thick blankets, rolled up on the right side of the little fort. There was also a small metal folding chair, and sat upon it was a man with dark ebony skin with gray in his curly hair and beard, dressed in a tattered poncho. His brown eyes looked up as Vallus walked through the entry.

"Well, well. Yet another Seeker come to test the vault? Come, sit. I'm Shiloh. What should I call you?" He said with a gruff and tired voice as he handed Vallus a cup.

"Vallus," he replied as he took the cup to find it filled with water. "Were you expecting company?"

"Seekers have been coming through here for a while. I failed in my task, so I stay here and await those who may need aid."

Vallus took a tentative sip of the water and found it was cool and clean. "You were a Seeker?"

"Oh, yes. I had been through a couple of vaults before this one. Couldn't even get past the security floor on the next level down," he said with a chuckle.

"What happened? You look fit enough," said Vallus.

"Took two bullets to my left leg. There were automated guns at the security entrance, caught me by surprise." Vallus saw Shiloh's hand grip his left leg ever slightly. There was a pained look on his face.

"So I take it you don't know much about this vault, then?"

"Not particularly. Like I said, I couldn't get past the guns. But I do know that this vault is in security lockdown right now. I've seen it before. There should be an override switch in the central security office."

"How operational would you say this one is?"

"Barely. From what I can tell, the lights, air conditioning, and minor systems are alive and well. But that view out the window is unsettling, to say the least. Watch your footing, and keep your wits about you, young Seeker."

Vallus nodded as he stood.

"You mind if I leave some things here for safekeeping?" asked Vallus. "Not at all," replied Shiloh with a wave of his hand.

Vallus reached back with both hands and pulled two small levers attached to his bag. The bag clicked, its metal frame unlocked, and Vallus pulled down to remove the bottom half of the bag, along with the attached bedroll. He set it to the side, the metal frame serving as a sort of tray for the bag.

"That half of my bag contains my food and various tools of use that won't be necessary as I move through this vault. Can I trust you to keep an eye on it?"

"Of course. Do what you must, Seeker. I'll be here should you need anything." Vallus nodded, then turned to the elevator. There was a sense of trepidation in him, the knowledge that a step into the elevator could be the last step he ever took. But that fear was outweighed by the strength of his conviction. He had pledged his life to his mission, and he intended to finish it. Vallus pressed the elevator's call button and waited. After a few moments, the elevator dinged and the doors slid open on a large elevator car. Vallus took a deep breath and stepped inside.

Looking at the inside control panel, all but one of the buttons were blinking red. That one button was labeled 'S', which Vallus assumed meant 'Security'. He pressed the button, and the elevator doors slid closed. With a groan and a thump, the elevator began a slow descent, and Vallus pressed his back to the wall of the elevator.

"Stay away from the door, Pip. We should avoid getting shot," he said. "Of course."

A faint *ding* sounded from the elevator as it groaned to a halt, then the doors slid open. Vallus waited for a moment, then peeked around the door. Then he walked out of the elevator, Pip following as she chirped at him.

"Wait! What about the…"

She trailed off as she saw why Vallus had left the elevator so confidently. They were in a long, wide hallway with a single door at the opposite end. A sign above it read 'Security', and to either side of the door were two wall-mounted machine guns. The gun on the left was hanging from its mounting by a single thick braided wire. The one on the right was also pulled from the mounting, but not nearly as far. The hall was littered with what seemed like thousands of bullet casings, and not far from the elevator door, there was what appeared to be a very old, very dried blood splatter.

"So it appears as though Shiloh's story is trustworthy aside from one minor detail. How did the guns shoot him if they were inoperable?" said Vallus, his arms crossed over his chest as he peered around the scene.

"Perhaps the guns were damaged after they shot him?" replied Pip as she hovered about and examined the area.

"But by what? If it was another Seeker, they would have had

to have left. They couldn't have gotten deeper into the vault with it on security lockdown. The elevator won't go to any other floor."

Pip chirped and wheeled to peer at Vallus.

"I am detecting trace evidence of damage in the walls where the guns were mounted.

It appears something overloaded the circuits connecting the guns to the vault. Too much power could have destroyed them."

Vallus considered Pip's findings for a moment. He looked at the bloodstain, then back to the guns. From the far end of the hall, Vallus could see that the wall around the elevator door was riddled with bullet holes, but the doors were unscathed. The walls and ceiling were similarly coated in scars.

"Seems probable. Vaults tend to be faulty. They are old, after all. You think we can trust him?"

"Shiloh? Perhaps. I believe we should see how he can aid us, but we should always be wary," Pip replied.

"If you want to move forward in a vault, make sure no one behind you has a knife," said Vallus, almost whimsically.

"What's that?"

"Something my father taught me. Never mind," said Vallus. "Let's get moving. The sooner we override this security lockdown, the better."

Vallus walked to the door flanked by guns. A small red button to the right was the only visible control. Vallus pressed the button and the door slid upward to open. Over the threshold, Vallus found himself in another hallway, although this one was shorter and diverged at the far end, with a metal staircase leading up to another hall to the right of another door. Next to the door was a small black box with a slit in it.

"How do I open this?" Vallus asked Pip.

"That's a card reader. We need an authorized key card to get through," replied Pip. "All right. Only way to go is up."

Vallus climbed the stairs with his hands loosely gripped around his swords' hilts in preparation. At the top of the stairs Vallus found a long hallway extending into shadows. Most of the lights were out, save for what little came through the dust-coated window on the left wall of the hallway that extended along its entire length. He tried to look through the window into the room beyond, but the dust was too thick to make out any details. The right side of the hall was lined with doors every few feet. Seeing no immediate threat, Vallus returned his swords to their sheathes and approached the first door.

There was no visible door control that Vallus could see, but he didn't think it would matter, anyway. The door appeared to be dented inwards and sat awkwardly in its frame.

Vallus could see a sensor bar on the top of the door's frame and a small blinking light on that. The door was jammed. He moved on to the next to find it in similar disrepair. Vallus continued on, passing two doors marked 'lavatory' and a third marked 'storage'. Vallus approached the next door, which slid up and led to a room filled with computer banks. Many of them were severely damaged, either hanging from their mountings by wires or missing connectors altogether. The room was littered with junk, mostly papers, but some odds and ends here and there of little interest.

Vallus took a closer look at some of the papers and found them to be about as useful as the random assorted junk scattered about the room. Most of them were files on detainment procedure, with one noting directions to a set of containment cells behind the security station.

There was one desk and file cabinet in the room. The cabinet was knocked over with all three of its drawers pulled out. Vallus guessed that the various papers on the floor probably came from it and had been scattered about by another Seeker, perhaps one who had visited the vault long ago. There was nothing on the desk save for a broken computer, a pile of papers, and a dusty, cracked mug. The desk had two drawers attached to it, but upon inspection they held nothing except old office supplies. Thoroughly disappointed, Vallus turned to look around the room for anything else that might help, and found his disappointment deepened. He left the room.

Pip floated out of his bag as Vallus returned to the hallway and, with a quiet hum, turned on a flashlight mounted under her optic lens. She moved with Vallus, shining the light wherever he looked. The pair walked past several doors, finding them all either broken or marked as something obviously of no use. Vallus passed several of these doors before he came to one marked 'clerk', and heard faint sounds coming from within, something akin to scratching and gurgling. He placed his hands on the pommels of his swords.

The door opened on a very dark room, lit only by a single flickering fluorescent light.

Pip shined her light around the room, revealing it to be filled with several desks and filing cabinets. In the center of the room, at the edge of Pip's light, was the crouched form of a thin, hunched man. He seemed unfazed by the light, and continued the scratching and gurgling Vallus had heard. As Vallus approached cautiously, he noted that the gurgling was coming from the man himself, but the scratching was coming from his hands as he continuously dragged the tips of his fingers across the metal floor. Then the man turned.

Vallus flinched backwards for a moment, and the man

screamed a primal, mad scream.

The man lunged forward with his hands outstretched before him. Vallus reacted quickly and drew both of his swords. He side-stepped the man's lunging attack and swung his blades in wide arcs that cut across his chest and abdomen. A thick, oily blood gushed from the wounds as he tumbled past the Seeker. Fueled by the momentum of his lunge, he flailed and slid across the room to come to rest near the door. Vallus shook the unusual blood from his blades and returned them to their sheathes.

"Well this is a first. Let's see what we can learn, Pip," said Vallus. "Starting with what in the void he was doing. Put your light where he was."

Pip followed the instruction and the light revealed a pool of the same gooey blood on the floor in a wide swath. The bits of floor visible between the uneven pool were covered in thin scratches. There appeared to be nothing else of interest.

"Perhaps he was absorbed by some delusion? This doesn't seem like rational behavior to me," said Pip. "Perhaps the body can yield more information."

Vallus stood and walked to the body of the madman. It was motionless, and more of the blood had pooled under it. Both wounds Vallus had inflicted seemed to have been lethal, having nearly cleaved the madman in two. He drew one of his swords and used it as a lever to flip the body over onto its back. Under Pip's light, Vallus saw that the man was quite emaciated, and he wore nothing except a pair of extremely tattered slacks secured with a makeshift belt that was simply a long wire tied through belt loops. His flesh was pale, and at least a dozen machine parts and several hoses were grafted into it, and the areas around these implants were necrotic and oozed blood and pus. Within the wounds, Vallus could see that the mechanical implants extended even further, with another dozen or so parts visible behind the man's extensive lacerations. The skin on his face was stretched back over his skull to the point that almost no discernible facial features were visible, and his eyes were glazed over.

When Vallus examined his fingertips, he found that their flesh was shredded nearly to the bone and caked with blood.

"All these machines… and the craftsmanship is shoddy, to say the least. Looks like a few of them are in his head. Probably drove him mad."

"It would seem so. Whoever did this to him is a madman," said Pip. "Let's wait and see if it was even a man," said Vallus.

Pip pointed her flashlight around the room and looked in as many directions as possible to assure they were now truly alone. After a few minutes of this, Pip beeped.

"We are clear," she said.

Vallus nodded and, with what little light he had, began to look about the room for anything that might have the key card he needed. There was a long counter to one side of the room, and evidence that there had once been a large wall that had at one time separated the front of the room from the back at that counter. In the back of the room was a dozen or so desks and a large shelf containing a hundred or so thick binders, with many of them scattered around the floor. Vallus heard a strange sound he couldn't identify as he approached the counter, and he realized that the sound was panicky breathing almost too late. An explosive report echoed through the room as a person who had hidden behind the counter fired a shotgun. Fortunately for Vallus, the man missed his shot and hit the ceiling. Vallus drew his blades and approached as the man screamed and crawled on his back to the wall. Vallus stopped.

"What are you doing? What's wrong with you?"

"By the Gods... No no no no no no..."

The man was trembling, his face stuck in a horrified cringe. He clutched his gun with the barrel unnervingly close to his chin. Vallus quickly realized the man was terribly afraid.

"Hold on. Calm down," said Vallus as he returned his swords to their sheathes and held his hands out in front of him. "Tell me what happened. Were you trapped in here with that thing?"

The man continued to tremble and cry. As Vallus got closer, he could see that the man was more a boy, no older than eighteen, and dressed quite similarly to himself. He had a messenger bag on his side, a long brown coat, and leather gloves on the hands that had begun to tightly grip the shotgun. Vallus suspected he was a fellow Seeker. And this had been his first vault.

"Can't help. Can't help. I've seen them. They never loved us," he muttered through his tears.

"Wait," said Vallus. "I'm a Seeker. I can help you. I can get you out of here."

"I didn't find truth. Their eyes burn red. They locked me in here." His eyes were lost, distant, and glazed over.

"Please. I can lead you to the door. I can protect you."

"They'll kill you," he said, his cheeks drenched in tears. "Grind you, crush you. No man can fight them."

"Wait!"

The young Seeker whimpered before he pulled the trigger. His body slumped over along with the smoking shotgun. Vallus bowed his head as his ears rang. After a moment, he knelt over the young Seeker's body and held his hand above its chest.

"Farewell, Seeker. Your journey is at its end," he whispered mournfully. Pip followed as Vallus left the body and continued his search. She chirped. "Shouldn't we see if he had anything useful?"

"No," replied Vallus over his shoulder. "It would be disrespectful to take his things. They were part of his journey; not mine. Let him rest."

"Oh. I didn't know…"

"It's fine, Pip. Let's get to work."

She beeped and followed. As Vallus searched through each desk's drawers, Pip shined her light so he could see the contents, which turned out to be mostly nothing. Vallus quickly tired of seeing paper clips and staples and pens. One desk had a pack of cigarettes.

Another had a pornographic magazine hidden under several papers that Vallus tossed aside in his search. Nothing of use. At the back of the room, Vallus found yet another desk, although larger than the others. It had a large computer at its center, and three books stacked on one side. Vallus looked at each book. *Tax Law. Advanced Accounting Reference Guide. Payroll Procedure Manual.* The top drawer of the desk was locked, but it was a simple lock, easily picked. Inside the drawer was more of the same office supplies, but also a small, plastic card. Vallus looked at it to find it had only three words printed on it: Gamma Clearance Card.

"This must be it. Guess we'll find out," said Vallus.

Vallus jumped to attention at the sound of metal clattering against the floor. He looked up quickly, but he couldn't make out much in the darkness. Pip's light aimed forward, and in the beam Vallus caught a glimpse of something climbing into the ceiling. It looked like a leg. A moment later, a clanging sound like something skittering through the vents passed over Vallus' head. Soon after, the sound faded into the distance. Vallus' heart pounded in his chest.

"What was that?"

"I don't know, but whatever it was left significant damage on the ceiling from where it was grasping, and it tore off the vent cover. That was bolted on."

"It's strong. But it sounds like it left."

"Why would it do that? It had the advantage."

"Maybe it was gathering information. Maybe it just didn't feel like it," said Vallus with a shrug. "But I'm more concerned about how he managed to clear a fifteen foot jump from the floor to the ceiling. And how he got there without my noticing in the first place."

"Our list of questions grows," said Pip pensively.

With the card in hand, Vallus rounded the desk and walked back to the door. He glanced over at the dead Seeker with a frown and stepped around the puddles of syrupy blood and back into the hall, then back toward the staircase. Once he had returned to the door, Vallus swiped the card through the reader on the wall. A bell chime sounded from the door and it slid open. Vallus walked through it and into an expansive, dimly lit room. There were some twenty desks in neat rows near the door, and a small shack at the back right corner with a sign on it that read SECURITY STATION. In the left corner was a large pile of rubble from the ceiling above, and resting in the rubble was a very large machine with a bulbous orb covered in cameras and five long, jointed legs covered in armor plates. Vallus walked toward the Security Station cautiously, his hands resting above his swords. Before he could open the door, an extremely loud, blaring siren sounded, and lights attached to the ceiling flashed red. A computerized voice over a PA echoed through the room.

"INTRUDER ALERT! INTRUDER ALERT!"

Vallus looked around frantically. He didn't hear the machine in the rubble stir over the sirens. He didn't notice it stand shakily to its five legs and raise its orb several feet in the air on a stalk over the screaming voice. But out of his peripheral vision, he did see it raise and swing one of those legs directly at him. Vallus quickly dove to the floor and the leg swept over him and smashed through the wall of the Security Station. Vallus rolled to his feet and drew his swords. He quickly attached the swords at their pommels and twisted the hilts to lock them into place and form a single, double-bladed weapon. The machine swayed on its legs for a moment. The siren and screaming voice had fallen silent, but the flashing lights remained, reducing the Seeker's visibility. Vallus stood at the ready as the machine began to move while the orb on top of it spun back and forth with its cameras extending and retracting. It covered some ten feet in a single step and swung another leg at Vallus. He stepped back to avoid the leg, but another leg caught him from behind. The impact was hard and knocked Vallus off his feet. He skidded across the floor and groaned as he jumped to his feet just in time to avoid the machine attempting to step on him. Vallus found himself thankful for the armor plating and light padding in the back of his coat; without it, the machine's leg could have killed him or snapped his spine.

Vallus bobbed back and forth on his feet as he prepared to avoid the machine, which he had silently dubbed the 'Observer'. The Observer, on the other hand, wobbled as it walked, and it shook and twitched with each movement. It rushed Vallus and tried to bulldoze him.

He had nowhere to dodge but forward, through the machine's legs. Underneath the Observer, Vallus saw nowhere his blade could penetrate to disable it. He did, however, take the opportunity to swing one end of his sword through a hose behind one of the Observer's legs.

The blade cut through cleanly as a putrid liquid poured from the severed hose. The floor hissed and burned, as the liquid was apparently some type of acid. Vallus ran forward, hoping to get out from under the Observer past the leg that now hung weakly and dragged along the floor.

"Pip!" he shouted as he escaped the machine's underbelly.

Pip flew to him and kept pace with him as he ran. The machine swung another leg but missed, and it appeared to have lost some potential momentum thanks to the leg that had become dead weight.

"What's your plan, Vallus?"

"The hoses on the back of its legs seem to be my best bet. If I can't get them, I'm going to need your help. Think you could get under it?"

"Of course. I may be able to shut it down, and I should be too small for it to detect. Tell me when."

Vallus nodded, and Pip flew off at speed and began to circle the Observer, looking for an opening to duck underneath it. Meanwhile, Vallus continued to dodge around the machine's haphazard attacks. It was clearly not designed for combat, but Vallus was quite aware of the sickness that seemed to corrupt the minds of machines. It was a concept he had become all too familiar with.

Vallus noticed Pip maneuver through the machine's legs and hover underneath it, but this distracted him long enough that another leg slapped into his chest. The impact was weaker than the first one Vallus had taken and struck him on the thickest part of his armor, but it was still enough to take the wind out of him and knock him off his feet and across the room. Vallus scrambled to his feet, clutching his chest as it throbbed with pain. He dodged another leg swipe, then had to roll to avoid another of the Observer's legs as it stomped to the floor and left a dent in the metal tiles. Vallus ducked a third swipe and had just enough time to swing one of his blades through the hose behind the leg. Some drops of acid landed on his chest armor, but they were minor and didn't eat away too much of the metal. The Observer, meanwhile, began to wobble on its three remaining functional legs. The other two dragged along the floor, still spilling small amounts of acid with each step.

The Observer poised to strike, but Vallus was faster than it. He noticed the machine had begun to lose power to its functional legs, perhaps because it had spilled too much of the acidic fluid which seemed to be some kind of hydraulic fluid. Vallus' swing against that leg missed the hose and glanced off the Observer's armor plates. He stepped back and tripped over some debris, and the Observer took the opportunity to try and step on Vallus with one of its broken legs. Left with no other option, Vallus dropped his swords and grabbed the leg with both hands. It may have been non-functional, but it was still quite heavy, and the joint that held it to the Observer's body was still active. Vallus strained under the weight as sweat began to pool on his brow. Then the weight became lighter, and the Observer made loud whirring and clicking sounds for a few moments as its cameras wildly spun and extended.

Then it slumped and fell over to its side and hit the floor with a heavy thud. Floating where the Observer had been a moment before was Pip, slightly tilted to the side as if to say "look what I did!"

"Thanks, Pip," said Vallus as he stood to his feet, detached his swords, and returned them to their sheathes.

"You're welcome," said Pip cheerfully. "Curious as to what

I did?"

"You found an 'off' switch?"

"No. Machines like this don't have anything like that. I overloaded its motherboard by forcing it to log and process pictures of your face on repeat," she replied.

"Weird," said Vallus, amused.

"It worked," she said.

Vallus climbed through the hole in the wall the Observer had made. The inside of the room was fairly plain, with two desks and a large computer in the back. Vallus went to the computer and looked it over. There was a large, red button labeled 'Lockdown'. Vallus pressed it. There was a loud alarm bell, then an automated voice over an intercom said "Security lockdown lifted."

Vallus recalled the directions he had found before and scanned the room. He quickly found the lever he was looking for. It was attached to the wall, and marked 'Cells'. He pulled the lever, and through the adjacent window, Vallus saw the back wall of the room begin to separate and open. He left the Security Station, rounded the building past the broken Observer, and walked toward the wall door. The remaining presence of the siren lights bothered him, but he moved on. Within the wall was a long corridor lined with cells. The first room on the left was marked 'Armory', but was visibly empty, seemingly cleared out long ago. With Pip floating behind and pointing her flashlight ahead, Vallus continued down the hall. The cells were all empty, and their doors were all opened. At the back of the room was a desk and rolling chair. On the desk was a badge, an ashtray, and a small plastic case. He opened the case to find a handgun inside, along with two full magazines and one loaded already for a total of twenty-seven rounds. Vallus pulled back the slide to find a round already chambered, and further inspection of the weapon showed it was a .45 caliber pistol. He took a holster from the case, put the spare magazines in the pouches on the holster's belt, then secured the holster around his waist, clear of his other belts that held his tools and his swords.

"A gun? Think it will help?" asked Pip.

"Perhaps. Guns aren't exactly common, either. In the right hands, it can be a useful tool," replied Vallus.

Vallus looked around the area one last time to assure he hadn't overlooked anything. His attention snapped back to the door at the sound of metal clanging to the floor. Then came the sound of something heavy falling to the floor with a bang. There was a hissing sound as Vallus sprinted to the door, Pip in tow. Vallus reached the door as he heard a scraping sound from the ceiling. Back in the room with the dead Observer lying still, Vallus frantically looked around as Pip aimed her flashlight in every direction. Then the hairs on Vallus' neck stood up at the sound of low growling. With some hesitation, he looked toward the ceiling. It was too far for Pip's flashlight to do much good, and the lights were all broken, and no light came from the hole in the ceiling. But between flashes of the security strobe lights, Vallus could barely make out a figure. On the first pass, Vallus learned the thing was big. On the second, he learned it was grasping the ceiling in one clawed hand. And on the third, he learned it was looking at him. Vallus couldn't see its left arm. The lights flashed again and it growled, then on the next pass it scurried into the nearby vent, scraping and tearing the ceiling viciously as it went.

Vallus waited quietly for a few moments, his hands clutching his swords and his heart pounding in his chest. He remembered the eyes. They were burning red. He shook the image out of his mind as he put away his swords. His eyes lingered in the direction of the vent for a moment before he turned toward the door he had entered from and made to exit the security wing.

***

An hour or two had passed, Rhald supposed, since the Seeker had entered the vault. He sat in the dirt on his knees, the castle in his sight. He debated back and forth on walking up the pathway. Maybe, just maybe, the King would grant him an audience. He was thankful he could even think. He had had trouble thinking with all the noise that had been coming from the entryway. All that gunfire. It was deafening.

Rhald shakily took a pack of hand rolled cigarettes from his pocket and an old lighter, then lit one and took a long drag. His hands shook as he thought of the walk along the path to the castle door. Then he rubbed his eyes and waved the smoke from in front of his face, for he thought he had seen an illusion. But when he looked again, Rhald noticed that he really had seen the door silently open. He sat still for a few heartbeats, quietly looking at the doorway and carefully puffing on his cigarette. He flicked the cigarette to the side and bolted toward the pathway. It was thin, with a sheer drop on either side leading to piles of jagged boulders at the bottom, but Rhald was unperturbed.

He stopped abruptly in front of the door. It was too dark inside to make out anything other than a short hallway. His heart pounded and his breath came rapidly, and with some hesitation, Rhald stepped over the threshold and into the old castle. The hall was lit by four small, dim lights, and the door at the end of the hall was open. Rhald passed through the door and into a larger room, lit by two slanted windows on the ceiling. The room was half the size of the castle, and at the center was an abnormally large throne.

Sitting in the throne, bathed in shadow, was a tall, intimidating figure covered in heavy, tarnished plate armor. It wore a full helm like that of a knight, and welded to the top of the helm were five long metal spikes, almost like a crown. Dozens of hoses ran under his armor, through small bits of the exposed flesh that could be seen through his mechanical body, and into his helm. Through the visor on the being's helm, Rhald could see nothing.

And sat beside the being, leaning against the throne with one end of the cross guard propping it up, was a massive sheathed sword, almost as large as the being itself. The figure shifted in the throne as Rhald entered the room, and startled him. When it spoke, it was with a man's voice, although like distant thunder and tumbling boulders. There was authority in it, an almost demanding tone, and a slight hint of immense wisdom.

"Day in, day out, you stare at my castle. Have you dreamed of my return? For how long?" he said, almost whimsically.

"My whole life, my lord," said the man nervously as he prostrated himself at the foot of the throne. The being stood and looked down on Rhald.

"What is your name, mortal?"

"Rhald, my lord," he replied.

"I suppose you've come to tell me a Seeker has come to the vault, yes?"

"Yes, my lord."

"King," he said bitterly.

"My lord?"

"I am the Ashen King. You will address me as such," he replied as he crossed his arms behind his back.

"Of course, my King. Apologies." He dared not look up at the King.

"Save it. I am aware of this Seeker. The time has come. Our new dawn is approaching."

The King took a single step down from the throne, his boots placed firmly in front of Rhald, only inches away. He stooped down toward the still-prostrated man and placed one hand on top of his shaggy-haired head.

"We thank you for your service, Rhald," said the King as he moved his hand along Rhald's face and lifted him onto his knees, forcing Rhald to look up at his helm. "You have been a man of great faith in your Gods. But your services are no longer required."

The Ashen King wrapped his hand around Rhald's throat and lifted him into the air. Rhald struggled and writhed against the King's grip, but it was too much to overpower and too sudden. The King slowly closed his grip as Rhald scratched at his armored forearms, choking and gurgling. Tears welled up in Rhald's eyes as his face went blue. Soon, there was a crack and Rhald's struggling ceased. The last thing he could see, just over the King's shoulder, was another tall, armored, mechanical being standing near the throne.

The King dropped Rhald's lifeless body to the floor and turned to the being next to the throne. He was much like the King, but wore bone white armor with several small grooves in each plate, with black armor plates layered underneath. His helmet was more like a mask, with dozens of pipes running from it to his body, as well as to his gauntlets and boots. A light trail of steam hovered around him like an aura. He bowed slightly at the King's approach.

"Have Aurien clean this up. Tell her to be ready. I must

confer with the Wizard," said the Ashen King.

"Of course," replied the second being, his voice gravely and wheezing. "Orders?"

The King stopped as he passed him. He turned his head over his shoulder and let out a deep sigh.

"Simple, Vakka. Wait."

The King walked through an archway at the back of the throne room and down a long, dark hallway. He quickly approached the back of the castle and a wooden door on his right, barely cracked. The King rapped his knuckles on it twice, and after a moment, it creaked open. The room inside was pitch black, with a single lantern casting a sliver of light from a dying candle. From within the darkness, the King could see a pair of burning red eyes near a desk. The eyes moved through the darkness like a wraith before a second, brighter light came on at the back of the room. The King stepped through the threshold to see a tall, thin being that seemed to be entirely mechanical, down to the details of his face and the fibers of his muscles, complete with plates that simulated a sort of robe, etched with numerous archaic symbols and trimmed with deep crimson paint. His face was thin and almost serpentine, with a sharp nose, thin eyes, and a razor slit mouth. Wires and hoses were connected to his strange, electronic component-covered head and several other points of his body. He also had long, thin fingers tipped with sharp claws, and a half dozen cables connected to his back hung loosely behind him. He stood at the center of the room, surrounded by shelves, machines, and tools, his bladed fingers laced together. His voice was almost predatory, with a sort of superiority and narcissism hidden just under the surface.

"We have a Seeker problem, it would seem," he said with a hiss.

"So it would."

"Ask."

"What do you recommend, Wizard?"

The Wizard tapped the tip of his claw against his pointed chin in thought for a moment. He looked back to the King and the thin metal plates that made up his eyelids narrowed as he spoke.

"Take our time. See what he can do. Assess the threat, then we can properly prepare for how it may affect our plans."

"And if this one is different?"

"They never are," said the Wizard, taking a step closer to the King. "He is but a man. And what is a man when standing against the might of the Gods? He is a leaf in a hurricane."

"I will keep an eye on him, then. Our new dawn approaches," said the King as he turned to leave.

"Yes. Close the door on your way out," said the Wizard as he shut off the second light and his eyes like fading coals coasted back to the corner of the room as the sound of his cables gently clanking on the floor followed along.

The King closed the door and stood outside it for a few moments. His thoughts were racing. There was still much to be done, but he played with half a dozen ideas. He began to feel something, like a tightness in his chest. Perhaps excitement? He had forgotten what it felt like. With much on his mind, the Ashen King marched up the hall, back to his throne, and sat in silence once more, contemplating the rapid arrival of the day he had been awaiting for so long.

Chapter 3

Vallus stood still and quiet as the elevator ascended back to the lobby, regarding a poster framed on the wall of the car. It was labeled 'Sector Map', but it was as generic and bare-bones as imaginably possible. Vallus inspected it and saw that there were supposedly twenty floors of offices below security. As he was looking over the map with what little light the lone bulb in the elevator car had, it slid to a stop and the doors opened.

The lobby was as Vallus had left it; quiet, dark, with Shiloh's tent sitting peacefully to the side. Vallus looked out the window. It was still quite bright outside, probably an hour or two after noon by his estimation. He stepped into Shiloh's camp, looking around for the aforementioned former Seeker. Vallus found him reclining on a cot at the far back of the camp, a tattered book in hand. He looked up over the book at Vallus with a smile, then a frown.

"You look like you've been through it already. Take a seat, eat something," he said, pointing to a bag on the table which contained several apples. He took one and bit into it to find it was fresh.

"This come from the town?" asked Vallus after swallowing, holding up the apple.

"Yes. If you walk past the elevator to the right, there's a hallway there. It's collapsed and impassable, but there's a hole in the ceiling above it that is, as I've been told, easily accessible by a pathway up the backside of the cliff this vault is built into. I paid a local boy in advance to drop food here every so often. Before, you know. The bullet."

"Right," said Vallus, somewhat absently, as he relished each juicy bite of the apple.

He looked up when he noticed Shiloh observing him with concern. "What is it?"

"There was an announcement. Security lockdown lifted. Wanna talk about it?"

Vallus nodded, then began to recount his experiences in thesecurity level. The madman, the Seeker, the Observer, and whatever the creature on the ceiling had been. Vallus noticed that Shiloh seemed to grow more horrified with each event, but was particularly shaken by the young Seeker. Once Vallus had finished speaking, they both sat in silence for a few moments, their heads bowed.

"That's a lot for one man to take in. If you wanna run out of this ghastly place screaming, I wouldn't blame you."

"No. My need outweighs my… discomfort," replied Vallus as he rooted through the half of his bag he had left behind.

"Still set on your task, eh? All right, then. What's your next step?"

"There's a map in the elevator, but it isn't very helpful. I need a better one. Any idea where I should start looking?"

"Well," said Shiloh, scratching his beard in thought. "You could try Logistics. It's the lowest floor the elevator goes to. If there's anything in this vault, it's gonna be deep."

Vallus nodded, withdrawing his box of power cells from his bag. He placed it in the bag he still had on his back. He stood and was about to leave when he turned back to Shiloh.

"What do you suppose that creature was? The one that was on the ceiling?"

"Never heard of such a thing. I honestly couldn't tell you," he replied. "Whatever it is, though, I wouldn't mess with it."

"I don't 'mess'," said Vallus with a tap of his fingers upon the pommel of one of his swords and a slight smirk on his lips that betrayed the intensity in his eyes.

Shiloh chuckled heartily as Vallus walked toward the elevator. With a deep breath, he stepped inside. With only a moment's hesitation, Vallus pressed the button on the control pad marked 'Logistics'. Pip hovered out of his bag as the doors began to close. Slowly, it churned past security. Not long after, the elevator lurched. The lights flickered. The buttons on the control panel lit up in a random order. Then the car began to fall. For a moment, it was almost as if Vallus floated. His stomach lurched. There was a terribly loud grinding sound, possibly the elevator's brakes. They weren't working. Then the elevator stopped. Vallus hit the floor with a hard thud. He was jolted by the impact, but not seriously injured. He stood as the doors opened, groaning slightly as he rubbed his shoulder. A sign on the wall read 'Offices Level 7'.

Vallus was puzzled by the sign, but even more so by the fact that none of the buttons on the elevator seemed to be working. Not even the button for the lobby. He had no choice but to enter the office. Ahead of him, Vallus could see very little in Pip's flashlight. The area was only lit sparingly by the odd functioning fluorescent light, and even those were sketchy at best and flickering wildly at worst. There were large partitions scattered throughout the room with a walkway between them, through which Vallus could barely make out a glowing sign pointing to stairs on the far side of the room. He took a step forward into the area and picked up a sound, one he could barely distinguish. It was like a clattering, or a scratching.

Then a low growl. Something moved in the darkness.

Vallus signaled to Pip to turn off the flashlight and she flew into his bag as he hugged the partition and moved through the walkway. He peeked around the corner after a few feet to see another walkway leading to the far left side of the room. About ten feet away were two men who looked much like the madman Vallus had been attacked by in security. Their movements were random, disorganized. They groaned and growled to themselves, and Vallus saw one of them walk straight into one of the partitions, weakly bang into it and stagger, then walk away as though nothing had happened. They didn't seem to notice him, but he clicked the safety on the pistol off just in case.

He began to creep silently past the branching path, keeping an eye on the madmen who still didn't seem to be aware of his presence. His heart thumped in his chest with each step. Vallus was almost completely across to safety when he heard a crunch. Then a growl as the madmen turned in the direction of the sound. Vallus moved his foot and found he had stepped on the remains of a broken coffee mug. The growling grew louder. Vallus placed a hand on the grip of the pistol. One of the madmen screamed and rushed toward Vallus, his hands stretched out in front of him, drool flying from his mouth. Vallus drew the pistol and fired three shots. The first shot missed, but the next two hit their mark, right in the chest. He kept running, apparently only momentarily fazed by the shots. Growling echoed from deeper in the room, along with shuffling as whatever was there searched for the source of the noise that had been Vallus' gun.

Vallus had only a moment to draw his sword and decapitate the madman, who fell to the floor behind the Seeker. He glanced at the body to see it leaked the same thick, syrupy blood as the other madman, and quite profusely at that. The second madman drew nearer, having been momentarily staggered by the sound of the gunfire. Still several feet away from Vallus, the madman dove at him. He wasn't ready for the maneuver. The madman crashed into Vallus with surprising force, enough to knock Vallus off his feet despite the fact that he was considerably larger in both height and mass compared to his attacker.

Vallus scrambled to his feet and drew his second sword as he and the madman tumbled apart. Out of the corner of his eye, he glimpsed movement down the corridor opposite where the two madmen had been. There was something down the hall, still relatively far away. Vallus guessed there were more madmen heading his way, but the one who was staring at him with glazed, mindless eyes, contorting its emaciated body with snapping joints, drew most of his attention. It screamed again and charged at Vallus. He had braced for it this time. The first swing missed its mark but took off the madman's right arm at the elbow. He staggered and screamed again. He swiped at Vallus with his left, but the Seeker sidestepped it.

With as much strength as he could muster, Vallus swung one of his swords into the madman's abdomen and cleaved him in two. It wasn't as hard as he had anticipated, considering Vallus' swords were designed to cut through metal plates.

Vallus began to hear groaning and growling as the madmen down the corridor grew ever closer. Vallus debated for a moment. *I can break for the stairs,* he thought. *Or I can fight.* He listened intently in the dark, trying to focus on the movement. He couldn't discern much, but he guessed there were at least two more by the growling. Fighting could be risky, as the noise could draw even more if any were in the maze of partitions. Making a run could potentially get him cornered if he alerted any more along the way.

He weighed his options for a moment, and decided to risk a bigger fight for the chance to get away.

He took his first running step and the growling intensified. Vallus didn't often run, as the gear he carried tended to make noise when he did, and the weight of his gear made it somewhat difficult. The former was becoming a problem. Vallus could hear growls welling up from deeper within the room, and he glimpsed stirring as he ran past another intersection in the partitions. Vallus glanced over his shoulder and counted four of them not far behind him. Another two steps and he counted ten. Yet another few steps, and they numbered too many to quickly count. They were all wailing and screaming, clawing and scrambling over each other to get to him. A tide of horribly twisted, deformed flesh chased after Vallus as he closed in on the door at the back wall.

The door slid open slowly enough that Vallus had to reduce speed to a jog to not run into it. Once through it, he caught a glimpse of the madmen before the door closed and Vallus hit the red 'lock' button on the wall. The door held as what Vallus guessed was thirty or forty madmen slammed against it like a breaking wave, scratching at it and screaming wildly.

Vallus wiped a few drops of sweat from his brow and proceeded to walk down the staircase, twenty steps down before a turn down twenty more. He did so quietly, hoping not to alert anything that may have been in the next room.

"Pip, best you stay in the bag. There seem to be a number of the madmen here; I'd like to limit my noise production," he whispered.

A low affirmative beep from his bag told him Pip understood. Vallus drew the pistol from its holster, checked the chamber, then clicked the safety on and holstered it again. He assumed he wouldn't need it again since it had seemed ineffective before, although he was curious to know how the madman could have survived the bullets it had taken. There was a thin vertical window on the door in front of Vallus. The room ahead was darker than the last, and Vallus couldn't see anything more than a few feet in. He took a step closer to trigger the door's motion sensor and stepped into the room.

There wasn't much he could see in the darkness, which was only broken up by the odd scattered fluorescent light, and even those were visibly on their last legs. A thought flashed through Vallus' mind that it was odd how the vault was simultaneously amazingly intact and falling apart at the seams. He had already stowed away his weapons, but he kept his hands near them just in case as he took in what little he could from the area.

There were more of the partitions. A dusty, stale smell hung in the air, and the carpet underfoot was coated in a thin layer of dust. Vallus kept his ears open for more sounds in the dark, but this room was quiet. Perhaps, Vallus surmised, the madmen hadn't gotten farther into the vault yet. He walked slowly as he moved through the room, and with no madmen to fight or run from, he was free to inspect the area in detail. Vallus couldn't see an exit sign or a stairway anywhere, so he decided to spend some time investigating rather than search for the next staircase. He still had to get to Logistics, but he didn't need to do so quickly. Vallus took his first left, and as he walked down a hallway formed by the partitions, he noticed there were openings in them every few feet. When he looked in one of these openings, he found that they were cubicle offices. In the first one he looked in, Vallus could see only a desk, a dead computer, and a broken and overturned office chair.

"Pip, let me get a light," said Vallus, and the little drone flew out of his bag and hovered at his side with her light on.

"Thought you'd never ask," she said with a playful beep.

Vallus chuckled lightly and pointed Pip to the next cubicle, now out of range of the nearest building light. Within was much like the last cubicle; a broken chair sat on the floor beside a desk and computer. This desk had items on it, though. There was a framed photograph of a man with a small child, a boy by look, although it was faded and cracked. There was a pen that had been snapped in half on the desk next to a small tool Vallus couldn't identify and a hand-scrawled note, faded with time, that read:

My dearest,

I might not be home tonight. There's a problem. Don't got the clearance to know the details, but the ... is being weird. I'm gonna have ... drop this note off if I have to stay late, which I probably will ... scanners are going nuts. ... are blocked, too. No outgoing.

Don't wait up, and give my little boy a hug for me. I'm sleeping in tomorrow; not feeling well and this day isn't helping. Love you.

Vallus put the note down and picked up the tool, turning it over in his hand. It looked like an infrared thermometer, but there was a thin metal coil at the tip of it and a small black button just below the screen above the handle. When it finished booting up, the tool's screen read 'no detection'. Vallus pointed the tool at the computer on the desk and clicked the trigger. It read 'no connection detected'. Inspired, Vallus pointed the tool at Pip. She bobbed in the air, tilted to one side curiously. Vallus began to understand the tool when its screen read 'Systems functioning. No errors detected'.

"I think this tool detects problems in machines. Might be useful later."

"Perhaps. Don't be surprised if it says they're broken, though," replied Pip.

"Of course."

For a brief moment, Pip's light flashed on the floor. Vallus held up his hand. "Hey, put that light back on the floor."

Pip did as instructed, and in her light, Vallus could see something on the floor just out from under the desk. He looked closer. It was a large stain, just under the layer of dust. It was dark and radiated in every direction.

"There isn't much there, but my scanner tells me this stain was most likely from blood."

"Something horrible happened in this vault. Let's keep moving," he said as he walked out of the cubicle.

The pair wandered through the maze of cubicles for some time looking for an exit. Vallus looked in cubicles as he passed them, but most were quite similar to the first two. A few were a little larger, and used the extra space to hold things like printers and filing cabinets. Vallus had learned in his first vault not to bother looking for the truth in ancient documents that used terms no one understood or contained redacted or damaged text. If he was ever going to get his answer - in his mind - he would need to get them from something more concrete, so he passed these by as he looked for the staircase.

Vallus stopped when he heard something glass break nearby. Vallus crept along the wall of the partitions, one hand on the hilt of a sword. He drew the blade as he rounded the corner into a cubicle, but he refrained from taking a swing when he realized what had made the sound. There was a picture frame on the floor, its glass face shattered with the remnants lying under it. Sitting on the desk, purring and licking its leg, was a small, brown cat.

It looked up at Vallus and meowed, then hopped off the desk and ran down the hall. Vallus chased after at a jog. About twenty or so feet ahead, the cat stopped and looked back at him.

He got near, and the cat kept running. This went on for some time as the cat led Vallus through twists and turns all about the cubicles. Eventually, he came to the end of a hall and found himself outside of the cubicles. A lone bulb fixture hung above, casting a light Vallus was surprised he hadn't seen earlier.

Vallus realized he was at the wall he would have been at had he turned right at the fork instead of left and went straight. He wondered how long he had been walking. Then he saw the cat. It was sitting near the door which was marked 'Floor 9', softly whining. Propped against the door was a body, and the area was covered in sprays of blood. The body was severely wounded, with two large bullet wounds in the chest and one in the stomach. The head was mostly intact, with a large cut down the left side and a chunk missing from the right. The body was also covered in stab wounds. The cat looped around Vallus' feet as he approached the body to inspect it. Judging by what remained of its attire, it was the body of a man who had been a Seeker.

"Think this cat was his companion?" asked Vallus.

"Most likely, based on the animal's behavior," said Pip as she inspected the head wound. "This wound was caused by a high-caliber bullet. It shredded him. The bullet is lodged in the door."

"Who did this?" asked Vallus, more to himself than to Pip.

"Not sure, but there was a fight," said Pip as she floated about the immediate area. "The dust on the carpet has been disturbed by heavy boots. There's blood from fresh wounds. And this only happened a day or two ago, at most."

"Shiloh never mentioned seeing a Seeker that recently."

"To be fair, you didn't ask if he did."

"Fair. Benefit of the doubt. Perhaps this Seeker got in through some other entrance I'm not aware of, considering the front door was locked when we got here. I entered my second vault through a damaged external vent, maybe this one did the same."

The cat rubbed against his boot, and he looked down, staring at the animal for a solid thirty seconds as a thought dawned on him.

"Why did he have the cat?"

"Same reason you fixed me?" replied Pip.

"Sure, but I don't have to feed you. The resources he would need... not to mention the constant attention... you'd have to constantly monitor it in a vault. Too risky."

"Perhaps, but it seems it was a risk he was willing to take," said Pip. "Even if it did seem to be the reason for his death."

"What makes you say that?"

"You can't tell a cat to be silent. Whoever killed this Seeker was most likely alerted to his presence because of the cat. And I'd bet the killer is still here, too. Maybe not this room, but this vault."

"Think it was that thing on the ceiling earlier?" asked Vallus, as a fleeting image of the creature's claws passed through his mind.

"Maybe."

Vallus walked to the body, pulled it around so that he could pick it up under the pits of its arms, and gently pulled it away from the door. He rested the body next to the wall and crossed its arms over its chest. Vallus repeated the same honorary rite he had performed for the last Seeker, then used some water from his canteen to wash the blood from the body off his hands. Quickly, he set to work on opening the door to the staircase, since it was apparently jammed. The cat stopped rubbing against his boot halfway through and turned, staring down the hall behind Vallus. It meowed several times, then began to growl and hiss.

Vallus stopped what he was doing and looked behind him. He saw nothing. He returned to his work, then a few moments later, a clanging sound interrupted him. There was a loud thud, as though something heavy had fallen to the floor. Vallus held still, his eyes struggling to adjust to the dark. Then he saw them. Two red embers, glowing from deep within the darkness. It moved, the thing. It was closing in on him. The cat hissed loudly and ran off into the darkness, away from the creature.

"Shit," said Vallus as he turned back to the door and worked faster. "Pip! Bag!"

He could hear the thing's heavy footfalls, even over the whir of Pip's fans as she flew into his bag pocket. It was coming closer, although slowly. Vallus heard a loud metallic sound, like two metal plates sliding against one another, and found the sound familiar. A dangerous kind of familiar. The door slid open and Vallus ran through. He caught one last glimpse of the thing's eyes burning in the darkness as the door closed. Vallus slammed his hand against the emergency lock button. Vallus stood against the wall in the stairwell, out of the thin window's line of sight. Vallus could hear shuffling outside the door. The thing was there. After a few moments, there was silence, then an enormous bang as something hit the door hard enough to dent it. Then there were several echoing, banging sounds followed by silence.

With his heart pounding in his chest and his hands slightly shaking, Vallus walked down the staircase to the next door. It slid open to another dark room full of cubicles. Vallus could once more hear the sound he had heard when he entered the vault, like a large fan slowly thumping as it spun. It was slightly louder than before. There was almost no light in the room, save for maybe three or four scattered and dying fluorescent bulbs. Vallus called for Pip, and she flew out of his bag and turned on her flashlight. There, just ten feet away from where Vallus stood in front of the door, were five madmen, gathered together in a circle.

They were perfectly still, and absolutely silent. Vallus drew his swords. They didn't react. Intrigued, Vallus slowly and cautiously approached the group.

They showed no sign of reaction to Vallus' presence, nor to Pip's light. They were breathing, but they appeared otherwise catatonic. He sheathed the sword in his left hand, then waved it in front of one of them. No reaction. Upon further inspection, Vallus found there were thick streaks of dried blood in and around their ears, as if it had suddenly burst out from within. Vallus noticed they were all groaning slightly, as if dazed. Then he heard something moving in the darkness. He carefully stepped around the madmen, Pip following closely behind with her flashlight illuminating his path. After passing a few turns to avoid whatever was moving in the dark, Vallus came to a dead end. He looked at the partition wall for a moment, debating whether or not he could jump it, when he heard the distinct sound of mechanical joints moving from behind him.

Vallus turned his head to see a humanoid machine no taller than five feet, with thin arms and legs. The arms were tipped with hands that had three long, spindly fingers. The feet resembled those of a large flightless bird. There was a faded logo painted on its chest, but Vallus couldn't make out what it was with what little light was afforded him. The head was of an unusually oval shape, like an almond, with two thin, red eyes mounted above what appeared to be a mouth. The machine stood in the darkness, illuminated by Pip's light, then began to open its mouth. As it did, a series of layered metal rings within shifted and spun along metal wires as a loud whirring sound emanated from it along with a bright blue glow. Then Vallus heard what sounded like a woman screaming, and was blasted off his feet by a wave of powerful, invisible force. Vallus careened through the partition wall behind him and crashed into the desk within the cubicle on the other side. His sword, knocked loose from his hand, fell under the desk just out of reach.

Dazed, Vallus scrambled under the desk to grab his sword. He couldn't hear anything over the high-pitched ringing in his ears, and he could barely open his eyes without wincing. There was an excruciating pain in his head, punctuated by an agonizing throbbing. He caught a glimpse of the machine as he struggled to climb over the debris to get to stable footing, and noted it was walking toward him slowly. The rings in its mouth were issuing a thin trail of steam.

Vallus was beginning to regain some of his senses when he finally clambered his way over the desk and onto the floor of an adjacent hall. He took a quick inventory of his surroundings, or what little of them he could see. He caught a glimpse of a sign for the door to the next staircase, but could not make out the door itself. There was a hallway behind him, and one to his left, and a solid wall to his right. And the machine was approaching from in front. Vallus motioned to Pip to take cover in his bag as he sheathed his swords.

"What about light?" asked Pip as she flew into the pocket.

Vallus noticed the machine perk up at the sound of Pip's speech. It hunched over for a second, then sprinted toward him.

"I'll explain later," he said as he turned and ran down the hall behind him.

The machine leaped over the desk and sections of partition before it bolted after Vallus, its metal feet clacking loudly with each stride. Its hands were open and outstretched, as if it was trying to grab Vallus. He ran, harder and harder with each step, pushing himself to ignore the weight of his gear and the discomfort of his hanging swords slapping against his legs. He could hear distinctive mechanical sounds behind him, just barely as the ringing faded from his head. Then he began to hear the charging sound as he rounded a corner. There was another explosive scream, and Vallus ducked his head under his arms as the corner of the partition wall was blasted to pieces behind him. The machine stopped for a brief second, then continued chasing after Vallus. With each step, he grew closer to the door. And with each step, the machine grew closer to him.

Vallus had almost reached the door. It was maybe forty feet away. The Seeker sprinted toward it, his head still throbbing and his muscles aching from the exertion. He could almost feel the machine's fingers on his back. As he ran, Vallus drew the gun from his belt and clicked off the safety. He took aim over his shoulder as he kept running. The machine was somewhat further away than he had anticipated, but he had hoped for that. He pulled the trigger. The machine was knocked off its feet by the bullet, giving Vallus enough time to hit the lock button. Huffing, Vallus holstered the gun and made to walk down the stairs. The glass of the door's window shattered, making Vallus jump. He turned to see the screaming machine's arm pushed through the window, scratching at the door. Vallus left it and walked down the stairs. This staircase had two flights, a feature Vallus found quite annoying as he massaged his aching thighs at the bottom of the stairs.

Vallus could still hear the machine, which he had silently dubbed 'the Screamer', scratching at the door. Occasionally, it would slap the door, as though it was trying to hit the lock button. He ignored it and pressed on. Once in the next room, Vallus was surprised to find it much more well-lit than the previous floors. It was also smaller, with a homier sort of atmosphere, although the air still smelled stale with a touch of old paper. Vallus jumped at a loud bang from behind him. With the stairwell still echoing the sound, Vallus guessed the Screamer had tried to scream the door down. Pip flew out of his bag and hovered inches from his face.

"Why are we running? You're bigger, stronger, and more equipped than that thing," she said, confused and frustrated.

"I planned to run when I saw the madmen. The way their ears looked - something did that to their brains. Then that thing screamed and I realized it was the cause. I can't get hit by that scream too much. Could do to me what it did to them. Or worse."

"Oh... I..."

"Forget it. Eventually, I will need to fight this thing. But for now, I need to get it to stop chasing and start searching."

Vallus found that the partitions had been replaced with actual walls, forming halls that led to various rooms. He wished he could explore them all, but he knew he couldn't risk letting the Screamer catch up. Vallus advanced into the area, keeping his eyes alert ahead of him and his ears alert behind him. Old pictures lined the walls, most of them faded with time and depicting long-dead people dressed for a bygone age. Vallus tried several doors, all to no avail. They appeared to be locked. Vallus waved Pip on, choosing not to try and bypass any door locks. He assumed he didn't have time, anyway.

There was a distant banging sound that echoed through the walls. Every few steps he took, bang. Every few breaths, bang. Bang. Vallus came back to the main hall. To his left was a long hallway that appeared to lead nowhere from where Vallus stood; to his right was the door he had entered the floor from. Another bang. Then another, louder. Then a scraping, as of metal against metal. Silence for a moment, then the door opened. The Screamer walked through the door and stood still in front of it, seemingly staring down the hall. Vallus stood still and silent himself, ready to run. The machine's head twitched randomly, as if trying to detect some sound. Upon closer inspection, Vallus could see bits of glass embedded in the joint connecting its right arm to its torso, and a thin liquid dripping from a hose in that joint. The arm twitched as it raised. Vallus shifted his boot on the carpet. The Screamer's head snapped still, then it ran.

Vallus turned and sprinted down the hall. He could hear the machine's metal mouth open as it charged another strike from its weapon. The Seeker rounded the corner just as it fired. The wall exploded as the sound wave struck it. The Screamer turned the corner and ran through the cloud of debris, hot on Vallus' tail. He looked back to see a thick cloud of steam issuing from its mouth. After rounding another corner and avoiding another explosion, Vallus came to a hall, at the end of which was a door with a large window to the left of it that presumably overlooked the staircase. The machine was gaining on him. His heart pounded as hard as his legs. Left with nowhere to run, Vallus drew his swords.

As quickly as he could, Vallus turned. His boots slid against the dirt-coated carpet as he wheeled around and swung his blades at the Screamer. He realized too late that he had been so focused on his plan that he hadn't heard the machine charge its weapon. It screamed, blasting Vallus off his feet and crashing through the window behind him. He fell ten feet and hit the bottom of the stairwell with a hard thump as a hail of glass fell around him. He jumped to his feet, sheathed his swords, and pushed on through the door to the floor marked 'Offices Floor 11', his back still aching from the fall. He locked the door, the Screamer still relatively far behind him.

The next room was like the others before it: dark, musty, and filled with cubicles.

Vallus quickly rounded a corner and ducked inside one of them, tucking himself under a desk. A few moments later, he heard the door to the room slide open, then the metal clacking of the Screamer's weird bird feet. It clicked and buzzed for a second or two. As quietly as he could, Vallus slowly drew one of his swords.

He could hear the thing moving in the dark. It took each step slowly. Clack. Clack. Clack. Clack. He heard a thump and a partition wall shake. Clack clack. It was in the hall. Clack. Clack. It was outside the cubicle Vallus was hiding in. Clack. It took a step inside. Vallus could see the connected parts of its leg assembly. The machine seemed to give up and turned to leave, and Vallus poised to strike. His hand steady despite the thumping of his heart in his chest, Vallus thrust his blade forward and cut straight through a hose that ran through its leg. The machine whirred and screeched as though in pain as it stumbled. It began to charge its weapon. Vallus kicked it hard in the side of the head and took off out of the cubicle at speed. He found himself thankful for the steel plating in the toe of his boots. Farther down the hall, Vallus ducked into a cubicle and pressed his back to the wall as best as he could despite his bag.

The machine wasn't running any more. It was limping down the hall. It groaned and hissed. It passed the cubicle. Vallus took a silent step out. The next step gave him away as he stepped on a shard of glass. The Screamer whirled on him and charged its weapon once more. Taking one more long stride to close the gap, Vallus thrust his sword forward as the machine began to scream. The blade pierced the inner mechanics of its mouth and sliced cleanly through the weapon. Its arms flailed at him, but they couldn't reach. It tried to scream, but couldn't make the severed rings move. With a roar he pushed the blade deeper through the machine, then twisted the blade to the side. The Screamer sparked, steamed, and groaned, then Vallus pulled the sword. Much of the Screamer's inner parts came with it. The machine crumpled to the floor in an inert heap.

Vallus dropped to the floor in a seated position next to the machine, exhausted, and dropped his sword on the floor next to him. He wiped sweat from his brow before he pulled out his canteen and took as big a drink as he was willing to take of what little water he had. Pip flew out of his bag and looked around the area with her light.

"We appear to be alone."

"Good. Thank you, Pip. I didn't have time to explain my plan, and I apologize," said Vallus as he slowly returned to a resting heart rate.

"Don't worry about it. You beat it."

Vallus nodded.

"It was following me by sound, I think. It seemed unaware of its surroundings until something made noise. I realized it when we were on the floor with all the locked rooms. It stared at me in that hall, but it didn't seem to notice me until I made noise."

"I see," said Pip.

"I needed you in my bag so you wouldn't attract its attention, and so you wouldn't get knocked away by the screams. Essentially, I was trying to avoid the same situation as that cat's owner."

"And you needed stealth on your side. I understand now. You always planned to damage the leg."

"Yes. Its biggest advantage, aside from the weapon, was its speed. I can't run forever. It can. I needed to damage a leg so I could force it to fight me up close where its weapon is less useful because of the charge time. And I couldn't let it corner me."

"So what's next?"

"I'm going to rest for a moment and catch my breath. Then I'm going to salvage what I can from this thing. Then we need to get out of here," said Vallus, rubbing his eyes. "Thank you for your help, Pip. We make a good team."

Pip made a high-pitched, cheerful beep and flew in a small loop. Vallus unbuckled the straps of his bag and removed it from his back, then laid down. His entire body ached, and his head was heavy.

"Pip, keep watch for an hour. I need…"

He trailed off as he fell asleep, Pip hovering nearby, her flashlight aimed into the surrounding darkness as she kept watch over him.

***

Vallus awoke at the sound of Pip's alarm. Groggily, he sat up and looked around. It was still pitch dark in the room. He rubbed the sleep from his eyes, then strapped his bag back on. With an achy groan, he stood and stretched.

"Gotta pee," he said absently after a deep yawn.

Vallus saw no reason to stand on ceremony nor to treat the vault with some level of reverence beyond the caution he took within. Vaults were clearly quite old, and didn't afford many amenities. Vallus walked to a nearby cubicle to have walls protecting his position and relieved himself onto the carpet. Awake and somewhat rested, Vallus stepped out of the cubicle ready to continue onward. He motioned to Pip, then stepped over to where the Screamer's body was lying motionlessly, the sparks and steam from it finally gone as the last bits of power the machine had running through it had long faded away. He pulled out his tools and got to work.

The Screamer, Vallus found, was not particularly difficult to disassemble. It had very little armor, and what it did have wasn't very strong at first glance. But as he took the machine apart and set aside whatever pieces might have been useful, he noticed that the bullet he had fired into the Screamer's chest was still lodged in the armor plate. The mechanics underneath the armor plate were relatively simple as far as Vallus was concerned, but it was the weapon assembly that intrigued him. There was a thin black box in the machine connected to eight braided cables. Each of them ran up through the neck into the head, bundled inside and around the neck assembly. Although he had destroyed the machine's weapon in the fight, the cables were still salvageable and easy enough to detach. He took three to break down and use to make twine at a later date. Within an hour, Vallus had the machine completely disassembled, save for the damaged head, and had set aside several useful parts. He put them in his bag and stood.

"Logistics shouldn't be far off now. Let's go," said Vallus, walking toward the door.

Pip followed along, keen to stay quiet to avoid detection. The door opened automatically and Vallus walked through to find himself in a long staircase. Darkness shrouded the stairwell, but Pip provided ample light so Vallus could see. Vallus walked down four flights of stairs but didn't see a door, so he continued down. He had lost count of how many stairs he had taken by the time he reached the bottom. He walked through that door to find himself in a small room that looked like a boiler room. There was a hole in the floor and a ladder that led down into it. At the bottom of the ladder, Vallus found himself in a hall made of metal frames with hundreds of thick wires and cables running through them like creeping vines. There was steam in the air, and some machine Vallus couldn't see or identify was making a gentle hissing sound. Vallus followed the hall for about fifty feet before he came to a hole in the floor. He could see the floor below in a somewhat well-lit room, so he dropped down.

The room Vallus found himself in was narrow with a grated metal floor. Below the grate was a large tank of water with several hoses fed from within it leading deep into the vault. The water was bubbling. Along the walls were dozens of computers, many of them quiet and inactive. The few that were functional whined incessantly. Behind him, Vallus could see a door that appeared to be severely damaged. Ahead of him was a door with a sign above it that read 'Logistics Entrance B'. The door also had a key card reader next to it. Vallus withdrew the clearance card and swiped it, and the door opened.

Vallus entered a very large, circular room. At least a hundred computers were set up all about the room. At the center was a machine built into the floor. It was the largest machine in the room, covered in switches, buttons, and lights, and it had dozens of cables attached to it. Those cables fed into both the floor and the ceiling, and into the network of cables and thick pipes Vallus had seen before dropping down, and he guessed he had been in the ceiling of this room. There was a light steam cloud all throughout the room, but it didn't reduce visibility by much, and Vallus could easily navigate the room, having assessed the floor to be sturdy. All of the computers looked about the same to him, so he decided to start with the closest one to try and find a map. Closer to the machine in the center of the room, Vallus could see the elevator entrance on the other side.

Many of the computers didn't seem to be functional. Some were physically damaged, others were stuck in strange loops and seemed to be trying to either update software or reboot. From near the center of the room, Vallus looked around and eventually saw one computer across the room that appeared to be operational. He began to walk toward it. There was an odd sense of trepidation in him, and the hairs on the back of his neck stood up. He heard a clattering in the ceiling between the light puffing sounds of machinery in the floor. He waved it off as just machinery within the vault. Before Vallus could close in on the computer, something fell out of the ceiling and landed not far from him with a dull thud. Vallus jumped a bit and drew one of his swords as a precaution. He slowly approached. The Seeker soon realized what the thing that had fallen was as the clattering grew louder and something hissed that wasn't steam. The thing was the cat, mangled and coated in a copious amount of its own blood. It looked as if something had squeezed it to death. A feeling Vallus hadn't really felt in some time welled up within him. It was fear.

With a thunderous and heavy bang, a being fell out from

within the cables in the ceiling to the floor, then stood to full height as it growled deep in its throat. The thing was at least seven feet tall and appeared as if its body was entirely comprised of machinery. It wore thin plate armor made up of overlapping scales with a large piece of cloth draped over its shoulders and head like a hooded poncho. Its large, powerful arms appeared finely crafted, and dozens of cables and wires ran through its body. The right arm had five long fingers protected by a thin plate and tipped in sharp, grasping claws. Its left arm stopped near the elbow before it became what looked to be a heavy assault rifle with stand and shield attachments. Strapped to the thing's side was a long, sheathed sword similar in form to a katana. Its eyes were entirely mechanical, like camera lenses, each one back-lit by lights that burned red. The area that surrounded those eyes appeared to be made of dull, gray flesh covered in scars. Its mouth and nose were covered by a metal mask with thin vents in it.

A few scattered pieces of information began to coalesce into a complete picture of the situation in Vallus' mind as several realizations dawned on him in the space of a few seconds. Firstly, the thing, as Vallus had ascertained, appeared to be almost entirely mechanical, yet it appeared to be breathing as the overlapping metal plates beneath its armor undulated slowly. Secondly, Vallus realized this thing was what he saw both in security and in the darkness of the Offices. And finally, he realized it was hostile as it reached its right arm across to its sword. It drew the blade and held it at its side.

"What are you?" said Vallus, the words almost catching in his throat.

The creature stood still for a moment, regarding Vallus evenly. It spoke with a growl, a deep and grinding hiss lying under a labored and bloodthirsty groan.

"I… am Nirav. God of Murder, patron of killers. Your end has been ordained, mortal," he said.

Thoughts and emotions exploded inside Vallus. Those words, akin to what he had only heard in dreams, shook him, sent fire through his nerves. This monster, this creature, stood before him, and named himself the God of Murder. His hands shot up and he held them in front of himself, waving them frantically.

"Wait. I don't want to fight you. I am a Seeker. I seek a Forgotten God. Is it you?" Nirav took a single heavy step forward, and spoke with a grunt.

"Forgotten? No… I don't think so."

"But you say you are a God? What happened to the world? Where did you go?"

"Go? Hmm… No. No more talk."

Nirav raised his gun arm and took aim at Vallus. The Seeker was momentarily stunned, but he quickly overcame it and ducked behind a computer before Nirav took his shot.

A loud crack echoed through the room before a second loud crack announced the bullet hitting the wall opposite Nirav.

"Cowardly mortal. Face your doom!"

Vallus was shaken. This monster called itself a God, and yet it fired a gun upon him. This was not the machine-gifting God Vallus had been taught of. How was he to fight a God? He didn't know, but he did know that he needed to figure it out, and soon. He ran toward the center of the room and the large machine just before Nirav delivered a powerful kick that demolished Vallus' original cover and sent computer parts spilling across the floor. Vallus spun around to face Nirav as he drew his swords. For a moment he contemplated attaching them, then hesitated.

Something in the back of his mind told him he needed both swords separately.

Nirav stared Vallus down as his gripped hand fidgeted with the handle of his sword.

Vallus could just barely see small mechanical parts moving between his armor plates as Nirav stretched and poised to attack. His eyes narrowed as he leveled his sword toward Vallus.

The latter swallowed hard and took a steady breath to calm his nerves. Time seemed to screech to a crawl, with Vallus only faintly aware of the rhythmic beeping and crackling processing sounds of the computers in the room. The strike was fast. With a savage roar, Nirav lunged at Vallus, his sword outstretched. Vallus sidestepped the blade, but Nirav punished the dodge with a kick to the stomach that knocked Vallus off his feet and across the room. He threw himself to his feet and flourished his swords.

"Gonna take a lot more than that. It would be much easier to just answer my questions, seeing as you're a God."

"Will knowledge change your fate? You will still die here," hissed Nirav in reply. "I have a duty to uphold. You can either help, or be pushed aside," shouted Vallus with more gusto than he felt he had, as Nirav's kick was beginning to ache his abdomen.

"Insolent!"

Nirav planted his booted feet and raised his rifle, but Vallus was ready for it. He took quick cover behind a computer just in time for the bullet to miss him and hit a desk off to the side of the room. Vallus got lucky when a second bullet struck his cover as he ran out and back toward the center of the room. Vallus turned to close distance with Nirav, but his luck ran out as a bullet struck his left shoulder and pierced through his armor. The pauldron popped loose as one of the straps holding it in place tore apart. Vallus went dizzy for a moment, then a searing pain shot through his arm, then numbness. He dropped his left-hand sword. There was a loud, metallic click sound. Vallus looked up to see Nirav loading a new magazine into his rifle. A warm, wet sensation began to fill Vallus' sleeve. He reached down, picked up his sword, and gripped it as tightly as he could. He winced.

"That the extent of your wrath? Are you truly a God? You need a gun to wound me, and yet I still stand, still seeking my answers. We can drop these weapons and speak, as our kind did before," he said, shaking and trying with ferocious effort to ignore the blinding pain in his shoulder.

"Before? Ha! Find your answers in your grave, mortal. My task is to slay you and nothing more."

"So you're just a cheap assassin. Pity. I hoped to find a God here; instead I found a murderer playing pretend."

Nirav snarled and screamed with rage. His eyes narrowed and he visibly shook. He poised to strike. Vallus snapped his fingers the moment Nirav moved. At the sound, Pip flew out of the bag and followed Vallus' pointing finger, flying past Nirav's head by mere inches. He turned, distracted by the little drone. The moment was ripe, and Vallus took his opportunity. He closed the gap in two steps. With a roar, he swung the left sword and struck Nirav between the plates of his armor, although he could tell his strength with the arm was diminished, but not gone. There was a scraping kind of sound as the blade dug into flesh and metal. Nirav roared and turned back to Vallus. He dodged under a swing from Nirav's sword, then swung his own in the right hand. Nirav blocked the blow with the rifle shield, but Vallus' blade found purchase in the mechanisms near the elbow and cut through a cable.

Nirav took aim as Pip flew back into Vallus' bag.

Nirav's shot missed its mark and hit a wall, but his scream wasn't frustration at his inaccuracy; Vallus recognized it as pain. A thin, blue liquid was dripping from the cable Vallus had severed, and a metal rod of about six inches in length protruded from the rear of the rifle. Nirav gripped his sword tighter and stared at Vallus.

"You think this stops me?" shouted Nirav in rage. "You are already wounded. It is only a matter of time before you lose enough blood to die, mortal. Your flailing does nothing but delay the inevitable!"

Somewhere in the back of his mind, Vallus knew Nirav was right. He couldn't feel the wound any more, and his arm was beginning to feel weak. He sheathed his left sword, and pain shot through his arm as his hand released its grip. He winced. The blood had reached his glove, but he knew he had no time to patch it. Instead, Vallus pulled the glove off and tossed it aside. Nirav quickly sheathed his sword and pushed the metal rod back into the rifle with a loud click. He growled. Then he raised the gun and it cocked, ejecting a casing that had been jammed in the chamber by the misfire. Nirav drew his sword again, then lunged at Vallus.

With some difficulty, he jumped backwards onto the machine in the middle. Nirav swung the sword horizontally, but Vallus spun his sword flat against his arm and parried the blow.

Vallus dropped off the machine to avoid the backswing, which sliced through several of the thick cables running into the ceiling. One of them ejected a stream of bright blue liquid that drenched Nirav's left arm. It distracted him long enough for

Vallus to drive his sword straight into Nirav's side. He kicked Vallus in the chest as he roared with pain and a thick, oily substance poured from the wound. Vallus slid across the floor before he dropped his retrieved sword. Slowly, he pushed himself onto his knees. Twenty feet away, Nirav slumped to one knee. He dropped his sword and gripped his wound, then looked at Vallus with narrowed eyes. Then he pointed his rifle at Vallus.

"Insolent mortal. You dare wound a God? You fight for nothing. There is nothing you can do to stop our new dawn," he hissed, the rifle trembling more from rage than from pain. "You should… run while you still can."

"Please… I never wanted to fight you. I only seek… answers," said Vallus, panting and in great pain.

"The Gods don't answer to you, mortal," said Nirav with a growl.

The mechanisms engaged, the rifle chambered a round, and the gun fired, but Nirav's arm exploded in a hail of fire and metal. The explosion ripped through his body and tore his armor apart, and shredded his face. Vallus was struck by the blast wave and was knocked back against the wall. His head spun and his body ached, and he nearly faded out of consciousness before he shook off the fuzz in his head and shakily stood to his feet. The debris was still raining from the explosion, and Nirav had crumpled to his knees, smoke pouring from his body. He shakily spoke through his shredded mouth, his mechanical jaw barely held on.

"Will… die… Leave this vault… mortal. Or it… will be your… grave," he choked out before his body fell sideways to the floor in a smoking heap.

Vallus felt his knee buckle, but held steady on his feet. He took his bag off his back and rifled through it for medical supplies. He withdrew the bag of supplies he had bought from the merchant. Moving quickly, he removed the armor and groaned.

"Pip," he said as he slumped and sat on the floor.

She flew from the bag, turned on her light, and aimed it toward the wound on Vallus' shoulder. She hovered there as Vallus peeled back his coat. The shirt was torn, and along with his sleeve, was soaked in blood. Vallus removed his right shoulder armor, then both sleeves of the coat, then unstrapped his chest armor and laid it aside with the other pieces, along with his glove. He then removed his shirt. Some of his light chest hair was soaked in blood, too, covering the scars that made his body hair grow in patchy. He supposed this would be another scar. With only slight hesitation, having hoped to conserve it, Vallus took the bag of water from the supplies, opened it, and poured about half of it over the wound to wash away as much of the blood as he could. Although each movement stung and burned, Vallus muscled through as he wrapped a cloth around it to slow the bleeding.

"Good news is that there is an exit wound, and my scans find no trace of shrapnel in it. Bad news is you've lost quite a lot of blood. Disinfect the wound while I prepare my suture, and keep the arm raised," said Pip evenly.

Vallus drew a bottle of clear liquid from his bag and opened it and a strong, stinging scent wafted forth. Vallus poured some of it over the wound and winced. The alcohol seemed to be doing its job. He pressed the cloth to it again and held his arm up. Pip floated closer and a small machine similar to that of the tip of a sewing machine extended out from her tool kit. Vallus moved the cloth and waited, clenching his teeth, as Pip went to work sewing the wound shut. He had gone through this process with Pip a number of times in the past, but found it never hurt less. Pip had the entry wound sutured in under two minutes and got to work on the exit wound. Vallus stared at Nirav's smoking corpse across the room as Pip worked.

"Why wouldn't he answer me?"

"Perhaps he just didn't want to? Or maybe he wasn't truly a God," said Pip as she continued to stitch the wound shut.

"Maybe. Wouldn't think a God would die that easily, though," he said.

Pip finished her work, then flew around and held her light still so he could wrap a gauze bandage around his shoulder. It still ached, but the pain was drastically reduced. He took several minutes to change his shirt to a spare he kept in his bag, then redressed and reattached his shoulder and chest armor. Vallus made a mental note to repair the armor's strap at a later date.

Vallus picked himself up off the floor with great care. He was tired, wounded, and hungry, but he was more committed to going onward. He picked up his bag bu' didn't put it on his back. Instead, Vallus approached the still smoking remains of Nirav. He stood over it for a moment, feeling uniquely out of place. The flames were beginning to die down, leaving only blackened, twisted metal and seared flesh. It felt almost like a grave sin, but Vallus knew he had to inspect the body. If it wouldn't give him answers while living, perhaps it would while dead.

With a deep, steadying breath, Vallus knelt down beside the burned out corpse and withdrew his tools from his bag. He took a long metal retractable rod and used it to shift the body and inspect it. A large pool had formed under it, although Vallus wasn't entirely sure it could be called blood. It was thick, syrupy, and nearly black, and filled with what appeared to be tiny flakes of metal. His cursory examination of the body led him to conclude that the insides were too burned to have anything usable still within. However, despite being the focal point of the explosion, the rifle Nirav had used was still largely intact. It had been torn from the arm, and much of its rear was sundered, but Vallus reckoned he could repair it. He checked to make sure it wasn't still hot, then pulled it away from the few wires and cables that kept it attached to the body and picked it up, along with the two magazines strapped to what remained of Nirav's arm, miraculously still intact. The rifle was heavy, much heavier than he had anticipated, which probably accounted for its survival. He made a mental note to fix that, and to add a stock, then checked the ammo. Fifteen rounds still remained in the loaded magazine, and each spare held twenty more.

"It feels almost wrong to claim a God's weapon, but then again, so does having to fight a God. Let's see if we can verify that, shall we?"

Pip flew over the body and shined her light as she scanned the remains. The application ran slowly, as there was quite an abundance of information to process. Vallus had never been quite sure how it worked, but Pip's scanner had never led him astray before, so he had come to rely on it. Pip hummed and beeped for a few minutes as Vallus looked over the remains for any clues. Eventually, Pip beeped twice.

"Scan concluded. The liquid is, in effect, blood. I can't detect any traces of DNA in it, however. The base is certainly blood plasma, but there are so many assorted particulates in it that I can't sort them all, and the attempt is causing severe lag in my systems," she said.

"Don't overwork yourself. Did you identify what those metal flakes in it are?"

"Yes. Those are a fine mixture of aluminum, copper, and zinc alloys. Although it should be noted that they aren't supposed to be in the blood. From what I can tell, they wouldn't serve any purpose but internal harm, so they must have spilled in just before the explosion when the body was initially ruptured. It is also possible they had been mixing in for some time before the fight, as my scans determined that there were a number of extensive damages that indicated they had been made before the explosion. God or not, Nirav was already quite wounded."

Vallus was silent for a moment.

"You don't think him being injured is a sign he wasn't what he claimed to be?"

"Not particularly. We have no way of accurately determining if he was or not, but I wouldn't say having some amount of organic body would disqualify them. He seemed quite adamant in his assertion of the idea, though."

"He was also quite adamant about killing me. But considering the state of the world, I'd say I probably should have expected to encounter a God like this."

"One more thing of note, Vallus. The vast majority of his machinery is extremely old, based on wear. At least a thousand years."

"Why would a God's body contain so much machinery? They did create artificial intelligence, but did they derive it from themselves?"

"Perhaps that was their secret to Godhood?"

Vallus nodded. He had just begun to notice the smell emanating from the corpse; a sickening, rancid scent, like burned rubber mixed with sewage. He retched, picked up his tools, and stepped away from the body. He glanced around the room, apparently safe for the time being, and searched for a functioning computer. There were several to choose from, but the one that caught Vallus' attention was a particularly large station at the far side of the room that had several thick hoses running to and from it. He crossed the room, careful to step around Nirav's corpse, and began to try and operate the computer.

He pressed a button and the screen lit up, displaying various meters and a feed of numbers. Many of them seemed to be pressure and heat readings for the computers and machines scattered about the room. There was a mouse to the right side of the keyboard, and Vallus tried using it. A cursor appeared. He clicked on a tab at the top of the screen that read 'tools'. A drop-down menu showed a list of subjects, but near the bottom was what he was looking for. He clicked on 'maps'. Doing so brought him to a screen with a list of files. He clicked the first one, which brought up, to Vallus' surprise, a large and detailed map of much of the vault. He quickly looked it over.

"Pip, can you start downloading this?"

"Yes. It should be quick work."

"Good. Strange, though. By the looks of this map, that section that appears collapsed is the historical records department. They kept knowledge here. It appears there's a massive machine that feeds all the way through the center of the vault, too. It feeds into… the system core? And there's a sub-level beneath it. That might be our objective, Pip. Let's get back to the lobby and figure out our next step."

"Right. I've completed the download."

Vallus put his bag on his back, picked up the rifle, and walked to the elevator. It appeared to be shut down, and the car wasn't there. He pressed the call button, but to no avail. He pressed it a few more times for the same result. An inquisitive look on his face, Vallus glanced around the immediate area. There was a console not far from the elevator door.

Vallus moved to it and began navigating its screens. An emergency sign was flashing under a heading labeled 'elevator status'. Vallus clicked a button that said 'override emergency'. A distant thumping sound echoed through the vault, and Vallus watched the control panel next to the elevator doors come alive. He walked back to the elevator and pressed the call button. This time, there was a thumping sound from behind the doors, and within a few minutes, the elevator car came to the room and the doors slid open. With one last glance back toward Nirav's smoking corpse, Vallus entered the elevator and waited as it ascended back to the lo.

***

"Gone and got yourself killed, eh, Nirav?"

Several minutes had passed since Vallus had left Logistics and the Ashen King stood over the scorched remains of the dead God, pondering events. Disgust rose in him, along with an almost obnoxious sense of disappointment. He shook his head.

"I handed you the keys to the kingdom, and you opened the door to failure. How pathetic. At least you died standing. More than could be said of you before now. Rest in peace, coward. No rafters to hide you in the after," he whispered.

As he was about to leave, the Ashen King noticed an active computer off to the side, the very one Vallus had used to find his map. The King approached it and looked it over for a moment. Rage seethed in his chest. He shook. Then he roared and smashed his broad hands down upon the computer, destroying it in a hail of sparks, plastic, and smoke.

"The rats are in the walls," he said, turning back to Nirav's body. "Plenty of time yet."

Chapter 4

The late afternoon had begun to cast its growing shadow along the broken road, marching slowly to dusk. A light breeze pushed a tumbleweed over the road where it rolled down the incline and came to rest against the remains of the Pursuer that had crashed off to the side. The Seeker and the merchant he had crossed paths with had been long gone for hours. If anyone had been on the road at the time, they might have heard the rumbling, growling roar of three motorcycles approaching the area. They might have seen them on the horizon, a pin prick in the distance that grew ever larger, riding with one bike out front of the other two.

The motorcycles were quite old, and had been modified with a number of attachments and upgrades to keep them running. Each one had two saddlebags made of pitch-black leather, and mounted upon all but one bike was a rider in a long, dark coat and one in thin armor.

They grumbled to a stop near the scraps of the Pursuers and shut off their engines. The front rider dismounted his motorcycle and took a few steps toward the destroyed machine in the road. He stood there, staring at it with his thin, dark eyes for a moment before he brushed his long, black hair back and grunted.

"Vault nearby. We can't follow them, but we can follow the road," said the man with a low, ominous growl, his voice cold and venomous.

"Who ya think did it, Yashir?" asked a man who sat upon one of the bikes, smoking a cigarette. He wore no coat like his compatriots, and wore black leather armor. He was tall, bald, and had several scars around his eyes, and he spoke with a thick accent.

The man called Yashir spoke without turning, only glancing slightly out of his large hood.

"Don't know. Don't care. Let's go, Volya."

"About damn time," said the third rider with a high, feminine voice that had a cackling quality under it.

"Patience, Hecate. We still have work to do," said Yashir as he mounted his motorcycle and started the engine. The other two riders followed suit, and the trio rode off toward Ashenvale, their engines thundering across the barren wastes toward the town, and toward the vault.

***

Once more, the elevator doors opened with a gentle whoosh on the lobby and Vallus stepped out, visibly taxed and carrying the broken rifle at his side. His shoulder pained him, but he blocked it out. As he neared the small encampment of blankets, Vallus glanced out the window to see the sky growing darker as afternoon crept toward its end. He was surprised the sun was still up. He walked into Shiloh's camp and sat down heavily on a pile of blankets in the corner while Shiloh regarded him with curiosity and a little worry.

"It got harder?"

"It got harder," Vallus affirmed as he began pulling tools from his bag. "Wait a second, did you get shot?" asked Shiloh, only slightly panicked. Vallus looked at his shoulder absentmindedly, then back to Shiloh. "Yup," he said.

"What happened?"

Vallus told Shiloh of his encounters in the offices and his battle with Nirav as he worked on disassembling the rifle. The parts were easy enough to manipulate, but several components were severely damaged. Shiloh still seemed concerned when Vallus finished recounting events.

"You should let me check that out," said Shiloh, looking around for his medical kit.

"It's fine. Pip sewed it up and I cleaned it. I'll live," he said, Pip floating out of his bag at the sound of her name.

"Well, either way, you've been through a lot. You should get some rest."

"When I'm finished with this. I have my doubts, though. I don't think Nirav was really what he claimed to be."

"I do," said Shiloh solemnly.

Vallus was taken aback. He looked up from the rifle at Shiloh, inquisitive.

"I'll have to tell you a story. It's one I heard when I came to this town. Have you ever heard the legend of the Ashen King?"

"No, but I have heard that name. They say he rules the town."

"Yes that's what I was told as well. I spoke with several people who live in the town, especially the older folks. The ones who kept the legend alive. They say he was called Farran, and known as the greatest soldier who ever lived; an unstoppable force on the field of battle. He won wars for his homeland, and they repaid him accordingly. He ascended to Godhood, and they granted him Ashenvale as a home to rule. They say he built that castle with his own two hands on the day he claimed his title. But then the Fall came, and he vanished along with the other Gods."

"So what about the legend makes you think Nirav was speaking the truth?"

"The legends say Farran had a number of loyal lieutenants, warrior Gods who had earned his favor. They don't know the names of all of them, but they do know of one called Nirav. Known as the Reaper, the Shadow, and the God of Death," replied Shiloh grimly.

"Odd. He called himself the God of Murder. Perhaps these Gods are more malignant than I anticipated," said Vallus, hiding how deeply he was shaken by the tale as he continued to work on the rifle.

"Perhaps. After all, they did burn the world. I believe you met one of the King's honored subordinates."

Vallus continued his work on the rifle. He had repaired its inner mechanisms with considerable ease and set to work on removing the odd metal plate Nirav had used as a shield from the gun. The task was easy enough, only requiring that he remove three screws from the plate and two more from the mounting. As he worked, Shiloh began gathering ingredients to cook. Vallus looked up.

"You're welcome to some grub. You're gonna need it."

"Thank you," said Vallus. "You wouldn't happen to have something I could use as this gun's stock, do you?"

Shiloh looked toward a large box at the far back corner of the camp. "Well, you could always use my rifle," he said.

"Something wrong with it?"

"No. I ran out of ammo before I even came here. It was old to begin with, but things like that are hard to come by."

Shiloh crossed the room and opened the box. Vallus couldn't see anything that was in it from where he sat, but the dejected and withered look on Shiloh's face told him everything he would need to know about it. The latter dug through the box for a moment, then drew an old, tarnished assault rifle from it. Its magazine was missing. He handed the gun to Vallus, who grasped it firmly and nodded to Shiloh in thanks.

"That box contains your old Seeker gear, doesn't it?"

Shiloh sat down with a small frown on his face.

"Yes. All the things I owned that I believed made me one, anyway. My weapons included."

"I hope you don't mind that I need to disassemble this," said Vallus, his hands on the stock, a touch of regret on his face.

"No problem at all. I'm not using it," said Shiloh with a chuckle that only sounded half-pained.

Vallus continued his work as Shiloh cooked a mixture of vegetables, spices, and meat. The aroma made his stomach growl, reminding him that he hadn't eaten in hours. As the two worked in silence, Vallus became lost in thought. He had faced much already, more than he had ever seen in a vault. He had noted that many of the vault's functions seemed to be either in immense disrepair, or completely disabled, and yet there were enemies around every corner as if it were more a tomb being guarded than an abandoned facility. A thought then occurred to him.

"What does 'he is coming' mean to you?"

"Ah, I forgot about 'hat. It's another part of the legend. They say one day the Ashen King will return, bringing a new age of Gods. His so 'called new dawn'," replied Shiloh solemnly. "They believe that day is coming soon. Sort of a prophecy."

"Strange. I've never encountered such specific worship of the Gods. Terms have always been ambiguous in my experience," said Vallus.

"It's to be expected of people who live where Gods once stood, surrounded by a place those Gods once called home. They can feel his presence in the ground. They feel it around the castle."

"All I felt from that castle was dread," said Vallus.

With a sharp, relieved exhale, Vallus loaded a magazine into the rifle and cocked it. It slid a round into the chamber with a loud click. He turned the gun over to the left, then to the right, inspecting his work. It had been a challenge to mount the stock, but one he had completed successfully, although the weapon was stuck in semi-automatic mode. Vallus clicked on th' weapon's safety and set it to his side on the floor, just within reach. He sat for some time, inhaling the sweet and spicy aroma of the cooking food and watched the steam from the pan waft gently out the broken window. Once he had finished cooking, Shiloh filled two worn plastic bowls with the food and handed one to Vallus. He savored the rich, spicy, sauce-covered vegetables and warm, juicy meat. It was probably the best meal Vallus had eaten in a long time. When he was finished, Shiloh took the bowl.

Vallus was refreshed and energized, ready to head deeper into the vault. He pulled a long, thick, fabric strap from his bag and called for Pip as he began attaching it to the rifle. The little drone floated out, bobbed in the air toward Shiloh as though nodding, then turned to Vallus.

"Yes?"

"If I ask you a question regarding that map, do you think you could answer it?"

"Most likely. Ask away," she replied.

"That's quite the neat thing," said Shiloh.

"She's not a thing," said Vallus evenly, although there was a hint of a growl in his throat. "Pip is my friend. My ally. She goes by 'she', and she's been with me on almost every step of my journey; she's earned respect."

"Apologies. I meant no offense," said Shiloh, visibly mortified. "None taken," said Vallus, waving a hand

93

dismissively.

"Also none taken," said Pip with a cheerful beep.

"Where did you find her, anyway?" asked Shiloh with an amused smile just barely visible on his weathered face.

"The first vault I entered. There wasn't much there, but there was a laboratory that had a plastic case in it. She was in there. Took me days to get her operational. Almost gave up. But it was worth it."

"Did you have a question, Vallus?" asked Pip, almost impatiently. "Of course. Where do you think I should go next?"

Pip hummed quietly for a few moments, then beeped.

"Well, this map shows alpha and beta clearance levels are required for many of the lower floors, so we need to find a key card with higher clearance. However, the lowest levels are sectioned off separately from the elevator, so you will need to find another route. I recommend the library floor. We may find information there, but it also connects to the far side of the vault."

"What's over there?"

"There appears to be a significant amount of space allocated for military storage, but there is also a public tour area. I guess the Gods brought people here to let them see their creations? Maybe a form of worship?"

"She's smart. Must have gotten you out of some bad spots," said Shiloh in amazement at the little drone.

"More than some. By the void, Pip's already saved my life twice today."

"And happy to do so," said Pip with a cheerful beep.

Shiloh and Vallus laughed heartily for a few moments. Pip beeped rhythmically, as though laughing right along with them. With a strap affixed to the gun and the removal of the shield having reduced the weapon's weight to a comfortable level,

Vallus stood and slung the rifle over his shoulder, then mounted the strap to a hook on his bag. He nodded to Shiloh, who returned the favor, then turned and walked to the elevator, Pip hovering along behind him. He stepped inside and pressed the button for the library. The elevator doors slid closed and the car chugged down the shaft. It stopped three floors down and the door opened, then Vallus stepped out and looked around. He was in a massive lobby, although much of its size was diminished by the collapsed wall t' Vallus' left, its slate gray walls rent apart and twisted by tons of debris that lied scattered across the room. A large sign hanging from the ceiling read 'Library'. The lights were mostly, as usual, damaged or missing, aside from the few that still worked. But this was more than could be said of the library's main door, as its frame had been crushed and warped.

Vallus scanned the room for another way he could proceed. To his right, Vallus spotted a ladder welded to the wall that led to a large vent, sizable enough for a man of his stature to fit through. He climbed the ladder and directed Pip to point her flashlight toward the vent. It appeared to be made of a thin, lightweight metal. Vallus grabbed hold of the vent with his right hand, supporting his wounded arm's grip on the ladder with his legs, and gave it a few firm tugs, finding it pliable and secured by pins that were likely weakened by time.

He tightened his grip, then jerked his arm back as hard as he could. The vent cover tore loose, along with the pins. He dropped it to the floor, where it fell with a dull metallic clap. He pointed to the vent and Pip flew in ahead of him to light the way, then he climbed up into the vent. It was large enough that he could crouch, but not stand. With a hand on the hilt of his sword, Vallus followed Pip closely through the vents. Soon, they came to another vent cover.

"Down there is the other side of the door to the library," said Pip.

He nodded, then leaned back on his palms. Vallus kicked the vent hard and easily broke it from the wall. It clattered to the floor within the room beyond, and Vallus waited in silence for a moment, listening for any movement by anything that might have heard the noise. Instead, he heard only a soft mechanical whooshing, followed by whirring servos. He peeked out of the vent into the library. Mounted to the ceiling down the length of the room was a layered mechanical track, with as many as three dozen pairs of long, segmented arms attached along it. Each arm was tipped with a large grasping hand consisting of four segmented fingers, and many of them held various items. The arms moved up and down the track, removing items from the shelves and sorting them to other places.

Vallus turned around and climbed out of the vent, down the ladder on the wall, then dropped to the floor. He was in awe of the sight before him. Stretched beyond into the darkness was a massive hallway-like room. It was lined with hundreds of shelves on their own separate floors, each filled with endless books and plastic cases, all being moved about by the arms. The side of the room Vallus stood on was well-lit, and he could see rubble and books scattered all around. The floor was different from the usual metal sheets or dirty carpet; it was tiled with intricate designs painted upon it, although aged and cracked. Tattered banners were draped against the large pillars that ran the length of the hall to either side, emblazoned with broken symbols that no longer held any meaning. There was a smell in the air, like that of musty paper and dust.

Vallus walked down the hall slowly, taking in all the sights.

He watched the mechanical arms above sort and move. He felt the tiles of the floor crack beneath his boots. Soon, he approached the center of the long hall, where there sat a circular desk with two computers on it. As he got closer, he could see that there were two openings in the desk to either side of the room and a control panel in the center of the floor. The floor within the desk had a large tile in the center, painted with a seal too faded to read, that appeared to be made of metal rather than ceramic.

He ran his fingers across the surface of the desk, disturbing the thick blanket of dust that coated it like paint. With Pip following behind, Vallus rounded the desk and stepped into its center. He examined the computer to find it running, much to his surprise. There was a chair next to the desk, but it was unfortunately too broken to use. Vallus looked over the screen carefully, but found there was no way to interact with it. There was, however, a disc port on its side.

Grrrrrr.

The growling emanated from the walls and echoed through the hall. Vallus jumped to attention as a scrambling, thumping sound filled the hall, its source indeterminable. Then, just as suddenly as it had begun, it stopped. He waited, quietly scrutinizing every small sound that he could. After a few moments, he relaxed.

"What was that?"

"Not sure," replied Pip. "Nothing good, to be sure."

"Keep an eye out. I'm going to try some of these discs," said Vallus as he turned to the computer on the desk.

There was a shelf under the desk, and it held several cases with discs in them. The first one Vallus checked was cracked. He picked up the next one and looked it over. There was no identifying title on the case, only a number: 17156. Vallus opened the case to find the disc intact, so he took it from the case and slid it into the computer's port. The computer hummed to life and began to load a program. After a few seconds of loading, a recording of a man appeared on the screen. The man looked tired, with a thin face to match his eyes and mouth. He brushed his curtain of greasy black hair back and spoke with an even and intelligent voice.

"The tests are going as planned. We hit a few speed bumps in the upgrade process, but the system shouldn't go critical again." He sighed. "I've revamped the code, so it should be able to handle greater usage, and the cooling network has been expanded to solve the overheating problem. The greater issue is the override protocol. I'll be here for two more days. Two days to teach them how to maintain this, how to fix it. I knew they should have contracted my company. I knew he couldn't handle the demand."

The video stopped and the disc ejected. Vallus returned it to its case and took another.

The disc was once more intact, and Vallus inserted it into the computer. The machine processed for a few moments, then displayed a document with a red arrow on either side.

Vallus scanned over the document. Then the next page. Then the next. It was a collection of a year's worth of shipping manifests for weapons. The next disc was just about as informative. Vallus began to walk down the hall toward the shadowed end. He looked at various books and discs as he went. He found that deeper within the library there were several smaller desks with computers similar to the others. After a few more discs, he found himself becoming increasingly frustrated.

"Here I stand, in the great repository of the Gods'

knowledge, and all I can find is maintenance logs and tax records!" he yelled as he chucked a disc case into the shadowy hall.

Vallus heard the case hit something metal. Then there was a loud, groaning beep like a computer booting. Then hydraulic pistons hissed and a light shone out of the darkness.

Walking off of a podium at the far end of the library was a large machine with a humanoid structure. Each of its arms were tipped with a large gun, and two launchers were mounted to the shoulders. Its head was built into the body, with two lights flanking its single optic lens. The machine stood to full height and pointed its guns at Vallus.

"Oh, shit," muttered Vallus.

Vallus dove behind a nearby desk, narrowly avoiding the machine's first shot. It took a step forward, groaning and beeping as it searched for its target. Then another step. And another. Vallus realized the machine was lumbering, plodding. He rounded the desk opposite the machine and, still crouching, walked along the desk to the far end of the room. Hidden behind the desk, Vallus glimpsed the machine's light sweeping back and forth as it searched. He grabbed the rifle from his bag, clicked the safety off, then called for Pip quietly.

"Can you tell me anything about this machine?"

"I have records, although minimal. It's a war machine. The Gods called it a Mech. It's slow, but if it hits you with any of those weapons-"

Vallus was blasted across the room by a massive explosion that obliterated the desks he had used as shelter. He rolled to a stop with just enough time to shield himself with his arms from a large chunk of a desk that had been careening toward him. He pushed it aside as he tried to gain his bearings. His head spun, and he could barely hear anything. His vision was blurry, but he could just barely make out the Mech across the room, smoke billowing from its launchers. It seemed it had gotten bored of searching and decided to fire rockets. Then Vallus realized he had dropped the rifle. He searched for it frantically as the Mech took aim. Pip chased after Vallus as he ran toward the rifle, having spotted it about twenty feet away, near where the desks had been. Ten feet away, he dove for the gun as the Mech fired its own. The bullet hit a pillar behind Vallus and put a ten-inch wide hole in it with a deafening crack. The Mech fired again and missed, hitting a shelf behind Vallus.

"Pip! Weak point!"

"Shoot the joints in the legs," she shouted.

Vallus aimed. The Mech began to walk toward him, crushing the rubble of the desks beneath its massive feet. Vallus took a deep breath, steadied himself, and fired. The rifle had a surprising amount of kick, and an even more surprisingly loud report. Vallus' first shot missed by a few inches, but he had time to fire a second. This time, his aim was true. The bullet broke through the Mech's left leg joint and shattered its machinery. It fell onto the joint as though it had dropped on one knee. It took aim and fired. Vallus found himself once more surprised, as the Mech had missed once more and hit another pillar. He looked at the huge hole in the pillar, then back to the Mech as it struggled to try and move. Vallus considered for a moment that he should be dead. He was completely still, had no cover, and was in a crouched position.

"Its targeting is messed up. It should have hit me."

"Well, kill it before it does."

Vallus chuckled as he aimed the rifle directly at the Mech's optic lens. It took aim once more, but it didn't matter. Vallus fired first. The bullet tore through the lens and exploded out the back of the Mech, scattering shards of metal and bits of wire. The Mech swayed for a few moments, tried to aim, then fell over with a mighty crash that cracked and bowed the floor beneath it. Vallus breathed a sigh of relief, clicked the rifle's safety on, then slung it back over his shoulder and onto the hook on his bag. After a few moments, the echo of the Mech's fall died out and Vallus was left in silence.

Vallus walked toward the smoking heap of 'he Mech's wreckage, but before he even had a chance to take his tools from his bag, he was grabbed from behind and yanked off his feet. He struggled against his attacker, flailing as the thing carried him higher through the library, Pip frantically chasing after him. He was about to draw one of his swords until he realized what had grabbed him. It was one of the many sorting arms attached to the ceiling. He quickly weighed his options. Cutting the arm would result in a steep fall to his death; fighting it would amount to about the same. With no other options in mind, Vallus simply allowed the arm to do its work. But soon, that too became a problem as it carried Vallus toward an empty slot on the shelf; one much smaller than him. The gruesome idea dawned on him that the arm intended to sort him, even if that meant crushing him into the slot.

He threw his feet up as he got close to the shelf and planted his boots against the wood. The arm exerted immense pressure on him as he pushed back with as much power as his legs could muster. His muscles strained against the machine as he drew a sword. The angle at which he had to swing the sword was awkward, but he was able to cut through the machine, which dropped him to the floor of the subsection. He landed on his feet and quickly checked to make sure the 'rm hadn't damaged anything in his bag. Reassured that the bag's protective lining had held, he continued onward.

His reprieve was only a brief one. Vallus had been lucky enough to hear the movement of another arm and dove out of the way just in time. The mechanical arm smashed into the shelf as though it had punched it. The arm caught in the shelf for a moment before it ripped itself away, sending a cloud of torn books and shattered disc cases flying. Pip flew around it in a wide arc.

Vallus ran, avoiding two more arms as they swung wildly at him. A third arm caught him hard in the ribs on his right side and he hit the shelf with force. He cried out in pain but scrambled to his feet and kept running. As yet another arm barreled toward him, Vallus drew his pistol and took five shots. A few rounds hit, but they glanced off the arm's metal plates with no noticeable effect. However, the shots had changed the arm's trajectory and it smashed into the subsection's railing. Vallus avoided the rubble and reloaded the gun as he kept running, but soon came to a dead end. To his left was a short hallway, cut off by a wall of rubble. A metal sign painted with alternating black and yellow diagonal lines was hung from the ceiling that read 'Gov Records: Alpha Clearance Required'. He pointed down the hall to direct Pip in that direction. Vallus turned to look for a way down, but found another mechanical arm as it hit him hard in the chest. His breastplate absorbed most of the blow, but it still knocked Vallus off his feet and down the collapsed hallway.

Achy and annoyed, Vallus climbed to his feet as Pip hovered to his side. The arm that had hit him was still in the subsection, trying to reach out to Vallus. It shook and thrashed, wildly slapping the walls and grabbing at air. Vallus decided to ignore its whining servos to inspect the hallway. He took several steps back to make sure he was out of the arm's reach, then turned to face the rubble.

"So that's what the collapsed part is. What does 'Gov' mean?"

"It's an abbreviation for 'government'," Pip replied.

"Ah. Not much of that left any more. Still, I could have learned so much from this place."

"Yes, it's quite unfortunate. We really should do something about these arms, though. Before another one tries to shove you into a bookshelf."

"Right," said Vallus as he turned back to the arm that was still reaching for him in vain, scratching and clawing at the walls.

"Shooting them has so far proven rather ineffective," said Pip. Vallus nodded in agreement.

"There must be controls for it somewhere. But I can't get to them if the arms are going to grab me again. Does the map show you anything, Pip?"

"Nothing. This map is only a layout map; it only shows where rooms and pathways are."

"Damn. Well, they wouldn't put them on the ceiling. That would make it harder to perform repairs. I didn't see anything that could be a control on the ground floor. It must be in one of these subsections."

"So we have our destination. Now how do we get past this arm?" asked Pip.

"Hmm… I was going to ask you the same thing," replied Vallus.

"Perhaps a well-aimed shot through the arm with the rifle could deal it enough damage to force it to retreat."

Vallus nodded and drew the rifle. The arm was still reaching, unrelenting in its pursuit.

The servos in its joints groaned with the strain. Vallus took aim, planted his feet, and took a deep breath. He fired. The gun's explosive report echoed down the hall, as if chasing the bullet that tore through the arm and sundered its insides. The bullet completely destroyed the third servo joint and the arm fell to the floor with a heavy thud, twitching for a moment before losing power. With the arm disabled, Vallus crept along the cold, steel wall back to the adjoining subsection.

The remaining arms seemed to be unaware of the damaged one, but they had no intention of ignoring him. With one foot out of the side hall, Vallus was forced to dive to the floor to avoid a deadly swipe from another arm. A hail of debris and books behind him, Vallus rolled to his feet and ran as fast as he could manage. Two more arms joined their compatriot in swiping at him, trying unsuccessfully to grab him. Soon, Vallus could see a dead end ahead. He muttered a quiet expletive, and with no other options, he jumped over the railing, and the mechanical sorting arms did just as he expected. An arm snatched him out of the air with a sickening jerk. Fortunately all of his gear was tightly secured, and the arm had grabbed him by the coat and not his bag, which remained intact and on his back.

The arm carried him across the library to the highest subsection. Vallus felt the arm twitch, then it threw him at the bookcase. Vallus shielded his face with his hands and slammed into the shelf. He fell to the floor, a cascade of books crashing on and around him. Rubbing his head, he groaned as he pushed the books aside and rose to his feet. He ducked under another hostile arm, then ran in the only direction he could, toward the rear of the library. Narrowly avoiding several more strikes from the arms, Vallus searched for a way out, the controls, or at the very least, a good source of protection. Pip chased after, being forced just as much as Vallus to bob and weave through mechanical arms.

Running out of options, I was trying to quickly communicate that Vallus was rapidly losing a path to flee the sorting arms, not that he was exiting an area. He made to turn down it, but was helped along by a strike to the back just under his bag from a sorting arm. The strike hurt, but the armor lining in his coat held steady, although he was launched down the hall several feet and knocked to the floor. Out of reach of the arm, he rose to his feet. He watched the machine strain and scratch at the walls for a moment before he turned away to look down the hall. He found a short hallway to a dead end, with a large bank of computers and controls at the far wall. Pip floated alongside him as he examined them. There were dozens of switches and keys, mostly labeled with symbols Vallus didn't know the meaning of, but one bore a symbol that resembled the arms. Vallus flipped the switch.

With a robotic whine followed by loud and heavy thumping, Vallus looked back to see the arm in the hall retract and slump down toward the floor. He walked back to the main hall and watched the rest of the arms shut down. Vallus let out a sharp sigh.

"Wait… what is that?" he asked, looking toward the back end of the library. "What?" asked Pip.

Vallus walked to the end of the subsection closest to the back wall. He noticed there was a ladder mounted to the balcony that led to the ground. But the thing that had caught his attention was something wrapped up in the track above the deactivated sorting arms.

Intrigued, Vallus hurried down the ladder and back to the

ground floor. He approached the center of the room and looked up toward the object. In the dim light, Vallus could only make out its shape, and see that something was wrapped around it, holding it to the track. Then, with the final streams of power running through them, the arms lurched and the object above was jostled loose. It came tumbling to the floor, spinning as it unraveled from the rope that held it.

The object's identity became all too apparent to Vallus as it hit the floor with a heavy, wet thud and part of it ripped away. The object was a corpse. Vallus stared at the body for a few moments in amazement, then to the ceiling. He looked back and forth several times, absolutely astonished.

"Pip, can you imagine what horrible chain of unlucky events put this body up there?"

"I can imagine a few scenarios. None of them pleasant," she replied.

Vallus took a step closer to examine the scene. There was little blood, and the body was severely withered. He concluded that it had been there for quite some time. The part that had torn off was the body's arm, and it had a device attached to it, hanging loosely from the ceiling by a thin braided cable. He inspected the device and found that it was a grappling hook launcher. He took hold of the cable and jerked it, but it wouldn't budge. He shook the cable several times, then shook it a few more but harder. The cable came loose and a metal hook fell to the floor. He removed the device from the arm and set it aside before turning back to the body. By the tattered and worn clothing and gear, Vallus surmised the body must have once belonged to yet another Seeker.

"We seem to have found another Seeker. Why are there so many here?"

"Not sure. Shiloh did say they've been coming here for some time, didn't he?"

"In not so many words, yes. I suspect we will find these bodies with less frequency the deeper we move into the vault, though."

"Most likely."

It was difficult to glean any further information from the body as it was severely emaciated and dry. Little blood came from its torn arm. Upon closer inspection, Vallus found a large - nearly ten inches wide, had the body been in fresh condition - hole in the chest.

"So bear with me," said Vallus, looking up and down the library in sheer disbelief. "I think what happened is this guy tried to use his grappling hook to get to a subsection, probably got harassed by the arms, then that Mech shot him. I think the momentum from all of that jostled the void out of him, and he got tangled up in his own cord as he bled to death. The arms could have wrapped him up, though, for all I know."

"But wasn't the Mech's targeting off? It couldn't hit you for anything."

"Maybe he managed to damage it before he got tangled? But I didn't see any damage on it before I shot it. I think we can chalk that one up to time. This body looks old; it's probably been here for years, at least."

"Either way, we should keep moving," said Pip.

Vallus nodded. He performed last rites for the Seeker, then turned toward the Mech. However, he hesitated, looking back toward the body over his shoulder. Pip hovered beside him, looking curious.

"It would be disrespectful to take a dead Seeker's gear... but that grapple hook seems too useful to leave behind."

"I believe you should take it," said Pip. Vallus turned to her, curious himself.

"I agree that it would be disrespectful, and I think you should stand by your convictions. But is it not Seeker tradition to pass along what you learn? Where did you learn your skills?"

"My father."

"And where did he learn them?"

"His brother. The actual Seeker in the family. Garin was his title."

"Yes. Yours is a heritage of learning. If the Seekers do not pass along their knowledge, then what's the point?"

"Fair," said Vallus as he turned to where the hook laid upon the floor.

He picked up the launcher from the floor and looked it over. There were loops for fingers, and the frame would fit cleanly over a glove. The mechanism was quite compact, and had three buttons on it. Vallus pressed one and the cord began to retract. After several seconds, the cable was fully retracted and sat inside the mechanism. The hook itself collapsed on itself and slid underneath. Vallus turned the device over in his hands, learning how to use it as he inspected each part. With a thankful and solemn nod toward the body, Vallus slid the device over his right glove. It fit tightly, but comfortably, with the trigger resting under his palm. He wrapped the hand around the hilt of his sword and found he would be able to grip it and draw the weapon without triggering the hook.

"This is an ingenious design. I wonder if he built it or found it," said Vallus to himself.

Vallus turned once more to the fallen Mech. With the library quiet, he pulled out his tools and got to work. The first thing he discovered was that the armor plates of the Mech were incredibly light and flexible, as though they had been made of a softer metal. They were easy to remove, having only a few screws holding them in place over the machine's larger, significantly heavier frame. With several plates removed, Vallus began inspecting the surprisingly bare insides of the Mech.

"Well, this is odd. Just like the sentry turret, this machine has no power source. It also seems to be missing most of its inner weapons assembly. This thin' shouldn't have been able to function."

"Another functioning machine with no power source. I feel as though there is something bigger at play here," said Pip.

"What do you mean?"

"I think there may be someone behind this. Making these dead machines come alive."

"It does feel as though we are not wanted here," said Vallus as he glanced around. He thought he heard growling again, but chalked it up to the air of the conversation.

Vallus continued to poke and prod inside the Mech, taking parts here and there for future use. As he worked, he found a faded and singed sticker on the inside of an armor plate. It said only three 'words: 'Display Model Only'.

"Display Model'," said Vallus curiously. "No wonder. This machine wasn't even built for combat. It was built as a display. To look at. Strange."

"Perhaps the vanity of the Gods ran deep? They had great power; it would stand to reason that they would want to show it off," said Pip.

"And so they have," said Vallus as he packed his tools away. "Time to g'."

"You're going to want to return to the round desk. According to the map, there is a platform elevator in the center of it that will take us deeper into the vault," said Pip as she followed behind Vallus.

Frustrated with the library's lack of useful information and ready to leave it behind, Vallus followed Pip's directions and returned to the large circular desk. He flipped the switch and prepared himself as the slow, lurching platform began its descent into the depths of the vault.

***

The sun had begun to set on the horizon, blanketing the town of Ashenvale in bleak twilight. The children who had been playing in the streets returned to their homes for dinner, the workers began to finish up their chores, and the guards finished their shift change. It was simply another day, with all of its little motions for each person to go through.

The front gate guard had been replaced for the night by a much more serious man, armed with a hunting rifle and a lit cigarette in hand. From his simple chair on the shack that served as a guard station, he could see what looked like three vehicles approaching rapidly, and the sun seemed to move along the sky as though it were fleeing them. His hand gripped the stock of the rifle a little tighter.

Within several minutes, the riders approached. Their bikes rolled to a stop some ten feet from the front gate where Yashir peered at the guard from under his hood. The guard flicked his cigarette aside, took his rifle in hand, and stood. He spoke with a drawl.

"Welcome to Ashenvale. I'm gonna have to ask ya to leave the bikes 'ere. Can't have 'em makin' all that noise."

The riders were silent for a few moments until Yashir nodded once, shut off the engine, and dismounted the vehicle. The other two riders followed suit. Expressionless and silent, Yashir approached the guard slowly.

"Any other rules we should be aware of?" he asked, almost mockingly.

"Not really. Just don't bring any trouble, and ya won't find any. Can I ask your business here?"

"The vault. Where is it?"

The guard looked unsettled. He pointed toward the path.

"It's down the left path from the courtyard, past the castle, in the valley. But I wouldn't recommend..."

"We've done this before," said Yashir bluntly.

The guard pursed his lips for a moment before he nodded and set his rifle against the chair in the shack. He motioned off to the side of the road with one hand.

"You can leave your bikes here. They'll be h l l l aw anna ya wanna leave."

The riders did as instructed and pushed their motorcycles off the road to the side where they propped them up on kickstands. Yashir lingered there for a moment, staring at the large, red letters painted to the wall. Volya walked over to Yashir and lit a cigarette.

"What do you suppose that means, Volya?"

"No fuckin' clue," he said with a grin, revealing a row of dirty, grimy teeth. Yashir grunted, scowling. With a nod to Volya, he walked back to the road where Hecate stood waiting, staring with a blank face at the guard, who was quite visibly uncomfortable. Yashir stopped in front of the guard and nodded to Hecate, then to the guard.

The guard nodded back before he returned to the little shack, and the riders proceeded under the arch and into the town.

In lock-step formation, the three riders walked through the town. What few people were still in the street avoided them, and people in their homes closed their windows. They passed by a pair of men sitting in front of an inn, one clutching a severed hand. They stared at Yashir and his compatriots, who paid them no mind in turn as they kept walking. They continued their walk past the castle with next to no interest, then entered the valley. After briefly examining the scene, they stood in front of the inert heap that had been the sentry turret. Yashir looked at it with intensity.

"A Seeker did this," he said. "Could still be in there. Hecate, open the door."

Hecate walked to the control panel to the side of the door and pressed the button. The riders stood in front of the door as it slowly opened, then stepped inside. They walked through the entry hall to the lobby door and entered. Careful to walk quietly once they noticed the tent structure, Yashir and the others moved to its entrance. Yashir peered inside to see a lone man on a cot, apparently sleeping. He signaled with his hand to the others and they walked to the elevator, stepped inside, and waited for the doors to slide quietly closed.

Chapter 5

"There is something different about this one," said the Ashen King, his mechanical fingers laced together in front of him with his elbows resting on his knees. He sat in his throne, leaning forward as he spoke intently to his subordinate.

"There is always something different about them," said Vakka, standing only feet away from the base of the throne, his broad arms crossed over his chest plate. "We needn't worry; he will not be strong enough to stand against you."

"That is not the source of my concern, Vakka. He has proven to be a pest, and even in the face of Nirav he persists."

"That's why we sent the weakest of us first. His false sense of security will be his undoing."

"And your hubris will be yours," said the King. "I trust my instincts. My instincts tell me this Seeker is more than he appears."

"And I do not? You know where my loyalties lie. We all do. As for hubris, I will allow my strength to speak for itself," replied Vakka with a low growl.

The Ashen King shifted and leaned back in his throne.

"Do we know where he is now?" he asked with a heavy sigh.

"Leaving the library. If he is truly as concerning as you believe him to be, why not send me now? I can destroy him, and we can never speak of it again," replied Vakka.

The King shook his head. "The time isn't right."

"Do you doubt me? Or yourself?"

"You know better…"

"Yes! I do!" shouted Vakka as he waved his arms in frustration before quickly regaining his composure. "How long have we fought beside each other? Of course I know better. I bled for you! So of course I know. The only reason the time wouldn't be right is if…"

Vakka trailed off, then nodded. He crossed his arms again. "I see. We have a better play."

"We do. I will judge this Seeker. We shall see what he is truly made of. But until then, we have work to do that cannot wait. Be ready, old friend. You shall play your part soon."

Vakka nodded, then bowed. As he departed the room, the Ashen King rested upon his throne. He was uncomfortable, anxious. Dreams of golden spires and glorious battlefields danced in his mind, just out of reach. The time was nearing.

***

The platform slowly descended down a dark shaft as Vallus prepared for what lied ahead. Pip hovered next to him, silently keeping speed with the elevator. He couldn't tell how deep the elevator had gone or how long it had been moving, but after some time it came to a stop with a hydraulic hiss. He was still in the shaft, but there was a door in front of him. The door stuck for a moment as it tried to open, then it unstuck itself. Vallus walked into an area unlike anything he could have expected.

Before him was a Stygian nightmare. He seemed to be in a sort of large spillway, with a central catwalk flanked by large, sloped ramps. They were filled with murky, flowing water, which in turn was filled with junk and detritus. But what truly horrified

Vallus was the sheer amount of blood. Although the flickering lights scattered about the room weakened visibility, the area was littered with hundreds of bodies, stacked haphazardly all about the place, over railings and on the several hanging platforms set along the catwalk, and even over each other. The path was all but obscured by these corpses and the massive pool of ichor that had filled almost every inch of the area. In the flickering lights, Vallus noticed movement, not only of stray madmen walking, but from the piles of corpses as well. The cascading water in the ramps made a loud, echoing crash, but it wasn't enough to drown out the seemingly constant moaning and growling that filled the room.

Vallus was stunned for a moment. Then he felt sick to his stomach. Pip seemed to have no reaction, although Vallus hadn't expected one. He took a few tentative steps forward, water and blood sloshing under his boots, sticking to their soles.

"There's so many…"

Vallus looked back. Pip was still hovering in place, seemingly refusing to move. "Pip? You okay?"

"Yes… sorry. It's just… there's more than five hundred DNA samples here. It's too much for me to process."

"Don't worry about it. Where are we going?"

"We're in the cooling exchange. These ramps carry water away from the core after being used to cool it. Although, I have no idea where the water is coming from. We need to move forward. There should be a staircase nearby that connects back to the main floors."

Vallus turned back to the path ahead. Gathering his resolve, he began to walk forward.

With as much care as possible, he stepped over and around any bodies in his way. He felt a tug as a hand grabbed his boot.

He jumped and kicked the hand away, cursing. He kept moving forward as more hands reached out from within the piles to grab at him. He brushed them aside as he went, unwilling to draw his swords and unsure if they would be helpful, anyway. As he approached the center of the room, he came upon a massive pool in the center of the walkway. It appeared to be a runoff pool for collecting water spilled by the ramps, with large hoses visible between the bodies that snaked their way up the walls and into the depths of the vault. But the pool was churning and filled with bodies. He stood at the edge of the pool, looking into its swampy contents.

"I can't tell how deep it is," said Vallus.

"It's too cluttered to tell with my scanner," replied Pip.

"What?" Vallus was taken aback. "What do you mean by 'cluttered'?"

"These pools are supposed to drain, according to the map. They feed into the vault's water purifier. It used to make clean drinking water. Something is clogging the drain, and it is filled with bodies. But it is shallow enough that you should be able to cross it on foot."

Vallus was about to take his first hesitant step into the pool when a hand wrapped around his ankle. Pip's light couldn't illuminate the entire area, but she could see more hands grab at him as she turned to see why he had yelped. Vallus thrashed against the hands, but they held tight as more emerged from the piles of corpses that flanked the pool. Vallus reached out to Pip, but she was suddenly knocked away by a madman who charged out of the darkness and slammed into Vallus. The madman was neither large enough nor heavy enough to move him, but Vallus had to use his hands to protect his face from the clawing, screaming man nonetheless. Vallus threw him over the side of the catwalk into the ramp. He tried to draw his sword, but hands had wrapped around his wrists. They tugged harder at his coat. He hadn't recalled seeing as many bodies this close. He tried to think about how they could have grouped up on him, but had to banish it as more hands began to pull him down. Hands wrapped around his chest, his waist, his arms. He fell to his knees as more of the madmen dragged themselves out from beneath corpse piles. Vallus thrashed against the hands, focused on calming his mind to avoid panicking. More and more madmen emerged, seemingly spawned from within the endless bodies, grabbing at him as they wailed and gnashed their teeth.

He could feel their fingers on him, trying desperately to claw through his jacket and armor. They pulled at his bag and even his hair. Pip came flying back to help, but there was little she could do. Vallus knew he would need to fight, but every time he struggled, a new hand reached out. Faces began to emerge from the darkness, twisted and malformed, wailing and screaming in his ears. Blood and water soaked his clothes as more bodies churned around him, enveloping him in screaming madmen. He was close to giving in when his right arm finally broke free. He sucked in a deep breath and drew a sword. Swinging the blade frantically, but carefully enough to avoid hurting himself, Vallus sliced through whatever he could reach. Thick blood splashed him as he cut his way through the madmen like vines in a jungle. He felt the grips loosen as he cut, and he thrashed his way out of the pile. Finally free, he stepped back to the edge of the pool, let out a gasping breath, and spat. Then he wiped the blood from his face. In the light of Pip's flashlight, a dozen or so madmen crawled along the floor toward him, groaning and hissing.

The vault made the decision to fight or flee for him. A hand reached out of the pool behind him and pulled him into its murky depths. Startled, he thrashed his way back to the surface. He gasped for air, spitting the mixture of water and blood out of his mouth as he gagged and kicked away madmen who tugged on him from underneath. A hand broke from the water and reached for him, but Vallus was quick enough to cut it away. Pip flying along above, Vallus trudged through the pool toward the other side. The water was warm, and with each step Vallus felt the squishing of dead limbs under his boots. Vallus had to fight to calm the nausea bubbling up in his stomach. Then he tripped.

Some loose limb had caught around his leg, and the disturbance in the water alerted its denizens. At least a dozen arms broke the surface and grabbed at Vallus as he struggled to steady himself. He was too off-balance to fight back as they dragged him under the surface. There was thrashing and flailing and blood-filled water splashed, then stillness as Vallus was completely submerged. Pip floated above, frantically sweeping the pool with her light.

"Vallus!" she shouted to no response.

The water was still for several moments, save the occasional bubble. Then Vallus broke the surface, spraying bloody water all around. Several madmen, their skin pruned and their eyes empty, hung from him as they scratched and clawed at his face. He threw one off into the pool, then cut another in half as he continued to struggle through the water.

"Pip! They're still grabbing my legs!"

"What do I do?"

"Pop a flare!"

"What?"

"They burn in water! Shoot it now!" he shouted as he

struggled against the last madman who was clung to him.

Pip loaded a flare into her mini-launcher and took aim. She fired, igniting the flare and sending it into the water below. The flare worked to some degree as Vallus began to feel hands coming loose from his legs. He threw the last madman off as he made a mad dash for the opposite end of the pool. Despite the flare that burned brightly in the water, more arms reached out to grab at him. Vallus hacked at them with his sword as he scrambled for dry land. A few managed to gain a hold, but Vallus was able to wrench himself away and plopped onto the walkway on the other side, panting and spitting out the rancid water.

However, he had no time to rest.

Disturbed by the flare and enraged by Vallus' escapes, the madmen began to crawl from the pool, dripping wet and growling a throaty, gurgling growl. Their hands clawed at the floor and his boots. Vallus kicked at them as he backed away, swinging his swords to force the madmen back themselves. He climbed to his feet in time to slice a madman in half, who had been rushing him from the side by running over the bunched up corpses of his fellows.

Vallus soon felt a metal railing bump his back. The end of the walkway. And he was surrounded by madmen.

They were less than a foot away when Vallus heard a loud whistle and the madmen retreated back into the darkness and the bloody water. There was silence for a moment before he heard the whirring of mechanical tools. Vallus slowly and hesitantly turned. The railing overlooked a large platform that rested over more water, filled with blood and body parts.

There were two stairways on either side that led down to the platform, with two concrete walls to separate the water ramps, and two large work lamps were positioned around the area. Standing between them in front of a large medical table was a man, although his back was turned as he focused on his work.

The man was at least a foot shorter than Vallus, bald, with a brown duster coat covered in grime and blood. Vallus mounted one of the staircases and descended it slowly, his hand perched on the grip of his pistol. The man turned when Vallus reached the foot of the stairs. His face was thin, with pale skin covered in small scars. One of his eyes had no pupil, just a large, sky blue iris. The other eye was brown. He was wearing simple metal armor under his coat, and wore heavy boots and gloves that were as wet with blood as his coat. A sick and cruel smile broke across the man's face when he saw Vallus. He took a step back from the table, revealing a young nude woman lying upon it. Vallus couldn't see much of what the man had been doing, but he could see a massive, crude incision through her midsection. Frightened and enraged, Vallus drew the pistol and leveled it at the man's head.

"Who are you? What have you done to these people?"

Pip floated over to Vallus as the man let out a mad, cacophonous laugh. "Welcome, Seeker. I am Jaral. I've seen you through the eyes of my children."

"You mean these madmen? What did you do to them?"

"Oh, only what must be done. I have given them the power to ascend. Can't you see? We can all be Gods," he shouted wildly, his arms outstretched to the sky.

The woman shifted on the table. Both Vallus and Jaral looked at her, the former stunned and the latter annoyed. Her eyes opened, deep and brown and filled with agony and tears as she stared at Vallus, her thin lips quivering.

"Kill... me... Kill...me..."

Vallus pulled the hammer of the pistol back with a loud click. He glared at Jaral, shaking with anger. He had seen countless atrocities and horrors on his journey. Nothing had ever shaken him so much before. The woman squirmed on the table and Jaral turned back to her, raising one of the bladed tools still in his hand. Vallus fired the pistol.

Jaral jumped, startled by the shot. And by the blood of the woman that had splashed across his face. He wiped it away to examine the bullet wound in her head. Now his turn to shake with anger, Jaral stared at Vallus.

"You bastard! Now I have to start all over!" he screeched.

"Stay back. The only reason you don't have your own bullet hole to match is because I want you to face the town. To face justice," Vallus spat.

Jaral tossed his tools aside. He grinned a wide and twisted grin. "Really? Well, waste not, want not."

Vallus watched, confused, as Jaral stood absolutely still, grinning and cackling. Vallus could see numerous machines grafted into the flesh of Jaral's head and neck. A thought began to occur to him. Jaral had experimented on himself as well as whoever had become his madmen. The thought had barely passed through his mind when Vallus was grabbed by several thick, segmented metal cords that came from seemingly nowhere and wrapped themselves around him like anacondas constricting prey. They bound his arms and he dropped the pistol. Vallus tried to fight against them, but they were too strong and he could not reach his swords. He couldn't see or hear Pip, and assumed she had been knocked away by a tendril.

As the cords coiled and Vallus watched the end not constricting him slither toward Jaral, he realized where the cords had come from. They had been submerged in the pit of water behind him. *Stupid,* he thought. *If you want to survive in a vault, make sure no one behind you is holding a knife.* The machine slithered across the floor to Jaral and climbed onto his arms. Vallus realized the machine was essentially gloves with ten long tendrils for fingers, each about an inch thick and made of durable, glossy black metal. The grip grew tighter as the machine mounted itself onto Jaral's hands. One of the tendrils was wrapped over his left shoulder, and it squeezed his bullet wound to the point that the stitches threatened to unravel. The warm sensation of blood soaking his shirt accompanied the shooting pain. He screamed as Jaral screeched in uproarious laughter and the cables grew tighter, ever so slowly. It was everything Vallus could do to choke out one word, as loudly as he could, as his muscles and bones ached.

"Pip!"

In an instant, the little drone flew over the concrete wall on Vallus' right. She hovered over Vallus and Jaral silently for a moment, but that moment distracted Jaral and loosened his grip on Vallus. Although the cables still held him tightly, he had enough room to struggle against them. Jaral's attention was quickly pulled back to Vallus, but the latter had had enough time to grab hold of a tendril. He pulled on it hard and Jaral's foot slipped on the wet floor as he tried to regain his grip on Vallus. Both of them fell to the floor. Vallus, coughing and in tremendous pain, climbed to his feet. He contemplated drawing his swords for a moment, but decided they wouldn't be useful.

Regardless of his strategy, Vallus had no time to employ it. Frantically, he looked about for the pistol, but his search was interrupted when a tendril flew at him from across the room. He narrowly avoided the whip-like metal cable, but its tool hit him on the way back.

Fortunately, it was merely a thin blade, but it cut Vallus' cheek nonetheless. Warm blood trickled from the wound and blended with the water and blood that soaked the rest of him. As Jaral continued to assault Vallus with the whipping tendrils, the latter dove for the gun. His back took several lashings, but his armor held. His hand wrapped around the pistol's grip as a tendril did the same to his ankle. Rolling against the cable's grasp, Vallus shakily aimed the pistol and fired two shots. The first shot missed, but the second struck Jaral in the arm. Jaral screamed with rage and began to pull Vallus toward him. Vallus drew a sword and slammed it against the cable. The blow glanced off its hard metal carapace. He swung again, harder and with great desperation, and severed the cable. The grasping tool at its tip flexed for a moment before it fell still. But Vallus still had nine tendrils to worry about.

Another tendril lashed him before he could fully climb to his feet, and the impact knocked him back to the floor. He dropped the gun again and it slid across the wet ground and out of his reach. Vallus dove after it as another tendril crashed into the floor next to him.

The pistol in hand, Vallus aimed and fired, but a last-second strike from a cable threw him off. The shot echoed through the room, barely audible over the crashing water, as Vallus made to bring his blade to Jaral. Then he felt a sharp pain erupt in his abdomen and he stopped, struck. He looked down to find one of the tendrils was buried in him, although not lethally deep, and blood gushed from the wound in his abdomen. With a sharp cackle, Jaral threw Vallus against the concrete wall where he slumped to the floor. As Jaral slowly approached, Vallus unbuckled the belt that held his swords and quickly removed the sheaths and remaining sword. He balled up a piece of cloth from his jacket pocket, placed it over the bleeding wound, then tied the belt over it.

"Only a matter of time, Seeker. That little trick of yours won't hold up. Soon, you will see. He is coming, and you will either bow before the Gods, or burn with everything else," said Jaral.

Vallus shakily climbed to his feet, supporting his weight with a hand on the wall behind him. His makeshift patch held, although precariously. Jaral raised his tendrils, poised to strike.

"Pip!" shouted Vallus. "Flare!"

The little drone descended from up high at speed and fired a flare that struck Jaral in the face. She bobbed and weaved between the cables to escape back to Vallus, where she injected him with a medicine she kept loaded to slow his bleeding. Reinvigorated, Vallus charged Jaral, hoping to catch him off balance as he reeled from the flare. Although he had dropped the gun in their previous exchange, Vallus still had his sword firmly in his grasp and ready to bring to bear. Jaral tried to block the sword with a tendril, but the blade sliced through it cleanly. Before Vallus could levy another strike, Jaral extended the tendrils to grasp the metal railing that surrounded the stairs to the area and pulled himself up onto the walkway and out of Vallus' reach. The Seeker gave chase, grabbing the pistol and holstering it as he went.

At the top of the stairs, Vallus was forced to push back several madmen that Jaral had rallied. They crawled from the murky pool, grasping and flailing at his coat, and wailing in what Vallus now recognized as abject suffering. Focused on Jaral,

Vallus pushed past as he pulled the rifle, disengaged its safety, and steadied it upon the blade of his sword since he couldn't sheath the blade. He found that his aim was worsening, and his head was becoming heavy thanks to the blood loss. Jaral retreated back to one of the platforms that hung over the crashing, thundering water in the ramps. Vallus took his shot, but the dizziness caused him to miss by mere inches. Jaral cackled.

"Running out of time, Seeker. How much more blood can you lose before you submit? When you do, you're mine to play with."

The tendrils lashed forward, but Vallus was able to throw a madman in their path, then put the rifle away. He edged forward toward Jaral, clutching the madman as he used its body as a shield. The tools at the tips of the cables tore, slashed, and burned the madman's body. Feet away from Jaral, Vallus pushed the madman toward his opponent. Jaral grabbed the body with the cables and threw it aside, but Vallus' feint had already worked. The cables couldn't come back fast enough. Vallus swung his blade in a wide arc that cut straight through Jaral's left shoulder and severed his entire arm. He reeled, streaks of crimson blood shooting from the wound as he screamed in a mix of rage and pain. He quickly regained his composure.

"Heh... What... about justice, Seeker?" he panted.

"What about all these people? What about their justice?"

Jaral tried to strike once more, but it was too late. Vallus had already drawn the pistol, already taken aim, and already pulled the trigger. The bullet hit Jaral square between the eyes. He stood still for a brief moment, twitching and blinking rapidly as though completely shocked. Then he fell backwards into the water, the tendrils flailing helplessly as he plunged in and was carried out of sight. Vallus collapsed to his knees, the madmen still crawling from the pit to encircle him. With what little strength he still had, Vallus pushed them away as he climbed shakily to his feet. His vision had begun to blur, but he managed to find his way back to the medical table with Pip's help. Vallus regarded the dead woman for some time, saddened but in crisis, before he lifted her body off the table and set it as gently as he could on the floor.

"We don't have much time, Vallus," said Pip as she hovered around examining the jars and plastic cases stacked neatly on shelves that sat around the table.

Vallus groaned as he lifted himself onto the table and laid back. He carefully removed the belt and tossed it aside, but continued to keep pressure on the rag that had become drenched in fresh blood. Pip's injection had begun to work, but it wouldn't be enough to stop him from bleeding out. As Pip worked on creating a temporary patch, Vallus handed her materials from nearby at her direction. With the major wound patched, Pip quickly tended to the smaller lacerations that had been inflicted upon Vallus.

"That patch should hold steady, but you're going to need a blood transfusion since you lost so much. Jaral seems to have had all the necessary materials to perform one, but there's just one small problem."

"No blood?"

"No *clean* blood. Plenty of B-type blood around here, but it's all mixed in."

"No way," said Vallus, jolting upright with a slightly panicked face, panting and wobbly. "No way are you... putting that sludge in me."

"It might be fine. I'm detecting a signal coming from it."
"What?"

"A signal. Something mechanical is in the blood. I've been sensing this signal since the first madman you encountered, but I couldn't isolate it or trace it to the source. I think there are nanites in the blood."

"Nanites? Microscopic machines? Think I'd rather die. In fact, there's... no guarantee that I won't, anyway."

"Well, considering all of the blood available is mixed and contains hundreds of different samples, that would normally be the case. But since the signal is so strong here, I think... Vallus? Vallus!"

As she spoke, Vallus slumped back onto the table, panting hard. The gauze patch had sprung a leak, and Vallus began to once more lose blood. He could barely see, but he caught a glimpse of Pip flying about in an agitated manner as she tried to help him. He passed out, Pip's screaming of his name echoing through his mind.

The weight was almost more than he could take. His muscles strained against it, young and pliable but burning nonetheless. He kept pushing, relentless in his exhaustion. It felt so familiar; so fresh. Vallus quickly realized there was no real weight on the bar. The bench was a facsimile. He had already done this. He stood and looked around. The courtyard had been more of a small, dusty patch of dirt set aside in the encampment for potential Seekers to train their bodies. Vallus had spent every day for some ten years in the yard, using the crude weights made of scavenged machine plates and the track lined with stones to build himself; to become as strong as he believed he would need to be.

"Machines hit hard. You need to be hard enough to take it. Because you will not always be fast enough to avoid it," his father had said.

"But why will they try to hit me?"

"There's something wrong with them. Their minds. Something in their artificial intelligence makes them hostile and violent. There is great darkness in this world, son. That is why you come here. The only way you survive, mission or not, is to become strong. Strong enough to look into that darkness and not blink."

Blink.

Vallus opened his eyes and found himself standing at the center of the encampment he had called home, which had come to be known as the Huddle, completely alone. It was as though the Huddle had been abandoned long ago, but everything had been left behind. Vallus was older now, as old as he was when he began his journey, and had all of his gear. But he knew it was all set dressing. He could almost feel the edge of the illusion, the haze that fogged his mind. His jacket felt unnatural, almost wispy. His swords had no weight.

Vallus was pulled from his musing reverie by a slight giggle. He turned to look behind him to find a very young girl, no older than five, standing several yards away. She held a crude, makeshift doll and her bright blonde bangs obscured her eyes. She grinned as Vallus stared at her, taken aback by her presence.

"You're gonna die," she said as she lifted her head to reveal the crusted, empty sockets where her eyes should have been.

Vallus gasped as the floor was pulled out from beneath him. The soft light of the sun above was replaced by darkness, the walls of the Huddle replaced by cold steel. Vallus was lost in a torrent of unpleasant sensations for a few moments before he returned to equilibrium. Lights flickered above his head and there was junk scattered all about the hallway that stretched out before him. He was still for a moment, then he took a few tentative steps toward the doorway he could barely see at the end. He looked at the wall to find a vault designation stenciled onto it: JA-1685. The first vault he had entered. He touched his hand to the letters, and a sort of itching urgency overtook him. He remembered what had happened in the hall, what had been there. What had forced him to take shelter in the laboratory where he found Pip. He didn't dare look behind him. Instead, he sprinted full speed toward the doorway. He ran, and ran, and ran, but no step seemed to bring him closer to escape. The lights flickering above dimmed his view, and he was caught by the briefest sensation that something large, writhing, and furious scratched at the walls just behind him.

The world seemed to collapse around him each footfall pulling the floor back instead of moving him forward. The walls began to fold and crumple as a deep panic wormed its way into his mind. He lost his footing and fell for what seemed like at least a full minute before he hit the hard, metal floor. The lights had all gone out, leaving him in complete shadow. Vallus carefully pulled himself to his feet as he waved his hands in front of him to search for stability. Suddenly, a blinding light filled the room. His eyes stung, but it was more like a mental pain, as though the light was screaming at his brain. For a few moments, an impossible pressure gripped him, then an unbearable release as the light dimmed and he found himself in a small room lined with steel walls. He looked behind and found there was no door in the room. He was trapped. The girl's words rang in his mind.

"You're gonna die. You're gonna die. You're gonna die."

The words became a chant. Vallus frantically searched for a way out, or at least for the source of the sound. He found nothing. The walls began to crack and splinter, and the floor felt marshy. With nowhere to go, Vallus watched as the cracks in the walls began to issue thick streams of blood. It was everywhere, bubbling up from beneath the floor and dripping from the ceiling. Gradually, the room continued to fill with an ocean of crimson as Vallus beat at the nearest wall to try and break through it. His efforts were to no avail. The blood continued to seep in as the singing grew louder in his mind. As the blood threatened to overtake him, Vallus screamed.

Vallus gasped as he awoke. He was still in DA-0708, still lying upon the table. He was groggy and light-headed, but he quickly noticed the three tubes connected to him by IV. His stomach ached, but the rudimentary patch had been swapped out for a clean one. He sat up, and Pip turned to face him from where she had been hovering, checking vitals.

"Vallus!"

"Pip... What happened?"

"You passed out, and I had to stop the bleeding and fix the patch. You seized for a moment, but I managed to stabilize you. Tough to do with just this tiny arm. Luckily, Jaral had most of the tools I needed."

"The blood... The nanites..."

"Almost gone. I managed to reprogram them by connecting to the signal they were transmitting. They were looking for instructions. So I told them to clean the blood and filter out anything that wasn't B-type. Then I ordered them to disassemble and pass through the digestive system. They should all be out of your system within twenty-four hours."

Vallus sat up as the fog began to clear from his mind. The water was still rushing, echoing through the tunnels, but there seemed to be no other sound.

"What of the madmen?"

"They seem to have all ceased functioning. My guess is that Jaral kept them moving. Killing him must have severed their connection."

"Need to keep moving," said Vallus as he pulled the tubes out. Pip rushed to bandage their holes.

"Now you wait a second. You just lost almost enough blood to kill a man. Rest. Now."

Vallus stopped and looked at Pip for a few moments before he grunted and hopped back onto the table. She went to his bag, which had been removed and set aside, and withdrew a wrapped parcel from it. She tossed it to Vallus with her tiny arm.

"Eat. You need to replenish your blood sugar and energy. At the foot of the bed is a relatively clean shirt I found. Seems Jaral kept all his stuff here. Might as well take it considering how much blood was on the other one," said Pip as she floated about cleaning up medical supplies.

Vallus unwrapped the ration parcel and slowly began eating the thin strips of jerky within. It was dry and spicy, but flavorful. Vallus recognized it as gluk meat, that of a sort of small, flightless bird that had been cultivated in the Huddle, although he was aware they could be found in other human settlements. They had been one of the few animals Vallus had ever seen for the most part, as most animal species had long since vanished with the Gods.

The Seeker had always found that to be incredibly odd. Vallus ate six strips of the meat, then set the parcel aside. With some strain, he pulled the new tunic over his head, careful to mind his bandages. He then strapped his chest armor back on before he stood, shakily for a moment, and picked up his coat.

"Keep in mind that you may experience some fatigue, physical weakness, dizziness, and nausea for the next several hours. You should also try and take it easy for a while, perhaps rest somewhere. You want to avoid damaging that bandage. I also changed your shoulder dressing. The wound is still bad, but at least it isn't infected. Also, you may find metallic bits in your urine or droppings, but they will only be the minor remains of the nanites, so don't worry about them. And as a final note, you may notice some residual effects from the nanites for an indeterminable amount of time. Their programming is extremely sophisticated, and I am not sure what the full extent of their abilities are."

"I'll take it under advisement," said Vallus, grimacing. "Let's see what we can scavenge from here before we move on."

"We shouldn't need any more medical supplies. I put a few rolls of gauze, some scissors, some medications, and some basic first aid tools in your bag while you rested."

"Thanks. Maybe he had some food or water," said Vallus as he gathered up his weapons and returned them to their proper places on his belts.

Vallus pushed the large medical table aside to get to the set of shelves that had been placed behind it, careful to avoid the woman's body. He gave her one last pained look, as if to apologize for not being able to give her a proper burial, before he returned to his task. With the table out of the way, Vallus found that there was yet more concrete wall behind the shelves, with a chain link gate built into it. The shelves held several dozen unusual tools and mechanical parts, but nothing of use or interest. With a frustrated grunt, Vallus pulled one of the shelves out of the way.

With Pip following closely behind as she monitored his vitals, Vallus walked through the gate into what looked to be a service tunnel. Vallus could still hear the thundering water in the ramps, but they were walled off and quieter. The tunnel was short, terminating at another chain link gate about thirty feet from the first gate. There was a lone construction lamp in the tunnel, with several belongings scattered about. Pushed up to the wall was a cot made of stacks of blankets. Several plates and eating utensils, a duffle bag, a jug of water, and a small leather-bound book all sat beside the cot on the floor.

"Looks like Jaral lived here for quite some time," said Vallus. "At least he kept this part clean."

"No qualms about taking Jaral's things, I see," said Pip jokingly as Vallus undid the duffle bag's zipper.

"Fuck him. He shouldn't have stabbed me," said Vallus, tossing Jaral's stray clothes aside as he shot Pip a coy grin.

"True. Anything useful?"

"No. Just clothes and toiletries. He traveled light. If there wasn't a noticeable lack of weapons and scavenged gear, I'd say maybe Jaral had been a Seeker. At some point, anyway. No food either. Don't wanna know what he ate, to be honest."

Vallus picked up the journal and flipped through the pages. Pip watched him silently as he read through it. She held silent until she noticed Vallus' expression becoming more and more disturbed.

"What is it?"

"He... he was planning this for quite some time. He uses a strange dating convention, but it looks like he had been here for at least five years. And all these people... they were mostly passersby that he lured here, but some came from the town. He doesn't mention how he got them down here, but it seems as though he knew of a way to circumvent the doors and security protocols. Maybe the water pipes?"

133

"Not surprising. There are hundreds of tunnels and service vents in this vault. This one's big."

"Ya. It doesn't seem like he knew much about the Gods, but he does mention that he met one. Says it didn't mention its name, but gave him things he would need. And a purpose. He was doing all of this for the Gods. He even has diagrams in here. Fuck."

Vallus tossed the journal aside with disgust. He felt his stomach lurch, probably from the nausea Pip had warned him of, and he leaned away from the cot as he vomited on the floor. He coughed for a moment before the nausea subsided, and he wiped his mouth with one of the blankets.

"That water clean?" asked Vallus, pointing to the jug as he tossed the blanket over the pile of puke.

"Scans indicate it is filtered. Should be fine to drink," replied Pip.

Vallus uncapped the jug and took a large gulp from it, swished it around, then spat it onto the blanket on the floor. Then he drank down as much of the water as he comfortably could. He hadn't realized how thirsty he had been, but the water was like a healing salve for his parched throat. He felt some of his strength and energy return, and he stood on legs that were more firm than they had been in hours. Vallus took his canteen from the clip on his bag and topped it off with water from the jug, then recapped it and set what little remained on the floor.

"Not going to take the rest?"

"No. Leave it for anyone else who may come here. Let's move."

"Do so carefully," said Pip, ignoring Vallus' slightly raised eyebrow.

With one final glance over the camp to assure he didn't miss anything, Vallus walked toward the gate at the back of the tunnel.

There was a chain holding it shut with a padlock, but it was old and rusted and easy enough for Vallus to break with a well-aimed blow from his sword. He pushed the gate open and proceeded into what appeared to be an old machinery room. Many of the room's machines were disassembled, with parts and tools scattered all about. The room looked almost like a house in the midst of construction, with tarps tacked to walls, boards laid out, and several work lamps set up in corners. There were also two more tables like the one Jaral had been using, and Vallus guessed he must have gotten the things for his experiments from the room before locking it up. Lying on one of the tables was a blueprint for a tool like the weapon Jaral had wielded against Vallus, although the blueprint implied it was a tool for working on out of reach places. Vallus surmised Jaral had gotten his weapon from the room as well.

Vallus spent some time sorting through the miscellaneous junk strewn around the area, finding little of use aside from metal plates and a roll of ballistic fiber that he could use to repair or upgrade his armor. In one corner of the room, Vallus found a large cutting tool next to a box of wires and spare blades. Carefully, he lifted one of the blades from the box to inspect it.

"Lightweight, but sturdy. Look how sharp this is. Pip, you think I could change the blades on my swords to these?"

"Most likely. They look almost like your current blades. Although I can't identify the metal these are made with, my scans indicate that this metal is highly dense. It should take quite a ridiculous amount of strength to break them."

"Hmm... They're a few inches longer than mine. Might make dual blade mode a little unwieldy. I'll have to test the weight. Are you sure you can't tell what it's made of?"

"Yes. The only reason I can think of that my scans would

come out like that would be if the blade is made of a synthetic material."

Vallus nodded curiously and took a large nearby tarp in hand. With surprising ease, he used one of the blades to cut a section of the tarp away, then he wrapped two of the spare blades in it and stowed them in his bag. He also took a box of screws and other assorted metal parts and put them in the bag along with the blades, hoping they would come in handy if he didn't already have the parts to affix them.

"So where to now?" asked Vallus as he meandered toward the center of the room.

"Well, it appears the only door out is blocked off. The area below is redacted... That's odd. There is a vent that leads down to the next floor above the blocked door, but there is also a cooling fan halfway down the duct. No indication if it is on," replied Pip as she scanned the map inside her mechanical mind.

"I'll just have to break it, then," he said over his shoulder.

Vallus took another step in the direction of the door to hear a slight creaking sound. There were several large planks of plywood set on the floor. He noted that it seemed strange to leave them lying about, yet he wondered why there was a large circle with a slash through it spray painted over them. Then he took his next step, and the boards broke. Vallus was stunned for a moment before he fully realized he was falling. Fast. Pip's yelling was like background noise, a distant echo. She chased after him as he dropped into a deep hole that appeared to have been caused by something extremely heavy falling through it. He didn't remember seeing any holes above him, but he had no time to muse on causation. Flailing desperately, Vallus grabbed onto a stray pipe. It only momentarily stopped his descent. The pipe lurched, then tore loose from the great wound in the vault as

Vallus ducked to shield himself from the falling shards of plywood. As he once more began to fall, Vallus noticed there was no light beneath him. Then he hit the floor. Or so he thought. The broken plywood was under him, but he had landed on a large piece of metal, which was beginning to sag slightly under Vallus' weight and from his impact. He guessed it was a sort of patch. Vallus nervously chuckled at the irony, a patched wound in the vault to match that of the Seeker.

His chuckling ceased when the metal buckled, he was quickly followed by the sound of a screw popping loose. Vallus quickly checked the grappling hook attached to his hand, assuring it was on his right. His left shoulder still ached. Pip caught up with him just as the metal patch broke loose from the ceiling below. Vallus writhed to spin his body, then aimed his arm, noting that the floor was fatally far below him, with what appeared to be an extremely massive object in the center of the room. With a silent prayer to any God that would hear him, he fired the hook.

Chapter 6

Vallus held his breath for a heartbeat, bracing for the worst. But the hook found purchase and held strong. Vallus gripped the brake and his arm jerked up. It hurt, but he ignored it as his descent slowed. Gradually letting go of the brake, Vallus eventually dropped low enough to let go of the brake and fall to the floor. Feet planted firmly on solid ground once more, Vallus jerked on the grappling hook's cable, but it wouldn't come loose.

Frustrated, Vallus pulled his knife and cut the cable. He then put the remainder of the tool in his bag.

"Expecting to find more cable?" asked Pip as she finally caught up with him. "No. Spare parts, maybe. I was hoping this thing had more than one use in it."

"Perhaps that same failure put its previous owner in the predicament we found him in?"

"Maybe. You said this floor is redacted?"

"Yes. It appears on the map, but its function is not marked," Pip replied.

Vallus inspected the machine at the center of the room to discover it was an automated tank. He looked up toward the hole he had fallen through, comparing the size of the hole and the tank. The machine, from what Vallus could tell, had most likely been the cause of the wound. Its treads were destroyed, its gun bent, but it appeared to have been left alone since falling to the floor. Vallus found himself perplexed as he withdrew his tools and began salvaging whatever he could, caught up in wondering why the tank had been dropped through the floor.

"Hey, Pip? Any idea how this got here?"

"My best guess is that this tank was being moved. I did notice a very large break in the ceiling of the room you fell from; I would guess it came from there. Maybe whatever they were moving it with broke?"

"There does appear to be a very large chain stuck under it… Why would they cover that hole with plywood, though?"

"They probably didn't count on us being there."

"Fair," said Vallus as he stowed his tools and the minor mechanical components he had taken. "The sign above the door says 'Restricted Access. I'm guessing the Gods didn't want us there, either."

"Probably not."

"One more thing. Did you notice a hole above us before I fell? This thing couldn't have come from that room."

"Yes. I was about to tell you about it," replied Pip. "Well, that's a little less weird. Let's go."

As Vallus approached the door, he noticed additional words stenciled onto it.

TESTING LAB. AUTHORIZED PERSONNEL ONLY. He looked around the door for a few moments, but found no way of opening it. Then he noticed a small plate to the side, mounted to the wall adjacent to the door. He pulled the clearance card from his jacket and pressed it to the plate as was instructed by a small icon etched above it. A loud affirmative chime issued from the door, then it slid open. Vallus walked through the doorway.

Inside was much of what Vallus had expected, a rare and somewhat welcome treat. He was in a long hallway flanked by rooms made by glass walls in metal frames. The area was relatively dark, with several fluorescent lights serving as the only sources of light. There was an aged, musty odor in the air, and many of the glass walls were busted out. Vallus was struck by the silence most of all. He had almost become accustomed to the sounds of the madmen aimlessly wandering in the shadows, but he reckoned he wouldn't encounter any more of them and would have to grow used to quiet.

The sectioned rooms nearest the door were filled with laboratory equipment, much of it knocked over or silent. Vallus couldn't identify what any of the experiments might have been, considering the thick layer of dust that sat on pretty much every item in the room, and most of the equipment was broken. After passing several labs, Vallus came to the first intersecting hallway. He looked down either side to find darkness and silence. Vallus moved toward the door at the end of the hall, and the labs began to look as if they had been used.

Curious, Vallus entered a room on his left through an open door. There was a pile of several dead and dismembered madmen in one corner of the room, and one madman chained to the table at the center. The table was set upon a mechanical arm attached to the ceiling, and was tilted so the body was nearly at a right angle with the floor. His entire body, from the neck down to the genitals, had been sliced open, and entrails left to rot were still lying upon the floor.

"Look at the wounds over the limbs. These were tortured. Why torture madmen, though?" Vallus asked.

"Fun," replied Pip with a somber voice. "The way the marks are made; the needless savagery. It all suggests the perpetrator wasn't doing this for information or retribution, but for gratification."

"What kind of sick monster…"

"Judging by the state of these bodies, we may soon find out. This couldn't have been done more than a few days ago."

Looking around through the surrounding labs, Vallus could see several more torture sites set up throughout the back half of the laboratory. Each had similar circumstances, although the methods of dismemberment and disembowelment varied by room. The stench lingering over the area was almost unbearable, rancid and metallic. What Vallus found most striking, however, was the distinct lack of any tools left behind. No blades, blunt instruments, or firearms could be found, and certainly none holding evidence of their use.

"They must bring the tools with them," he said pensively.

"Most likely. Seems strange, though," said Pip as she floated behind Vallus and the pair returned to the main hall.

Although he was still more than sixty feet from the door at the end of the hall, Vallus could vaguely make out a figure standing in the doorway. It was hard to tell for sure, but the figure appeared to be about as tall as Vallus, with broad shoulders, a long hooded coat, and very thin eyes. As he grew closer, he could see that the figure was in fact a man, with a long curtain of jet black hair like drapes made of blades and what looked to be a permanent scowl. Although he hid his discomfort well, Vallus prepared for the worst.

"You... Are you a Seeker?" asked the man.

"Yes... I am called Vallus. And you?"

"Not a Seeker. I am Yashir. I recommend you leave this place, Seeker. This vault's story ends in flames." There was venom in his voice.

"Can't do that," said Vallus, trying to keep his cool and not reveal that he was doing so.

"Unfortunate," Yashir hissed through his thin lips.

141

"Nevertheless, my plans here won't be impeded. Seek what you will, but know that one way or the other, this vault will meet its fate."

"What are you going to do?"

Vallus didn't get his answer. Yashir had already slipped into the shadows and vanished from sight. Vallus sprinted down the hall toward the door, passing more labs that had been converted to grisly torture chambers. He passed over the threshold to find an empty second atrium. There was only one door, straight across the room and undisturbed. There were two vents, but neither looked bothered.

"Where did he go?" asked Vallus quietly, his hands hovering over his swords. "I'm not sure, but I think he's gone. Perhaps he went through that door?" Vallus looked from the door he entered through to the door at the back.

"Maybe. Let's keep moving, but keep an eye out for that guy. I got a bad feeling about him."

Vallus eased up and inspected the door. It was marked 'CHEMICAL TESTING', with the large letters stenciled in white, chipped paint. Reading the words, Vallus hesitated for a moment before he raised his gas mask to his face. The mechanical mask hissed lightly as it sealed itself around his mouth and nose. His voice came through it muffled.

"Good of them to warn us. Let's see if it's as bad as it was in GR-1375," he said with a shiver.

Vallus pressed the button on the side of the door and it slid open. Within was a dark, quiet room filled with rows of odd machines composed of large barrels with a number of hoses and control boxes attached. At the top of each machine, about ten feet off the floor, was a tip like a shower head. These sprayers would occasionally emit a low hiss while they sprayed a fine cloud of translucent dust, meant to land on the empty planters below. The dust hung low in the air, filling every inch of the room. He noticed it was clinging to his skin on his face, but he felt no pain, nor any reaction. He pressed on into the room as the door behind him slid closed with a thud.

"What is this stuff?"

"Not sure," said Pip. "I'll run a few test scans."

Vallus continued on into the room, examining the things left behind. There was little Vallus considered of use, but he did pocket a few stray tools he needed as he moved about the room. A growl filled the room, low and anticipatory. Vallus prepared to draw a sword. Then a loud thumping sound echoed through the vents above and a clattering, scratching racket filled the room for a few moments before silence once more blanketed the area.

"What the...?"

"Unsure, but my scanners have finished their tests. I still cannot identify this dust, but it looks like a mild hallucinogen or perhaps a psychoactive in structure. And it will activate if enough of it sublimates through the skin. We - or more accurately, you - need to get out of here. Fast."

"Where to?"

"This way," said Pip, floating ahead of Vallus toward the back of the room. He noticed that Pip's fans seemed to be pushing the dust away from her. "Climb that ladder to the catwalk over the sprayers unless you want a thick coat of poison dust. The doors in this room triggered a lockdown when we entered and won't open again until the room is decontaminated," she continued on as Vallus followed via the catwalk, which creaked and shook under his weight. "There's a control panel over here that should turn off the sprayers. Then we need to vent the room."

Get out.

143

"Pip?" he said quietly, too quietly to hear through the muffling gas mask.

Vallus found that a strong sweat had built on his forehead. His muscles no longer ached, and the pain in his shoulder and abdomen was greatly reduced. His head was somewhat light.

"Pip, I..."

The dim lights began to take on a different quality, almost textured. Vallus' breaths came ragged and stiff, and a strange and intoxicating lightness came over him. He stumbled.

"Vallus? Vallus!" Pip's voice was distant, almost ethereal.

"You need to get out of here," a voice said from behind him.

Vallus turned to see a woman in a white sundress with bare feet not far from him, her face obscured and smudged, but kind and bright. Something about her calmed Vallus, and slowed the horrible thundering of his heart in his chest. He shivered and clenched his hands several times. He was overcome with the sensation that he could feel the organs and tissue in his body. He clenched his jaw.

"I feel... sick... Who are you?" he said as he struggled to unclench his jaw.

"You know."

"Do I?" He raised an eyebrow. "I can't just 'get out'. I have... work... to do," he huffed.

"Your father raised you well. Be a shame to see *his* work wasted here."

"I... can't."

"This road only ends in one place, Vallus. Huh. Vallus. Good choice."

The shivering not only continued but intensified as tears welled up in the corners of his eyes. The woman came closer. A powerful warmth radiated from her. His breaths were sharp, rapid. Her hands extended out to his face, cupping his cheeks. A tear fell. Then a sharp pain struck him, coursing through him from his neck. He shouted.

"Vallus!" Pip screamed.

He whirled around to face the drone, rubbed the back of his neck, then ripped away the gas mask so he could copiously vomit over the railing. Once finished, he quickly replaced the mask. He looked around, but the woman was gone.

"Sorry. Had to give you a depressant to counteract the psychoactive effects of this dust, apparently. Who were you talking to?"

"I... I'm not sure," he stuttered. "I think it was... Never mind."

Vallus continued onward, his head still feeling fuzzy, then dropped off the catwalk to the floor near the control panel. The room was once more filled with the clawing, banging noise from the vents, but it persisted. The ceiling sagged, bending and straining the metal plates that lined it.

"Get down," Vallus said.

"What?"

Vallus didn't reply. He grabbed Pip and tucked her to his chest before he dove behind the control panel. At that same moment, the abrasive sound of tearing metal filled the room, followed by something heavy falling to the floor. Vallus was motionless, his hand covering Pip's flashlight until she turned it off. The thing's weight had destroyed a number of the sprayers, so Vallus could hear each step it took in the rubble. It took four steps, slowly, growling a low, bestial growl along the way. There was a sound as of something sniffing the air. The growling intensified. Then another four steps. The thing dropped something on the control panel, and Vallus looked up to see a massive paw, about the size of a tire and tipped in five curved claws like sabers, gripping the desk next to the panel. He held his breath. The thing continued to sniff the air for a few moments, growled, then withdrew and leaped back into the vents. It banged and clattered through them until the noise faded away.

Vallus let go of Pip and climbed to his feet. He scanned the control panel for several moments before he found the switch to deactivate the sprayers and pressed it. Within seconds, the machines ceased functioning. Through his gas mask he breathed a sigh of relief, hit the button to vent the room, then moved back into the room to inspect the hole in the ceiling as the gas began to dissipate. Pip followed, with Vallus guiding her light by pointing. "That hole is enormous. Think you can measure it?"

"Way ahead of you. The hole is about twenty feet in diameter. With the damage to the ceiling taken into account, I estimate that whatever that thing was, it was probably around fifteen feet in length. And very strong. That steel is forged to prevent these gasses from seeping through the minute spaces in the plates."

"Any idea what it was? What kind of machine would crawl through air vents and behave like that?"

"None. I cannot identify exactly what it is, but I did detect a heartbeat. Whatever it is, it is organic."

"An animal? How?"

"I cannot say for sure. But we should be careful, and expect to see that thing again."

Vallus nodded, then turned to head to the door at the back. However, upon arriving at it, he found it was jammed. He tried the control panel on the wall, but the door simply wouldn't budge, although it would open about an inch wide. With Pip's light shining through the crack in the door, Vallus could see it would be a waste of effort to open the door, anyway, considering there was a very large and very visible hole in the floor in the room beyond.

Looking around, he saw only one other door, perpendicular to the jammed one. "The map say what's beyond that door?"

"It appears to be a repair room of some sort. Look at the door, though. It's broken."

Vallus looked closer and found Pip was correct. Sitting within the frame were two sliding doors like the one to the broken room, but one was stuck at a slight angle and was jumped off its track. He approached and looked through the thin crack in the door to see it was relatively safe and that the doorway was clear. Then an idea occurred to him. He motioned to Pip to get far from the door, then followed her. Once he was some twenty feet from the door and behind the cover of the nearby control panel, Vallus took one of his two remaining grenades from his belt. With a deep breath, he pulled the pin. He held the trigger for a few moments, then rolled the grenade across the floor toward the door where it came to a stop against the track at the base. Within a heartbeat, the cooked grenade exploded. Vallus ducked behind the control panel along with Pip as the room was filled with noise, fire, and smoke. Once it had cleared, Vallus rounded the panel to inspect the damage. The loose door had been blasted completely from the wall, and the other was bent back from the bottom. He cautiously stepped through, one hand on a sword.

The room was dim and quiet, with only several large florescent bulbs on the ceiling left functioning. There was a plethora of machinery, much of which Vallus was unsure of the purpose of. A half a dozen large steel tables were scattered around the room with a variety of mechanical implements and tools strewn about them, and each table had a mounted lamp.

There were six tall metal cabinets filled with drawers near the tables, as well as a metal drum beside each table. The floors were covered in dust, ash, and detritus. Overall, it reminded Vallus of the workshop in the Huddle, only larger with significantly better stock. The workshop in which he had forged his swords.

"Let's see if one of these lamps work. If you can watch my back, I can put these new blades on," said Vallus as he removed his bag and set it on the nearest table.

Vallus flicked the switch on the lamp and it weakly buzzed to life. The light was dim, but it was good enough to work under. Pushing aside some of the junk and tools, Vallus cleared a decently sized workspace, then drew his swords and laid them carefully on the table. Reverently, he ran a hand along the blade of each one. The faint sound of a hammer clashing against forged steel rang in the back of his mind. He thought of the words the smith had told him as he set to work, beginning by pulling the new blades from his bag along with his tools.

"Careful, now. Draw out the steel evenly. Twenty inches long, but set aside some metal for the handle assembly," the smith had told him as he hammered away. "It isn't shaping. Put it back in the heat. Hold it steady; the fire won't hurt you."

"It's… heavy," a thirteen-year-old Vallus had said as he pulled the steel from the heat and quenched it in the tub beside him.

"Good, good. You want it heavy. Dense. Won't cut through machine plates otherwise. File it. Now shape that steel, boy. Keep it even and straight. Twenty inches long, four inches wide, a half centimeter thick."

Vallus continued his work, the memory floating in his

148

subconscious. He drew the pins from the hilt, set aside the discs with the etched initials, then carefully removed it from the tang. He then removed the screws that held the blade to the tang and gently pulled the blade from the slot that held it to the grip. He set the blade aside, then unwrapped the new blades and carefully inspected it. Setting the new blade in a vice, he took a drill from the table and put a bit in it, then set to work drilling new pin holes to line them up with those of the handle. With the blade set to fit, he mounted it in the hilt, and replaced the discs, pins, and screws.

With the sword rebuilt, Vallus picked it up and tested its weight, then gave it a few swings through the air.

"Perfect. This blade was made with precision. A little longer than the old blades, but they don't throw off the balance. Good," he said to himself. "Fits the sheath as well."

With the first sword finished and sheathed, Vallus set to work on the second. He found solace in the work. It was almost like a ritual of sorts, one to build devotion to the life he had chosen. The work became a distraction from the intense stress that recent events had lumped upon his shoulders. His focus had been bred by years of study, often under the meticulous eye of his father. Having been a learned man himself, and assigned to teach the Huddle's children as his duty, Vallus' father had been a stern but encouraging educator. And it had paid dividends, as evidenced by the numerous children who would stop by their home regularly, seeking even more knowledge from him. And it had earned him the unerring respect of his son as well.

With the second blade affixed to his sword, Vallus drew the first and attached them at the pommels to assure the modification still worked and had not been hampered by his changes. He was pleasantly surprised to find that they not only worked, but it had in fact given better balance to the swords. Satisfied, he separated the swords and returned them to their sheaths. Then he stopped dead in his tracks as a thunderous crash echoed through the walls, as though deep within the vault. Dust fell from the walls as they shook.

"What was that?"

"No idea, but whatever made it, it's either extremely heavy, or extremely strong," replied Pip, a worried tone undercutting her usual cool demeanor.

BANG.

The sound reverberated through the walls again, knocking more dust loose and gently rattling tools on the tables. Vallus approached the door at the back marked 'Emergency Stairwell'. The walls shook again as he opened the door and walked down the stairs in the dark. There were eight flights of stairs total, and yet another crash resonated through the walls at the bottom of each, growing louder with each step.

BANG.

The sound grew louder and more frequent. Vallus came to a door labeled 'P-1 Maintenance Access'. His hand hovered over the control panel to the door, hesitant and anxious. Another bang. He flinched, only slightly. Then, with a deep breath, Vallus opened the door. His entry was greeted by yet another reverberating crash, deafening as it echoed along the hallway that stretched out before him.

Vallus found himself in a long hallway with a high ceiling. Long tracks attached to the ceiling stretched the length of the hall, with a number of machines hanging from them that Vallus couldn't identify in the weak light. At least twenty doors on either side flanked him, and the area was littered with more junk and construction equipment. He walked down the hall slowly, hands above his swords and at the ready, as the banging sound

150

continued.

About halfway down the hall, a door on either side of Vallus opened and two humanoid machines entered the hall through them.

The machines appeared to be around five and a half feet tall at Vallus' best estimation, with jointed limbs covered in smooth, gunmetal colored armor plates. They had what could pass for a head, with two ocular lenses that served as eyes. They walked with a stiff, jerking manner as their pseudo-heads twitched back and forth as if searching the area. Each of them held a short machine gun with a wire that connected from the gun to the back of their necks.

A strange, static-filled gurgle emanated from them as they slowly began to enter a patrolling formation. Then their apparent programmed routine was interrupted when they noticed Vallus. The closer machine raised its weapon, and the second soon followed suit.

"Oh, no," said Pip. "Battle droids."

"What?"

Vallus had no time for answers. He was forced to dive behind a work table which he had to flip onto the side to form makeshift cover. The gun's firing made an unusual, high-pitched noise, and though he could feel the rounds impact against the table, they left no dents or damage that he could see from his side of the barricade.

"What are they shooting with?"

"Energy weapons," said Pip, peeking ever so slightly around the edge of the table. "Probably laser-based. If they were plasma, we'd be dead already."

Vallus smirked morosely and drew his rifle. He quickly

checked the ammunition remaining as he waited for the droids to stop firing, then clicked off the safety.

"Careful. They don't need to reload since their weapons draw power straight from their on-board supply, so you'll need to take your shot quickly and return to cover," said Pip.

Soon, the firing ceased and Vallus took his opportunity. Careful not to expose too much of his body to the second droid, Vallus peeked over the table with the rifle aimed at the left side droid and fired. Vallus quickly ducked back to cover as the second droid returned fire. He hadn't had time to check his shot's lethality, but judging by the lone shooter firing back and the loud clanking of metal smacking against the ground, he surmised his aim had been true.

"Uh oh," said Pip.

Vallus didn't need to question her. The table he was using for cover had begun to warp, and he could tell it was heating up. The battle droid's weapon was beginning to break through. Muttering an expletive, Vallus ran out from behind the table toward the side of the hall. The droid gurgled and screeched as it ceased firing to adjust its aim. It fired, and several lasers caught Vallus in the metal plate on his left shoulder. The impact forced the plates to strike his bullet wound, but the layers of clothing reduced the pain by a small degree and the stitches held. Vallus fired back before he took cover behind a steel pillar, getting off two more shots that missed. As he returned the rifle to its spot on his bag, the battle droid continued to fire and Vallus drew his swords. Pip, hovering above, whistled.

"As good a time as any to test the new blades. You're going to need to round this pillar as quickly as you can and aim for the chest. The power supply is housed there," she said.

Soon, the droid ceased firing and it took a few steps closer to reposition. Vallus didn't give it the chance to attack. It was a solid six steps to close distance with the battle droid, but Vallus' height and speed gave him the advantage. He pushed the droid's gun away as it tried to aim and drove both blades into its chest. They pierced the metal chest plate with a renewed ease, sending sparks flying from the destroyed power supply. The machine gurgled, whined, then fell to the floor in an inert heap. Vallus let out a deep sigh of relief as he returned the swords to their sheaths.

With Pip keeping watch, Vallus leaned down to inspect the destroyed droid. Although the chest was too damaged to salvage anything of use, Vallus was able to take a few pieces of scrap metal he deemed useful. He picked up and inspected the droid's weapon and pulled the trigger in the direction of a wall, but nothing happened.

"The gun won't fire without an active power supply. You could scrap it, though," said Pip.

He shook his head.

"Not worth the effort. Let's keep moving. But keep an eye out; I'd rather not be caught by surprise by one of these things," Vallus replied.

Vallus continued walking down the hall, all the while the banging sound echoing through the walls, as he searched for an exit. It was a long and uneventful walk to the next doorway, with Vallus flanked only by empty cells and scattered trash. Broken tables and abandoned construction gear littered the entire length of the hall, but Vallus was thankful for a lack of any more aggressors as the junk would make poor cover. At the end of the hall, with an unusually large door set in the wall, the banging intensified. Whatever its source was, Vallus knew it was beyond the door. He took a deep breath, then opened it.

As the banging continued, Vallus entered a large, circular, dark room filled with empty cells that would fit better in a prison than a vault. There was a second level of cells above, with a flight of curved steel stairs on either side of the room leading to them. Scattered about the floor were several madmen, all in various states of dismemberment, and the floor was splattered with their blood. Toward the far end of the room was more construction equipment, and three living madmen. However, these madmen were not long for the world.

They were bitterly embroiled in combat with what appeared to be a female figure of about seven feet tall, with broad shoulders, intricately-carved armor, and wires that flowed from her mechanical head like silken hair. Leaning against a table near her was an enormous hammer.

The madmen dove at her, but they were no match as she grabbed the first and slammed him into the ground with such force that his head essentially exploded into a grisly paste. The next to attack was lifted into the air and torn in half, its blood and guts soaking the floor. She turned as the third madman attacked, and she tore the madman's head clean off. Soaked in blood, the mechanical woman stood to full height and regarded Vallus with curiosity. Although she appeared to be made of machines, her chest undulated as though she drew breath.

"Took you long enough, Seeker. I have eagerly awaited the man who slayed Nirav," she said with a grating voice like lightning, a cruel laugh deep in her throat.

"Are you another God?" he asked as he cautiously approached, the hammer in his peripheral vision. "Like I told Nirav, I have no intention of fighting. I come here seeking answers."

"I am Aurien, the Lioness, Goddess of Justice. You have already been judged, Seeker, and you have been found wanting," she replied as she picked up the hammer and hefted it with both hands.

"As I said, I seek only answers. I have no quarrel with you," said Vallus, ready to draw his swords nonetheless.

"Answers will not change what is coming. Face your end with dignity, Seeker," she replied bitterly as she charged forward, hammer held aloft.

Vallus drew his swords, but knew that attempting a parry would be hazardous. As Aurien swung the hammer, he dodged to his left and narrowly avoided it. The hammer slammed into the ground, producing a much louder version of the banging sound he had heard in the hall as it crushed the metal flooring under it. Vallus moved to strike, but Aurien had already recovered from her miss and took a sideways swing at the Seeker. The weapon only grazed his chest, but the tremendous force behind it was still enough to knock him off his feet and send him careening across the room into an errant pool of blood. He slipped as he tried to climb to his feet, with Aurien fast approaching. Desperately, he rolled out of the puddle just in time to avoid yet another calamitous hammer swing.

"Slippery one, aren't you? No matter. You will tire. I won't," she said as she raised the hammer yet again.

"You're right. It would be much more relaxing if you would just tell me what happened. All you need to do is tell me what caused the Fall and I'll leave," Vallus said as he continued to avoid the deadly swings of Aurien's hammer.

"Even if I wanted to, I couldn't answer your questions, Seeker," she replied with a growl.

"Can't, or won't?"

155

"Does it matter?"

Aurien swung again, and Vallus dodged again, but he could tell that the first strike to his chest had begun to tax his breathing. His other wounds were of little concern, as their dressings held tight and he felt very little pain. As he continued to avoid the slow but powerful strikes from Aurien's hammer, he noticed a sweat building on his brow and on his chest. Aurien seemed to tire of Vallus' endless dodging, as she leveled a kick at his head. She missed, but struck him in the chest. The wind ripped from his throat, Vallus was knocked across the room once more and collided with a wall where he dropped his swords as he gasped for air. Once he finally caught his breath, he had little time to cough before the Goddess was upon him. He hastily rolled out of the way of her hammer, grabbing his swords along the way, as the weapon slammed into the wall and tore apart the metal. Vallus drew the pistol as Aurien wrenched her hammer from the wall, and fired a shot at her head. The bullet bounced off the metal plating around her mechanical face. She laughed, a hearty and cruel laugh.

"Foolish mortal. The might of the Gods is before you, and you think that tiny thing will help you?"

Vallus back-peddled as he sheathed one of his swords. He fired off four more rounds, aiming for her burning red eyes or the hoses that ran through her armor. The bullets bounced off, and the pistol clicked. He had no time to reload, as Aurien was on him already. She grabbed the pistol from his hand and crushed it into pieces, tossing them aside like so much dust. Vallus was only momentarily stunned. He drew his second sword again as he directed Pip to stay clear of the fight. The drone flew to the ceiling as Aurien watched her.

"Interesting. I've seen one of those before," she said, her

eyes fixated on Pip. "It will be a pleasure to crush your tiny little body."

"You will not touch her!" Vallus screamed as he charged forward.

He dodged her attempt to push him away and took a wild, powerful swing. It was a glancing blow, but the new blade proved sharp enough still as it sliced through one of the thin armor plates that protected Aurien's side. She roared as the blade cut through, yet there was no blood. Instead, a bright blue fluid poured from the wound, although only a small amount.

Aurien tried to retaliate, but Vallus was already behind her. He swung his second blade, and it found purchase in the plating around her leg. The sword cut deep, causing Aurien's leg to buckle. She dropped to one knee, but was not to be deterred. She reached back and grabbed Vallus by the top of his chest plate with her intricately engineered mechanical fingers, and with a mighty roar, she threw him across the room.

Vallus rolled across the floor, but the distance between himself and Aurien was only a brief reprieve. She ran toward him, hammer in hand. As Vallus jumped back to his feet, he was knocked back again as Aurien closed the gap and kicked him in the chest. He maintained his grip on his swords, but it was of little comfort. Aurien was upon him yet again, but this time she pushed away his sword and lifted him into the air by his throat. He struggled and thrashed against her grip, tight enough to hold him but not enough to cut off his breathing entirely. Vallus tried to punch her in the jaw with his right arm, now free since he dropped his sword as she lifted him, but the strike did nothing. With an eager growl, Aurien slammed Vallus into the floor. She pinned him there with one of her powerful arms as she traced her claws across his cheek.

"Little mortal… So fragile, yet you struggle as if you can change your fate," she said as she increased the pressure and her claw cut into his skin.

Blood trickled down his cheek, adding to the uncomfortable static sensation of Aurien's breath on his skin, her face mere inches from his own. Vallus' throat began to ache as he continued to fight against Aurien's grip. He landed several more punches to her jaw, but they didn't seem to faze her. His eyes began to water. As she cut his cheek again, Vallus screamed.

Next, it was Aurien's turn to scream, as Pip dove down from the ceiling and shot a taser round between the metal plates on her neck. It stung and shocked her, distracting her long enough to lose her grip on Vallus. He kicked her as hard as he could in the jaw as he squirmed out from under her. She dropped her hammer. Aurien struggled to pull the taser dart out of her neck, as the shock had disoriented her. Vallus grabbed hold of the hammer and found it extremely heavy, but not impossible to lift. With great effort and monumental strain, he roared as he lifted the hammer and smashed it into Aurien's face.

The blow broke away some minor chips of metal from her head and knocked her sideways. She quickly rolled to her feet and charged toward Vallus, screaming and wailing in unadulterated rage. Vallus had already dropped the hammer and dove for his dropped swords.

He dodged around the ferocious kick she had aimed at his chest as he stood, and was forced to leap out of the way as she had grabbed her hammer and swung it overhead and into the floor with explosive might. She wheeled on him, swiping the hammer side to side as Vallus stepped back to dodge.

"Stand still. There is so much pain I need you to endure," she said through a clenched jaw, swinging the hammer with mad ferocity.

"You must be the torturer. Why? To what end?"

"Found my handiwork, huh? Those things just won't stop crawling up from the muck Jaral made them in. I'm just sending them back. Slowly. Such is the will of Justice."

Aurien missed with the head of the hammer, but swung the opposite end at Vallus and struck him in the arm. The blow didn't hurt much, but it did knock Vallus off his balance.

Aurien took the opportunity to grab his chest plate again and slammed him to the floor. Vallus found himself silently thankful for the armor plating that lined his bag once more. Then Aurien raised the hammer high above her head, and Vallus had to roll out of the way before she brought the weapon crashing down onto the floor where his head had been moments before.

Vallus took several swipes at Aurien, but missed. The final swipe struck the handle of her hammer as she used it to block, then he was forced yet again to dodge out of the way as she swung the hammer into the ground where it stuck between two disjointed metal plates.

She yanked on the handle, but it wouldn't budge. Thinking quickly, Vallus sheathed his swords and drew the rifle. As he did, Aurien pulled the hammer from the floor and aimed another sideways swing at Vallus. He fired the rifle, and a round tore through her right arm. She yelled in anger and pain as more of the blue liquid seeped from the wound. The shot upset her swing, making it easier for Vallus to sidestep. Although she was wounded, Aurien showed no discomfort beyond the initial shock as she redoubled her efforts to swing the hammer at Vallus. He was forced to put the rifle away and retreat out of her range.

His back step was of little use. Aurien jumped forward, hammer in hand, and delivered a mighty kick to Vallus' chest. He was ready for it this time, and the blow took less wind out of him as he collided with a vertical table behind him. He found that it was coated in a thick layer of dried blood. Vallus had no time to dodge before Aurien was in front of him, hammer placed on the ground as she pinned him to the table with her wounded arm. Even with what seemed to be her blood dripping down her arm in thick streaks, she was strong enough to keep Vallus held to the table. She held the tip of one of her clawed fingers up to his eye.

"Where to start? Should I pluck out your eyes? Or I could just cut you all over and see how long it takes for you to lose your mind. You can stop fighting, mortal. This only ends as the King has ordained. You have been sentenced to cruel and unusual punishment."

"You... forgot..."

"What?"

Aurien followed Vallus' upturned eyes to see Pip hovering in front of her. She was struck for a moment, her metal mouth agape, before Pip fired a firecracker into her eye. The firecracker exploded in a hail of harmless but blinding sparks, forcing a disoriented Aurien to loosen her grasp. With his opponent distracted, Vallus drove one of his swords into her abdomen. She roared with pain as blue blood spilled from the wound. She reached for the hammer, but with his other sword, Vallus cut her right hand off. In retaliation, and slowly regaining her sight, Aurien punched Vallus in the face. She missed his nose, but the blow still stung as it cut his cheek and drew blood. She swung again, weaker, but Vallus dodged it as Aurien fell to her knees, a gurgling mixed with the grating of her voice. Before she could topple over, Vallus grabbed her by her armor and held one of his swords to the thick cables and plates that made up her neck.

"Tell me what I want to know! Where did the Gods go? What did you do to this world?"

"Justice... demands that... I follow orders..."

"Talk!"

"I... think not..." she said, cackling as her chest plate split open and slid apart to reveal a glowing white core mounted in an intricate series of metal frames with wires fed into it. Vallus realized it was her power supply. And it was beginning to glow brighter. And there was an immense heat coming from it.

Vallus let go of her and backed away as quickly as he could. Aurien's cackling grew into mad laughter as she convulsed. She screamed a primal scream laced with insanity. Then Vallus was knocked across the room as Aurien and her vibrantly glowing power supply violently exploded. The room was filled with fire, smoke, and raining shrapnel, and Vallus was slammed into a nearby wall on his right shoulder. He was dazed for quite some time before he noticed a piece of shrapnel had become lodged in his left forearm, drenching the sleeve in more blood. But he was too disoriented to do anything about it as he yelled out for Pip.

Luckily, Pip was unharmed by the blast and came speeding to Vallus. With her by his side, Vallus pulled the piece of shrapnel from his arm with a groan. Using her mounted tool, Pip glued the wound before Vallus wrapped it with a roll of gauze from his bag. Vallus shakily rose to his feet, his head still spinning. He wobbled as he struggled to hold his balance. His hearing had finally returned, but his head pounded like a drum. Rubbing his forehead, Vallus looked around the still smoke-filled room. He stepped carefully around the scattered and burned debris from the explosion and stood over the charred remains of Aurien the Lioness.

"There's not much left. Can you detect anything new, Pip?"

"No. The remains are too burned and damaged. I can, however, confirm that her body was made of the same metal as Nirav."

"Were you able to get any readings on that blue liquid?"

"A few. It was a seventy-four percent match to blood, but contained several unusual chemical components. It also contained nanites."

"So she had something close to blood," said Vallus as he knelt to inspect the wreckage. "Strange. But these remains aren't going to give me any more answers than it did while alive. Let's move."

Pip floated along close to Vallus as he moved toward a door at the end of the room opposite where Vallus had entered. The door led into a long hallway with a dozen or so thick pipes mounted to the ceiling and walls, each feeding into a different point in the hallway. The hall itself was filled with steam, emanating from an unknown point. Vallus cautiously approached the unmarked door at the far end of the hall and walked through as it opened by motion sensor. The sight beyond was truly unlike anything Vallus had ever seen anywhere.

Vallus stood in an incredibly large, sprawling area with a high domed ceiling and a stone path that wound through the room. The entire area was bathed in a warm light that seemed to radiate from the place itself, and the air smelled sweet and clean. Flanking the path were patches of grass, several bushes, and a number of tall trees of a variety of types, all alive and well. As he slowly walked through the room, Vallus looked around, in utter awe of the sight. There were bushes with berries and nuts growing on them, flowers in full bloom, and even dew drops on the grass. He rounded a corner and came to a wide and open field, with a long wall of rocks to the right and a waterfall that poured into a large, clear pool to the left.

Upon seeing the pool, Vallus looked down and noticed how dirty he was, along with his clothes. He approached the water and looked into it.

"Pip, keep watch, please," said Vallus as he removed his weapons and set them on the floor, along with his bag.

Pip tipped in air to nod, then began to circle the area, taking scans as she went. With Pip's watchful eye flying above, Vallus stripped down to his underwear and sank into the cold water in the pool. As he did, he noted how remarkably clean and clear the water was. It was cleaner than his canteen water to be sure, and even cleaner than the water he had traded for. He drank some, careful to avoid any that had been contaminated by the gunk he washed off, and found it cool and refreshing. He cupped his hands and poured it over himself, washing away the dried blood and fluids that had splashed him. The pool also afforded him the opportunity to clean his wounds and check their dressings. He noted that the stab wound he had received from Jaral was still clean and patched, and that its patch was made of a waterproof material that held tight even though it had been submerged for some time.

However, the dressings for the shoulder wound had peeled back, and two stitches had come loose. His chest was also heavily bruised, but Vallus was thankful to find that nothing was broken.

Vallus' eyes were closed, immersed in the comfort of the cool water and the peaceful aura of the place when he heard the door he had entered through open, accompanied by three sets of heavy boots walking along the path. He opened his eyes to find Yashir standing not far from the pool as his associates joined him. Volya walked to the far end of the room and sat down in the grass, then lit a cigarette. Hecate giddily climbed up the rock abutment and sat down on a boulder, her legs crossed and a devious grin on her face. He caught a brief glimpse of what appeared to be dozens of thin knives inside her coat. Vallus wiped the water from his eyes.

"Enjoying yourself, Seeker? I thought I warned you to leave this place," said Yashir.

"You did, but I don't answer to you," said Vallus as he climbed out of the water and pulled a towel from his bag. "Who are they?"

"He's Volya. She's Hecate. They work with me."

Vallus glanced up to see Pip patiently waiting, hovering above the waterfall. He kept an eye on Yashir as Vallus began to redress. He spoke as he did.

"You said this vault's fate ends in fire. What did you mean? Why are you here?"

"Simple. I'm here to destroy this vault. Like every other vault I've been to."

"That's going to be a problem. I need to get to this vault's core."

"You can seek your answers elsewhere," replied Yashir bitterly.

"My journey led me here, Yashir. I've met Gods here. I can find my answers; but not if you destroy this place."

Yashir scoffed.

"There are no Gods, neither here nor anywhere. Just demons. You'll find only death here."

"The fuck you waiting for, Yashir? Just kill this bozo so we can get outta here," hollered Volya from where he sat in the shade.

"He makes a good point, Seeker. I could just kill you. Wouldn't need your answers if you were dead."

"Then draw your weapon," said Vallus as he gripped the hilts of his swords. "I don't need one," he said as he charged forward.

Vallus wasn't ready for such an impulsive attack, but he managed to duck the first punch Yashir aimed at him. The second was a quick jab that struck Vallus in the chin. Vallus reeled as Yashir grabbed him with both hands by his jacket and threw him across the room and away from the pool. He quickly rolled to his feet, but Yashir had already closed distance.

Vallus blocked a few punches from Yashir's left, but when he struck with the right and Vallus blocked, pain erupted through his arm. Vallus stepped back as he shook the pain off.

"What kind of glove are you wearing?"

"Not a glove," said Yashir as he reached up and tore the sleeve from his right arm.

Doing so revealed an intricately built mechanical prosthetic, complete with armor plating and artificial muscle. He flexed the arm a few times, looking at it with, to Vallus' surprise, contempt.

"Whoa," said Vallus.

"That wasn't my reaction. You think these so-called Gods will give you answers? All they ever give is death and turmoil. That's what they gave me," said Yashir, holding the arm up as if to prove his point. "I was four years old when the cult took my arm in the name of their God. Since then, I've had to rebuild it eight times to fit as I grew. And each time was like torture."

"So that's why you want to destroy the vault? Revenge? Why not just move on? Why not just embrace your strength and forget the pain?"

"That's the problem, Seeker. I can't forget," he said as he touched one of the metal fingers to his temple. "I remember… everything. Every bit of pain and anguish. They told me my perfect memory would be a gift. They were wrong. I am cursed with the memory of every wound these pretender Gods have inflicted upon me. And on the world."

"Then find the God that did that to you. The vaults didn't do that."

"I would if I could. But these vaults are just mausoleums, crypts dedicated to monsters. They are a symbol of a dead world, and that world must be given its burial."

"So you would destroy the last thing that can bring closure to people?"

"There is no closure to find. Tell your people of the Gods' cruelty. That's all they have."

"Then we're at an impasse. I can't leave until I complete my mission, and your mission will prevent me from doing that."

"I suppose so. Only thing left to do is die."

"Wait," said Vallus as he held up his hands in surrender. "At least give me a chance. Give me time to get to the core and get out. Then you can do whatever you want to this place."

Yashir stood still. Volya stood up and tossed his cigarette aside, his hand reaching for his holstered pistol, but that stopped with a single stern glance from Yashir. Meanwhile, Hecate seemed lost in her own world and completely uninterested in anything else as she sat leaned back upon a boulder with her arms folded behind her head.

"Six hours. You have six hours to get out. If you're still here after that, then you can join the vault in its grave."

Abruptly, Yashir turned and walked to the end of the room. Volya lit another cigarette and gave Vallus a dirty look as he followed, and Hecate grinned a wide grin and stared at him, not entirely without lechery, as she hopped down from the boulder. Without so much as another glance, they passed through the door and Vallus was left alone with Pip, surrounded once more by only the crashing of the waterfall. After picking up his bag and sitting on the grass nearby, Vallus called Pip down and had her repair the two stitches in his shoulder that had come loose. He then wrapped the shoulder with fresh gauze and checked that all of his gear was in place. Vallus gave the area one last broad look, taking in the peaceful, mellow energy of the place and basking in it for a moment. He then picked up the shredded sleeve from Yashir's jacket and Volya's cigarette butts and headed for the door. On the way, he came to one of the many trash cans like those he had seen scattered throughout the vault and deposited the riders' leavings in it. With one final longing, lingering look around the room, Vallus walked through the door the riders had walked through before.

Beyond the door was a straight staircase that led to a large, circular room lined with pipes and hoses. There were two doors to either side, but one was blocked by rubble from the damaged ceiling above and the other was labeled 'Maintenance Closet'. Directly across from the stairway he had entered from was an elevator door. He found himself once more puzzled by where the riders could have gone.

"This it?" said Vallus as he approached the elevator door.

"Yes," said Pip. "We might need to fix it, though. I am reading an error message from the console."

"Of course," said Vallus as he reached into his bag and withdrew his tools.

He went straight to work and pried the console cover away from the wall. As Vallus looked for a way to bypass the elevator and its error, a bang echoed through the room. There was a clattering in the ceiling that echoed through the vents from a distance. Vallus worked faster as he muttered expletives. Pip guided him, apparently unfazed by the noise. A scratching accompanied the bangs and thumps. There was a set of switches Vallus had to flip in a specific order that he didn't know, so he began flipping them at random. The sounds grew closer as Vallus flipped switch after switch, and he grew more frustrated. Finally, he flicked a switch and the three indicator lights in the console Vallus had been trying to activate turned green and the elevator began to move from wherever it was within the shaft. From the sound it made, Vallus guessed it was closer to the lobby. Yet another bump filled the air, closer still. Vallus prepared to draw his weapons. One more loud thump, and Vallus could see the ceiling bowing in places. Then a soft hiss from behind him told Vallus the elevator had arrived and he backed up through its doors and hit the button for the lobby. The doors slid closed and the car rose through the shaft away from the depths of the vault and the creature in the vents.

Chapter 7

The elevator churned slowly up the shaft as the thumping of Vallus' heart finally slowed. With a calming sigh, he bowed his head as he awaited his stop. He contemplated what he had faced below, and his plan for what he could face ahead. Pip sat resting her power cell in Vallus' bag, a small beep issuing every so often. He knew it would take some time for her to charge, but he hoped it would be long enough before the next leg of his journey. The elevator came to a stop with a soft whine, and Vallus opened his eyes with the doors. He immediately drew his swords.

Standing before him was a massive mechanical, armored being of at least eight feet in height. He wore bone white armor over black body plates, and he held an enormous shield with a sharp, stylized crest in the shape of a great bird emblazoned upon it. Staked into the ground behind him was a lance as long as he was tall. And in his free right hand was Shiloh's throat. The faceless being glared at him through the eye holes of his mask. At first glance, Shiloh appeared to be alive but in serious condition.

"Let him go!" Vallus screamed.

"As you wish," the being replied as he tossed Shiloh aside into the destroyed camp. "Stand and deliver, mortal, for you face Grand General Vakka, Knight of the Legions and God of Honor."

"This doesn't need to be a fight. Please, I seek answers," said Vallus, trying to restore his calm as he glanced at the camp in search of Shiloh.

Vakka laughed mockingly, but didn't respond. Instead he took a single great stride toward the elevator and swung his fist into Vallus' stomach. It blasted the wind from his lungs, but the Seeker quickly recovered. Vakka swung again, although with a weaker jab that struck Vallus in his jaw and spun him around. Vakka then grabbed Vallus and lifted him into the air. Vallus struggled, but to no avail.

"A question for you, mortal: do you think this will kill you?"

Vakka rose to full height with the Seeker gripped tightly in both of his hands, and threw him out of the skylight. Glass shards dug into his coat and cut small slits in it as he broke through what little remained of the window. Vallus hit the ground and tumbled across a massive pile of rubble, formed from the sunken dome roof of the vault. At the center of the area was a tilted metal spire about thirty feet tall. Shaken but unharmed, Vallus rose to his feet as Vakka leaped through the window himself, crashing through the metal structure like a charging bull. His shield and lance were in hand, and a cloud of steam followed him in a thick, billowing blanket. He landed upon the mountain of rubble, shield raised and lance at the ready.

"You have pestered us long enough, mortal. You are without honor. You scurry in the dark, picking at the bones of *our* world, demanding you be answered as if your life is worth more than the dirt you will be laid in. You mortals always were bottom feeders," he said.

"Are all of you monsters? What is wrong with you Gods?"

"Still with the questions. Go ahead and prattle on as I send you to the after."

Vakka charged forward, seemingly unburdened by his massive weapons. His strides were long, with the confidence of a seasoned veteran. Vallus had some difficulty finding footing, but he decided to give up the search to jump out of the way of his charging opponent. He sheathed the swords, drew his rifle, and took aim. Vakka took a moment to recover from his charge and turn, but it was enough for Vallus to fire three shots. The shield put a stop to them all. The Seeker quickly traded the rifle for his blades.

Vakka turned about face and thrust his lance at Vallus with furious speed. With little time to react and his boots still slipping through the rubble, Vallus crossed his swords around the lance and ground it to a halt, the tip mere inches from his face. The parry cost Vallus greatly. Vakka withdrew the lance, causing a minor roll on the edge of one of Vallus' swords. Then as Vallus tried to rally and deliver a cut to his opponent, Vakka quickly bashed his shield into Vallus, knocking the latter back several feet. Vallus stood and wiped blood from his chin as Vakka charged him once more, enveloped in a cloud of steam that barely reflected the weak moonlight above.

Vakka missed as Vallus dove out of the way, and drove his lance into the side of the tilted spire. While his opponent still had his back turned, Vallus fired three more shots at Vakka and heard the gun click on his fourth shot. Unfortunately, the shots seemed to have no effect, but Vallus still had enough time to reload and cock the gun. Vakka wheeled around and slammed the shield into the ground, obscuring his form as he ducked behind it and charged, the lance aloft. The shield slowed his run, but it dug up chunks from the rubble and launched a cloud of dust into the air. The dirt and steam clouds forced Vallus to put away the rifle and get out of the way. Vakka passed by him, then spun quickly on his heel and charged forward with the shield raised. He slammed into Vallus, hitting him in the arm. Although the arm didn't break, Vallus could tell that any more force would have done the trick.

He let loose a scream as he was thrown back.

Vallus hit the ground, but was able to quickly get back to his feet. It was of little use, for Vakka was upon him. Vallus managed to narrowly avoid the lance once more as he swung his sword at the weapon. His blade glanced off as Vallus took a swing with his right sword at the shield, which also bounced away. Vallus was growing frustrated, as Vakka's defenses seemed impenetrable. Vakka tried to bash Vallus again, but the latter was able to jump back and out of the way. But it wasn't enough. Vakka pushed forward again and chained a second shield bash that struck Vallus cleanly in the chest and knocked him back forty feet. Vallus rolled across the ground, his swords falling from his hands as he tried to protect his bag as well as Pip, who still rested within. Once he had safely, to some extent, come to a stop, he looked up to find that Vakka had done the same. He stood still, his burning red eyes gazing evenly at Vallus from within the blank mask. Vallus cautiously rose to his feet, spitting blood from his cut lip and possible internal bleeding, judging from how his chest stung.

"Lose your nerve?" he shouted at Vakka with more gusto than he felt he had.

"You dropped your weapons," he replied calmly. "It would be dishonorable of me to attack you while you are unarmed."

"God of Honor. Right," said Vallus as he guardedly approached his swords where they rested on the ground.

"I must apologize, Seeker. I'm not one for talking. I dislike niceties. But you have earned some of my respect. You fight well. Perhaps there is a shred of honor in you after all."

"Thanks," said Vallus incredulously, looking down at his swords. "You mind if I do something quickly?"

Vakka nodded.

Nodding in return, Vallus unbuckled his bag and took it off

his back. He turned ninety degrees to his right, walked about thirty steps to the edge of the sunken vault roof, and sat the bag on the rubble. He gently patted the pocket of the bag where Pip slept while recharging, then returned to his swords. He picked them up, gripped the handles tightly, and prepared himself.

"Another thing," said Vakka. "It has become clear to me that you have a unique style of fighting. My methods are not working. But that is of little concern."

Vakka slammed the tip of his lance into the ground. The rubble shifted, ever so slightly, under Vallus' feet. Vakka twisted the handle of the lance, and as steam billowed from it, he drew a long double-edged sword from within. He then raised his shield, and a dozen or so mechanical plates began to shift and move on it. The shield became smaller as the plates made it take on the shape of a kite shield. With the new plate configuration, the sigil on his shield changed as well. To a crown. And although Vallus could not see his face, as Vakka changed his stance and glared at him, he knew there was a smirk under the expressionless mask he wore.

***

Deep within the vault, the doorway to the core sat silent and bolted shut, the lights in its gateway and adjoining atrium all dark. It was uncomfortably silent in the entryway, more like a grave than an ancient testament to the power of the Gods. There, his hand on the door, stood the Ashen King. His head rested against the door, he whispered quietly.

"I will have what I came for... You cannot hide from me forever."

"We yet have work to do, Farran," came the icy, hissing

voice of the Wizard from behind him. "We will have our prize. In the meantime, we should protect this door."

"Vakka is solving that problem as we speak," said the King as he turned to face the Wizard.

"Contingencies, Farran," said the Wizard as he crossed his arms behind his back and coolly regarded the Ashen King, and his thin metal mouth curled into a toothless smile. "We believed Nirav and Aurien would succeed as well. They did not."

The Ashen King's hands curled into fists. He shook, only slightly, but held his temper at bay.

"Vakka has earned the faith I have in him. He will prevail. But I will satiate your paranoia for now."

Several tubes that wove through the King's armor began to glow blue as he raised his hands toward the ceiling. As if at his command, scrap and parts from the pipes and machines all about the room began to move toward him. They broke apart and dug into his flesh, slipping in between his armor plates. The King groaned as the machine parts absorbed into him. Then he hunched over, opened his helmet, and wretched violently. A thick jet of black liquid filled with metal chunks erupted from within his helm and coalesced into a puddle at his feet. The Wizard, who had looked away in disgust, turned back as the King's helm closed and he stood to full height. Farran reached out to the puddle with one hand as the pipes glowed again.

"I shall form a glorious Simulacrum in my image to be my fierce guardian. By my decree, none shall enter this door until the appointed time," he said, almost as if chanting.

The pool began to bubble and swirl as the metal took on rudimentary form. The beginnings of an arm emerged as the King stepped over the puddle, down the three small stairs near the door, and stood next to the Wizard. The puddle of liquid metal continued to bubble and churn behind him.

"Our new dawn approaches, Wizard. I want this Seeker dead."

"Of course," replied the Wizard. "We have much left to do. Pray that your faith in Vakka is not misplaced."

***

Vakka charged forward, sword held aloft and shield at the ready. He took a broad swing at Vallus, who parried the strike with the sides of his blades. The parry was costly, as the impact was powerful enough to push Vallus back. Even though his footing had been weakened, Vallus was able to duck under the next sword swing. Vallus went to slash at Vakka, but he parried with his shield. The move offset Vallus, and Vakka made his riposte. Vallus barely dodged out of the way, but the sword cut through his coat and dealt a minor laceration to his right side, just under his ribs. First came the briefest sensation of pain, then blood.

The wound wasn't too serious, and Vallus knew there was nothing he could do about it anyway as Vakka continued his vicious assault. He parried another sword strike, spun with the momentum of the attack, and took his own swipe at his opponent. The blade cut into one of the armor plates that protected Vakka's leg, but it was a superficial wound. Vakka held the blade flat and attempted to stab Vallus. The attack missed its intended target and instead cut through the left sleeve of Vallus' coat to deal another minor laceration. Vallus grit his teeth through the pain, refusing to show his opponent even a shred of fatigue.

Vakka jumped back and flicked the blood from his blade. Vallus took his own turn to charge forward, his swords at the ready. He rolled under Vakka's defensive sword swipe, then blocked a shield bash with the side of a sword. Mustering as much strength as he could and roaring viciously, Vallus drove his right blade into Vakka's side. Vakka roared in both pain and rage, then kicked Vallus away from him. Vallus rolled across the ground, then hopped to his feet. He was surprised at the sight as Vakka pulled the sword out of himself with a growl as the same blue liquid that had poured from Aurien's wounds began to spill from Vakka's. He threw the sword to Vallus, who caught it by the hilt and connected the two swords at the pommels.

"You are just full of surprises, aren't you, Seeker?" said Vakka. "You truly will die a warrior today."

"All of this could be avoided, Vakka. We could lay down our arms and talk this out."

"We could, but I have my orders, and honor dictates I follow," replied Vakka. "You want answers? Then get past me. Get to military storage."

"Why? What's there?"

"You are a Seeker, yes? Seek."

"What exactly are your orders?" asked Vallus.

Vakka shifted his shoulders, tightened his grip on his sword, and raised his shield. "Simple. Destroy you."

Vakka rushed forward, sword held in front of him like the bowsprit of a great ship, the moonlight reflecting off the clean, cool steel of the blade. Vallus had grown weary, and the fight had nearly drained what little stamina he had left. On legs that were not as sturdy as he would have wanted, Vallus stood his ground as the steam-laden God of Honor charged him, a great and thunderous racket filling the sunken arena. Gripping his dual-bladed sword tightly, he prepared for the trying fight ahead of him.

But it did not come. As he drew his sword straight back,

Vakka leaped over Vallus.

The cloud of steam that had been following him blasted Vallus in the face like a mighty gust. The heat was almost unbearable. But it did more than burn. The steam cloud disoriented Vallus, obscuring his sight and the sounds of Vakka's footsteps as the God landed on the ground and pivoted to attack. Vallus turned just in time, alerted as his senses came back to him. But Vakka's attack still landed. The blade cut across Vallus' left bicep. Although not a lethal wound, it still bled profusely and ached incessantly. But Vallus' determination was not broken. With the last of his remaining strength fading, Vallus drove his blade forward and into Vakka's abdomen. A spray of the blue liquid splashed the Seeker's face as Vakka roared with pain.

Enraged, Vakka threw his shield aside and grabbed at Vallus. He jumped back, his sword still lodged in Vakka's stomach. Vallus dodged another swipe of Vakka's sword before the latter grabbed him by the collar with his free hand. Vallus struggled, but Vakka's grip was impossibly strong. Vakka lifted Vallus off his feet and grabbed the Seeker by the throat after he drove his sword into the ground. As his windpipe closed under Vakka's enraged hands, Vallus kicked his sword with the steel tip of his boot. The God roared as the blade was driven further into his abdomen.

"Fight all you want. Struggle. Nothing will save you. I have had enough of this game. Now I'm just going to crush the life from you," said Vakka, his voice filled with seething anger.

"Not… very… honorable," Vallus choked out as his breaths became shorter and shorter. The God merely grunted in response.

Vallus' mind raced. Pip was still charging; he couldn't call for help. He guessed he had two, maybe three minutes if he could hold his breath to figure something out. He lashed out at Vakka with a punch to try and put the God off his focus, but he was unfazed. The grip tightened. Vakka was taking his time, and Vallus' was running out. Little else at his disposal, Vallus pulled his knife and jammed it into Vakka's neck. The God screamed in Vallus' face as his grip loosened, but it wasn't enough. Vallus was beginning to see spots. Then an idea occurred to him. He planted his right foot in Vakka's abdomen, just above the sword that was still stuck inside the God. Vakka tried to stop him, but with both of his hands full there was little he could do.

"Ah. Let me return that to you, Seeker," said Vakka with an exhausted growl. "Thanks," Vallus choked in reply.

Vakka released one of his hands from Vallus' throat, just as Vallus had hoped he would. He reached down, grabbed hold of the sword's handle, and pressed the small trigger under the engraved discs. The exposed sword quickly detached from the other, leaving the pommels behind. Vakka tried to shield his head as Vallus swung the blade up, but it pierced straight through Vakka's hand. With a roar of his own, Vallus drove the blade onward straight through the middle of Vakka's blank face mask. A jet of blue blood drenched Vallus as the pair fell to the ground. Vallus rolled off Vakka as the latter hit the ground, and with one final gurgle, fell silent.

Vallus laid there for a very long moment, panting as sweat and the strange blood stung his eyes. Every muscle in his body felt as though they were made of concrete. Unable to move, he stared into the blank night sky as the moon faded behind a cloud and blanketed him in pitch darkness. Vallus tried to keep his eyes open, but he was too exhausted. His last thought was of Pip as he drifted off to sleep.

***

Vallus awoke some time later and sat up. It was still dark outside, and Vallus guessed he had only slept for an hour or two. He stood, somewhat rested but still sore. He looked to his right to find Vakka's body was missing, though his swords and knife had been left behind. He picked up his weapons and returned them to their sheathes with their pommels back in place, then walked to his bag. He put it on his back, secured it, then called for Pip. Fully charged, the little drone flew from the bag and hovered in front of Vallus.

"You appear to be injured. What happened while I was charging?"

As Pip got to work tending to Vallus' wounds, he told her of his return to the lobby and his encounter with Vakka. With the cuts cleaned and glued, Vallus returned to where Vakka's corpse had been with Pip in tow, her flashlight activated and pointed at the spot. Under the light, Vallus found a number of unusual things. Firstly, the pool of blue blood was much larger. A half dozen mechanical parts sat in the puddle, seemingly shaken off the body. But the strangest thing was a trail from the puddle to about twenty feet away from where the body had been, as though it had been dragged. And judging by the deep gouges in the rock along that trail, something big with extremely sharp claws had done the work. Vallus followed the trail to where it terminated and crouched down to inspect the ground. There were a few more stray parts there he hadn't noticed before, in addition to an unusual warped pattern in the packed rubble that formed the ground. The rock had been worn smooth in a semi-circle and glistened as if it had been polished.

"What do you make of this, Pip?" asked Vallus, pointing to the rock.

"It appears as though it has been exposed to extreme heat, but the strangest thing is the molecular structure compared to the rock around it. It's as if it was always like this."

"How do you suppose that happened?"

"No idea. Without a proper laboratory, I can't study this rock in more detail."

"Okay. Well, let's get back to the lobby and check on Shiloh. Hopefully he's still alive," said Vallus as he moved toward the window to the lobby.

The window Vallus had been thrown through was some six feet above his head. From the broken metal framework around it, he surmised that the ground beneath his feet had once been a roof that connected to the windows to form a skylight that had been inverted in the dome collapse. A thick pile of rubble formed a wall which Vallus took some time to inspect. He ran his hand across it, then wiggled a few jutting chunks of rock to find them firm, settled tightly with time. As he prepared to climb, the moon emerged from behind the cover of the dense clouds above and basked the wall in light. He looked at it, mesmerized by its size for a moment, then set to work climbing the wall. About halfway up, a stone came loose and fell to the ground, but Vallus kept his hold and continued on. Careful to avoid any broken glass that may have been still in the frame, Vallus climbed through the window and dropped to the floor of the lobby. Pip followed closely behind.

Vallus rushed to the remains of Shiloh's camp and quickly found its owner lying on a pile of sheets. Carefully climbing over Shiloh's scattered belongings, Vallus knelt down beside the man and checked his pulse. He was alive, but unconscious, and he didn't appear to have any severe wounds that required attention. Vallus picked Shiloh up, moved him aside, then pushed the sheets off the makeshift bed and put Shiloh in it. He then got to work setting the poles up that had held the sheets. They had been held up with cinder blocks and mechanical vices, which Vallus positioned as close to what they had been as he could. Soon, with a little tidying, the camp looked relatively put together.

After some digging through the items that had been scattered by Vakka, Vallus found the other half of his bag and set to work cooking a heavy meal of vegetables and gluk meat. As the food simmered, Vallus drew his sword and got to work fixing the roll in the blade.

With that repaired as best as could be done, Vallus turned back to the food as Shiloh began to stir. He sat up in the bed and coughed before he took a seat in another chair across from Vallus, rubbing his throat and wincing.

"How're you feeling?" asked Vallus as he fixed Shiloh a plate and handed it to him.

"Well enough," he replied as he took the food and coughed again. "Throat's still sore, but that'll pass. I take it you dealt with Vakka?"

The pair ate as Vallus gave his account of his battle with Vakka. Shiloh looked over Vallus' sealed wounds, clearly more concerned about them than Vallus was. Once they had finished, Shiloh took the dishes and set them aside to wash despite Vallus' protests.

"So why did he attack you? He had nothing to gain from doing so."

"He was looking for you. I wouldn't tell him anything, so he tossed the camp. I tried to fight him, but he was too strong."

"So he just walked right in?"

"Ya. I figured if I tried to hide he'd find me anyway, so I confronted him."

"Well, next time you see a God, I'd recommend a different approach," said Vallus with a coy grin.

"What's next for you, Seeker?" asked Shiloh, his voice still hoarse but audibly improving.

"Vakka said something about a military storage area. Gotta get there. But there's another problem. There's a group of people here, not sure what to call them. But their leader wants to destroy the vault. He gave me six hours to get my answers and get out, and at least two have passed."

"You sure he can actually do that?"

"Yes. He said he's done it before. Can't take the chance he's lying," replied Vallus. Shiloh nodded solemnly. He coughed again, holding up a hand to allay Vallus' worries. Vallus handed him a cup of water poured from Shiloh's stock, which he took a long drink from.

"You should press on. Don't worry yourself with me," he said.

"Right. Pip, can you find a military storage area of any kind on the map?" She was silent for a moment before she chirped.

"Yes, but it is quite far away. There are several sub-rooms on the path, and it is on the far end of the vault."

"So it'll most likely be dangerous," said Vallus as he stood.

"We should expect no less, based on recent events," said Pip as she hovered up to follow Vallus.

"Elevator?"

"Yes," replied Pip.

Vallus stepped outside the camp but stopped for a moment over the threshold. He turned back to Shiloh, concern on his face. Shiloh nodded to him with a weak smile.

"I won't be back for a long time. Stay safe," said Vallus.

"Will do," said Shiloh with a pained cough and a chuckle.

"And you do the same."

As Vallus stepped into the elevator, he saw Shiloh stand, and felt that perhaps the former Seeker was in more pain than he had claimed. He limped to the bed, cradling his right side as he walked with a hunch. Forcing himself to focus on his path ahead, Vallus set the thought aside and pressed the elevator button. At Pip's direction, they began their descent to the Pathway Interchange. The elevator moved downward for quite some time, traveling to the deepest floors of the vault. When it finally came to a stop, the doors opened and Vallus stepped into a long, dark hallway.

The hall was much wider than any other Vallus had been in. To the left of the elevator was a long track attached to the ceiling, which was still operational and moving large freight containers by magnetic hooks. Throughout the hall were several piles of crates stacked up, their movement abandoned long ago. There were doors along the right wall every ten feet or so. Signs all about the area marked work stations and staging areas for the movement of freight, and were posted on not just walls but on most of the steel pillars that were spaced every ten feet or so down the hall. Vallus inspected some of the containers near the entrance but found them locked by code. He moved down the hall, then a door opened. Wanting to save resources and avoid a fight, Vallus ducked behind a stack of crates. There was a space between some of the crates that allowed Vallus to get a small view of the doors.

Two battle droids entered the room as their heads swept back and forth, scanning the area. Not far behind them was Volya, a cigarette in his mouth as he calmly looked around. Vallus was taken aback, as the droids seemed to be aware of Volya, but not hostile toward him. In fact, they appeared to be following his commands. Vallus noticed a small metal disc attached to each battle droid's chest plate, each with a blinking light. He focused on eavesdropping.

"Keep watch. He could be here soon," said Volya as he spat off in a corner.

Both droids nodded once, then walked past Volya and began to patrol the area just a little ahead of where Vallus knelt in hiding. Volya flicked his cigarette into a corner and walked down the hallway and out of sight. Left alone with only the gurgling processing sounds of the patrolling battle droids, Vallus began to formulate a plan to proceed. Thankfully, the droids didn't seem very intent on patrolling too close to the elevator. Vallus directed Pip to take cover in his bag as he drew one of his swords and quietly maneuvered around the stack of crates. As one of the droids came near, Vallus took it by surprise and sunk his blade deep in the machine's neck. The battle droid screeched and sputtered, drawing the attention of its cohort. As the second droid took aim, Vallus pulled the sword out, gripped the droid by the back, and pushed forward toward his attacker with the droid serving as a shield. A bolt from the droid's laser rifle pierced the dead droid and grazed Vallus' side. The shot stung, but Vallus pushed on. When he was only a few feet away, Vallus pushed the first droid toward the second. It moved out of the way, but the move distracted the droid long enough for Vallus to decapitate it with a swing of his drawn sword. With both battle droids decommissioned, Vallus looked down the hall. It was still empty, and Vallus assumed Volya had moved on already. With an exasperated huff, Vallus sheathed his sword and moved onward down the hall.

Pip floated out of the bag with her flashlight at the ready and followed Vallus down the hall. There was little of note there, short of a massive opening in the wall that allowed the large freight containers to pass through on their way to their destinations deeper within the vault. Farther down the hall, the lights grew more and more scarce, and Vallus relied more and more on Pip's light. He kept a hand on each of his swords, unsettled by the deep silence broken only by the clanking of the freight track. Vallus kept a brisk but cautious pace as he tried to focus on any background noises. He also kept in mind that he had no idea where Volya had gone, and he was wary of every door he passed. None of the doors had windows, and the lack of forewarning unsettled him. Then he heard the growling.

Vallus froze in place, unsure if the growl had been genuine or just the track that had begun to fade behind him. Then it came again. A low, guttural, almost hungry growl. Vallus took his breaths slowly, quietly. It was at that moment that he truly began to feel as though he were being hunted. He pushed the thought aside as the growling came again, a little closer and a little louder. Along with it came a crunching sound, like thin metal bending. Vallus wrapped his hands around the hilts of his swords. Then a strange, high-pitched whistle echoed through the hall, followed by a clattering and thrashing as something moved quickly through the vents above. Then silence once more. A chill ran down Vallus' neck, but he brushed it off, loosened up, and continued onward down the hall.

It wasn't long until Vallus came to the end of the hall and Pip's light shined on a lone door. It was simply labeled 'G-7'. He supposed it was a label for workers. The door opened by motion sensor and Vallus walked into another section of hallway, although much wider and with a higher ceiling. The lights were on in the area, bright florescent bulbs in parallel lines along either side of the angled ceiling. There were several loose crates scattered about along the hall, along with three small mechanical cranes for lifting light freight. They appeared to be automated, but were inactive and had a thin layer of dust on them. As Vallus passed by the first one, he noticed something out of the corner of his eye. Along the crane's arm were four thin lines through the dust, as though someone had wiped their fingers across it. Recently.

Vallus had just realized this when doors on either side of the hall opened and six battle droids entered. They surrounded Vallus, their weapons drawn and trained on him. They halted about six feet away from him. They stood there, still and calm as they processed with their signature gurgle. All of them sported the same metal disc on their chest Vallus had seen before. He focused on the droids, but he also noticed that not far ahead of him was a crate with a thin line of smoke issuing from behind it. With a cackle Volya stood up from where he had been lounging, cracked his back, turned around, and rested his elbows on the crate as he held his cigarette between his fingers.

"Great fuck but you walk slow, don't ya?" he said with a rude smirk and a drag of his smoke. "Like my friends here? Took years to figure out how to override their brains. Took about the same to figure out how to get close enough to strap it on 'em."

"Neat trick. You'll have to teach it to me. What do you want? Do you not remember the deal your leader and I made?"

"Leader? That's rich!" yelled Volya, laughing like a drunk hyena. "You think we have a chain of command? No way, man. Destiny is an illusion, and so is anyone's authority over me. Yashir only calls the shots 'cause he has the plan. I only stick around 'cause it keeps me alive. If everything is pointless, I might as well fuck shit up for as long as I can."

"What do you mean 'pointless'?" asked Vallus, bemused. "You know what? Never mind. I couldn't care less about your philosophy. You going to honor my deal with Yashir or is this going to get needlessly messy?"

"You'll come around. You still got plenty of time, Seeker. Why not burn an hour here? Kill him, but make it fun."

Volya jumped up onto the crate and stood, his cigarette held tightly between his lips and his arms folded over his chest. Vallus didn't get a chance to assess Volya's weaponry before the droids began to attack. Vallus was forced to duck. Fortunately, one of the droids missed Vallus and instead hit one of its associates. Vallus quickly ran to the dead droid, grabbed hold of its limp and heavy metal body, and used it to shield himself as he drew one of his swords. The droids continued to fire for a moment before they let up. Two of them deployed forearm-mounted blades.

Vallus pushed the dead droid at the shooter in front of him as he buried his sword in the one that remained behind. It fell to the ground with a loud *thunk*. He back-peddled quickly to distance himself from the blade-wielding droids as he slung the rifle over his shoulder. He aimed at the shooter droid, which had begun to stand after being knocked back by Vallus' feint. One well-aimed shot put a hole in its head, and put it on the ground. Pain surged through his arm, as he had fired the rifle with his left arm, and the shot hurt his bullet wound especially. Still, he took the pain as he fired a second shot to incapacitate one of the two remaining droids. The final droid raised its blade arm as it approached, but before Vallus could react its head exploded in a flurry of metal shards and fire as a deafening gunshot echoed through the room. Vallus looked over to see Volya aiming a short shotgun, its single barrel issuing smoke.

"I told them to make it fun. What a shame they couldn't

deliver. Guess I'll just have to do it myself," he said as he pointed the gun at Vallus.

Vallus dove behind a nearby crate, Pip in tow. Volya fired the gun just as he did and hit the floor. From behind the crate, Vallus saw shards of metal basked in flame. He sheathed his sword and gripped the rifle with both hands as he heard Volya hop down from the crate to the floor. He was taking his steps slowly, a predator on the hunt. Vallus steeled himself and took a deep breath. He stood, wheeling on Volya as he aimed the rifle. Volya aimed back, but Vallus fired first. Vallus hadn't accounted for his target moving and the shot missed, but Volya was distracted for a moment. Vallus fired another shot, but his target had picked up speed and the second shot struck the wall. Volya aimed and fired. Vallus had managed to take cover behind a nearby support pillar, and the incendiary shrapnel from Volya's gun struck a crate which caught fire.

Smoke began to fill the room as Volya reloaded his shotgun. Vallus checked the rifle's magazine. Fifteen rounds were left in it, one in the chamber, and only one more spare magazine remained on his belt. Vallus heard Volya draw a blade as he approached the pillar. Vallus smirked to himself, put away the rifle, and drew his swords. A few more steps and a repugnant giggle followed as Volya came closer. Vallus rounded the pillar, swords in hand. Volya aimed around the pillar where he thought Vallus to be, but found nothing. Vallus swung horizontally at Volya from behind, having circled the pillar. Pip flew out of the bag, and Volya became distracted. But not too distracted to avoid being beheaded. Vallus' blade struck the pillar and bit into the metal. Volya wheeled around, a short, single-edged falchion in hand, and swung. Vallus blocked the dull blade with his right bracer, then wrenched his sword out from the pillar. Volya tried to aim the shotgun, but Vallus was too close. He pushed the gun aside, but Volya fired anyway. The shot missed, but some of the shrapnel cut Vallus' face and burned his neck. Dazed by the blast's report and the burn, Vallus staggered backward with a pained yelp.

Volya took the opportunity placed before him and drove his blade forward toward Vallus' abdomen. Seemingly saved by sheer luck, Vallus tripped over a stray cable that fed into one of the cranes and fell backwards to the floor. Volya's stab missed, and he himself tripped over Vallus. He hit the ground a few feet to the side, not wanting to fall on the Seeker's blades. Fighting off the searing pain in his neck and face, Vallus stood, blades in hand and tears in his eyes from the stinging. He gritted his teeth, furious and impatient. In the back of his mind, his father's voice rang out weakly.

"Calmness is the greatest weapon of a Seeker," he muttered through his teeth to himself. "Master thyself, and you master everything else."

"What the fuck are you?" said Volya rhetorically as he stumbled to his feet. "I've seen Seekers before. Shit, I've killed a few of 'em. But none of 'em were like you. None of 'em were this ferocious."

"I need to be. I need to survive. There are people counting on me."

"Why do you even care? They want answers so bad, maybe *they* should come get 'em. There's no reason to throw yourself to your death so these weak people can sleep at night."

"I'm the only one who *can* do it," said Vallus as he began to calm. "And I aim to bring them more than a good night's sleep. I want to give them hope. So they can start fixing what the Gods did to this world."

"Fuck that. You want to rebuild it, but here you are, not rebuilding it. You can't cure the world by fuckin' around in its bones. You care so much about all of these things, yet you do nothing. And that's what you need to understand. They will all die eventually, for no reason, having done little with their short, pathetic lives. All of us. In the end, all we amount to is dust. You. Me. This vault. Even the Gods. I mean, look around some time. When was the last time it rained? When was the last time it rained and the rain wasn't poison?"

"It wasn't always like this. It doesn't have to be. But we need to know how it got this way before we can fix it. Knowledge is strength. The strength to keep living."

Volya laughed.

"You believe that? Think for yourself for a minute. You think you're gonna get outta here alive? If I don't kill you, something will. I've been deeper in the vault. Well, as deep as you can go before all the doors are locked. This place is a cesspool. And even if you do, what then? You just gonna walk around tellin' everybody? You'll just die on the road in the middle of nowhere."

"Then so be it. My job isn't done until I can return home. And if you need to die for that to happen, then so be that too," said Vallus as he flourished and readied his swords.

Vallus rushed toward Volya, hoping to give him no chance to aim his shotgun. Vallus swung both of his swords in a deadly whirl of blades. Volya was able to parry one slash, but the next few found purchase but didn't cut very deep. The next few swipes cut through Volya's chest armor but didn't go deep enough to deal real damage. The final slash cut Volya's right arm, drawing blood but not victory. He stumbled back as he tried to parry Vallus' new wave of strikes, but it was of little use. Volya back-peddled, fell back, and aimed his shotgun.

Vallus' chest plate caught most of the blast, and his swords protected his face. But the shot was powerful enough to knock Vallus off his feet, sending him flying across the room and into the hard metal arm of a nearby crane. Vallus fell to the floor on his hands and knees, brushing flaming shards from his chest armor. He was still winded when Volya shakily rose to his feet. Vallus spat as he steadied himself. He had lost his swords when Volya's shot hit him. Volya raised his shotgun and pointed it at Vallus. Then he noticed Pip hovering above, watching the fight and awaiting Vallus' call. He took aim at her.

"NO!"

An explosive report echoed through the hall. Blood dripped down Vallus' shoulder as his stitches had come loose when he slung the rifle over his shoulder and fired. His haste had cost him a clean kill, and Volya stumbled backward before he collapsed against the nearby wall. He clutched his gut as blood spilled over his fingers and down his chin. He sat there, twitching, as he began to weakly cough and sputter. Shaking, he pulled a cigarette from his pocket with his open hand. He did the same with a lighter, lit his cigarette, and dropped the lighter. Still chuckling to himself, he took a few drags as Vallus ran to him.

"All right. If you're done being a psychopath, let me get you out of here," he said, wary of the small pool of blood Volya sat in.

"Still... trying to... make something matter, huh?" said Volya with the cigarette in his mouth. "Get it... through... your head... This... changes nothing."

"No time for a debate, Volya. Let's go," said Vallus as he moved to pick up the blood-soaked man.

"No... Like I said... Doesn't matter. Changes nothing. Let

me show you." Vallus backed off.

Volya pulled the pistol from his side with his blood-drenched hand. Vallus was caught off guard and unarmed, having set his rifle aside before coming to Volya's aid. But he didn't point the pistol at Vallus. Before Vallus could react, Volya tucked the pistol under his chin, and with a final gaping grin and a raucous laugh, he pulled the trigger. There was a loud *bang*, Volya's head smacked into the wall, and he slumped down sideways to the floor in a pool of blood.

His quickened breath slowing, Vallus sighed heavily and stood. He stared at Volya's body for a few moments in silent contemplation, Pip quietly hovering over his shoulder. Then, with a silent and disappointed shake of his head, Vallus turned and began to walk away. Pip beeped in confusion.

"This man is no Seeker. Perhaps he left something we can use?" Vallus stopped in his tracks.

"Doubtful," he said. "But you make a good point."

Vallus returned to Volya's body and knelt down. As he did, pain shot through his arm and he was reminded of the blood that soaked his sleeve. He motioned to Pip and exposed the shoulder so she could repair the stitches. As she worked, Vallus looked over the gear strapped to Volya's armor.

"Maybe the pistol to replace the one Aurien destroyed?" said Pip.

"No. The last pistol proved to be less than reliable. If I need anything, it's not weapons. Wait, what's this?"

Vallus noticed a small, open pouch in Volya's belt. Within were a number of the small metal discs Vallus had seen on the battle droids. He took one and inspected it.

"Any idea how this would work?"

"It looks as though you would need to simply touch it to a machine and it will mount itself. However, you would also need a control device."

Vallus carefully patted Volya's body down. Further disappointment appeared on his face.

"The device was in this pouch on his armor. And I shot him right there. My bullet destroyed his device before it hit him."

"Take a few discs. When you use them I will try to connect to them," said Pip as she finished the suture and Vallus wrapped it in gauze.

"You can do that?"

"Probably."

"Hmm…"

With Pip's work completed, Vallus turned to continue onward but soon stopped. He turned to look at Pip, pity and disappointment etched on his face. He scowled.

"You know, in a way, he was right. None of this mattered. What a waste."

"I think he was wrong. You learned from this. And now, Yashir has one less ally. It may have not mattered to him, but it aided our cause. Meaning isn't objective."

Vallus nodded. He supposed Pip was right. But with some introspection, he thought that perhaps all of them were, in some small way. But he knew he still had a long road ahead of him, and he had no time for philosophy. He pointed toward the end of the hall and pressed on as Pip followed, gently bobbing through the air as she went. At the far end of the hall, about two hundred feet from the entrance, Vallus came to a large door. It was marked 'TRAM'. The door slowly slid up as Vallus approached, its motion sensor apparently functional. It took nearly a full minute for the door to open far enough for Vallus to step through, and it groaned and whined the entire time. Vallus had to cover his ears, as the sound was not only incredibly annoying but extremely painful to hear.

Pressing onward, Vallus came to an expansive tunnel with tracks below the platform he walked on. The tunnel was dark and musty, with only a few scattered florescent lights and even fewer flashing signals. There was a tram on the tracks not far from the doorway, but upon inspection Vallus found that it was not powered. Another fifty feet down the platform, Vallus found that it terminated with only a single door on the adjacent wall. The door would not open, but Pip pointed her light down the tracks.

"This tunnel is the only way to the military storage sector. Fair warning, it is quite a long walk," she said.

Vallus peered down the dark tunnel. With only a little trepidation, the Seeker hopped down from the platform and onto the tracks. From what he could tell, none of the trams were operational, so he walked at a brisk pace as he followed Pip's light. It was not only pitch dark in the tunnel, but silent as well. Occasionally, some odd object would fall in the distance and lightly clatter. The sounds didn't bother him, but he did question what could possibly be making them, and whether they would become a threat.

After quite some time walking in the darkness, a strange sense of impending doom settled in the back of his mind. He felt almost as if he was marching toward some horrible, inexorable fate. It wasn't that he believed himself to be in danger; but that something terrible awaited him, perhaps just through the next door. He pushed the thought to the back of his mind and chose to focus instead on his surroundings. There was no power running through anything around him, and the tracks were relatively free

194

of debris.

After what Vallus guessed must have been an hour, he came to another open boarding area with a platform on his right. There were yet more blinking signal lights, but fewer working building lights. With Pip keeping watch, Vallus climbed up onto the platform. He checked his surroundings, and satisfied that he was relatively safe, he pressed on. Soon, he came to the door to the military storage sector.

Or at least where the door should have been. In Pip's light, Vallus found that the set of double sliding doors to the area had been torn from their tracks and dropped to the floor next to the frame. Upon closer inspection, Vallus found the impressions of very large hands on each one, pressed deeply into the thick metal. Whatever had torn the doors free had gripped them so hard that they bent.

"The Gods have been busy, it would seem," said Vallus. "What makes you think it was one of them?" asked Pip.

"What else have we encountered that was strong enough to do this? No telling when it was done, so I can't tell which one did it. Wasn't Nirav, though? Each door has a different hand imprint. He didn't have a left hand."

"This area does not seem safe. You should stay alert," said Pip, a hint of concern in her usually even voice.

Vallus nodded and walked through the doorway into a much smaller but very dim hallway. The hall was quite short and led to another door. This one was still intact, and opened with a swipe of Vallus' clearance card. Through the door, Vallus came to an area that very much resembled the entry to the Security wing. Again, there was a door with a key card scanner and a ladder leading upward. Vallus approached the key card door and swiped his card, but the panel buzzed and the door sat still. Pip interfaced with the console.

"This panel only accepts Beta level or higher key cards. I can't bypass it, either. We should check the offices; perhaps someone left a key card behind."

"This again," said Vallus with a huff and a roll of his eyes.

Regardless of his vexation, Vallus took Pip's advice and climbed the stairs to the door.

It was locked, but Vallus easily overrode it. The door slid open and Vallus entered another long hallway. It was dimly lit by dying florescent bulbs, and there was a dusty, dead scent that hung in the air. Unlike the security offices, this hall had no overlooking window and instead was bare save for a faded horizontal stripe of paint that either had been gray, or was grayed with time. The first door Vallus came to was cracked open, stuck on a metal paperweight, and was marked 'Shift Commander'. With quite some effort, Vallus pried the door open and walked through. The door remained motionless behind him, having most likely lost power long ago.

The room was a very small office with a nearly bare desk. There was a chair on either side of the desk, as well as a musty rug. On the desk was an empty and cracked coffee mug, a computer, and a single framed photograph of a remarkably gorgeous woman with bright blue eyes and brown hair. The glass in the frame was broken. In the top drawer was a card much like the one Vallus already possessed, although it had a blue stripe and was labeled 'Beta Clearance'. Vallus smirked as he picked up the card.

With little motivation to search the rest of the area, Vallus left the room, walked down the stairs, and back to the key card door. He took a deep breath, then slid the key card. The door beeped loudly before it slid open with a loud groan. Vallus walked through it into another expansive room basked in shadow. From the top of the staircase he stood upon, Vallus could see several large shipping containers in a corner, three mechanical tracks on the ceiling, and a massive bay door that extended nearly the entire length of the back wall. Vallus mounted the stairs and descended to the concrete floor. Once there, he could see off in the corner an ancient jet plane covered in a thick layer of dust. In the opposite corner was a wide guard tower attached to the wall. As Vallus approached the center of the poorly-lit room, he noticed something odd about the guard tower. All of the windows were broken out, and standing within was an enormous figure in heavy armor with a steel crown welded upon its head.

"Welcome, Seeker," said the Ashen King evenly. "You have become quite an imposition. Let's see if you are truly worth all this trouble."

The King raised his hand as blue light emanated from the tubes that were visible through his armor. As he did, a port in the wall opened and a massive shipping container entered the room suspended from one of the ceiling tracks. It stopped at the end of the track with a loud *thump*. Then the Ashen King snapped his fingers, and the bottom of the container dropped open.

What fell from the container with a deafening crash was an enormous machine unlike any Vallus had ever encountered. It was made of an armored body almost like a tank but twice the size, with a smaller "head" at the front with a single optical lens. It had eight heavily armored legs laid out like those of a spider. The machine's carapace was equipped with at least two dozen visible heavy guns, all aimed in different directions. The machine whirred and clicked as it came to life and it began to slowly shuffle its legs. From the guard tower, the King chuckled lightly.

"Prove your worth, Seeker. Defeat my siege engine, or die."

The King snapped his fingers again, and the siege engine's attention immediately turned to Vallus. Two guns on what Vallus could only think of as its shoulders began to spin up. With little cover around him, Vallus ran. The siege engine opened fire. Vallus didn't want to look back, but he knew the siege engine would take a long time to lock in its aim. He could almost feel the massive bullets fly past him as they impacted the concrete floor beneath his feet. Quickly, Vallus took cover behind a small shipping container. A huge bullet tore through the container and flew over Vallus' head before it slammed into the wall across from him and put a chest-sized hole in it. Then the machine stopped firing. Over the violent ringing in his ears, Vallus could hear the King taunting him from the tower.

"Afraid, Seeker? Has the enormity of your situation finally dawned on you? Has your place become clear?"

Vallus huffed as he struggled to formulate a plan. He had faced plenty of large machines before, but never anything as well armed or as protected as the siege engine. Vallus peeked around the crate to see the head of the siege engine lower as a long gun barrel extended from its back. Then an extremely loud whining sound issued from the machine as the inside of the gun barrel began to glow bright red. Vallus ran from the crate toward the jet.

The siege engine fired a blazing beam of blinding red energy. Vallus wasn't sure what the energy was, but it destroyed the shipping container with explosive force and blasted it through the wall. The force of the blast was so strong it knocked Vallus off his feet and he slid under the jet. He watched as the siege engine searched for him, withdrawing its massive cannon as it did. But what struck him as odd was the fact that high up in the guard tower, the being that seemed to be another God remained completely still, almost statuesque. Vallus had assumed the being would aid the machine, but he appeared to be giving it no assistance. From under the jet, Vallus pulled his rifle and took aim. He steadied himself and fired.

The first shot missed its mark and bounced off the siege engine's thick armor plates. Vallus quickly fired again and hit a joint within one of the machine's forward legs. The shot seemed to do minimal damage. Vallus put the rifle away, having seen that it would be of little help. And the shots had drawn the attention of the siege engine. It turned on him as its forward guns spun up. Vallus ran once more, and was once more just barely fast enough to get to the cover of another nearby shipping container. Behind him, the jet went up in a fireball before the siege engine ceased firing. He peeked around the corner of the container as before, and watched as the siege engine looked toward him and buzzed. Then ports on either side of its main body opened, revealing rows of small missiles.

With nowhere left to hide, Vallus ran to the only place he could: straight toward the siege engine. It fired the missiles, but they had already found their targets and hit the container and the dock door behind it. The resulting massive explosion blasted Vallus forward off his feet and he slid underneath the siege engine. From his prone position, he found enough space to crouch under the machine. Pip hovered beside him as he did.

"We should get out from under this thing quickly. It may try to crush us."

"No. Look at the legs. If it tried to do that, it wouldn't be able to get back up. It would get the kill, at the cost of itself. Its programming won't allow that."

"Perhaps we could try the discs?"

"We'll have to. This armor is too thick for my swords."

Vallus pulled one of the discs from his pocket and placed it onto the siege engine's body. The disc clicked and buzzed as it attached itself magnetically and clung tightly. Vallus motioned to Pip and she began her attempt to activate the disc. Soon, she let out a low, disappointed beep.

"It's not working. Something seems to be interfering with the signal, cutting me off somehow."

"I bet I know who," said Vallus, motioning in the direction of the guard tower. "How do we do this?" asked Pip.

"You fly out and meet me up top. There must be a way to get onto this thing, maybe a way to shut it down."

"I will run scans as I go," said Pip before she turned and zipped out from under the siege engine and into the air.

Vallus carefully moved toward the rear end of the siege engine. As he emerged, he looked up at the tower. From his position, he couldn't see the being. He grew increasingly worried. Nevertheless, he crept behind the siege engine in search of a way to stop it. His search was quick, as there was a ladder at the rear of the machine that led to a mounted platform. He climbed it quickly, and by the loud and aggressive whir coming from the siege engine, he guessed he had been found. Fortunately, none of its guns could safely aim at him. As he reached the platform, Pip zipped around to him.

"The being in the tower is still motionless. He seems much more dangerous than the others."
"Yes. Let's focus. What now?"

"There should be a service panel here. Try that handle."

Vallus pulled the handle, but found it to be a storage space. There was a gun inside, and Vallus pulled it out. It was, by looks of it, some type of energy rifle. The meter on the side showed it at half charge. Above him, a port on the siege engine opened and a small laser canon emerged to aim at Vallus. He aimed the weapon back and fired. The rifle emitted a burst of laser beams that shredded the canon apart. But the weapon began to heat in Vallus' hands, and he realized it was damaged. He threw it at the siege engine's head. It bounced off, then immediately exploded in a cloud of black smoke filled with red lightning. The blast seemed to not affect the machine, but there also seemed to be nothing it could do about Vallus.

Running out of ideas, Vallus drove his blade into the side of the machine between two plates. There appeared to be another panel that could be pulled away, but it was jammed.

Using his sword, he pried the panel away to reveal the intricate machines and computers inside the siege engine that gave it life.

"What do I do?"

"We need to disable some critical system. If you can find its BIOS chip or another similar part, you might be able to shut it off entirely."

"What if I just stab into it?"

"You could hit nothing important at all, or set off its weapons. You could even possibly set off its power supply."

Vallus closely inspected the parts within, grasping the side of the panel to keep steady as the siege engine constantly shifted under him. He tried to read the tiny letters printed on one of the computing parts, but a bundle of wires was in his way. A tag on the wires told him they were responsible for sending the order to reload. He disconnected them and pushed them out of his way. On the card, in nearly unreadable letters, were the words 'Main Control Unit: Do Not Touch'. He ignored the warning and tried to pull the card from its mount, but found his efforts to be unsuccessful. It was secured to the slot by two screws, and Vallus had no time to rummage for tools. Then he heard ports on the siege engine open. He pulled out of the panel and looked toward the head. It was shaking, swaying side to side like a mule trying to fight off flies. And the ports it had opened were filled with fresh missiles.

"Wait, how did it reload?"

"It probably did that earlier. But why is it… Oh no. We need to get away from this machine."

"Why is it aiming up…? Oh shit."

Vallus jumped off the platform, Pip following behind, and rolled as he landed from the considerable fall from the machine. Then it fired the rockets, which shot into the air, then curved back down. Vallus ran. Several of the missiles struck the siege engine, as it had been in their flight path. Two more missiles flew over his head and struck the wall and the staircase he had entered the area by. As the siege engine went up in a cloud of flames, it exploded further and released a shock wave that blasted Vallus off his feet and sent him skidding across the floor.

As he stood, shakily, he took in the scattered and burning debris that filled the room.

His heart pounded, more from adrenaline than fear, but there was something else. He was angry. Still holding his sword, he pointed it toward the tower and spat as he screamed.

"Come down here and fight me yourself! I'm tired of these 'tests'! I'm tired of your silence! I will tolerate no more obstructions to my mission!"

"Fine," replied the King with a low growl.

He appeared to crack his neck, then jumped out of the guard tower window. He was much larger than it, and as he jumped out, he tore completely through the metal frame like a great whale breaching the surface of an ocean and fell to the floor with a thunderous crash. Metal and glass shards rained down around him as he stood to full height. Vallus noticed that he had no weapon.

"We have not been properly introduced. I am Farran. You may address me as the Ashen King, Hero of Ashenvale and the God of War. You would do well to bow," he said as he extended his hand, palm laid flat, as if to command the gesture.

"I am called Vallus. You know what I am. You know why I am here. Why won't you answer me?"

"All in due time, Seeker. I have simply come to show you the cost of your intrusion. Like you, I will tolerate no obstructions to my mission. The new dawn comes. Whether you live to see it is entirely up to you." His voice was deep, gravelly, and filled with a powerful authority. Vallus trembled, just slightly.

"Look, I don't care what you plan to do. I came here for answers, and I don't intend to leave without them. I just need to know what happened to my world. And where the Gods went."

"The Gods died, just like everyone else. You should let the past lie, Vallus. There are only skeletons there. It won't matter when the new dawn arrives."

"But how? Why?"

"No more questions. Face me, mortal. Let us see what you're really made of."

Vallus couldn't react. Before he could fully process any of it, the King charged toward him. Vallus tried to defend himself, but the King was too fast. He struck Vallus in the side with a powerful punch that rocked his entire body. He screamed out in pain as the Ashen King drew back another fist. He tried to swing his blade at the King, but the latter dodged the sword and struck Vallus in the chest. The armor protected Vallus from a great deal of the force, but the punch dented his armor and knocked the wind out of him. He staggered backward and the Ashen King kicked him hard in the chest. The blow sent Vallus sliding across the floor again. Pip hovered above, powerless to intervene. Vallus motioned to her, and she knew it to be the familiar signal to stay out of the way. Vallus only ever used it when the risk of her being damaged was too great. She could only watch as the Ashen King slowly walked toward Vallus.

The Seeker tried to stand on shaking legs and dodged a quick swipe. He tried to fight back, but the King grabbed his arm with his left hand and gripped Vallus' chest armor tightly in his right hand. So tightly it bent the metal and left a hand print. The King lifted him into the air. There, he held Vallus at his eye level, peering out through an expressionless helm.

Vallus caught, only briefly, the sound of his raspy breathing. The thought occurred to his dazed and weary mind that it was strange that a God would need to breathe.

"You reap what you sow, Seeker. You belong in the trash with anything else that would stand in my way."

"I don't... want to... fight," said Vallus through a mouthful of blood. He was sure the King's kick had broken one of his ribs. "Just... answers."

"Seek them elsewhere," spat the King.

Without so much as a warning, the Ashen King slammed Vallus into the concrete floor. Fortunately, the protective lining of his bag protected his things, but the impact sent an explosive wave of pain through his whole body, and he spat blood as he screamed. Vallus couldn't move; the slam had taken the last bit of fight out of him, and he was overwhelmed, his body wracked with pain. His breaths came ragged and weak, and every muscle and bone in his body ached with each one. The King crouched down over him.

"One more thing, Seeker. You need not worry about...

what's his name? Yashir? Just like you, he will meet his fate. And he can't get into the core, anyway."

Vallus watched as the King stood, powerless to move or fight or even beg for mercy. The King closed his right fist, peered down at Vallus, and drew back. Vallus watched as the fist came barreling toward him, then everything went black.

Chapter 8

By Pip's count, two hours had passed since Vallus fell and the Ashen King left through the nearby receiving door without so much as a word to her. Since the vault remained intact, she guessed the Ashen King had been correct about Yashir. For much of that time, she had sat still on Vallus' chest as he laid unconscious. She had done so once she had realized that there was nothing she could do for him. Occasionally, she would turn slightly to assure nothing crept up on them. The silence didn't bother her, nor the darkness pierced only by the dying flames that still coated the wreckage of the siege engine. The only thing that disquieted the otherwise calm drone was the shallow, ragged breaths Vallus took as he slept. She had checked his wounds and assured that their dressings held up, but there was nothing she could do for his rib. Instead, she resigned herself to wait for someone, anyone, to come and help her.

Around the three hour mark, Pip began to detect a distant sound, down a hallway under the guard tower. She checked the map, but could not be sure where it led. All she knew was that the sounds coming from the hall were violent. She processed a few thoughts. Firstly, that there were still dangers nearby. Secondly, that she had little in the way of defenses. And finally, that whoever won the fight in the hall would determine her fate, and that of Vallus as well.

***

Vallus stood in an expansive field of grass, a bright and vivid sun shining down on him through a cloudless, clear sky. He looked himself over and found that his Seeker gear was gone, and his clothes had been replaced by a simple tunic and pants. There was a breeze, calm and gentle unlike the harsh, biting winds he was accustomed to. He was at ease, peace, for the first time in seven years. There was almost a sense of elation in the place, of careless whimsy, a fitting end to a long journey.

This peace was interrupted by a rumbling, far away and barely noticeable at first, but it grew quickly with time. Vallus turned to see smoke in the distance, just over the horizon. He could barely see through the glare of the sun, but something was approaching. Vallus squinted against the sun. As the thing came closer, Vallus realized it wasn't just one thing. It was many. Hundreds of siege engines, surrounded by thousands upon thousands of battle droids. The rumbling in the ground grew stronger as jets blasted by overhead, and the air screamed from the resulting sonic booms. There, among the marching mechanical legion, was the Ashen King. A trail of flame and destruction followed in their wake, the field burning with each step they took. Vallus watched with wide eyes as the God of War approached, shaking, unable to fathom the enemy before him. He turned to see no one at his side, no weapon, no salvation. Soon, the army was upon him, but it passed him by. They marched onward, oblivious to his presence. When finally the last battle droid walked by, he was left alone, surrounded only by scorched dirt and silence. He fell to his knees as tears began to well in his eyes. He gazed into the sky, its warm light replaced by darkness as the sun faded.

Hecate had grown bored. She had been mulling about the vault for the last two hours, looking for a fight that she couldn't find thanks to Vallus' recent exploits. Everywhere she went in the vault she found the remains of the things that had stood in his way, if she found anything at all. She decided to move deeper into the vault. She hadn't seen Yashir in some time and assumed he was off somewhere trying to get into the Core Systems Sector, but she couldn't care less about that. She needed entertainment.

She had been following signs to the military storage sector for nearly an hour when she checked around a corner and found what she had been looking for. Action. Patrolling the hallway ahead were six battle droids, all well-armed and on high alert. She would need to be fast. From the holster under her coat, Hecate drew a heavy revolver with a grin on her face.

With the revolver extended, she rounded the corner as she reached into her coat. The battle droids were caught flat-footed and had little time to react. Hecate fired at the nearest droid. The shot slammed into the droid and exploded. As it did, Hecate threw two knives from her coat. Each knife struck a droid with deadly precision and pierced deep into their chests. By the time the other droids began to fire, the corridor was already filling with smoke and fire which weakened the droids' aim.

Hecate threw another knife into the smokescreen, and grinned to herself at the sharp sound of her blade piercing another droid. As she pranced whimsically down the hall, she retrieved her knives from the destroyed droids and returned them to her coat. The lasers flew past Hecate as she calmly waltzed down the hall and aimed her revolver. As the smoke began to clear via the vents, she fired and destroyed another droid. The remaining droid continued to fire, missed, and was in return destroyed by another head shot.

With the hall cleared of everything but smoke, Hecate continued onward as she reloaded and holstered her revolver. She stepped over the smoldering remains of the droids and walked to the door at the end of the hall. She looked at it for a few moments, inspecting every inch of the door. As if looking for something hidden, Hecate ran her hands over the door, along where it sat in the wall. Then she drew one of her knives and wedged the long, thin blade between the wall and door. She fidgeted with it for a moment, then heard a popping sound as the door began to open.

***

Pip began to worry when the violent sounds from the hall intensified. She registered gun shots, energy weapons, and tearing metal through her audio receptor for a few minutes. Then, all at once, silence. Pip turned off her light. She waited, there in the dark with Vallus quietly breathing. Then a door at the far side of the room opened and a cloaked figure entered. Pip magnified her vision and scanned the individual. She recognized her as Hecate, the absentminded woman from before. Pip readied her flare launcher as Hecate approached.

"Stay back! I'll shoot!"

"Whoa there, drone," said Hecate as she raised her hands. "I'm not gonna hurt ya. Or him."

"You're with Yashir. I can't trust you," said Pip.

"With Yashir' is a stretch. Traveling in numbers is good for someone like me. Come, little one, lemme help. He looks like he's in a bad way."

Pip silently considered the offer for a moment. She didn't

know Hecate's true intentions, but she had no way of getting Vallus to safety. She made her decision.

"Okay. Take a look, but I doubt I missed anything."

"What happened?" asked Hecate as she approached and knelt down at Vallus' side. "He fought a God. The Ashen King. It did not end well. I believe he may have some internal bleeding, but he also has a broken rib and some severe lacerations. I need help to patch him up."

"No way. A God? Interesting. Okay... Do you have medical supplies?"

"Yes. He keeps them in his bag. Main pocket in the white plastic case. You will have to move him. Be advised; he is quite heavy."

"I got it," said Hecate.

Using both hands and a considerable amount of strain, Hecate angled Vallus into a seated position. His head drooped as Hecate rummaged through his bag, supporting his weight on her knee. She quickly found the medical supplies and set them on the floor. When she did, she noticed the cracks in it underneath him. A twinge of fear shot through her.

"That God was pretty strong, huh?" said Hecate, trying to hide the slight tremble in the question. "I can't believe your friend is alive. He must be one tough son of a bitch."

"We have been through much. We just need to get him to safety, then he can push through this. I hope."

Hecate nodded and got to work. Pip watched and assisted, impressed by Hecate's apparent medical skill. Hecate glanced sidelong at the drone as she worked on Vallus' ribs.

"What's up?"

"You know medicine. Doctoring. How?"

Hecate cracked a thin smirk.

"I've been a loner most of my life. Grew up with no one, so the only person I could count on was me. I had to learn how to fix myself. Picked up things here and there. And encampment life isn't for me."

"Were you not born in one?" asked Pip.

"I was," replied Hecate as she continued her work to fix Vallus' rib as best as she could. "My parents died when I was eight. They got sick, never got better. I didn't want to stay in that place after that. So I left."

"So you're not a Seeker? Who taught you to fight?"

"Lots a people, here and there. Most of what I do is self-taught."

"But you aren't a bandit, either?"

"No way. I'd have to answer to some heaving asshole with no manners and a stench. And I may be mean, but I'm not *that* much of a bastard. I'd rather just wander. There's nowhere good to set down roots, so who needs 'em?"

"I see. In a way, you too are a Seeker. You seek belonging."

"All I seek is a good time. One day, probably soon, I'm going to die. Everything has an expiration date. Might as well have fun along the way, and maybe help someone out once in a while."

As Hecate finished her work, Vallus began to come to. He yawned and rubbed his eyes, and Pip was taken aback. Supporting his own weight, he spat blood and looked at Pip.

"What?" he said, still groggy.

"Were you sleeping?"

"I don't know. I guess? Wait, what is she doing here?" asked Vallus as he tried to crawl away backwards before he growled with pain.

"Helping you," said Hecate as she maintained a grip on the

Seeker to steady him. "You're welcome, by the way."

"Calm down, Vallus. You have been injured and she helped. We need her so we can get to safety."

"Good," said Vallus wearily. To Pip, something about him seemed off. Like he was more tired than usual. He almost seemed sad.

"Can you stand?" Hecate asked.

"I think so," said Vallus as he made the attempt but slumped back to the floor. His legs were jelly, and his back didn't feel much better.

"Let me help," said Hecate. She wrapped her hand around his arm and pulled him to his feet, then wrapped her other arm around his back as she draped his over her shoulder. "There somewhere safe you can think of?"

"The lobby," Vallus replied wearily. Hecate's narrow eyes widened. "That's pretty far away. Sure you're up for it?"

"Got no other choice," replied Vallus. "Pip, can you find us a shortcut?"

"I already checked the map. There's no quick way that I am aware of," she replied sadly.

"The tunnel we took can't be the fastest way through, can it?"

"No," said Hecate. "It isn't. I'll take you. There's hundreds of service tunnels throughout this place; one of 'em has to be quicker than the tram tunnels. Those service tunnels are usually pretty empty and they go straight past doors and any collapsed areas."

"Very well. The faster, the better."

As they began to walk toward the door Hecate had entered through, Hecate holding up Vallus' weight with surprising ease, Vallus held up a hand and stepped away. He quivered for a moment, hands still up, but soon steadied himself.

"Before we move on, there's one more thing I need from you."

"Oh, yeah? I can think of a number of things I could do for you," said Hecate with a suggestive grin.

"What? Oh. No, not interested. Never have been. What I need from you is assurance that you aren't going to put a knife in my back and tell me Yashir sent you. What is he doing? Where is he?"

"Anyone ever tell you ya ask too many questions? Guess it comes with the territory. I can't give you assurance. I can tell you that I don't work *for* Yashir, I work *with* him. He lets me run free and cause all the mayhem I want; I point my gun at what he needs me to. At my discretion," she replied.

"That's something," said Vallus.

"As for Yashir, I got no idea what he's up to or where at. He knows what he's doing, and he doesn't need my help to do it. But I'm gonna be honest with ya. I think we might be in over our heads here. This place is a damn maze, there's all kinds of crazy shit running around, and I'm pretty sure we've heard at least three explosions within the walls at some point."

"Ah. Those may have been my doing. I'm not sure I can trust you, Hecate. But for now, I'll give you a chance. We can talk on the way. Let's go."

Vallus and Hecate moved on through the door and into the hall with Pip following closely behind, her optic lens tilting in the frame to keep an eye on Hecate. At first, Vallus tried to walk at his usual brisk pace, but his body twisted in blinding pain as he did. He was forced to move at a more measured pace, and walked with a limp. As they walked, Vallus inspected Hecate's handiwork, looking over the smoldering remains of the battle droids.

"You did this? Impressive," said Vallus.

"Oh, yeah. They weren't as much fun as I had hoped. Oh, well."

With Vallus and Pip slowly in tow, Hecate led the group through the hall and to a service tunnel entrance in the wall. The grate had already been broken off. They entered the tunnel, a long dark shaft built tightly between the walls of the vault. There were thick pipes running through it, but Vallus couldn't make out much more than that until Pip turned on her flashlight. The top of the shaft was nearly tall enough for Vallus to stand in, but the pain in his leg and back forced him to hunch, giving him plenty of room. The tunnel winded through the vault, with stairs in some places to allow passage up sharp inclines. Vallus found climbing the stairs somewhat painful at first, but quickly acclimated. He noticed that his pain was starting to fade, although it still lingered in his back and chest. There hadn't been much Hecate could do for his rib, but he could tell it would be good enough for the time being.

The group continued onward. As they did, Hecate walked in front to lead.

Occasionally, she would look at the walls closely between the pipes or check down crossing paths. It drew Vallus' attention at first, but after a while it drew his interest. Pip followed closely as Vallus hurried to walk closer to her.

"Looking for something?"

Hecate glanced over her shoulder at him. Her eyes were obscured to him by her hair, but he had a feeling they would have told him as much of what she thought as her silence.

"Sometimes there's signs on the walls between the pipes that tell you where the shaft leads. I'm not sure where this tunnel goes. That last turn threw off my sense of direction."

"We're on the right path."

"How do you know?"

"I've gotten good at orienting myself in these places. They're so big you almost have to if you want to get out. We should be close to a room with access to the elevator."

"All right. How's the pain?"

"Better. Thanks. There's something I should tell you, by the way. Volya is dead."

"Go figure. You or him?"

"A bit of both. He refused my help," replied Vallus.

"Well, good riddance. That guy was rotting his brain with all that 'nothing matters' shit. Never liked the guy."

"Those discs he was using to control the droids... Do you know how they work?"

"Nah. Volya built them. Think he got the idea from some old blueprints he found. Had to compensate for his lack of combat skill somehow."

"I take it your dislike of him was more than a passing distaste?"

Hecate nodded. "Yashir is pretty scary, but Volya was a genuinely bad person. He was a pervert who killed for nothing and had little to no conviction. I'm honestly glad he's dead, and he probably deserved a less honorable killer."

"Thanks. I think?"

"Don't mention it. By the way, sorry for the pass at ya," said Hecate as she looked at him with a coy grin and a wink. "Didn't mean to offend, if I did."

"No worries," he replied. "I thought nothing of it to begin with."

"So you've never been interested, huh? What about when you were a teen?"

"Never. My life has always been about my mission. Being strong enough, being smart enough, to complete it. While my friends in the Huddle talked about girls, I was busy learning about how the machines work."

"So it's a priority thing?"

"Not really. Sure, I spent my youth preparing for this, but as far as I can recall, I've never had any sort of desire for or thought of any sort of sexual interaction. It isn't as if I am unaware of the action; I just don't want it."

"How about a kiss? No way you were such a shut-in ya never had a first kiss."

"I did. When I was nine. There was a young girl who lived in the Huddle named Meira. I gave her some of my food because she had dropped hers and she kissed me."

"Like, on the lips?"

"Yes. Can't say I felt anything, but I suppose it was a kind gesture."

Hecate laughed. "So, where's little Meira these days?"

Vallus frowned. "Dead. Some bandits attacked when we were around fifteen. A few got in, one shot her before I could drop him."

"Holy shit, man. Your life is sad."

"I choose to think otherwise. There are many things I haven't experienced, but there are plenty of things I have done that most people cannot do. I consider it an even trade. And if I can bring hope to my people, it will all be worth it."

"Here," said Hecate.

To the group's right was another grated opening. Hecate kicked it off and they entered into a hallway that adjoined to the library. They followed the hall to a large door which opened into the library itself, about a quarter of the way down the long hallway. They were close enough to see the wreckage Vallus left behind on his journey through the area, but much closer to the front entrance. They passed through that door and down another hall that led to the elevator door.

"This is where I leave you," said Hecate, the strange and disturbing grin that usually plastered her face appearing once more.

"Thank you, Hecate. Really," said Vallus. Pip detected a hint of weariness in his voice.

"No problem. Didn't have anything better to do, anyway," she said with a low chuckle.

The pair nodded to each other, then Vallus called the elevator and boarded it with Pip in tow. The doors closed, leaving Hecate behind as they began to ascend toward the lobby.

Pip observed Vallus as they went. He was uncharacteristically quiet, and much more stern than usual. And although she couldn't feel in the traditional sense, Pip could tell that something was wrong. She was about to broach the subject when the elevator made its gentle *ding* sound and the doors opened onto the lobby.

Vallus calmly walked to the makeshift camp and gathered up the other half of his bag. Pip bobbed about, watching with curiosity. Shiloh was sleeping, but Vallus' work roused him from his slumber. With an extended groan, the former Seeker stirred and climbed off his cot. He rubbed sleep from his eyes as he yawned.

"Ah, you've returned. I was starting to worry."

"No need. Thank you for all your help, Shiloh. I have greatly appreciated it," said Vallus, looking up only briefly.

"No worries, Seeker. Odd though. Sounds like you mean to leave."

"Vallus?" asked Pip, concerned by Vallus' brief and contemplative silence as he temporarily ceased his packing.

"Yes. I won't find my answers here. These so-called Gods want nothing but my death or my absence, so I will seek my answers elsewhere," he said as he checked over his bag.

"I'm sorry, Vallus, but that is probably the dumbest thing I've ever heard you say," said Pip, and from her voice, Vallus could tell that she was upset, to say the least.

"Excuse me?" he replied, taken aback by Pip's bluntness.

"You heard me. We've been in two other vaults; you've been in three. How many of those held your answers? Now we come to a vault where the Gods still walk and you want to give up?"

"They won't talk to me!" he yelled, his face flush with anger. But there was pain there as well. And a touch of guilt.

"Then make them!" she yelled back. "The mission means nothing if we run away!"

"The mission means nothing if I don't make it out alive! I have to bring the knowledge back, or it dies with me."

"I'm sorry, but what happened?" asked Shiloh as he quietly groaned. Pip noticed his pained movements, but decided it was a matter that could wait.

"I met the Ashen King," replied Vallus. "It took him all of twenty seconds to knock me out cold. I cannot beat him, and he either can't or won't tell me what I need to know."

"Well of course you didn't beat him. He's called the God of War for a reason," said Shiloh. "But that doesn't mean you should give up. It just means you should fight harder. Or did your teacher not tell you that?"

"He did. But he also taught me how to tell when it's time to move on. When it's time to acknowledge my shortcomings."

"What does your name mean?" interjected Pip.

"What? You know-"

"What does it mean?" Pip demanded once more.

Vallus sighed heavily. He slumped onto a nearby chair and ran his hands through his hair in frustration. He was surprised by the amount of grime that came away, blood and dirt that had gathered since he left the room filled with plants. He sat in silence for a few moments, regarding the grime curiously.

"Valiant," he replied with a heavy sigh. "It means valiant. It is what I vowed to return home as."

"And you cannot call yourself that unless you keep going."

"I… I can't, Pip. I can't do this. I'm not strong enough. You saw what he did to me." He shook.

"This isn't about being strong enough. It's about not giving up. What does this truth you seek mean to you?"

"Everything. But…"

"No. None of that. Get up, dust yourself off, and keep going. Your journey is not yet over, Seeker," replied Pip sternly. "Too much blood has been spilled here to give up. Make it count."

Vallus looked to Shiloh. He appeared to be in agreement with Pip.

"I know. I'm trying. But every time I try to tell myself it's time to press on, I think of that fight. How am I supposed to overcome that? How do I even begin to fathom what it would take to do that?"

Shiloh cleared his throat, and the other two looked to him with curiosity.

"If I may? I gave up, and it is the greatest regret of my life. I don't have long; I was never able to get the bullet out and my leg has been weakening ever since. And Vakka beat me up pretty badly. But I stood up to him because I believe in you. I have since the moment I first spoke with you. You are no ordinary Seeker; and this is no ordinary vault. Don't become like me. Think of all you have overcome. Why should this be any different?"

Vallus was stunned. He sat in silence for a few moments as he pondered Shiloh's words. Could he simply brush it aside? Forget the ferocity and overwhelming power of the enemy he faced? Then he asked himself a different question. Could he simply return home empty-handed? Or with something less substantial than the words of Gods?

His body ached, unrelenting in its torment of him. He had already sustained many more wounds than he ever had in a vault, and he worried that any more threats could seriously endanger his body. He recalled his ammunition count, and knew he was dangerously low. His blades had seemed ineffective before. He felt as though a mountain stood before him, and he had nothing but a rope and a coat. But his equipment woes were pushed aside by the nagging thought in the back of his mind, his greatest fear whispering in his mind.

Failure.

It wasn't fear that gripped Vallus' heart. He had learned long ago to push that aside. Fear was not an option. But there was always room for error, and despite all of his training and all of his mantras, Vallus had grown to fear failure, if only ever so slightly. It picked at the back of his mind most of the time, although he had learned to ignore it. But his encounter with the Ashen King had kicked open the door to that fear's little prison. Here stood the first thing that had ever truly defeated him, and yet it had allowed him to live so that the torment of that tiny fear could grow. Perhaps he did belong in the trash.

"Wait a minute," muttered Vallus.

"What?" said Pip.

"He told me I belong in the trash…"

"Come now, Vallus. He-"

"No. Wait. What if he meant it literally? Check the map. Is there a waste disposal area of some sort?"

Pip chirped happily at being asked to return to work. She quietly beeped for a few seconds before she spoke.

"There is a subterranean waste management sector. Getting there will be quite difficult. There is a large magnetic locked door that only opens once every thirty-two hours at the bottom of the vault that leads to a deep sluice-way. Then from there it leads to waste management."

"I bet the key card to get into the Core Sector is down there."

"But why would he leave you a clue if he wants you gone? Is it a trap?"

"Probably. But I either do this, or return home with nothing. You're right. I can't let all of this be for nothing. I can't afford to fail. So if it is a trap, then we spring it and figure it out from there," said Vallus as he stood and set aside the bottom half of his bag. "And if I can't beat the King… Well, I don't suppose it'll matter much after that."

From his bag he took out his medical kit, then took two pills from it. He swallowed them down with a gulp of water from his canteen, then returned all the things to their places. He hoped they would ease his physical pain. He would just have to deal with all the other types of pain himself.

Vallus took one more deep breath, which ached his broken rib. As he slowly breathed out, he ruminated upon the words Pip and Shiloh had spoken to him. He knew they were right. He knew he had no option but to move forward. And somewhere in the back of his mind, he knew that there would be grave consequences if he didn't. He gave one more thankful nod to Shiloh, then to Pip, then headed to the elevator door.

Both Vallus and Pip remained silent as the elevator descended toward the lowest floor. They both stared straight ahead at the door, too focused on what was to come. Vallus recalled his lessons, and found that he really didn't have any wisdom for what to do in his situation.

No one had ever thought he would meet a God, let alone several of them. The thought weighed heavily on him, constricted his chest. Then the elevator doors opened, and Vallus stepped in to a short hall that led to an expansive, dark room.

A few of the large light bars mounted around the room still functioned, although they had some broken bulbs here and there. Scattered all around the room were large piles of trash, mostly old and broken machine parts along with hundreds of black contractor bags between them. Attached to the ceiling were three large mechanical arms, much like those Vallus had encountered in the library, only heavier and with more plating. Luckily, they seemed to be inert. There was another door off to the side, but Vallus was more interested in the extremely large steel door at the back of the room that seemed to be more of a lid than a door. It sat on great steel hinges over a raised chute that was about two feet high and twenty feet wide. But there appeared to be no controls nearby to open the door. He looked around the room, searching for some control box or computer. There appeared to be none.

"Pip, scan the area. See if there's a way to get this door

open."

Pip beeped in affirmation and began to float about the room as she ran her scanner. Meanwhile, Vallus continued to look around the room himself. He thought that perhaps the controls had been covered by the trash and began to poke around in a nearby pile. He was amazed at the variety of junk he found. Everything from cleaning machines to dismantled battle droids could be found, as well as hundreds of bags taken from throughout the vault in the past. Many of the bags were torn open, which seemed to be the source of the strange, stagnant smell Vallus had been picking up since he got to the room. Unfortunately, there didn't seem to be much of use in the piles of junk. The vast majority of items in the pile were broken, and some of the larger machines were too deeply entrenched to be accessible without risking climbing. There were a few minor pieces of metal plating that he thought could be used to enhance his armor in the future, but nothing beyond that. He put the parts in his bag and continued to search through the pile.

Pip continued her own search, although she was growing disappointed at her lack of results. She had figured out most of the mechanics of the large door, but the piles of junk were too dense to scan through. With her scanner, she could see the electrical currents of wires that ran through the walls, but they disappeared into the junk on their route from the door and didn't appear to connect to anything.

With no other ideas, Pip flew into a gap in one of the piles. She was able to navigate through the pile by weaving through broken parts and ripped bags, but still couldn't find any control devices. She was beginning to think that it would only open on its predetermined schedule. Then she detected the sound of the side door opening and flew as quickly as she could out of the trash heap. As she broke out and ascended into the air, she glimpsed Yashir as he entered the room.

Vallus had also noticed Yashir's entrance and turned away from his search. The two men stood silent for a few moments as they eyed each other. They each began to pace the room, walking in a wide, calm circle, never taking their eyes away from the other. The weak lights in the room occasionally reflected off Yashir's cold steel arm. There appeared to be a curious amount of blood splattered along its protective plates, and Vallus quickly recognized it as the same thick, goo-like blood of the madmen. His eyes still had the same dark, venomous quality Vallus had noticed before.

Rooting through the trash, eh?" said Yashir with a low hiss. "Your time is up, Seeker."

"I honestly never cared about our deal, Yashir. I didn't expect you to uphold your end, so I can't be bothered to uphold mine. Besides, I must complete my mission," replied Vallus evenly.

"Figured as much. Who kicked your ass?" he asked, pointing to Vallus' face.

"Don't worry. You'll probably meet him soon enough if you keep poking at the core."

Yashir scowled, more so than usual. Vallus couldn't be sure, but he swore he could hear a low growl coming from Yashir's throat.

"Do you remember what I said before? How I could simply kill you?"

"You could. Or we could drop this shit and work together. I can figure out a way into the core. Help me get there and get what I came for, and I can clear the way."

"Are you suggesting I need you to do my killing for me?"

"No. But I doubt you can kill one of these Gods."

224

"I told you there are none of those," said Yashir bitterly.

"And I told you that I've met them. And killed them. You may have been right; they are demons. But they still have my answers. I almost died for this; I'm not leaving."

"Shame," said Yashir, flexing his mechanical arm into a fist as he looked at it. "By the way... Have you seen Volya?"

Vallus smirked slightly. He hoped Yashir hadn't seen it.

"Ya. He's dead."

"You?"

"Sort of. He tried to kill me with battle droids. That didn't work. Neither did his own weapons. I tried to help him, but he chose a different way."

"Hmm. It seems this place has cost me much already. And Hecate?"

"She helped me get back to the lobby after the Ashen King knocked me out. She's around here somewhere. That one can handle herself."

"The what? Never mind. I assume he's what you meant by 'meet him soon enough'. It also seems as though every time I turn around, you are once more in my way."

"I really don't understand what your problem with me is, Yashir. We can both get what we want, and all it would cost you is your pride!"

"I have no pride!" screamed Yashir. It was a violent scream, laced with bitter hatred; not toward Vallus, but toward everything. He held up his arm.

"See this? My pride died with this! With every time I had to change my arm because I grew. It died with every 'ritual' I still remember every single fetid detail of, as if it happened yesterday! You kill my partner, sway my other to your aid, and still refuse to leave here and you expect me to help you? No! No, I will not help you! Instead, I will simply kill you!"

With a primal roar filled with rage and hate, Yashir charged toward Vallus. The Seeker drew his blades, but the rider was already upon him. Vallus took note of the speed. He had barely enough time to side-step the first swing, but he had expected it to come from the mechanical arm. Instead, Vallus dodged the real arm and found himself at a disadvantage.

Yashir's metal arm slammed into Vallus' side. The blow shook his entire body and made him scream. With Vallus tilted, Yashir prepared another strike. But Vallus, this time, was faster.

He swung one of his swords, narrowly missed Yashir's chest, and clipped some of his long hair. A few strands were cut away and wafted through the air. Yashir was not deterred, but Vallus wasn't either. His second sword also missed its intended target of a clean stab through the chest and instead cut into Yashir's coat at the shoulder of his left arm. Although it wasn't much, his blade came away with blood. Yashir seemed to not notice the wound in his rage and once more struck at Vallus. The swing missed and launched Yashir past Vallus.

Vallus turned and tried to strike, but Yashir blocked the sword with his arm. To Vallus' surprise, the blade glanced off and left not so much as a mark. But he also noticed that Yashir's hood had fallen off, and there appeared to be a number of small tubes connected to the back of his neck, barely visible between his hair. He looked back at Vallus, scowling deeply as he pulled his hood back up.

"What did they do to you?" asked Vallus, deeply concerned.

"I'd rather not say. The details might make you lose your nerve. And I want you to struggle."

Yashir threw another punch. It caught Vallus by surprise, but he was able to dodge it. Vallus swung his swords, but to his surprise, Yashir rolled out of the way. He hopped to his feet and quickly attacked again. Vallus had little time to defend, and his swing missed. Yashir feinted to his right and threw another punch with his mechanical arm. Vallus blocked the strike with the side of his sword, and although it was a dangerous ploy, it absorbed most of the blow and protected his wounded shoulder. But he was knocked back and onto the floor.

Yashir wasted no time and drew back to punch Vallus where he sat.

Vallus rolled out of the way and jumped to his feet as Yashir's fist slammed into the metal flooring and dented it. With a mighty roar of his own, Vallus charged forward with his blades at the ready. Thoughts raced through his mind; every word of his father's teachings, every move his opponent could make. He let it all play in the background. Yashir dodged through each swipe of Vallus' blades. He swung them rapidly, hoping to force Yashir to slip up and make a fatal error while trying to avoid a flurry of blades. He kept up his attacks even as he dodged around Yashir's own counterattacks. Then Yashir made the error Vallus had been hoping for. He lost track of Pip.

From up above, Pip fired a taser dart from on high and hit Yashir in the neck. It wasn't enough to stun him, but it was enough to distract him. The first blade hit the metal arm as Yashir reached for the dart and glanced off, but the second blade sliced into Yashir's side through his coat. The wound wasn't as deep as Vallus would have liked judging by the long strip of blood that came back on his blade, but it was enough to make Yashir scream more in pain than in rage. He stumbled back as he clutched his side.

"You forgot about Pip," said Vallus with a smirk.

"Didn't forget about the stupid drone," said Yashir.

"Couldn't fucking see it."

"Her," Vallus growled.

"What?"

"You said 'it'. You call Pip 'her'. She goes by that. And watch your mouth when you speak of her."

"*She* shot me!"

"*You're* being an asshole! I don't tolerate obstacles in my way. And now you know what it feels like to be one. You can call me what you will. Fight me all you want. But you will be respectful of her."

"Or what?" said Yashir as he stood to full height, apparently fighting the pain of his wound with pure, seething anger.

"We both know how this ends, me more than you. It ends one of two ways. Either I kill you, or the King does. Either way, your story ends in this vault, Yashir. So I really have no need for threats."

"There's a third outcome. I kill you and turn this place into a smoldering crater."

"And you intend to do that how? You can't get to the core."

"Says you."

"You're right, says me. Because you're not leaving this room."

"How very astute of you, Seeker," came a rumbling, shockingly commanding voice.

Vallus shivered as a cold streak ran down his spine. His hands shook. Yashir was peering upward over Vallus' head, his eyes wider than usual and a slight tremble running through him. Vallus found it somewhat odd that Yashir's eyes were such a bright green. Pip was silent as she hovered above. Slowly, and with much hesitation, Vallus turned and looked upward. Above, on a mezzanine built over the main door, stood the Ashen King, his broad arms folded over his chest.

"Don't stop killing each other on my account," said the King. "Consider me a curious observer."

But Vallus had lost his will to do so. He turned to Yashir, pleading urgency on his face.

"Yashir. Listen to me. We need to end this now. It doesn't matter what we do to each other; he will kill whoever survives. We need to work together. Please."

"First you die, then he does. Shake in your boots all you want," Yashir spat in reply.

With renewed vigor, Yashir lashed out at Vallus as the King watched from the mezzanine above. His strikes were wild, unrestrained, and filled with rage. There was an animal ferocity in his eyes as he attacked at his dodging opponent. Vallus continued to plead with Yashir as he blocked his opponent's strikes.

"Enough! This is a waste of our time!" yelled Vallus as he landed a powerful kick to Yashir's jaw, knocking the latter off his feet and to the ground.

"I agree," said the Ashen King from above as he raised his hands and extended them forward. The pipes between his armor plates glowed brilliantly in the darkness.

What is he doing? Vallus thought to himself.

Quietly at first, the heaps of trash began to stir. Yashir noticed it as well as he climbed to his feet. The door off to the side opened as the piles stirred and Hecate entered the room.

She looked around quickly, taking everything in.

"Sup?" she said to Yashir. She nodded toward Vallus as well.

"We will talk later. For now, draw your weapon. We have trouble," said Yashir.

"Starting to understand?" asked Vallus as the source of the

stirring began to reveal itself.

From within the heaps of trash, broken and damaged battle droids clawed their way out. Some were missing limbs, a few had severe body damage, but almost none of them were actually armed. But their optic lenses glowed blue. They stumbled and limped as they moved, and they dragged their broken limbs along the ground, creating a horrible screech. Vallus turned to look at Yashir.

"Now is the time to choose, Yashir. Fight them, or fight me. Up to you, but my priority is these monsters."

"Fine. But we are not done," replied Yashir.

Hecate was already firing upon the droids, but the three she blew away were quickly replaced as more droids emerged from within the trash. She was already reloading when Yashir began punching droids hard enough to shatter and crush their hard metal carapaces. Vallus sheathed his swords, drew his rifle, and took aim. Careful to not hit either rider, Vallus fired and destroyed three more droids. But their numbers never seemed to dwindle. Then Vallus decided to make the risky attempt of disabling the King to stop the swarm. Still aiming his rifle, he wheeled around and fired a single shot at the Ashen King. The bullet struck his target cleanly in the center of the head and knocked it backward, but Vallus soon realized that it had bounced off and the King was completely unharmed. And he was laughing. Vallus looked back to see dozens more battle droids emerging from the piles. Vallus and Yashir backed away, but not Hecate.

The group continued to fire into the swarm of droids. Vallus emptied the magazine of his rifle and took several more droids down, but it wasn't enough. Yet more came, soon joined by other machines that Vallus did not recognize, but knew were just as dangerous.

Vallus backed away more as he reloaded the rifle. From within his coat, Yashir drew a large pistol and fired into the crowd. A strange machine with mounted saws fell to the rider before he punched another that resembled a snake. But the group was running out of bullets, energy, and time.

With a coy grin on her face, Hecate looked back at the other two. The crowd of machines drew ever closer, slowly but surely. Vallus was confused, but Yashir seemed taken aback. That was when Vallus realized that there was something in her hand, and that she had put her revolver away. Vallus had counted his shots, and had only ten rounds left. Not enough to destroy the ever-growing swarm of broken machines that continued to emerge from within the depths of the trash heaps. And as the machines began to encircle them, not fully but blocking off escape to either side, Vallus realized that the object in Hecate's hand was some sort of grenade, and the pin was gone.

"Get out of here alive, Yashir. And don't freak out. I'm cool with this," she said.

"Stop! Now!"

"You know that won't work. Oh, and Seeker," she said, turning to look at Vallus. "You looked pretty trashed back there. Don't give up."

Vallus fought against his instincts, because all of them said to approach. He covered his eyes as Hecate let go of the switch. There was a thunderous explosion, and a flash of light. The blast knocked Vallus and Yashir back, near the mezzanine. It took Vallus a moment to shake off the disorientation, but a ringing remained in his ears. He looked up to see the machines all lying inert, basked in flames and smoke. Among the pile, Hecate lied on the ground motionless. Her coat had been burned to rags. Vallus didn't get a chance for a better look, but he was sure he didn't want one. Yashir was upon him.

The ringing in Vallus' ears had begun to fade. He could finally make out Yashir's screamed words as he wildly and clumsily swung at Vallus. He could barely tell, but under the hood and between his strips of blade-like hair, Vallus could see tears in Yashir's thin eyes.

"...Took everything from me! I will crush you! Then, you will pay for her life with your own!"

As he finally came back to his senses, Vallus dodged a punch and slammed the butt of his rifle into Yashir's face. The strike cracked his nose and drew blood as the rider staggered backward. Before Vallus could continue to attack, the Ashen King jumped off the railing of the mezzanine and landed on the floor between the two. Vallus stepped back, but Yashir swung his mechanical fist at the King with an enraged scream. The King caught the punch in one hand, twisted the arm, and lifted Yashir off his feet. The latter struggled against the King's grip as he spat profanities laced with venom and hate. He emptied his pistol's magazine toward the King's helm, but the bullets did nothing.

"Let go of me, bastard!" screamed Yashir desperately as the King's grip began to crush his arm.

"Quiet. Your words are as useless as your weapon," said the King. He looked at Vallus. "I see our previous encounter didn't teach you the error of your ways, Seeker. No matter. You persist despite your weakness, and for that I shall reward you with truth. The truth that any who stand in my way, no matter how trivially, shall perish."

With a terrible ripping sound, the Ashen King shoved his free hand straight through Yashir's back and out of his chest. Yashir tried to scream, but his impaled lungs drew no breath. He tried to struggle, but his spine had been torn in half. Blood poured from his wound like a geyser, soaking the floor and the King's hand in a fountain of crimson. He then withdrew his arm, dropped the still-gasping Yashir to the floor, and without so much as another word he jumped back to the mezzanine and vanished from sight. Vallus heard the door above close, then a loud metallic crushing sound. And in what felt like a sudden moment, Vallus was left alone in a silent room, with only the burning embers and bodies of the dead.

Chapter 9

Failure.

Vallus and Pip were both silent and stunned for some time. Some of the trash had caught fire and the room had developed a much more offensive odor, but Vallus couldn't be bothered by it. His side throbbed from the blow Yashir had landed on him, but he almost didn't register it. All he could focus on was that once again, the Ashen King had bested him. He was relatively unharmed, but he was surrounded by the small defeats the God of War had laid before him.

Hecate's body still had streams of smoke wafting from what remained of it, and a large pool of blood had formed under Yashir's. The room was littered with the remains of the destroyed droids, although a few yet twitched as energy still ran through them. All around Vallus was silent, but his mind was filled with sounds. The explosion that tore Hecate to shreds. Yashir's final, frail gasp for breath. The whirring, gurgling of the droids. Yashir's screaming. The words began to finally process in Vallus' mind.

Why did you have to shoot him?

Vallus couldn't think of an answer. Desperation? Was it really the best strategic option? The words of his father came back to his mind, distant but distinct. Ever present in his mind, yet so far away, his father's face clear in his conscience. His father would be disappointed.

"Every room in a vault will present you with new challenges.

You will never know what may be there, or what may happen. But you must always be mindful of your options. You must know where to run. Where your enemies are. You must know the right tool for the job. And always know the best strategic option," his father had said.

Vallus couldn't say he had. He knew he didn't have enough bullets to destroy every machine. He had counted Hecate's reloads at a total of five. Yashir had reloaded three times himself, and Vallus recalled him shouting about low ammunition in the chaos of the fight.

What could that bullet have been better used for? He had hoped to hit one of the glowing pipes, but they had been a hard target thanks to the King's thick armor plates. He had hoped that it would somehow disrupt the King's power. Instead, it had cost him potentially two allies and much of his own ammo.

"He was controlling them. That's why he's the God of War. Anything can be his army," said Vallus absentmindedly.

"It would seem so. That is why I couldn't use the disc to control the siege engine. That was the signal that was blocking me. But that would mean his power is derived from a machine or a program of some sort. What exactly are these Gods?" asked Pip.

"Good question. The more I fight these things, the more I am split on what I believe of them. In some ways, their power seems to be based in machines. In some ways, I question if they are Gods at all."

"Well, at least we only have the one to deal with. It would seem he has no other Gods to send against us. Otherwise he wouldn't have come here himself."

"I wouldn't rule out any others. We must consider the possibility, at least as a precaution," said Vallus as he finally began to calm down. He felt as though he had once more hit his stride, a sort of return to work. But he reminded himself to learn a lesson from the burning remains that surrounded him.

Vallus took a sharp breath out and put on his gas mask, hoping it would filter out not only any harmful chemicals in the air from the fires, but also the horrid odor of the room in general. It helped greatly, but the stench was still mildly present and Vallus was beginning to find breathing slightly difficult. Although he supposed that could be thanks to the hit he took from Yashir. He shook off the pain, and decided to do the same to the room.

Thanks to the Ashen King calling the droids from the trash heaps, a ladder to the mezzanine had been uncovered. Vallus was able to climb over the scattered trash and up the ladder. There, he found the door the King had left through. It was crushed in the middle, clamped shut. By the railing there was a control panel. It took Vallus quite some time to find the door control in the large number of buttons and dials, but he eventually pulled the switch and the massive steel door slowly opened with a loud, heavy thump.

With Pip quietly in tow, Vallus hopped the railing to the floor and approached the pit. Looking into it was to peer into an empty void. Total darkness, and no indication of its depth. Pip's flashlight hardly pierced the shadows, but it did reveal a ladder attached to the inside.

Vallus checked to make sure it was sturdy, then mounted the ladder and began his descent. Pip followed along, lighting the way as best as she could.

"This ladder goes down some one hundred and fifty feet before it will come to a slope. Be careful, and watch your footing," said Pip.

"Right."

As Vallus climbed, he made sure to focus on his surroundings. He listened for any noises, any growling or movement in vents. Occasionally, he would peek behind him at the wall he could barely make out. The only sound that broke the utter silence was that of his boots on the metal rungs.

"I have a question, Vallus. What makes you so sure the key card is down here?"

"It was strange to me that the King was so specific in his choice of insults. He could have insulted me in any way, but he chose to do so in a way that seemed to reference a sector that just so happens to exist within this vault. He seems to want me to get answers, but he wants me to hurt for it. I just don't know why he wants to test me like this."

"Gods test mortals," said Pip.

"I suppose so. There's also the matter of Vakka's body. Where did it go?"

"We can't be sure."

"Well, I have a sneaking suspicion that we may find it soon."

Near the bottom, Vallus began to hear the sound of rushing water. He climbed lower to find several large ports to either side of the tunnel, with water pouring from them into the depths. He soon came to the end of the ladder and a small platform that stood above a sloped ramp. There was some trash gathered in the corners, and the ramp was directly under the water.

"No way I survive sliding down this," said Vallus. "Ideas?"

"That access panel to your right. It should lead to the bottom," replied Pip.

With some effort, Vallus tore the grate off the access panel and climbed inside. It was a tight fit for one of his stature, but not too uncomfortable as to prevent progress. The panel led to a small tunnel that winded and twisted downward. There were several ramps and ladders, but the journey was unhindered. He soon came to another access grate. Pip nodded in air at Vallus, and he kicked the grate off. From within the wall, he emerged into a long, dark tunnel surrounded by pipes and filled nearly to Vallus' knees with murky water. Behind him, the cascading water from the ports formed a sort of waterfall.

The water was filled with trash and debris, much of it similar to the trash above. It was dark and slimy, and Vallus noted more than a few corpses strewn about as well. None of them appeared to be Vakka's. Most of them were Jaral's victims. He continued onward, only slightly discomforted by the water seeping into his boots. Farther down the tunnel, he came to an area with raised walkways and climbed out of the water. Vallus pressed on, thankful for some drier land. The concrete walkway was slick, but Vallus' boots had good traction and he found walking much easier.

Vallus walked on for another twenty minutes before he heard a low growl echo through the tunnel. Then the vents above clattered and groaned as something moved through them. Vallus put his hands on his weapons, but whatever was in the vents passed him by. The echo of its growling followed behind it, then silence again. Vallus continued onward. But his walk was quickly interrupted. All along the walls, dozens of wires began to spark and crackle with lightning. The electricity surged through the wires in a line, then jumped into something that was submerged in the water ahead of Vallus. The lightning branched out and struck scattered machines for a few seconds, then vanished. Vallus thought the whole affair strange and was about to move on when the water ahead began to churn. Something heavy and almost serpentine moved through the water, then a figure began to rise from its murky depths.

It was the figure of a man, bald with one arm missing. Mechanical tendrils sprung from the water as he rose, coalescing around him in a strange sort of stasis. Then the figure looked up and Vallus looked into his dead eyes. There was a small bullet wound between them. Vallus recognized the man to be Jaral. He screamed a violent, bloody scream as the tendrils began to attach to his body, tearing and ripping into his flesh. More and more machines rose from the murky water to surround Jaral's somehow reanimated corpse and began to reform his severed arm. Soon, Jaral stood before Vallus, his body more machine than man, and his eyes still empty and dead, but with a light blue glow. He groaned, spilling blood and water from his limp mouth as the writhing machines embedded in his flesh bloated his body.

"What the–"

Jaral charged forward, his speed and ferocity enhanced by the machines. Vallus knew not how or why Jaral had been resurrected, but he was left no time for questions. He drew his swords and side-stepped Jaral's vicious lunge. Vallus was forced to remain on the defense, however, as Jaral swung his hefty mechanical fist at him. The blow struck Vallus' blades and knocked him backward and into the water. Pip chased after, narrowly avoiding Jaral's attempt to swat her out of the air.

Vallus quickly emerged from the water, soaked but infuriated. Not only was he angry that he had already killed the opponent that he now faced, he was angry that he didn't know how that could be possible. Then it dawned on him how it could be.

"The King," said Vallus. "But how can he do this? He's not here."

"Perhaps he can use his power over a distance. But we have

no time for questions," replied Pip.

Pip was right. Jaral was already barreling toward Vallus, the deadly mechanical fist raised high. Before he reached Vallus, he extended the arm and several metal tendrils erupted forward from it. Vallus dove out of the way with not a second to waste, but one of the tendrils tore his coat. As he scrambled out of the water and onto the opposite walkway, Vallus began to formulate a plan. His enemy was strong but slow, but also probably wasn't making any plans of its own. Vallus decided to try and end the fight quickly.

However, that was easier said than done. Jaral still swung wildly and ferociously at Vallus. And Vallus had to be extra wary of the arm, as he was unsure of the full extent of its abilities. From the additional strikes Jaral attempted against Vallus, it seemed as though he wasn't particularly keen to use them, anyway. Jaral swung the large mechanical arm again, but Vallus dodged and the punch slammed into the wall of the tunnel, breaking a large hole in the concrete. Vallus now had some idea of how hard it could hit.

Jaral tried to get Vallus more intimately acquainted with the fist, but Vallus was quick enough to dodge. The reanimated corpse continued to swing wildly at Vallus to no avail.

Then it did something new. Jaral reached his mechanical arm forward and it tore apart into dozens of tendrils as it spread open. Vallus had no place to retreat to, and hacked viciously at the tendrils as they began to wind around him. The slashes did little to stop Jaral, and the tentacles wrapped tightly around Vallus. Then Jaral slammed Vallus into the nearby wall.

Vallus' armor protected him from the wall, but a chunk of concrete still hit him in the face. But as Jaral pulled Vallus out of the wall, the tendrils began to loosen. Vallus' arm came free and he was able to slash away at the mechanical arm. The metal was thick, and remarkably tough, but a few strikes cut apart some of the cords and caused Jaral to recoil.

The arm broke apart into dozens of tendrils, each grasping at Vallus as they tried to capture him in their coils once more. However, doing so caused them to drop Vallus, who began slashing at any tendril that got too close.

Vallus had been so focused on the fight he hadn't noticed the disgusting gurgling sound that was building in Jaral's throat. It was as if he was trying to speak, but the machines that were woven through his body couldn't control speech. His attacks were maddened, wild, and uncoordinated. But no amount of hacking and slashing from Vallus seemed to slow Jaral's assault. Each tendril Vallus cut away was quickly replaced by two more, regrown as more machines were added to Jaral's body. Vallus continued to cut the tendrils, hoping to overwork Jaral's reanimated body. Each strike forced Jaral to draw more and more detritus from around him into his body, even pulling machines from the holes in the concrete wall.

Soon, his body was near to bursting, filled with machinery that didn't seem to be helping him much at all, even as more slithered their way into him. Soon, he slumped with the weight of the metal in his body, and with a single clean swing of a sword, Vallus cut his head completely off.

To Vallus' surprise, not a drop of blood spilled from the wound as the body slumped to the ground. Only junk and broken machine parts spilled out, like a satchel full of metal tipped over. Vallus sheathed his swords and rubbed his aching neck, then he knelt down to inspect not only the severed neck, but the head itself.

"Seems I must have severed the connection somehow..."

"The King must have been controlling Jaral's movements

through the implant in his head. I'm reading fading signals from it. It was responsible for motor control."

"Why would Jaral need an implant for that? He moved just fine when I fought him before."

"Well, now that I can scan the body, I've found evidence that Jaral was suffering from some sort of degenerative disease. I can't accurately diagnose it, but he was losing his ability to walk."

"Perhaps that's why he came here? Maybe he was searching for a cure?"

"I don't think so. He didn't have any testing equipment or anything to help synthesize any medication. I think the implant kept him moving, and his madness did the rest."

"Perhaps," said Vallus as he stood and prepared to move on. "Either way, he can't hurt anyone any more. But I am tiring of the King's games. We need to get to the core as fast as we can, then get out of here."

"Agreed," said Pip as the pair resumed their journey down the long, dark tunnel.

It was a long and quite disgusting walk down the remainder of the tunnel, but Vallus was relieved to find it an uneventful one. Eventually, the tunnel ended and opened on a massive area lit by several lights mounted above, each the size of a car. However, much of the area was cast in shadow by the enormous machines that were mounted to the walls. There was also a spire in the center of the room that connected to the ceiling. The room was filled with water, with mountains of trash all around.

"Any idea what those machines are, Pip?"

"I have no comprehensive data on them, but they appear to be for waste disposal. We seem to be in the right place."

"So they burned their trash?"

"No, I don't think these are incinerators," said Pip as she followed the wandering Vallus. "I think they must have converted trash into something useful. Perhaps they broke it all down into base components to be used for energy?"

"Well, I'd put trash disposal at the bottom of my list of questions about the Gods. Let's get to work."

"We should avoid those trash piles. If we unsettle them, we could find ourselves buried. And we should look for anything recently thrown down here. If your theory is right, then we will find our card on something accessible."

"Right," said Vallus as he began sifting through the water.

Vallus grew impatient as he looked through the scattered trash. The water was filled with all sorts of unpleasant and unidentifiable liquids, and the stench was overpowering even through his gas mask. His search brought him closer and closer to the pillar in the center, but there was no key card anywhere he looked. As he approached the spire, the shadows shifted and the light cast down upon something tied to it, about ten feet above Vallus. Upon closer inspection, he realized that it was the burned skeleton-like remains of Nirav, God of Murder. His own sword had been shoved through what remained of his chest plate and driven into the side of the spire. Vallus stared at the strange display for a few moments before Pip joined him, her own gaze caught by the horrid sight.

"It's almost as if he's been crucified," said Pip.

"What's that?"

"A form of torturous execution in which the victim is affixed to a large beam by nails or ropes. The victim usually dies of suffocation as their body weakens. Whoever did this felt immense malice toward Nirav. They wanted to inflict pain upon him that we robbed them of the chance to inflict."

"We know who did this. But why does the King hate Nirav so much?"

"Who knows?"

"I suppose the minds of Gods are beyond us mortals, huh?"

"Speak for yourself," said Pip playfully as she returned to her search. "We can't learn much from that body, but there isn't a key card there."

"Right," said Vallus as he too returned to the search.

There was yet more junk to sift through, but not much of interest. Vallus soon began to question his judgment. He had been operating on a simple assumption: that Gods test mortals. They had been testing him since he entered Logistics. By his reckoning, the King had made their intention to do so clear in the military storage sector. But he had begun to wonder if he had made a miscalculation. Perhaps he had been wrong, and the King had just been cruel for the sake of being cruel. Or perhaps the ancient God's agenda was beyond his comprehension. He tried to allay his worries by telling himself that Nirav's body was some sort of sign, perhaps an indication that he had indeed followed the hints down a path laid before him by the Gods themselves. But with each piece of worthless metal and discarded plastic he sifted away, he lost a tiny shard of hope.

Vallus' mind was so preoccupied that he didn't notice the shuffling and thumping in the vents high above. The sounds of the creature emerging from them was lost in the echoes of Vallus' boots sloshing through the water, as were the scraping of its claws as it wove its long, slender body around the spire, clinging to the side. The thing's low growling was indiscernible as it slowly climbed down toward the water. Vallus noticed none of this until he pulled a thin metal plate from the water. He looked at it with disdain for a moment and was about to cast it aside when he saw a reflection in its slimy surface. There, its long body wrapped around the spire with its claws gripping the metal, was an enormous, almost lupine creature. It stared at him with glowing red eyes, barely slits, and a long snout lined with two rows of fangs that dripped with spit. The thing growled, then roared as Vallus wheeled around and drew his swords.

"Pip!" Vallus yelled as the creature lunged off the spire toward him with another ferocious roar.

Pip spun around in air to see what all the commotion was, and quickly flew to Vallus' aid. She soon realized there was little she could do. Vallus had managed to dive out of the way of the creature's lunge, but it had begun to pace as it prepared to attack again. In the light, Vallus got a good look at the creature that stood before him. It looked almost like a dog, although Vallus had only ever seen one of those. Except unlike the friendly mutt Vallus had met, this creature was much larger and far more muscular. By Vallus' estimation, it was maybe thirty feet long from head to tail, and six feet from floor to shoulder. It looked more machine than animal, with hundreds of hoses weaving in and out of its flesh and armor plates that seemed bolted to its hide. As it took each slow, prowling step, it brandished its long, hooked claws. He took in the thing's low, vibrating growls. And a realization dawned upon him.

"This is the creature that's been hunting me. The one that was in the laboratory. The thing that's been in the vents."

"It seems we have a good nickname for it," said Pip, floating above and hoping to avoid the creature's notice. 'The Hunter' has a nice ring to it."

Vallus chuckled and prepared to fight. The Hunter still eyed him, its head low as it took slow steps in an arc around Vallus. Without warning, it pounced. Vallus was caught off guard, but not enough to give the beast a successful attack. It landed in the water, splashing the dirty muck all over Vallus' coat and in his hair. He shook it off as he wheeled around and swung his blades. The first blade bounced off the Hunter's armor plating, but the second blade cut a shallow slice in its hide. From the wound, thick, oily blood oozed out onto the beast's matted fur. However, the creature didn't seem to notice or be bothered by the wound and spun around, sending a spray of water flying all around it. It roared furiously as it pounced again.

As the Hunter dove for Vallus, it swung its clawed paws wildly through the air, but Vallus dove out of the way. He immediately regretted the decision, as doing so landed him in a slightly deeper part of the vast lake of swill. He struggled to climb out of the water while still maintaining his grasp on his swords, all the while fighting the urge to vomit as some of the water splashed into his mouth. He spat before he was forced to roll out of the way through the disgusting mire as the Hunter pounced yet again.

Vallus' roll didn't get him very far from the Hunter, and it was quickly upon him. Vallus lashed out with his swords, and the creature recoiled as one of the blades cut its leg. Fighting against the water, Vallus jumped to his feet but was quickly knocked back down as the Hunter slammed its whip-like tail into him. And to add to his problems, the blow had knocked him into the side of a massive pile of trash. As he struck the mountain of detritus, it wobbled and shook for a moment before it cascaded down like an avalanche. Fortunately, it was the smallest of the mountains littered about the area, and it fell in a fork around a large protruding pole and left Vallus unharmed. But he still had to contend with the Hunter, who had been clear of the trash slide, as well as the massive amount of scattered junk which he would need to navigate around if he were to have any hope of felling the creature.

The Hunter began to pace once more, its dead eyes focused on Vallus with an intense hunger. Vallus stared back just as intensely, his swords skimming the water as he waited for his moment. Then it charged. But Vallus was ready this time. Quickly, he hooked a bag of trash on the tip of one of his swords and flung it at the beast. The bag hit it square in the face and exploded into a cloud of garbage and dirty water. The bag partially wrapped around the Hunter's head and it roared in animal rage as it tried to shake the trash away. Vallus had hoped it would claw at its face to remove the bag, but it seemed smart enough to not make that mistake. Instead, the creature slammed its face into the floor beneath the shin-deep murk.

With all due respect for the severity of his situation, Vallus fought the urge to laugh at the seemingly silly behavior of the Hunter. But as it raised its head from the water and growled heartily, all of Vallus' humor melted away. With another ferocious roar, the Hunter charged toward Vallus, finally free of the bag's remnants. He tried to prepare for the attack but his boot got caught in a broken trash bag and he tripped. Fortunately, his blunder caused the Hunter's sharp claws to miss him by mere inches, but he still fell hard in the water. The creature wheeled around as Vallus hopped up and its large paw slapped him hard in the chest. The claws raked against his armor, but merely scratched the plate. But the force of the strike knocked him back into the water.

"I'm not seeing the key card," shouted Pip as she continued her search and left the wet work to Vallus.

Before Vallus could escape the gross water filled with trash, the Hunter pounced on top of him. He fought not only to keep his head above water, but to avoid the gnashing fangs of the beast. One of its powerful paws clamped his left arm under the water, but his right was still free and still armed. But with his attention focused on avoiding the Hunter's maw, he had a difficult time aiming a decent slash. He screamed out as he thrashed against the beast.

"Keep... looking!" he shouted as his head was repeatedly dunked under the water.

Pip took the direction and left Vallus to handle the Hunter. Meanwhile, the beast continued to try and bite the Seeker. But Vallus could feel its paw losing its grip. He swung the blade again, not at the Hunter's head, but at its leg. The attack didn't have much force behind it thanks to the water, but it had enough to gash the beast's leg and force it to leap back and off of Vallus. As he tried to stand, Vallus tripped over a piece of metal under the water and was caught by the Hunter as it swung its tail again. The blow wasn't as powerful as the one before, but it still knocked Vallus back into the base of the trash mountain that had spilled. As Vallus tried to stand, with the Hunter staring him down and growling, he tripped yet again. But this time it was no simple bag of trash or chunk of discarded metal detritus that caused him to do so. It was a large, mechanical body. And as he slowly and carefully rose out of the water, Vallus realized that the body was that of Vakka, fallen God of Honor. Sitting wedged within the face wound that had killed the God was a key card soaked in blood. Vallus barely had time to pull the card from the wound before the Hunter pounced again. "Found it!" Vallus yelled as he dove out of the beast's path.

Pip came flying back from the other side of the room as fast as she could. With the key card safely tucked away in a pocket of his jacket, Vallus focused his full attention on the Hunter. The beast continued to rampage through the trash as it swung its claws at Vallus, but its soaked fur obscured its vision and gave Vallus a wide open window of attack. Instead of trying for another weak attack, Vallus sheathed his left sword and grabbed hold of the creature's side by one of its armor plates. The beast ran, trying to shake off the Seeker, but Vallus climbed his way onto its back.

The Hunter thrashed and kicked, trying to throw the Seeker off from where he straddled it. The beast's claws could not reach Vallus, nor could its tail. It roared as it flailed wildly, and the motion made Vallus hesitant to strike. He had to make it count. Vallus swung his sword around and stabbed it straight into the creature's back. He missed the spine, but he was sure the machines mounted to the Hunter would have protected it. The sword sunk deep into the creature's flesh as it roared in pain. But it continued to run and thrash.

"Sorry, beast," said Vallus quietly as he struggled to maintain his grip on the Hunter's back. "But it's either you or me."
Frustrated but not deterred, Vallus forcefully drug the blade through the creature to open a long wound in its back. More thick blood poured out, filled with puss. With one final roar, the creature fell and slid through the water as Vallus was thrown from its back.

The Seeker stood and shook off the muck. Whatever Hecate had done for his rib had worn off, and the pain had returned. In addition, the burning ache was amplified thanks to the Hunter's tail. With a few shakes of his sword, Vallus cleared the blade of most of the gunk before he sheathed it. He then checked the rifle, hoping that it hadn't been damaged by the water. Finding its condition satisfactory thanks to the weapon's shielding, Vallus turned his attention to the Hunter's still body. Pip hovered down to join him.

"What do you make of this thing, Pip?" he asked.

"My scans indicate that it is a dog. Or at least, it was. I'm not quite sure how it was done, but something heavily mutated it. There are extremely high levels of hormones in its blood. Oh, and all that puss? That's coming from hundreds of tumors. Poor creature."

"There are so few animals left... What kind of monster would do this?"

"Vallus, it seems to me as if much of what we have endured is connected. And there is a common thread: the Ashen King."

"So what was this? His pet? Why wait till now to sic it on me?"

"Perhaps he perceived you to be vulnerable?"

"He was wrong," said Vallus, turning away toward the spot where Vakka's body sat motionless. "But I'm more interested in that."

Vallus trudged through the water to the body. He examined it to find that it was in much the same condition as it was when their fight had ended. However, there were deep teeth marks in one of the ankles. From the look of them, they assuredly belonged to the Hunter. There was only one other difference, and it confused Vallus. On the right hand, the tips of all of the fingers except the thumb were missing. The stumps were glazed over with a silver metal that was absolutely smooth and clean, as if polished to perfection.

"What happened to his fingers?" asked Pip.

"I was about to ask you the same thing. They're almost like the rubble... as if it was never there. Odd."

Vallus continued his inspection of the body, but found nothing telling. He looked into the wound in the face, but it was clogged with what had once been Vakka's blood, which had congealed into a dark blue gunk. Vallus inspected the helmet, but found no way to remove it. He pulled his tools from his bag, but none of them seemed to be able to pry the mask away. Vallus was hesitant to cut into the body, mostly so he could avoid damaging his own swords, but also because of the uneasy sensation that rested in the pit of his stomach.

With a more concerted effort, Vallus finally managed to peel back the mask. It was pinned on with long screws that bore into the God's metal skull. Vallus couldn't see much behind the mask, even under Pip's light. The inside of the head appeared to be entirely mechanical, almost like the inside of a computer but more cluttered, and they wrapped around organic brain and muscle. Vallus had decided to see if he could pull back Vakka's breastplate when it split down the middle and opened, much like Aurien's had done. Inside was Vakka's own core, and it glowed just as Aurien's had. Vallus stumbled back over the trash and through the water and fell to a seated position. The body shivered as a blue light ran through it, then it exploded with thunderous force.

Vallus was just barely clear of the explosion, but was blasted back by the aftershock regardless. His head throbbed as he rose from the water. The explosion had caught much of the scattered trash on fire, most likely more fueled than quenched by the sewage around it. Pip had also quickly cleared the blast radius, but she had flown high enough to avoid the aftershock. She sped to the Seeker's side as Vallus pulled the card from his pocket and wiped away the gunk that was smeared on it. Printed clearly on the card were the words 'Alpha Clearance'.

"So we have the card. Now we just need to get to the core," said Vallus as he rose from the water.

"We need to go deep. I can guide you," said Pip.

"Seems he had one more trick," said Vallus, nodding toward the wreckage. "I believe the King did this. Did you see that blue light?"

"Yes. That's who I meant," said Vallus with a smirk. "Let's go. I mean to put an end to this. Whatever 'this' is."

With Pip in tow, Vallus returned to the tunnel, and with the key to the deepest reaches of the vault in hand, made the long and arduous climb out of the sewers.

***

"Our defenses are in place, and the game has begun," said the Wizard as he approached the Ashen King's throne. "Nirav's remains were a nice touch, if I may say."

The King sat hunched forward in his throne, and only slightly lifted his head to acknowledge the Wizard's arrival. He seemed to be in deep thought, but snapped back at the Wizard's words.

"All is according to plan, then," he said, barely above a whisper. "Are you ready, Wizard?"

"Of course," he replied with a nod of his thin, serpentine head. "As you say, all the pieces are falling into place. Soon, we will have our victory. And the door shall open upon a glorious new dawn."

The King stood and walked down the stairs in front of his throne to stand before the Wizard. They stood quietly, face to face, then the Wizard nodded and walked past him and the throne. Before he vanished from sight, the Wizard stopped, placed one of his clawed hands on the side of the throne, and looked over his shoulder at the King.

"We are Gods, Farran. Forget not that we may dispense our judgement as we see fit. This mortal shall tremble before the rising flames of our wrath."

Without another word, the Wizard disappeared from view to leave the Ashen King alone again with his yearning thoughts.

***

It was quite a long, uneventful, and disturbingly quiet journey from the waste management sector, through Logistics, and through the long tunnels that led to the deepest levels of the vault. In Logistics, Vallus had debated returning to the lobby to assure Shiloh was safe, but decided that escaping the vault quickly was a greater priority. Vallus and Pip were mostly quiet as they navigated the maze of hallways that led to a large, heavily reinforced door with only two words stenciled onto it in thick black font. The door read simply:

RESTRICTED SECTOR

He looked at the words for some time as a strange anxiety settled deep in him. Vallus quickly pushed it aside. He pulled the card from his pocket and slid it through the reader on the wall. There was a deep buzz, then the thick door slowly churned open and Vallus walked through it to find himself in a long, fully lit hallway. The light burned his eyes, as he had become accustomed to the broken florescent bulbs and work lights throughout the vault. But this new area was strangely bright.

Vallus walked cautiously through the hall before him. It led to yet another door, but it automatically opened. Within was a sprawling network of laboratories and testing zones.

However, he was unable to inspect the area in closer detail

as he was forced to quickly duck behind a large nearby machine with a purpose Vallus couldn't guess. Pip followed closely behind when she realized that Vallus had taken cover because the area was swarming with battle droids.

Fortunately, none of the droids seemed to have noticed the Seeker or the drone, but he couldn't get an accurate count of their numbers. Vallus had, however, seen that the room afforded plenty of cover and that there were numerous paths he could take to avoid the droids altogether. He signaled his intentions to Pip, who took cover of her own in his bag, and he prepared to cross from the machine to a nearby lab table that was covered with tools and lab equipment. Before he could take his first step, a battle droid stopped right next to the machine and scanned the area as part of its patrol. Vallus stayed absolutely still, hardly taking a breath, and waited for the droid to walk away. Fortunately, it didn't seem to have noticed Vallus, and within a few seconds it turned away to continue its patrol.

Vallus knew he had no time for hesitation. He couldn't afford to second guess his movements, as any slight misstep could draw the attention of a horde of droids which the Seeker was confident he could not defeat on his own. It was a challenge to cross to the table, more so because of the light clattering of his gear as he moved than the droids themselves, but he managed to safely make it to cover once more. He ducked under the table and tried to get another look around the room. Vallus still couldn't count all of the droids, but he estimated that there were at least twenty of them based on the cacophonous gurgling of their processors.

Regardless of their numbers, Vallus still needed to cross the room to reach the door that would take him deeper into the Restricted Sector and onward to the core. Thanks to the numerous scattered and abandoned projects throughout the room, Vallus found that he actually had a relatively easy time crossing the room. Occasionally, a droid would come uncomfortably close, and he noticed that these droids were much more heavily armed than those he had encountered before, but they didn't notice him and he hid himself well, despite his large stature. As he neared the door, his coat brushed against a table and knocked a flask to the floor where it shattered.

Vallus froze. A few of the droids noticed the noise and had begun to move to investigate, but fortunately his blunder didn't attract more than three. But he soon realized that if he didn't move, he would be exposed when the droids arrived. He decided to risk drawing further attention and snuck as quickly as he could to the machine closest to the door, a large contraption that looked to be some sort of water filtration machine by the looks of the three large but shattered glass tanks on it. At the sound of his hurried movements, a few more droids perked up. They also raised their weapons in preparation. Not wanting to be caught out of cover, Vallus waited for his moment, then rushed to the door. As he reached it, the horde of droids saw him. They took aim as he swiped the key card, and luckily he was able to get through the door and close it behind him just as they began to fire.

The door held against the storm of laser bolts that thundered against it as Vallus continued on down the dark hall before him. His heart began to thump in his chest as he anticipated what he believed to be the rapidly approaching end of his journey. It was a strange feeling, to be so close and yet to feel so far away at the same time. He knew that the vault's core could yield nothing and leave him with yet more questions, and that there was no guarantee he would find his answers there, but he was impatient nonetheless. The shadowy hall did little to allay his impatience, but after a long walk down stairs near the end of the hall, Vallus came to a large door. Yet more letters were stenciled on it in the same font as before.

The door read CORE SYSTEMS. Vallus stared at the door for a few moments as he mentally prepared himself. Then, with only a little trepidation, Vallus swiped the key card and the door opened.

Chapter 10

The door took an unusually long time to open, and did so at an incredibly annoying and grating volume. When it finally finished, Vallus passed over its threshold and found himself in an expansive but nearly empty room. There were a few odds and ends, various pieces of junk and stray machines scattered about the room, but there was almost no indication that it had ever been used for anything. Along the far side of the room was a tinted window that ran the length of the wall, and there was a single door in the center of it. The room was also covered in a thick layer of dust.

Vallus looked around the room for a little while before he began to walk toward the door. As he neared the center of the room, the hairs on the back of his neck stood. He shivered. Pip, who had been following closely behind Vallus, beeped ominously. Vallus looked back at her, concerned.

"This is odd. I am detecting a slight shift in air pressure," she said. "Wait... What is that?"

Pip turned around to follow the Seeker's pointing finger. At the far end of the room, there appeared to be a strange shimmer, almost like a mirage. Then it started to expand. It was like a strange distortion in the air, and Vallus was almost sure he was imagining it. Then it expanded farther and through the distortion he could just barely make out what looked to be a dark room lit by a lone candle, as if through a fish lens. As the distortion expanded ever onward and neared almost ten feet in radius, the candle was blocked out by a shadow with a pair of burning red eyes. Then the room was filled with a deafening *crack* and a blinding light spilled out from the distortion. When the light began to fade, Vallus looked past his arm which had shielded his eyes. A figure had begun to emerge from what appeared to be a portal, one step of its mechanical legs at a time. As it passed through the distortion, Vallus began to make out details of the being.

It was tall and thin, and its mechanical body was draped in armor that resembled robes etched with ancient symbols and trimmed in blood red. He held his clawed hands outstretched to his sides, and sauntered with each step. His serpentine face showed no emotion, but his intricate mechanical eyes held pure loathing. His metal feet made a horrible clang against the cold steel floor. Then, all at once, the portal vanished and the room was filled with a loud *pop!* The Wizard cracked a tiny smirk in his metal lips as he folded his arms behind him.

"A pleasure to finally make your acquaintance, Seeker. I am Ishan Grimishar, God of Machines and the Great Builder. You may call me Grimishar," he said with a deep, grinding sneer of a voice. "Or you may address me by my formal title."

"What's that?" asked Vallus. Something about this God unsettled him deeply. There was almost an aura of evil wafting off of him. Then the Wizard raised his right hand in front of him and it began to glow as small parts of his mechanical arm shifted. Sparks of lightning gathered around it.

"The Wizard," he said as a bolt of lightning exploded forward from his hand. Vallus had anticipated the well-telegraphed attack, but he was still almost too late to dive out of the way. The bolt struck the opposite wall and blasted a small hole in it. With nowhere to run, Vallus stood and drew his swords as Grimishar raised his hand again.

"You have met your match, mortal," said Grimishar as he fired another lightning bolt. "Abandon all hope you may have held in your heart. The longer you fight, the more painful your death will be."

The Seeker rolled out of the way of the lightning just in time. He quickly stood to face the Wizard as his heart pounded in his chest.

"I've slain Gods already. What makes you think this will be any different?" asked Vallus.

"Not all Gods are equal within the pantheon," replied Grimishar with an ominous growl.

The Wizard dashed forward, closing the gap between him and the Seeker in an instant.

Vallus had anticipated that Grimishar would use his claws, but instead the Wizard slammed his fist into Vallus' gut. The blow was like being struck by a car and blasted the wind out of his lungs. Vallus struggled for breath as Grimishar swung again and hit him in the head.

Warm blood dripped down the side of his face. With the Seeker's head still reeling, the Wizard slapped his wildly-swung sword away and grabbed him by the throat. Grimishar lifted him off his feet and pulled the Seeker's face close to his own.

"So this is the mighty Seeker who felled my compatriots. Color me unimpressed," said the Wizard coldly before he threw Vallus through the large window.

Vallus went through the glass, hit the floor hard, then slid several feet before he came to a stop. He had finally started to regain his breath and his senses when the wall around the shattered window exploded and Grimishar emerged from the dust. Vallus was too amazed by the view to be concerned with his opponent.

He was not sure what to call the area he had found himself in. He stood on a platform that appeared to form a balcony in a massive circle around the center of the vault that overlooked a steep drop into its depths. There were thousands of massive, thick cables that connected to a spire that came from deep within the vault and rose up toward the top. Vallus looked over the railing around the balcony and was amazed by the sheer size of the central machine. He figured that it must have been part of the core. Whatever it was, it wasn't working. Grimishar's voice came from behind him, a vicious and grim rasp that chilled the Seeker's bones.

"Take it all in, Seeker. This is as close to the core as you will get."

The Wizard stood behind Vallus. The Seeker was frozen in place, unsure of what to do or how to do it. This was not an enemy he was prepared for, and it seemed as though Grimishar knew it, too. Vallus tightened his grip on his swords.

"Vallus," he demanded as he struggled to hide the shake in his voice.

"Excuse me?"

"You keep calling me 'Seeker', and while that is what I am, you will call me Vallus," he replied forcefully.

"I will call you whatever I wish, mortal," hissed Grimishar as he placed his hand on Vallus' right shoulder. The long claw on his index finger poked at Vallus' neck, just barely scratching him. "Your blasphemy will be your undoing. You tread with Gods, *Vallus,* and it would behoove you to mind your tongue."

"You could have just said 'shut up'," said Vallus with a smirk.

"Ah, impudent as well. I'm going to enjoy this." His grip

tightened, ever so slightly.

Grimishar hadn't noticed Vallus reverse his grip on his swords. Vallus only got a moment to feel lucky. He stabbed his left sword toward the Wizard's abdomen, but to his amazement, the blade tilted and glanced off. The Wizard took the opportunity to push Vallus forward hard and slammed his head into the steel railing. The Seeker screamed, and more blood soaked his hair as his head bounced off the rail. Grimishar then threw Vallus back toward the empty room. Vallus slid across the floor and hopped to his feet. Pip hovered to his side as the Wizard slowly approached, apparently reveling in the fight. There was a slight twitch in the metal plates that made up his sharp face and his eyes narrowed when he noticed the drone.

"Interesting. You have a Personal Interface Partner. Hello, little one. You may bow before your creator at your leisure," he said with a wave of his hand, a sense of pride in his voice.

"My... creator?" said Pip.

"Of course. I created many machines. You being one of them. Or, at least, your model. There were many like you."

"Hmm. I think I will pass on the bow, thank you," said Pip.

"You seem to know much, Wizard. This doesn't have to end in blood," said Vallus as he stood.

"You just tried to stab me, and now you want an interview? What have you come here for, Vallus?"

"I think you already know, and that's why you keep trying to kill me. I want to know what happened, and I want to know how to fix it."

"Then ask the right questions," said Grimishar as he stopped in place about ten feet away from Vallus. "Many things have happened to the world, and to fix something, you must know what the 'something' is."

261

"Fine. Then what scorched the world? What killed all the plants and animals?"

"Nothing that matters. You're still asking the wrong questions. But it changes nothing. The appointed time is near, and the new dawn holds no place for you."

The Wizard raised his hand again, but this time there was no lightning. Instead, his palm glowed white hot for a moment before a stream of fire burst forward. Vallus could do nothing but retreat from the flames. But the Wizard approached. The jet of flame licked at him as he tried to find a way out of the attack's path, but Vallus' coat protected him as it was thick and flame-resistant.

Soon, Grimishar halted the torrent of flames and took one large step that closed the gap between him and the Seeker. With barely a grunt, Grimishar swiped his claws at Vallus, but missed. But the Seeker was running out of room to retreat, and the Wizard showed no sign of relenting. Vallus tried once more to make use of his swords, but Grimishar grabbed his head tight and slammed it into the wall behind Vallus. He reeled from the force of the blow, but Grimishar wasn't done yet. With a cackle that was more cruel than humorous, the Wizard took advantage of the Seeker's disorientation and slammed his fist into Vallus' gut once more. The force of the punch made Vallus spit a small splash of blood.

"Come now, Vallus. You *can* do better than this, can't you?" the Wizard taunted as he spun the Seeker around and tossed him back toward the railing.

As Grimishar turned to face Vallus, he began to rise into the air on several loudly whistling jet engines. Vallus was stunned. With a hideous shriek, Grimishar dashed through the air toward the Seeker, but to Vallus' surprise, Grimishar flew over him and floated over the great pit below. He raised and extended his hand as lightning began to gather in it.

"No more games, Seeker. Make your peace before I send you to the after."

Vallus, with Pip in tow, ducked behind a nearby crate to avoid the lightning bolt that exploded from Grimishar's hand and filled the chamber with a violent, thunderous echo. The Wizard took aim again, but Vallus emerged from behind the crate as he himself aimed with the rifle. He could have sworn he saw a slight twitch of inquisitiveness in Grimishar's face.

Please let this work.

Vallus fired. The bullet smashed into Grimishar's outstretched right arm and tore straight through it and out the elbow. The Wizard screamed as lightning surged around him and branched out to strike at the walls, discharged from his shattered weapon. He clutched the sundered arm, then soon calmed and turned to Vallus, still hovering on his jets. His eyes narrowed and he spoke with a deep and wrathful hiss.

"Congratulations, Seeker. You are now the first and only being to ever wound me. Now allow me to make you the last," he said as he extended his other hand. Vallus took aim again, but Grimishar closed his hand and curled his arm back. It glowed with a vibrant light from between the plates and thick cords that made it up and a portal opened behind him.

Vallus was forced to shield his eyes from the bright flash and lost his aim.

The area was dead silent, but there was a chill in the air even though the lightning had only dissipated seconds before. Then came the same explosive *crack*. But it had come from above. Grimishar fell from the portal, his right fist drawn back, still wounded but functional. Vallus was unable to react. As he tried to retreat out of the way, he gave the Wizard a better target.

Grimishar drove his fist into Vallus' chest, dented his armor, and slammed the Seeker into the floor. It buckled. He drew the fist back again. Vallus had no time to react. Grimishar punched him in the chest again, and the metal plates beneath Vallus broke apart. He fell through them about ten feet to another platform. The Wizard followed, floating down on his jets as he laughed.

"I could destroy you so easily. You see that, don't you? When we commanded you to leave, you should have heeded us. We are the Gods, and we do not ask."

Vallus struggled to his feet and wiped the blood from his head away from his eye. He had dropped the rifle as he fell, and it sat on the floor a few feet away. Pip was nestled safely in her reinforced pocket on Vallus' bag. Vallus patted the pocket.

"Stay in there, Pip. You'll be safe," he whispered before he turned back to Grimishar.

He scowled. "I came here for answers, Wizard. I have pled, and I have begged, and I have bled and none of you have spoken a single word of use. You may be Gods, but I am not a worshiper. I am a Seeker. I seek absolution for my people. I seek hope for the future. And I seek salvation for the world that, as far as I can tell, you destroyed. And I will be denied no longer."

Grimishar cracked an amused grin, only slightly at the corners of his cold metal mouth.

"You are quite insolent, mortal. But it takes guts to speak to me like that, so I will think fondly of you when I crush you like the bug you are," said Grimishar with a deep scowl. Then his face lit up. "But I will grant you a boon. Go ahead, you get one question before you die, and I will answer. Better make it count."

Vallus thought for a moment. One question, one answer. He supposed he could avoid the rest of the deal, but it would be quite difficult. With some haste, Vallus took his bag off, patted the pocket again, and set it aside with the rifle. Vallus knew the Wizard's patience would not last, and he had to think of a question. But he had already been told to ask the right questions. Perhaps it wasn't about how or why? Grimishar had already said the what didn't matter. A question dawned on him.

"How long ago did it happen?" he asked.

"How long ago did what happen?"

"The Fall. Whatever did all of this to the world. The first event."

The corner of the Wizard's lips twitched slightly, almost curling into a grin again. "Interesting choice. The time is hard to evaluate, what with all the factors. We were asleep for some time. But my calculations say it was a thousand years, give or take a decade."

"You don't know for fact? Aren't you a God?"

Grimishar scowled.

"That makes three questions, Seeker. You're pushing your luck. But contrary to popular belief, we are not omniscient. We don't need to be."

Vallus contemplated the Wizard's words. But he didn't have much time to do so, as Grimishar had already extended his left arm and begun to charge another lightning bolt.

There was no cover around him, and he knew there was no way he would get to his rifle before Grimishar unleashed his attack. But then something strange happened. The Wizard lowered his hand.

"You know what? The lightning would be too quick," said Grimishar as he disengaged his jets and landed on the floor with a loud *bang* that shook the balcony. "I'm going to make this slow."

Vallus drew his swords. He saw no reason to make it a fair fight. The Wizard took two great steps forward and swung his right fist hard. Vallus ducked the punch but had to avoid the follow up and had no time to make his own strike. He dodged one more punch before he swung his blades, but the Wizard was faster and planted a hard kick to the Seeker's chest that knocked him backward twenty feet. He slid another ten before he hopped to his feet and connected his swords. The Wizard used his jets to burst forward and close the gap. Vallus was unsettled not by Grimishar's speed, but by his eerie silence. No screams, no battle cries, and not so much as a grunt. But there was a slight smirk. Vallus supposed he *was* enjoying it.

Vallus was forced to retreat backwards as the Wizard swung his sharp claws. The first swipe he deflected with his sword, but the second swipe raked through his coat and a few of the claws sliced his arm. Vallus growled through the pain as he stepped forward and ignored the blood that soaked his arm as he drove one end of his sword toward Grimishar. His stab missed, but Grimishar hadn't dodged far enough and the blade cut into his side. He didn't seem to notice, and the blade drew no blood, not even the strange blue liquid that had spilled from the wounds of the previous Gods. Grimishar drew back and swung a fist at Vallus, but the Seeker dodged it and swung the other blade toward the Wizard's arm. It glanced off.

Vallus staggered back as the Wizard continued to attack. He had no option but to dodge and hope Grimishar had no more tricks to deploy. His hopes were soon dashed. The Wizard feinted, and Vallus took the bait. He tried to swing his sword, but Grimishar pushed him back and raised his hand. There was no lightning or fire. Instead, he emitted a powerful wave of what seemed to be pure force. The blast was like a gale, and knocked

Vallus off his feet and through the window behind him. By the time Vallus struggled to his feet, the Wizard had already flown through the wall on his jets in a cloud of dust and rubble. He landed some twenty feet away and folded his arms over his chest.

"I expected more of you, Vallus," said the Wizard. "Not long now. Are you sure you want to make your death this agonizing? It will be quicker if you don't fight back."

"Not gonna let you kill me yet. There's still questions you can answer," said Vallus as he separated his swords.

"You still don't understand, do you? We aren't going to answer your questions. We aren't going to indulge you. We bring a glorious transmission, a new world born in the vast power of the Gods. We have no time for history lessons," said the Wizard, his voice raised and yet somehow still sneering.

"You wish to rule us, but not to inform us of why you should?"

"No, mortal. We don't wish to rule you. We already do."

Grimishar raised his hand as it began to gather electricity. Vallus had only precious moments to find cover, and was fortunate enough to have a large crate to dive behind. The bolt struck the corner of the crate and blasted a cloud of splintered wood over his head.

Vallus gripped his swords tighter, unsure of how to proceed. The heavy, clanging footsteps of the Wizard approached slowly, and Vallus had neither his rifle nor Pip's help. And the enemy before him was beyond his abilities. He shook that last thought off as he prepared to strike.

As if he were casually tapping his fingers, the Wizard placed his hand around the corner of the crate. With little effort, he threw it against the adjacent wall where it shattered into chunks. But Vallus had already begun to strike.

Vallus had sheathed one of his swords to grip the remaining weapon with both hands.

Mustering every bit of strength that still remained, Vallus drove the blade forward into Grimishar's chest. The Wizard roared with fury as the blade pierced his metal chest plate and dug into his core. But the wound hadn't been lethal. Grimishar laughed as a strange distortion formed in his throat.

"You think this will stop me? No, you fool. You have only made me stronger."

The Wizard grabbed the blade, and with a devious grin on his face, he pulled it deeper into his chest. The blade bit deep into his power supply as sparks of lightning discharged out from within the wound. Then he ripped the blade out of his chest and flames shot from within him. Some of his armor plates peeled away and fell to the floor, and more flames emerged.

Soon, the Wizard was engulfed in fire, the broken plates giving the impression of some macabre burning skeleton. He laughed slowly, like a hungering fiend.

"You dare to stand before Gods and make demands of us? Your every breath is a blasphemy. Every step you take is a sin. And now I will smite you, mortal, and drag you kicking and screaming into the darkness!"

Grimishar dashed forward, claws raised and a wrathful scream in his wake. Vallus was only slightly ready for the assault that followed. With the help of his sword, Vallus was able to parry away a few of the Wizard's strikes, but it wasn't enough. A series of rapid but powerful blows rocked Vallus' body and broke another rib. Then the Wizard grabbed the Seeker and slammed him into the floor face first. He held Vallus there, the force of his grip like a boulder on the Seeker's back. The heat from the flames was almost unbearable. A strange, oily liquid dripped from

Grimishar's body all around him and burned the floor. He knelt down to speak in Vallus' ear, a grim and vile whisper filled with malice.

"You cannot prevail, Seeker. Soon, my overcharged core will rupture and I will die, but you will be but a smear by then. And I am a God, with a God's mastery over death. What hope do you have?"

"None," Vallus choked out. "But I have a sword."

Vallus stabbed behind him with all his might. The blade dug deep into Grimishar's side and forced him off of Vallus. He ripped the blade from his side as the Seeker stood and flung it into a wall where it stuck. Vallus drew his second sword.

"Well aren't you the perfect image of the caveman waving a pointy stick," Grimishar sneered. His voice was choked, as if full of phlegm.

"You're running out of time, Grimishar. Now would be a good time to start talking."

Grimishar screamed with bitter rage. The flames pouring out of his body intensified and lightning arced around the room. He extended both of his hands as he sneered.

"Petulant mortal! I will hear no more of your demands!"

With a deafening explosion, a blast of lightning erupted forth from the Wizard's outstretched hands. Vallus dove out of the way, just barely avoiding the massive bolt.

However, an arc branched off and struck him. He screamed and rolled thirty feet across the room. The bolt slammed into the wall and blasted a hole in it before dissipating. Vallus couldn't move, and he couldn't hear. But he could see. Across the room, the Wizard had hunched over and yet more fire had begun to spill from his body. The plates that made up his robe were falling off, one by one. Slowly, he raised his head to look at Vallus, who had started to regain some feeling and could just barely prop himself up. Grimishar spoke, but Vallus could not hear the words. He then began to regain his hearing.

"… Didn't destroy this world. You did… Mortals… You took our gifts… and you squandered them. You all deserve… to… burn." There was fire in his mouth.

The Wizard issued one final raspy breath, then screamed as the flames consumed him.

A bright light burned at his chest, and he threw his head back as lightning arced off of him. Then, with violent force, he exploded. Lightning blasted off of the explosion and knocked out the few remaining lights, and Vallus found himself without hearing once again. Soon, the ringing in his ears subsided and he was able to drag himself to his feet. As he did, Pip flew into the room and examined the site. She then rushed to Vallus' side.

"Let me take a look at that head wound," she said.

Vallus stood still as Pip cleaned the wound and he wiped the blood away with a wet cloth. The wound wasn't bad enough to need stitches, but Pip did need to use her medical glue. Using her tools, Pip checked a sample of his blood to assure there were no underlying conditions. She beeped.

"This is odd. It seems there are still nanites in your bloodstream, and they are functioning. I think they may be slightly augmenting your physical attributes."

"Meaning?"

"I think you were able to defeat the Wizard because these nanites were making you faster and stronger, at least by a little bit. They should fully leave your system in a few hours, though. We should do whatever else we need to do here and get to the core."

Vallus nodded, and with some reluctance, he approached the

smoldering remains of the Wizard. The body looked almost like a charred skeleton, although there were bundles of wires and other mechanical pieces all over it, torn apart and sundered by the explosion. The chest cavity was completely shredded, and the head was mostly ripped apart. Then something caught his eye, as well as his nose. At first it was the smell of burning meat that intrigued him.

He knelt down by the body to take a look. He looked closer and found that there appeared to be something organic inside the Wizard's sundered head. He had Pip scan it.

"Well this is strange. My scans indicate that that is brain tissue. The brain seems to have been his, but there were probably a lot of wires attached to it based on the look of it. Weird. Why would he have a brain but no other organs?"

"Good question. But regardless of the answer, we need to press on," replied Vallus as he stood. As he walked back toward the door to grab his gear, he gave the Wizard's body one last kick to the jaw for good measure, collected his sword from where it was stuck in the wall, and left the room. He stopped in the doorway, as Pip was still hovering within the room.

"Something wrong?"

"No... I just detected a signal. Just for a moment. It connected to something... Never mind."

Pip quickly turned and flew to Vallus, and they continued on out of the room. Vallus tried to question Pip on what she had detected, but she seemed unable to answer anything conclusively.

Back on the platform walkway, Vallus put his bag back on and remounted the rifle on it. He took another long look at the area, peering down into the depths of the core. There was an eerie silence throughout the place, and it unsettled Vallus. He turned to Pip.

"So where to now?"

"The core itself is protected by a series of gates, but it is eight floors below us. We should be able to get past the gates considering we have the Alpha key card, but we should remain wary. We don't know what else is in here, and my map is showing no information on these floors."

"Has the data been deleted?"

"No. It seems to have been purposefully concealed, probably to prevent espionage. The doorway to the next floor is in the room with the Wizard's body."

Vallus nodded and continued on with Pip following closely behind. They passed through the room, past Grimishar's smoldering corpse, and through a door that led to a long staircase. Vallus descended the stairs. At the bottom, there was another door and a curve in the stairs that continued down. Tired and eager to end his time in the vault, Vallus skipped the room and moved on down the stairs. He continued to ignore the doors at the bottom of each staircase until he came to the last door. Vallus stood still before the door for a few moments as he prepared for what may lie ahead of him. Words were stenciled on the door: CORE GATE 1 ENTRYWAY. Vallus took a deep breath before he swiped the key card and walked through the door.

Vallus found himself in a long, dark hallway. There was only a single functioning light, at the far end, and it flickered incessantly. There were no doorways in the hall, only dust and stale air. His footsteps echoed through the hall as he approached the single door at its end. He passed through it.

The Seeker found himself on a long catwalk with rails over the pit. At the end of the catwalk was a massive dark steel wall and a control panel. Vallus approached the controls and inspected the wall, which only bore large, yellow stenciled letters: CORE

GATE 1.

Vallus then inspected the control panel. There was a large lever and a key card reader. Vallus swiped the card, and the console beeped. He pulled the lever and a loud, deep thump echoed through the chamber. With a loud *creak*, the wall slid out of the path and came to a stop far off to Vallus' right. The gap between the catwalks was short, and Vallus was able to easily step over it. He noted that there was a section that was supposed to move up to fill the gap, but it was broken. The Seeker continued on to the next gate. Once there, Vallus repeated the process of swiping the card and flipping the switch. The second core gate slid off to the left, just as loudly as the previous. Before Vallus got to the next wall, he stopped on the catwalk and called Pip to face him.

"Pip, I need to talk to you. I am almost certain that before we leave this vault, I will have to face the Ashen King again. I don't know if I can beat him. But I need you to remain safe, so if he shows up, I need you to stay in my bag unless I call for you. There is no reason you need to meet the same fate as me should the King kill me."

"With all due respect, Vallus, I will acquiesce to your request, but I disagree. We are in this together, no matter where your journey takes you. Grimishar called me a 'Personal Interface Partner', but I am your friend," she replied. "And I am just as determined to see this through as you are."

"That settles that then, I guess," said Vallus with a smirk and a shrug. "Any idea how many gates we still need to pass through?"

"Just this one," replied Pip.

Vallus nodded and continued along the catwalk as Pip followed closely behind. Once more, he swiped the card and pulled the lever, and the gate slid to the right out of the way.

The catwalk continued for another ten feet before it connected to a short flight of stairs. Before Vallus was a massive steel structure with an enormous door and two solid walls that extended out from either side of it. The walls each had doors on them that seemed to lead to other sides of the structure. There was also a short staircase that led to the massive door. The entire area was cast in shadow, only lit by a few remaining florescent bulbs that flickered and buzzed. And within the room, in front of the staircase, was a tall figure. Vallus carefully approached.

The thing appeared to be some eight feet tall, resembled an athletic man, and was completely smooth. It appeared to be made of some type of liquid metal that glistened like chrome. The face had no features, only the suggestion thereof, but had a pair of cold, gray eyes. Vallus took another few steps, and the eyes lit up with a bright blue light. The thing raised its slumped head and spoke with a booming, robotic voice.

"By decree of the King, none shall enter until the appointed time," the thing yelled in monotone from a mouth that wasn't there.

Vallus held his hands up.

"I mean you no harm. I only wish to enter the core," he said.

"By decree of the King, none shall enter until the appointed time," it repeated.

"Okay. It is the appointed time. Can I enter?"

"By decree of the King, none shall enter until the appointed time."

"Look, I just need to enter the core," said Vallus as he cautiously took another two steps. The thing didn't seem to like that. Its hands curled into fists and it took a step forward as it let out its thunderous yell.

"ATTEMPTING TO ENTER SHALL RESULT IN IMMEDIETE TERMINATION!"

"Okay! Okay!" yelled Vallus as he held his hands up. "When is the appointed time?"

"TARGETING... TARGETING..."

"Shit," said Vallus as he drew his swords.

The Simulacrum took two long steps and swung its bulky fist at Vallus. The Seeker avoided the strike and swung one of his swords at the Simulacrum's exposed midsection. The blade sliced through it like butter, but drew no blood. The thing didn't seem to register that it had been wounded. But it quickly became apparent to Vallus as to why. The Simulacrum's liquid metal body had already healed the wound. And it had turned around. It threw another slow but powerful punch. Vallus was prepared and side-stepped the attack. As he did, he cleaved the thing's arm off at the elbow. Again, the weapon cut through easily. The Simulacrum returned the favor by kicking Vallus in the chest. When Vallus came to a stop some twenty feet away and rose to his feet, he watched as the Simulacrum picked up the severed arm and held it to the stump. The liquid metal quickly bonded and restored the arm.

As the Simulacrum turned on Vallus, the Seeker drew the rifle and took aim. It took a single step before Vallus fired and hit it between the eyes. The bullet pierced straight through, but the wound barely slowed the thing before it quickly closed. It extended its right arm, and the metal began to undulate. From the twisting, writhing liquid metal, the Simulacrum formed a long rifle. Then the barrel glowed red. Vallus didn't dodge in time, and the laser that was fired from the cannon slammed into his right shoulder. The armor deflected the laser bolt, but its impact still knocked him sideways.

As Vallus recovered from the impact and tried to close in on the Simulacrum, he directed Pip to hover above and scan the thing. The results were interesting, to say the least, but she chose to withhold the information so as to not break the Seeker's focus on the fight.

Instead, she began to calculate the success rates of each of Vallus' weapons against the data she had collected. Those results were grim. With nothing else to do, she ran projections to develop some kind of plan that could stop the seemingly unstoppable machine Vallus faced.

Vallus was gathering his own results as Pip worked above. None of his weapons had done anything of significance to the Simulacrum, no matter where he struck. Decapitation proved futile, as it simply reattached its head after knocking the Seeker away. The rifle had proven ineffective, regardless of where the bullet struck, and Vallus was disappointed by his pitifully low ammunition reserves. It soon dawned on him that he had no weapon that could destroy the machine. He remembered the single grenade on his belt as he dodged another punch from the Simulacrum, but couldn't think of an effective way to use it. He also doubted it would work. The Simulacrum formed a blade from its left hand and took a swing at Vallus, but he parried the strike. The force of the blow knocked the sword from Vallus' hand. Thanks to another slash from the sword, Vallus was forced to dodge rather than retrieve his blade. He took a defiant swing at the Simulacrum with his fist, but it broke through and sunk into the liquid metal. However, he found it easy to rip his arm out.

With a reformed hand, the Simulacrum batted Vallus away. The blow hurt, and it cut his cheek slightly. He stumbled back, only a step, and picked up his sword. Vallus had begun to grow desperate when he got an idea, and a plan began to come together in his mind. The Simulacrum formed another laser cannon and took aim. But he was drawing against Vallus, as the Seeker had already sheathed his swords and aimed his rifle. Unlike the Simulacrum, his weapon didn't need to charge, and Vallus fired first. The bullet tore through the laser cannon and flayed it apart as it lost its form and returned to liquid. There was still no indication that the Simulacrum had felt it as it began to reconstruct its hand.

As the Simulacrum closed in on Vallus and formed an axe out of its hand, he began to solidify his plan. He could think of only one way to stop the machine, but he knew he had to execute his plan without fail. He dodged the axe, which slammed into the floor and caught.

As the Simulacrum began to reshape its hand, the Seeker closed in himself. Vallus lunged forward and punched the Simulacrum hard, piercing its midsection just as easily as before.

He hooked his arm upward to assure he didn't punch all the way through. The Seeker found it difficult to open his hand within the thing's guts, but not too much so. Vallus ripped his hand out and dove backwards to dodge the sword it had formed. The Simulacrum seemed almost confused. Vallus couldn't tell if it understood the gravity of the gesture when Vallus raised his right hand and spun the grenade pin around his finger, but he supposed it didn't matter. The grenade he had shoved into the Simulacrum detonated and shredded the machine from within.

Vallus worried that the Simulacrum would yet be able to rebuild itself, but as chunks of the machine's liquid metal continued to rain down around him and the explosion echoed through the chamber, his fears began to fade away. Vallus stowed his weapons, and with little motivation to inspect the thousands of tiny pieces of the Simulacrum, he turned to face the massive doorway that separated him from the core. Pip quickly flew to his side.

"You figured it out," she said, only slightly concerned by his solemnity.

"This is it, Pip. This is the last door that stands between me and the end of my mission. It feels… unreal."

Pip, for the first time, had nothing to say. Vallus nodded to her and took a deep breath. He hesitated for a moment, then swiped the key card. There was a loud thump before the door began to churn open. Vallus took a drink of water as he waited and a steadying breath before he walked over the threshold.

Chapter 11

Vallus passed into a massive room filled with enormous and complex machines.

Hundreds of thick pipes and cables ran from the ceiling to the central power source, which sat dim and weak. All of the machines seemed to feed into the center in some way or another, including the pipes that ran under the grated floor beneath. Mounted in front of the dead core was a large chair surrounded by a control console, and sitting within it was an emaciated man with extremely long, silver hair like spider silk and an equally long, silken beard. Many of the cords from above fed into his body, as wells as the console itself. To Vallus' surprise, the man spoke, his voice ragged and tired. He looked at Vallus with piercing blue eyes, the only part of him not withered with time.

"Welcome, Seeker. You have had quite the journey, yes?" He coughed as he spoke.

"Yes," replied Vallus, a light quiver in his voice. "Are you the Forgotten God?"

The man laughed weakly as he shook his head.

"God? No. My name is Domo. But I see they managed to push that strange mythology of theirs. How disappointing."

"Wait... Are you saying there are no Gods?"

"That's up for debate. There was only so much we could do. No, what I am saying is that they have sent you in search of a lie."

Vallus was stricken. By this man's admission, Vallus had

indeed faced no Gods. But what had they been? He decided to hear out the man, and perhaps press him for answers.

"Explain," said Vallus.

"This belief people have... I only have so much access to the outside, you understand. But I have gathered that the idea is that we, as in those from before the crash, are Gods and we once lived alongside you, as in mortals. We built grand cities, and you helped, so we gave you machines to make your lives easier, right?"

"About sums it up, yes. What's your point?"

"We were never Gods. We were just wealthy and powerful. We had access. I would know; I built the system. It was in every facet of our lives. It ran everything. Then it broke. It crashed. We tried to fix it, but..." He trailed off.

"But what?"

"How many of them were there? These Gods? I know they were here... Oh, no. He's here." There was something in his voice, like panic.

Vallus noticed a slight tremble in Domo as his eyes widened. The Seeker turned around to find the Ashen King standing in the core's doorway, his great sword mounted to his back. He slowly clapped his hands as he took a few steps forward. Pip took cover in Vallus' bag as they had planned.

"You have done well, Seeker. I knew he wouldn't open the door for me. But an overly-curious Seeker with an annoying habit of not dying? That would be too good to pass up. You played our game well, but like all pawns, you have outlived your usefulness. The appointed time has come."

"You can drop the charade. You are no God. But I would like to know what exactly you *are.*"

The King chuckled.

"As far as you are concerned, I am," said the King. "But I will show you."

The King's visor raised and revealed a pair of cold, blue eyes topped with bushy, scowling eyebrows. Then the helmet split in half and slid back around the King's head. Beneath the helmet was the face of a man, with a strong nose, a wide chin, and deep circles around the eyes. The face ended at the hairline and was replaced by the machinery that made up the back of his head and neck.

"I was once like you, Seeker. A mere man, capable of great violence. But I ascended; reborn by the power of a God. My machine body sustains me forever. It empowers me. You have already seen the feats it allows me to perform. I expected you to run, but I won't complain. You have delivered my new dawn to me. The only thing left to do is destroy you and that withered husk."

Vallus drew his blades.

"You could simply allow me to have my answers and leave. I don't understand why you need to fight me so badly when I could care less about whatever mad delusion you keep going on about. But you will not kill Domo. Because I won't let you."

The Ashen King drew his own sword and pointed it at Vallus, holding the massive weapon in one hand.

"I will give you no choice. Come, mortal. Face the power of the God of War!"

Vallus roared and charged forward, blades at the ready. Vallus had learned much along his journey, and he was prepared to use it and avoid a repeat of his first encounter with the King. With only slight effort, Vallus ducked the King's sword as he swiped it at the Seeker. Within striking distance, Vallus drove a blade forward as hard as he could. The blade glanced off the

King's thick armor plates. In rebuttal, the King backhanded Vallus across the face. The blow dizzied him, but he was still able to dodge the next swing of Farran's mighty sword.

"Quite the pathetic display, Seeker," said the King as Vallus continued to have no luck with his attacks. "I hoped you could do better. I can detect the nanites in your body; they should be making you stronger. And you are lucky I can't control them."
Vallus dodged the sword again but found himself at the mercy of the King's free hand.

The Ashen King grabbed the Seeker by the coat and threw him to the floor. He raised his sword, poised to strike. Vallus rolled out of the way just in time to avoid the stab. The blade of the King's sword stuck in the floor, lodged in between two pipes. With his thumb, he pressed a small button on the hilt of his sword. The blade began to gently glow red and he pulled it out from the floor. The air boiled around the blade, and steam rolled off of it as he pointed it at Vallus once more. Vallus hopped to his feet and quickly removed his bag before he slid it across the floor for safe keeping. The King was already upon him.

A radiant heat followed in the wake of the King's blade as it passed by the Seeker's face. Vallus' dodge cost him his defense, and the Ashen King slammed his knee into the Seeker's gut. He buckled hard and spat before he dodged the King's stab. Vallus took several more quick steps back to get out of the King's range, but the King raised his free hand. A machine arm behind Vallus activated and slapped him in the arm. The blow hurt, but it hadn't been intended to kill; the King used it to close the gap. Vallus dodged the sword one more time, but the devastating kick the King deployed slammed into his back and sent him across the room. Vallus spat blood as he pushed himself to his feet.

"Seems you learned from our first fight. Good. I want you to suffer before you die."

"You have a strange idea that I have come to stop your plans. But I don't even know what your plans *are*. And I could honestly care less. So shut up and fight, because I have grown tired of your posturing," Vallus yelled in retort.

The King screamed with rage and bolted toward the Seeker, his blade raised high and poised to strike. The first swing missed, but the second grazed his arm. The wound stung, but the heat of the blade cauterized it. Vallus just barely avoided the third swing and took one of his own. The strike wasn't deep, but it caught between the King's armor plates and drew a small amount of blood as the King recoiled. He screamed again as Vallus continued to push on to the offensive. He could afford to fight defensively no longer.

Vallus decided to rely on his speed, and made several quick steps forward to harass the Ashen King with fast but shallow slashes. He quickly received indication that his plan was working, as the King became increasingly frustrated. Vallus' movements were too quick for the Ashen King to accurately aim his blade, and although each slash did little damage, they upset the King's equilibrium. Finally tested beyond his patience, the King stomped his foot into the floor hard. The stomp crumpled the floor beneath and threw off Vallus' footing. Caught off guard, Vallus had no defense against the vicious backhand that the King hit him with. The Seeker slammed into a wall, fell to the floor, and groaned heavily. His nose bled, and had very nearly been broken.

"You have earned both my respect and my ire, Seeker. But no longer will you stand between me and my new dawn," said the King as he took steps, not toward Vallus, but toward Domo. "As for you... You have withheld the last piece of the puzzle,

Domo. Give it to me."

Domo appeared unshaken as the King stared down at him from behind his helm. "You can't have the Master Controls. It will not work, Farran."

The Ashen King leaned forward, his helm inches away from Domo. He placed his hand on the console that surrounded the so-called Forgotten God, then crushed it as his anger seethed to the surface.

"And you can't stop me from getting them. You lose," he said through gritted teeth. Vallus could stand, but he wasn't fast enough. With his rifle out of his reach, the Seeker had no way of putting himself between the King and Domo. And as the King lifted his sword, Vallus felt the last little bit of hope he held flee. Then, with a violent roar, the King drove his blade through Domo's chest. There was no blood, as the King's sword boiled it. Domo's eyes grew wide, but he smiled. Oddly, as he spoke, he looked not into the King's eyes, but at his chest.

"So... long... I've been trapped here... To stop... you," he said as blood poured from his mouth. "You will... fail, Farran."

The King roared as he ripped his sword from Domo's chest. And yet, Domo continued to speak, as if in defiance of death itself. As if there was still one thing he had left to do. He turned his head to gaze at Vallus.

"Chosen Seeker... You must... stop him," Domo wheezed. "Like it... or not... This is the path before you... Look... for the home..."

With one final laughing, wheezing breath, Domo slumped over and fell silent. Slowly, almost as if he was grieving, the Ashen King turned back to Vallus and opened his helmet to gaze at him.

"It is over, Seeker. I have won. And the new dawn arrives. I shall use these Master Controls to sunder this world again, and from its ashes I will raise my empire. I will save this world, and grant it a rebirth. Bear witness, *Chosen Seeker,*" he sneered. "This is the power of the Gods."

The King turned back to the console and the core behind it, closed his helmet, and extended his free hand. The bright glow seemed more intense. Then the machines attached to the core began to move, as if by the will of an invisible hand. They converged on each other and attached to the core. It was a spectacle to see, as machine parts from all around the room were drawn to the center and fed into the core. As it all unfolded before him, Vallus considered taking the opportunity to strike at the King while his back was turned, but he calculated that the distance was too great and the area too unwieldy to navigate. He had no way to make a clean strike.

As the machines continued to coalesce upon the core, they began to form a strange object. It resembled a long rifle aimed upward at a forty-five degree angle attached to a plinth, with a large vent to either side at the base and some forty or fifty hoses, and hundreds of cables attached along the barrel. Vallus then noticed that Domo himself seemed to be lifting machines into place. He caught a brief glimpse of Domo's eyes, and they glowed blue. The Ashen King turned back to Vallus once more. As he did, Domo fell to the floor, apparently dead for good.

"Behold, the World Machine. The instrument of this world's purification. We near the apex, Seeker. Soon, it will be fully functional, and my glorious empire will rise from its grave."

Vallus stepped forward and shook off the pain that ran through his body. With a flourish, he attached his swords, then spun the weapon.

"Do you not realize that you're not a God? Have you gone completely insane? You can rebuild buildings all you want; dead is dead."

"You misunderstand, Seeker," said the King. "This machine isn't just going to rebuild. It will reshape the world in the image of the Gods. There will be no more death because machines don't die. This is my new dawn. The dawn of the Age of Gods."

"That age already came and passed, Farran. Domo was right; you will fail."

"No, Vakka was right!" yelled the King as he wheeled on Vallus. "I should have destroyed you sooner. He was my friend, you know. My closest friend. And you killed him."

"And you sent him to me. Then you stuck a key card in his head and dumped him in the trash. Some friend you are."

"Enough!" the King screamed.

He charged forward, his sword hefted in both hands. He took a mighty swing at Vallus but missed as the Seeker jumped clear of the attack. Vallus swung back hard with a spin of his sword and cut into Farran's arm. The King responded by slamming his forearm into Vallus' chest. The blow knocked the Seeker backwards and off his footing. The King gave chase and swung his sword over his head. Vallus regained his senses - and his footing - just in time to roll out of the way. The sword slammed into the floor, but the King quickly hefted it again and took a great stride to close the gap.

Vallus continued to retreat as he looked for an opening to strike. Those openings were few and far between, as the King held his blade at a slanted angle when not attacking to defend himself. Besides that, his speed and strength meant that Vallus had to devote more energy to avoiding attacks than to making them. The cut in Farran's arm hadn't seemed to bother him much or affect his ability to wield his sword. But Vallus noticed that he was slightly slower, just by a barely-noticeable margin. The Seeker used it to his advantage as he ducked and weaved through the King's attacks. Although the blade couldn't catch him, the King's powerful follow-up kick did. Vallus rolled across the floor and came to a stop near his bag.

As the Ashen King approached, Vallus grabbed his rifle from his bag. Pip still sat within, protected but ever vigilant. Crouched on the floor, Vallus aimed the rifle at the King. By his count, he had some six or eight rounds left; he couldn't recall the exact number. The King continued to approach, regardless of the weapon pointed at him. Vallus had learned his lesson, though. He knew the gun would not help him. If he shot at the King, at least. With a smirk, Vallus turned to his left and aimed at the World Machine, which was still in the process of attaching parts. He fired two shots at its exposed core. The resulting explosion blasted both Vallus and the King backwards toward the door and sent an echoing thunder through the room. Vallus was deafened as debris rained down on him.

Vallus rolled over to his back and tried to stand, but he was still disoriented. His arms and legs were like jelly, and he couldn't hear a thing. But his sight worked fine, and by the looks of it, the Ashen King seemed to be almost as disoriented as Vallus. He had also been disarmed and the sword had been embedded into the wall nearby. It no longer glowed, either. Vallus himself still had his rifle, but his dual sword had been flung across the room into the corner between two trash cans.

The World Machine burned, and the King was beginning to come to his senses.

Vallus had little time to retreat and recover his weapon. But he quickly discovered that the King wasn't interested in him.

Instead, he walked toward the destroyed World Machine and opened his helmet. There were tears in his eyes. But his hands were balled into fists, and he visibly shook with anger. He moved only his head ever so slightly to address Vallus.

"You think this is a victory, Seeker? The power of my control module will remedy this in short order. I will simply rebuild it, then destroy you."

The King wretched, then vomited a stream of metallic liquid filled with chunks of scrap. The puddle it formed writhed and contorted as a shape began to emerge at the Ashen King's command. Vallus soon realized that it was forming another Simulacrum. With his swords back in hand and split again, and his rifle slung over his back by its strap, Vallus prepared for the fight to come. Within moments, a new Simulacrum stood, its eyes empty as though waiting to be filled with purpose. The King placed his hand on the back of the thing's neck and its eyes glowed blue as he whispered into its ear.

"You wake by my decree: keep the Seeker away from my machine, and show him the truth he so greatly desires."

The Simulacrum took two steps forward as the King turned to the burning World Machine. Vallus knew the machine wouldn't allow him to attack the King, so he turned his attention to it. He didn't have a chance to attack. The Simulacrum split open straight down the center of its body, and from its gaping maw several liquid metal tendrils rushed forth and grabbed Vallus. He dropped his swords and planted his feet firmly against the floor. Vallus struggled against the tendrils as they coiled tightly around his limbs, but to no avail. His footing was weakening, and the thing pulled him closer to it, one inch at a time. As the Seeker neared it, several tubes held by thin, wiry machines emerged from within the Simulacrum and stood at the ready. He had thought the thing was trying to eat him, but the machines told him something else. As he realized what it was doing, Vallus gave in.

As the tendrils wrapped tighter around him and the Simulacrum began to encase him in its liquid metal body, Vallus could faintly hear Pip scream his name, as though through the fog of a dream. But any sounds were soon replaced as something thick and uncomfortable jammed into his mouth. He struggled not to thrash against the tube as it moved down his throat and bothered his sinuses. Small spikes formed within the Simulacrum and slowly pierced his face in several spots, but they didn't hurt. To Vallus it seemed as though the Simulacrum was preparing him. Then his back arched as a needle pierced his spine, and he blacked out.

***

From the outside, it appeared as though the Simulacrum had devoured Vallus. Once it had pulled the Seeker into its body, the liquid metal closed up and the Simulacrum stood completely still. Pip had already admonished herself for shouting for Vallus, but it seemed as though her error hadn't caught the attention of the Ashen King, who was still busy with his Machine. Pip scanned the King, but found her scanner blocked. But she didn't need it to know that he was drawing massive amounts of power to rebuild the World Machine. From within the bag, she watched the silent Simulacrum and waited.

***

Vallus awoke with a start. His head throbbed as he sat up. He seemed to be in a large bed, although he had no idea where he was. With his head still pounding, Vallus stood and looked around the room. It looked unlike any shelter Vallus had seen. It had more in common, structurally, with the ruins of the cities Vallus had passed through. There was a single light; a lamp in the corner. The room was musty and needed cleaning, but there was very little else beyond a table and two chairs. His head stopped hurting, but a buzzing in his ear had replaced it. Then he realized there was something on his ear. A machine. He reached a finger toward it and touched it. A voice whispered in his mind.

"You're good to go, Farran. Get to the Cosgrove building. Instructions to follow." Almost automatically, Vallus began to walk toward the door at the end of the room.

He passed a mirror, and saw that he was not himself. It was the Ashen King in the mirror, although his armor looked newer and he wore no helmet and had cropped, brown hair. He continued on and passed through the door into bright light. He was blinded for a moment, but when his sight returned, Vallus found himself surrounded by activity.

He stood in a busy city center, surrounded by audacious skyscrapers and dozens of monitors. Thousands of people walked the streets toward whatever their destinations were, some talking on phones and some hardly paying attention at all. Vehicles of all sorts passed by in the streets, their windows down and their horns at full blast. The sun was bright and warm, and there was a gentle breeze. Two jets passed above, the report of their afterburners echoing behind them.

Vallus turned to walk down the street as if by force. He was intrigued by the unsettled faces of the people that passed him by, and the wide berth they gave him. Then he remembered the mirror.

They must have feared him, he thought.

"They did."

The King's voice echoed in his mind. Vallus tried to speak, but all he could do was think. It was as if he was trapped in someone's body, an unwilling possessor.

What is this?

"This is my world. The world we lost. I can bring this back. I can fix it all."

That machine can't help these people, Farran.

"One thing at a time, Seeker."

Okay. Then why did they fear you so much?

"They knew of me. They knew of the power I possess. The weak fear the strong."

Is that how you saw them? Weak?

"That is how they were. They cowered behind us as it all fell apart."

He continued on down several side streets, winding and weaving through people and traffic. There was so much to see, Vallus was sure he couldn't take most of it in. But there were things he saw, from the corners of his eyes. A realization dawned on him.

The mirror. The things I can see. This isn't some kind of vision; it's your memories.

"Very good, Seeker. Yes. The crash came three days after this. Be patient. You will see."

Vallus continued to move along the streets to his predetermined destination, but he was more interested in the things in his peripheral vision. It seemed, despite the glistening sun and warm light on the breathtaking edifices that surrounded him, the King could not hide the realities of his world. He couldn't hide the broken and desperate people who lingered in the margins, sheltered down dark alleyways and wrapped in tattered blankets. Next to a dumpster, a tired and frail woman held three emaciated children to her sides and shivered.

As he continued along, Vallus passed a store with screens in the window. They showed a news feed, a stream of headlines with a newscaster speaking. Only a few headlines jumped out at Vallus, as the King had apparently stopped to look at the screens for a few moments. Prime Minister deposed. Declarations of war. Governments deadlocked. Farran saw a prosperous world thanks to the glory he had been basked in, but Vallus saw something different. It was a dying world, choked by sickness and war. The countless destitute cried out for help, but none came. Between the clawing tips of the skyscrapers, a storm was brewing on the horizon.

He resumed his march until he passed by a large fountain and into the courtyard of a skyscraper that towered above the rest. The sign in front of the double staircase read COSGROVE BUILDING, but the building itself had a different moniker branded on it: GRIMISHAR ADVANCED CYBERNETICS. If he could have, Vallus imagined he would have shuddered. He mounted the marble stairs and passed through one of six glass doors to enter an expansive lobby, decorated with sharp and sleek machines and pop art. People hustled through the lobby toward the elevators and stairs, focused on their phones and work. At the reception desk were three people. One was a woman in a slate gray suit with thin glasses and short, blonde hair. The other was a man with a black suit, short brown hair, and five o-clock shadow. The third person Vallus recognized as the man from the video he had watched in the library. He was at least as tall as Vallus, perhaps taller, and his black suit was paired with a blood red tie. His greasy black hair was pushed back behind his ears.

He turned as Vallus, or rather Farran, approached.

"Ah. You're here," said the man. "Have you been briefed on the situation?"

"No, Mister Grimishar. This was a rapid deployment."

"Very well," replied Grimishar. "We need to transport the memory cards for the system. It would normally be easy enough, but rebel forces have threatened to intercept any shipments. Regardless of contents. We need an armed escort."

"Why not fly?"

"Can't. The cards need to be kept at a very low temperature, and we can't fit a big enough freezer on an aircraft. We're going to take them by road to the nearest node. The rest of the node captains are going to have to figure it out on their own, because if they don't, the system will crash."

Vallus felt himself pulled inexorably through what felt like a blur. The lights flickered out and were replaced by a rush of feelings and sounds. Explosions. Screams. A woman crying. It was as if the entire memory had been repressed, obstructed by something. When the memory continued, Vallus found himself outside of a collapsed building. The other Gods were with him, and he looked out over a dead world. Somewhere deep within him, he seethed. He could see the Wizard's mouth moving, but could not hear the words, nor could he hear the words of any of the others. There was a new, even stranger sensation. Obsession. The need to right the wrong. He had failed before. He couldn't accept it again. The mission was too vital.

Vallus couldn't be sure if that feeling was that of the King, or his own. But he was overcome by a burning, raging desire to be free of the dream. A thousand thoughts rushed through his mind. He didn't know how to fight against it. He could not command his body. He couldn't even speak. Vallus tried to scream, but nothing came out. His heart raced. The memory was too thick, like a weighted blanket over his mind.

Instead of trying to physically move, Vallus turned inward. Perhaps he could ignore the dream and snap back to reality. For a moment, everything went black and he coughed violently. He had managed to force the tube out of his throat. Then he blinked and had been pulled back into the memory. He was the King again, kneeling down in the dirt as he scooped a handful of soil up. There was a sense of unspeakable sorrow, an unbearable agony almost like the loss of a dear loved one. As if his heart had shattered. Vallus focused once more.

In the blank between the memory and reality, a strange and timeless spot where the solid and objective line between life and death blurred, Vallus could think. He had gained insight and knowledge to be sure, but he had gained more. Vallus had gained resolve. He reflected on himself, and understood that he had never seen himself as anything beyond an average man. His desires were simple and his ambitions plain. He had sought hope, and found blood and death. In his mind, he had resolved that allowing the Ashen King to accomplish any part of his goal would result in untold suffering. Therefore, it fell on him to prevent it. Vallus had never wanted to be a hero of any sort. He imagined a life after his mission, only briefly, somewhere in peaceful solitude where he could rest with the knowledge that he had lit the sparks to reignite the fire of humanity. His family had relied on him, and had ordained him a Seeker. And he realized that he would need to come to terms with the fact that if he didn't play the role of hero and stop Farran, he would fail his people.

As Vallus was violently ripped away from the empty between-place back to reality, he screamed. He thrashed and flailed to rip and tear away the machines that had wormed their way into his body. Above, in what must have been the Simulacrum's head, was a small glowing orb. Vallus pushed past wires and pipes toward the orb, and grabbed it. Hoping against hope, Vallus pulled on the orb and tore it from its mounting. His guess paid off, and as he pulled away the power source, the Simulacrum exploded apart, writhing and thrashing as it tried to rebuild itself. Finally free of the machine, Vallus fought the rest of his way out of its grasp, then threw the power source back into it.

"Pip!" he yelled.

At his command, the drone rocketed out of the bag and fired a taser dart at the orb. The dart hit, and the electricity excited the already unstable core. There was a bright blue light, then a vicious explosion as the Simulacrum was torn to shreds. Vallus was free, renewed, and finally filled with a clarity of purpose. But the Ashen King had completed his work, and the World Machine had begun to charge. The King wheeled around, drew his sword, and prepared to answer the Seeker's call.

"This ends now, Farran! I have seen your failures; both past and present. Here and now, I will stop you!"

Chapter 12

There was no more need for words. The King charged forward, his blade held high and a mighty battle roar issuing from deep within him. Vallus rolled under the horizontal swing, then dove for his swords. He managed to take hold of them and roll to his feet just in time to parry another strike. As the blades collided, sparks flew past Vallus' face. He took two steps back to avoid the King's blade and slung the rifle over his shoulder. He fired a single shot, and it finally struck true. The bullet slammed into the Ashen King's neck and tore through, spraying a thin stream of blackish blood. The King roared and hefted his sword again.

Vallus was forced to pick up his swords again and parry the King's attack. More sparks flew and forced Vallus to tighten his concentration as to not be blinded. As he backed away and looked for an opening to strike, Vallus quickly inspected his swords to find that small grooves had been seared onto the blades. Although he couldn't tell by looking, the Ashen King seemed pleased with himself in the way he sauntered toward the Seeker.

"Your useless, pathetic weapons can't take much more of that, can they? Soon, you will have nothing left to defend yourself with. And when you do, you will die."

"I'm not done yet, Farran," replied Vallus, although the words were gasped.

"I am the Ashen King and you will address me as such, mortal!" he screamed. "I have conquered a thousand battlefields and slain a million warriors to earn my place among the Gods and you will bow!"

Vallus was forced to abandon his plan to attack an opening and instead dodged away from the King as the Seeker's opponent swung his sword quickly and with great ferocity.

Each swing blasted Vallus with a wave of heat, and sweat poured down his face. His heart raced as he began to assess his options. He had to parry only occasionally, which meant he had no other option but to avoid the blade. Then he found his opportunity. The speed of the King's attacks slowed, only for a moment, but it was enough to allow Vallus to dash forward and strike. Vallus took a few swings, aiming between the plates of the King's armor. A few drew blood, but the armor was built to minimize exposure, and most of what was exposed was machinery that would not yield a fatal wound.

The Ashen King wheeled around and swung his sword. Vallus had no choice but to parry, but his heart sank as the blades made contact and his sword shattered. Vallus was knocked back but quickly regained his footing. With some disappointment, Vallus tossed the broken sword aside. He switched the sword in his left hand to his right and fitted the rifle more comfortably on his back as well. But the King was upon him quickly.

Vallus was able to just barely avoid the driving stab from the King's sword, but it cut through his coat. Thankfully, the heated blade cut straight through and didn't catch his coat on fire, but Vallus was forced to dodge again as the King swung once more. The King's relentless ferocity began to tax Vallus' endurance as the Seeker continued to dodge and duck the speedy and sure strikes. His opponent showed no sign of fatigue, nor doubt in his abilities. But the King's flurry of attacks was interrupted as his attention was turned to the World Machine. Vallus took the chance to regroup and prepare for another salvo, but the Machine had different plans. It began to whine at a deafening pitch, filling the room with abject chaos. Ports along the barrel of the Machine glowed, and steam and lightning issued off it.

The Ashen King had turned away from Vallus to bask in the glory of his Machine. As he did, he opened his helmet to gaze upon it. It was so close, just within his grasp. Those dreams he had chased for a millennium still danced in his head; still mocked him, just out of reach. He was almost stupefied, just barely able to comprehend that his mission was nearly complete.

While Vallus had had his reservations about trying a sneak attack against the King before, he no longer held such hang-ups. Vallus flipped his sword around and charged forward, hoping to land a quick and surprising attack at speed. He jumped, blade ready to strike at his opponent's exposed head. And all the while, the incessant whirring of the World Machine continued on. And like the Machine's first iteration, Vallus' hopes were dashed to pieces.

The King quickly whirled around and grabbed Vallus by the throat. The Seeker dropped his sword as his airway constricted beneath the Ashen King's grasp. His face was all bitter rage, and he scowled deeply as he peered into Vallus' eyes. But his grip soon loosened, and he turned back to the Machine. As he did he switched his grip to grasp Vallus by the back of the neck and held him aloft to look upon the World Machine.

"Gaze upon it, Seeker," shouted the King over the whine of the Machine as his fingertips dug into Vallus' neck. "Witness your end, and the beginning of a new age!"

The World Machine shook, then the barrel slid back and forth once, quickly, like the slide of a pistol. A massive wave of force slammed into Vallus as he tried to struggle his way out of the King's powerful grasp. The entire vault shook, then a heartbeat of silence. Then the floor beneath their feet was sundered as massive mechanical tendrils and metal spikes erupted from within the vault. The vicious maelstrom of steel threw the King and Vallus apart as they were forced to avoid the machines. More and more machines rose from within, undulating violently as they clawed their way toward the ceiling. Vallus hit the floor, grabbed Pip, and dove for his bag. He missed it, and it was carried up through the vault by a tendril.

Another erupting tendril slapped Vallus backwards as it rose from the floor and tore through the nearby wall. He spun around to find the Ashen King barreling toward him, but unarmed. Vallus dove out of the way, and another rising machine slammed into the King and sent him flying across the room. With Pip tucked tightly to him, Vallus ran to the World Machine, avoiding more machines as he went. He couldn't identify the purposes of any of them, but he knew none of them were good. And they had begun to tear through the ceiling of the room. They branched further and further through the building and destroyed floor after floor.

As Vallus approached, he had to shield his eyes with one arm from the blinding, pulsating lights that issued from the Machine. There seemed to be a forceful aura of energy around it, a sort of field that pushed back against the Seeker as he took each step closer. He reached out, squinting against the lights. He couldn't hear anything over the deafening scream of the World Machine other than the voice in his mind.

Keep going. No surrender. No failure. I have no other choice.

Vallus was mere inches from the machine when it violently shook and whined. Then blasts of lightning erupted from its vents, and another wave of force blasted the Seeker off his feet and across the room. He slammed into a tilted steel spire and fell to the floor. He panicked for a moment before Pip floated up to

299

his face, apparently safe.

The room had been basked in an eerie silence, and the World Machine had fallen quiet, including its effects. Off in the corner Vallus could hear the King stirring. A thick, billowing cloud of smoke issued from the Machine and had begun to fill the room. As Vallus struggled to his feet and turned, the Ashen King came into view. His sword had been shoved through his abdomen, and he pulled it out of him as he approached. His helmet had also been broken off. He raised the blade and heated it again.

"Come, Seeker. Your time is here."

Vallus had no weapon aside from his rifle. He drew it and took aim, then fired as the King charged forward. The first round hit the King's shoulder plate and bounced off, but the second and last bullet struck the sword wound and tore through the King. He continued to charge, but screamed with pain nonetheless. Vallus dove under the sword and slammed the butt of his rifle into Farran's wound. The King doubled over and slammed his sword into the broken floor. He tried to pull it back, but at the same time it caught in the floor, Vallus punched Farran hard in his exposed face. Farran let go of the weapon. As the King reeled, Vallus tried to fire his rifle again, but it clicked. He tossed the weapon aside as the King came back to his senses. He charged, and Vallus grabbed hold of the King's dropped sword.

Vallus' shook violently as electricity surged through his body. It was like being hit with a taser. With the help of his insulated armor and pure will, Vallus lifted the blade and ran it through the Ashen King's chest. Lightning surged around the King's body as his power core was damaged, and he screamed a primeval, bloody scream. Vallus pushed it aside as an illusion caused by fatigue, but he could have sworn there was a second, darker voice in the scream.

Vallus fell back to the floor, exhausted and tingling from the sword. The King pulled the blade from his chest and took it in hand. He grasped his chest, clearly on his last legs as he stumbled forward. He could barely raise his sword, and his words came in gasps.

"How did… you like that, Seeker? My hilt… is encoded to read my palm. Anyone… who tries to use it… gets shocked… But you took more than I expected…"

"You lose, Farran," Vallus wheezed as he dragged himself away from the King.

"Your core…"

"I know…" said the King with a mischievous grin as Vallus struggled to his feet. "But you still lose."

The King grabbed his sundered chest plate in both hands and tore the metal away to reveal his power source beneath. It had begun to glow as more lightning surged around his body. The Ashen King spread his arms as he shouted.

"I smite you, mortal!"

With a deafening boom, a beam of energy erupted forth from the Ashen King's chest.

Vallus just barely dove out of the way, his arm slightly clipped by it as he went. The beam missed Pip as well, who had flown high up. Instead, the beam slammed into the smoking World Machine and blasted it to pieces with a thunderous explosion. The blast sent Vallus flying across the room into the side of a steel spire once again where he collapsed to the floor.

The Seeker was dazed and shaken for some time, and rose shakily to his knees. The room was filled with so much smoke that he couldn't see much of anything. His head was ringing, and he couldn't see Pip anywhere. By the time he pulled himself to his feet, Pip had flown to his side and he had begun to regain some of his hearing.

"…You okay?" she asked.

"Ya… Gimme a minute," he replied.

Vallus regained his senses - at least for the most part - as the smoke began to clear. Vallus cautiously approached where the Ashen King knelt on his knees, a trail of smoke issuing from his burned chest and his head hung. He still lived, although his breaths were ragged and weary. Vallus clutched his burned arm as he looked at the King.

"It's… not over… Seeker. It is all… part of the plan."

"What plan?"

"I just wanted… to go home," he wheezed.

With one last sigh, the Ashen King fell to the floor. The smoke continued to roll off of him as he took his last breath. Vallus stood there for a long while, observing the King's body. There was so much he had to process. So many things to be learned. He didn't feel as though he had won; he felt as though he was still fighting. But the room was silent. Vallus looked back at the remains of the destroyed World Machine, and was surprised to find no desire to inspect it. He had seen enough. With some of his strength finally returning, Vallus searched around to find the remains of his swords. The first sword was not too far away. Vallus pried off the crests and put them in his jacket pocket. The other sword had been flung across the room and was wedged tightly between two of the spires that had been raised by the Machine. He pulled on the sword as hard as he could, but it wouldn't budge. With a sharp sigh, Vallus decided to cut his losses and removed the crests from the hilt.

Finding the rifle took some doing, but Vallus located it all the same, and intact. His bag, however, seemed to be lost. Vallus decided to keep the weapon and slung it over his back. Still aching, he walked across the room to the door, which had been torn asunder by the World Machine and blocked by rubble. From his quick inspection, there was no way to pass through it. Pip flew to his side and looked up at the door.

"We seem to be trapped," said Vallus.

"I hate to be the bearer of bad news, Vallus, but you're going to need to climb."

"Sure there's no cracks in the door to slip through?"

"None. The only part of all of this that we could fit through is at the top of that spire over there. It has pierced through the core shielding into the levels above. In fact, we may have to climb all the way out of the vault."

"The damage is that bad?"

"From my initial scans, it seems whatever the World Machine did spread for quite a distance. There are still minor aftershocks running through the ground."

"All right then. I'd better get climbing."

"No last words for our fallen opponent?"

"None. We need to focus. I don't have much strength left."

The spire had a number of exposed ports and protrusions that made for decent hand and footholds, but his sore muscles and wounded body fought against him. He could make the climb fine enough, but the effort was taxing and made him breathe hard. After a solid ten minutes of climbing, Vallus finally made it to the top of the spire to climb through the crack.

He found himself in the entryway where he had fought Grimishar, but couldn't locate the Wizard's body as the room had been tossed by the rising spires. Vallus continued on down the hall and back all the way to the elevator to find that it had been destroyed by the World Machine, and more tendrils snaked their way through the walls of the vault like great jungle vines made of steel.

With no other viable route at his disposal, Vallus began to climb through the elevator shaft. He made use of the winding tendrils to climb ever higher, and at times was forced to crawl through the innards of the vault's walls to make progress. At one point, he came out in the library to find it completely destroyed. However, the damage created something of a natural ramp toward the surface made of toppled bookcases. In some places, it was like a slightly taxing walk up a hill, and in others it was a sheer mountain climb.

Vallus continued his ascent through the upper reaches of the elevator shaft.

Occasionally, he would take some time to inspect the spires and machines created by the World Machine, but there wasn't much he could learn from them. Most of the inner machinery appeared to be inert or incomplete. Pip hovered along, but didn't scan anything beyond a few of the machines out of curiosity. Not much seemed to be of interest or use, so she decided to allow the Seeker to concentrate on his ascent. They moved on in silence, with it only broken by Vallus' grunting.

Vallus was running out of energy when he finally broke through the door from the elevator shaft into the lobby. The room was yet another casualty of the World Machine, as much of the roof had been torn asunder. Almost miraculously, Shiloh's camp was virtually untouched. Pip looked about the area, but couldn't find the second half of Vallus' bag. She alerted him to the fact, but he dismissed the thought.

"I can get new gear. Where's Shiloh?"

Vallus searched the camp and quickly found him. He was lying on a cot at the back of the camp, apparently asleep. Vallus called out to him.

"Shiloh? Wake up."

Vallus crouched down as he approached. The Seeker checked his pulse and realized that Shiloh was dead. He called Pip over and had her scan the body. His heart broke. Pip quickly beeped as she finished her scan.

"It seems he sustained much more internal injury than we were aware of. Vakka hurt him badly. From my scans, it seems he suffered organ failure as a result of internal bleeding. His immune system was quite weak; I am impressed he lived as long as he did," said Pip.

"He was a good man. He didn't deserve to die as a consequence of my mission," said Vallus in a somber tone.

"Agreed. Without his help, we may not have survived this place."

"Yes," said Vallus before he turned back to Shiloh's body. "I wish to bury him. He was entombed in this place for so long; he deserves to be free of it."

Vallus gently tucked his arms under Shiloh's neck and lower back and picked him up. He then left the camp, walked through the destroyed door, and down the hall. He sighed one last breath of the vault's musty air, then had Pip open the main door and walked out of DA-0708. As he passed by the destroyed turret, he quietly laughed to himself. It seemed so long ago that he was being shot at by it. The sun had begun to rise and made Vallus squint as his eyes readjusted to the light of day. Onward he walked, past the broken barricades in the shadow of the valley.

All around him was the evidence of the World Machine. Its spires and tendrils had torn through the vault itself, woven through the valley, and had even extended into the town. Where the castle had once stood was another massive steel tower. As Vallus passed the cliff side by the road, he peeked down to see the castle - or, what remained of it - lying at the bottom of a chasm. The screaming man he had passed on the way to the vault was gone. Just before the entrance into town, Vallus stepped off the road to where the ground had flattened at the base of the hill. Carefully, he laid Shiloh's body down.

He looked around for something to use as a shovel, and was disappointed to find little of possible use. There was a spire's tip nearby, protruding some ten feet out of the hillside.

Vallus approached it and ran his hands along its facets. He drew his knife and slipped it between plates on the spire and pried one away. It was easy enough for Vallus to tear it away from the spire. He turned the plate over and inspected it, and found it to his liking. It was serviceable, at least. He returned to the spot he had chosen, Pip watching over the body silently, and began to dig. The nearby town guard didn't seem to notice or be bothered by Vallus' work, and the Seeker didn't care if he was bothered, anyway. He dug, and dug, and dug, silent all the while save for his huffing from the work. An hour had passed by the time he had dug the hole to an acceptable depth.

Vallus climbed out of the grave and knelt down beside Shiloh's body as he tossed aside the makeshift shovel. He bowed his head in silence for a few moments, then gently rested his palm on Shiloh's chest. He then crossed the arms over the chest.

"Rest now, Seeker. Your journey is at its end," he whispered.

Vallus carefully lifted Shiloh's body so as to not move the arms, then gently lowered it into the grave. Once more, he picked up the makeshift shovel and got to work. He worked in silence as he refilled the grave, ignoring the stinging in his eyes from the sweat. After nearly another hour, Vallus tossed the last scoop of soil onto the grave and tamped it down. With a loud huff, he wiped the sweat away from his forehead and shoved the metal shard into the ground as a headstone. After one last moment of silence, Vallus turned and walked into Ashenvale.

More accurately, he limped into town. The adrenaline had worn off, and his many wounds had begun to catch up with him. The effects of the nanobots had subsided. The pain was nearly unbearable, yet the Seeker pushed on. The bandits who had harassed him before were gone, and the Seeker was thankful for it. In the courtyard, he stumbled and nearly fell over. A local, to Vallus' surprise, came to his aid. It was a young girl with long, brown hair and worried, brown eyes. She was much shorter than the Seeker, yet she still helped to prop him up. The pain had started to make him delirious, but he could just barely make out what she said.

"…Get you help," she said.

After gasping out a thanks to the girl, the Seeker wobbled again, then fell over. Before he hit the ground, he blacked out.

***

Vallus awoke in a small room, lying in a bed with sheets over him and much of his body bandaged. He was groggy, and his head pounded. Although he was still half asleep, he quickly noticed Pip, who came to his side as he sat up. A doctor was not far behind, a tall and thin man with kind eyes and stubble on his rectangular jaw.

"You're awake," said Pip. "Good. I was starting to worry."

"How long have I been out?" asked Vallus as he rubbed his head.

"Three days," replied the doctor. "And you're lucky to be alive at all. What in the name of the Gods did this to you?"

"The Gods, if you'd believe it. Your vault had a monster problem."

"Really? Well, judging by all that madness that came spewing out of it, I'm inclined to believe you. Not to alarm you, but you had quite a variety of wounds, so they were very difficult to treat. There was the gunshot wound, along with multiple lacerations, a concussion, two broken ribs, a fractured femur, a third degree burn, and a nasty stab wound. You're going to need to take it easy for at least a few weeks, maybe take a room in town and rest. You lost a lot of blood, and your body needs time to heal."

"No time. Need to get on my feet and back home. I found what I came for. Or at least some of it."

"What was that?"

"Truth," he replied.

"Well, I don't recommend it, but I can send you on your way with some medicine for pain and some extra dressings."

"Maybe… Maybe I'll just rest," said Vallus as he tried to get out of bed and failed miserably. "Gonna need supplies before I leave, anyway. But I should tell you that I have no way to repay your kindness. My bag was destroyed in the vault, along with all of my tools and travel supplies. I have nothing to barter."

"Please," said the doctor as he waved off the Seeker. "We've had so many Seekers pass through Ashenvale on the way to the vault that we don't charge for helping you. We consider it a tithe to the cause. Besides, you're the first one we've ever seen go in there then come back out."

"Thank you," said Vallus. "I greatly appreciate that."

"And I'm sure the locals would be willing to chip in to get

you provisions for the road. We must all help each other if we want to survive, isn't that right?"

Vallus nodded and leaned back into the bed. He decided to take the doctor's advice and rest, at least for a little while. He was eager to return home, but understood that he needed to survive to do so. As he lied in bed, Vallus peered out the nearby window and reflected on everything he had faced in the depths of DA-0708. There was much for him to consider, but he was weary. Pip hovered to his side.

"So what's next, Vallus?"

"We rest. Prepare. Then I must return home. But my mission isn't done. I need to tell people what happened here. They need to know. Those monsters called themselves Gods. They made the whole world believe it. That lie needs to die with them."

"Yes. It seems their manipulations were much farther reaching than we anticipated. They warped the world's history at a fundamental level."

"Every person we see once we leave this town needs to know what happened here. They need to know the truth."

Pip nodded. "Yes. In the meantime, there is much we still do not know."

"And I still don't know what caused the Fall. But they called it the Crash. I still need to seek, and plan to do so on my way home. But for now, I need rest."

Pip hovered down onto the bed and rested on the Seeker's lap as he drifted off to sleep. Vallus remained in the town for another week as he waited for his body to regain some sense of normalcy. When he was finally ready to leave, he thanked the people for their help and graciously accepted the small kit of provisions they had prepared for him. With one final broad, sweeping thanks to the people of Ashenvale, Vallus turned and left the town.

The long, broken road stretched out before him, and the sun sat at its apex as Vallus walked away from the town and the vile memory of DA-0708. His heart was still heavy, but he felt stronger than ever, and ready to seek anew. But he now sought true hope; the final piece of the puzzle. He relished the chance to bring his story to the world. With Pip floating behind him, gently bobbing on the weak breeze, Vallus the Seeker walked along the broken road toward home.

***

There was an unusual stale scent in the air of the vault, one far from Ashenvale, and Callum could smell it despite his mask. He had easily slipped into the vault unnoticed, and even more easily circumvented its security systems, but he still had a long way to go. As he moved through the ancient monolith and ever deeper into its seemingly endless maw, Callum was forced to traverse a number of obstacles, but nothing violent. Still, he had come prepared and armed. In the guts of the vault's wall, he used his sword to cut through a thick bundle of wires and pipes that appeared to be useless anyway and continued onward.

It was several hours before Callum finally reached the core. He gently placed his hand against the giant door that stood before him, a deep pride welling in his heart. Every success drew him closer to his master's final victory, and his ultimate reward. His ascension.

"You have slept for far too long," he whispered, as if speaking to the vault itself.

Callum had learned much in his own long journey, and those lessons made the door no trouble to open. Within the core,